SIX

USA TODAY BESTSELLING AUTHOR

K.I. LYNN

Six
Copyright © K.I. Lynn

This book is a work of fiction. Names, characters, places, and incidents either are products of the author's imagination or are used fictitiously. Any resemblance to actual events or locales or persons, living or dead, is entirely coincidental.

This work is copyrighted. All rights are reserved. Apart from any use as permitted under the Copyright Act 1968, no part may be reproduced, copied, scanned, stored in a retrieval system, recorded or transmitted, in any form or by any means, without prior written permission of the author.

Cover design by Lori Jackson Designs

Editor
Vanessa Bridges
Marti Lynch

Publication Date: June 6, 2016
Genre: FICTION/Romance/SuspenseCopyright © 2016 K.I. Lynn
All rights reserved

SIX

PLAYLIST

Killing Strangers—Marilyn Manson
Heathens—Twenty One Pilots
Dangerous—David Guetta feat. Sam Martin
Android Porn—Kraddy
Dark Star—Jaymes Young
She Wolf (Falling to Pieces)—David Guetta feat. Sia
Arsonist's Lullabye—Hozier
Gasoline—Halsey
Dangerous Woman—Ariana Grande
Me, Myself, & I—G-Easy and Bebe Rexha
Castle—Halsey
Way Down We Go—Kaleo
Out of the Woods—Taylor Swift
Take me to Church—Hozier
Alive—Sia
Earned It—The Weekend
Confident—Demi Lovato
Lies—Chvrches
Collapse—Zeds Dead feat. Memorecks
Animals—Maroon 5
Black Widow—Iggy Azalia feat. Rita Ora
Maps—Maroon 5
Hold Me Down—Halsey
First Person Shooter—Celldweller
Blackbird Song—Lee Dewyze
Adrenaline—In This Moment
I Miss the Misery—Halestorm
Heaven Knows—The Pretty Reckless
Dark Horse—Katy Perry feat. Juicy J
A Light That Never Comes—Linkin Park X Steve Aoki
Bad Romance—Lady Gaga

INTRODUCTION

RIGHT AND WRONG.

Morals.

Good versus evil.

All things I was taught as a child. Sides I persevered to belong to based on what society said, what the church said, you needed to be a decent person. These shaped me into the adult I'd become.

Bad people do bad things, but I never questioned why they did them. I never delved into the psychology of evil.

Politeness, manners, and courtesy made friends. Without them, the world was your enemy. Everyone lives with a charade for the public eye, acting the way a civilized person does.

But not everyone is civilized.

Monsters are real.

And they have their own version of the world.

I should know, I was kidnapped by one. Dragged down into the pits of their hell.

Changed.

Altered.

Forced to do *anything to survive.*

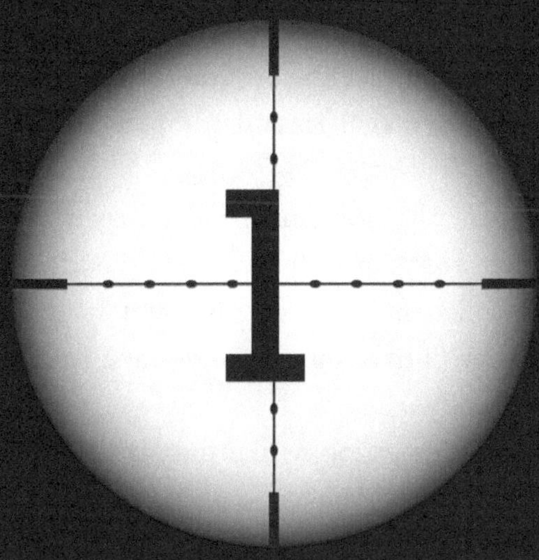

I LOOKED LIKE A VAMPIRE.

Maybe a zombie.

The vial was mocking me. In the slim reflection of the plastic, my dark-circled eyes looked back at me. I placed the vial into the centrifuge and sat back, rubbing my eyes with the palms of my hands, pressing in.

Zombie it was.

How long had it been since I'd slept?

Twenty-two hours? *What day is it?*

I'd done countless blood chemistry analyses, trying to catch up on the backlog.

"Paisley, do you have the blood work done for Dr. Patterson?"

My head fell back, and I got an upside down view of Marcy, my boss. She stared at me with her unconcerned brown eyes, freshly woken and showered.

She looked a lot like a pig from my skewed view. Not that she was. She was a damn good boss, friendly and helpful. Granted, I was the best technician the medical examiner's office had. Four years of college with a degree in biology went a long way. Which was one reason why I was still processing samples almost twenty hours after walking through the door.

I reached forward, feeling around for the stack of files containing the completed analysis and grabbed the top one, holding it over my head. "This it?"

She huffed, her lips forming a line. I'd say it was a disapproving line. "When was your shift supposed to end?"

"Murphy called in," I said with a frown that probably looked like a smile to her. "I'm pulling a double, and Rick wasn't able to come in."

"Shit. You only get loopy like this when you've been here too long. Do you know what time it is?"

I glanced over to the clock. "Seven."

"Morning or afternoon?"

I blinked at her. "Does it matter at this point?"

She rolled her eyes and pushed on the back of my head. "Sit up. Your face is turning red."

I let out a groan, my head spinning.

She settled in against the counter. "It's seven in the morning, which means you've been here for eighteen hours. Go home."

"Still two hours left." Most of the time I loved our ten-hour shifts because I had three days off a week, but two shifts in a row was too much.

"I don't care. Damon can fill in until Sandra gets in."

"Damon's a doctor. He doesn't *do* lab work."

"Well, he will today." She scanned the counter and the small stack of work that was left. "Anyway, you're pretty much caught up, so it can probably wait until Amanda gets in. Though I would love to see the look on Damon's face." A grin spread on her face. It was sinister.

"Why, Dr. Brenton, I'd say you have something against Dr. Douche." He was a pompous ass to everyone in the lab, even the chief medical examiner, Dr. Mitchell.

Her eyes widened, and she playfully slapped my shoulder.

"Shush, you."

"If you do, video it for me."

She let out a small chuckle. "As I was saying, go home. The party's tonight and Dr. Mitchell wants you there, mentally as well as physically."

Fuck…the party.

I hated parties.

Scratch that.

I hated work parties, loathed them.

Every year I prayed they'd forget about it.

Who ever heard of a year-end party in February? Granted, the medical examiner's office was especially busy during the holidays, so we'd never been able to hold one around that time. February sixteenth was the furthest out we'd ever gone in the five years I'd worked here.

"Do I have to go? Micah gets handsy when he's drunk." Micah was one of the ME's assistants. Nice guy, decent looking, but I wasn't interested in him. Plus, in his drunkenness, he was an equal opportunity groper.

She laughed, smiling as she shook her head. "I'll be there to pry him off."

"Then he'll just latch onto you."

She nodded. "True, but I could use a little loving, and he's not bad looking."

"Cougar."

She gasped. "He's only three years younger than me." I grinned up at her, and she rolled her eyes. "Enough. Tell me where you are and get out."

With a brief description of where I left off and what samples were in the centrifuge, I headed to my locker. Purse out, lab coat in, and I was gone.

In what felt like seconds later I was face down on my bed,

sprawled out on top of the comforter, scrubs still on. I didn't care how I got home, only that I was, and I could finally sleep.

The incessant beeping of my phone going off pried me from my deep sleep. I patted around the bed trying to locate it, half seeing out of my sleep covered eyes to turn it off.

Four in the afternoon.

It was my usual time for getting up if I was working the night shift, but it was my week for day shifts, and tonight was the party.

My face scrunched up, and I nuzzled against my comforter. All I wanted to do was cuddle on my couch, maybe watch a movie and order a pizza.

The phone next to me beeped again, this time with a text from Marcy telling me to get up. Or more precisely…

Get your ass out of bed. Don't make me come get you.

I pushed against the bed, propping myself up. Bright lines danced across the floor as my curtains blew in front of the window.

As I stood, aches in my body protested all movement. Every part of me was stiff. A bend of my neck led to a snap, crackle, some pops, and a lot of relief.

My feet shuffled across the floor, dragging as I made my way into the bathroom. The reflection greeting me in the mirror was horrific.

What was I saying about zombies earlier?

My strawberry blonde hair was still in the ponytail I'd put it up in, but it was a wild mess of loose strands. At least the dark circles were gone from under my baby blues.

A shower later, and color returned to my pale skin. Life seemed to be flowing through me again, doubly so when the numbers on the clock read much later than I expected.

Adrenaline pumped through me, driving me like a mad woman as I dried my hair at super speed before going through my closet.

I pulled out the few dresses I owned, all of them from the Digby days. Two were nixed due to being too fancy, another three because they were summer dresses. What remained was a cap sleeved flared dress and a body hugging, long sleeved sweater dress.

Due to the cold weather, the sweater dress won, and I decided to pair it with my knee-high boots.

So what if the front zipped up? And that Digby had pulled it down with his teeth before fucking me on his desk in the middle of a Christmas party?

Maybe the dress would get lucky again. I wouldn't be against it. A little live action in my nether regions. Just not with Micah.

Hair? Check.

Dress? Check.

Drink to calm my nerves and help get my ass there? There was an atrocity happening in my kitchen—the rum was gone. Along with the vodka and amaretto.

There were a few small shot-size bottles of rum somewhere. After finding them stuffed in the egg carrier in the fridge, I tossed them in my purse.

Eyeliner, mascara, lip gloss, and out the door.

Only ten minutes late, but it wasn't like I had to be there exactly at six.

Fifteen minutes later I was parked and slowly walking toward the hotel bar, downing my tiny bottles of rum while convincing myself the necessity of my being there.

"Wow, Paisley, you look hot." Marcy walked toward me, her short bob of brunette hair curled and pinned, bouncing with each step.

"Have you looked in the mirror?" I looked her up and down. "Damn, girl!"

A blush spread across her cheeks, and she smiled. Marcy was always self-conscious about her weight, but the skintight cocktail dress she wore highlighted her curves in all the right ways.

"Your tits look great." I waggled my eyebrows at her.

She slapped me with her clutch. "I'm still your boss."

I shrugged. "What? It's a compliment. You know I like the sausage."

Her brow quirked, and she stared at me for a moment. "Did you start drinking already?"

My gaze bounced around the room, glancing over to the trash can that held the two recently emptied bottles of rum. "Maybe."

"You have loose lips when you do. Come on." She waved at me to follow her into the hotel's bar.

"Marcy, I don't wanna."

She let out a sigh. "Stop whining like my five-year-old niece, and get your ass in there. It's just a party."

My shoulders slumped forward, and I groaned. "It's a *work* party, which makes it infinitely worse than any other party."

She put her hands on her hips. "What is your party malfunction, Warren?"

"I'm a social drinker. I get fucked up, horny, and sleep with whoever is available. And with my luck, it's the ugliest guy there."

Her lips cracked up into a smile. "I'll keep you ugly free."

"That's beside the point! I don't want a nighter with

someone I have to look at every day. Plus, Dr. Douche becomes extra douchey when he's liquored up. I had to file a complaint with HR after last year."

"Wait, what?" she asked with a furrowed brow. "I don't remember that."

"He called me a whore."

"Whoa!"

I pursed my lips and scrunched my brow. "Then again, I may have been hitting on him. I don't really remember."

She shook her head and wrapped her arm around my shoulders, tugging me along with her. "Even his hotness can't combat his horrible personality. What if we taped his mouth shut? He has a great smolder."

My head fell back in laughter. "Don't tempt me. It's been a while."

We walked in, and I took a deep breath as we crossed to the back. Most of the tables we passed were empty but would steadily fill in with the people filtering in. During the last few feet of approach to our group, I took a quick glance around the room for my exits before we reached the table where over half a dozen people already sat.

"Paisley, sit here." Micah's eager smile beamed at me as he patted the space on the booth beside him. The drink in his hand was half gone—sitting next to an empty one—which probably accounted for his rosy cheeks.

A hand reached out for mine and tugged me in the opposite direction.

"Paisley, dear, why don't you sit next to me?" The corners of Dr. Mitchell's eyes crinkled with fine lines and age, a knowing smile as he pulled out a chair.

"Thank you," I whispered, giving his hand a squeeze.

"No worries. You aren't the first victim of the night." He sat back down beside me, what looked like a brandy in front of him, which he gingerly sipped from. "How have you been?"

I glanced around for Marcy to make sure she hadn't been snared, only to find that poor Sandra had, then turned back to the older gentleman next to me. And that was exactly what Dr. Mitchell was—a gentleman. His once dark hair was white, but he still held a youthful appearance for his sixty years.

"Good. Work's keeping me busy."

"Not too busy for a social life, I hope," he said before taking a sip.

Social life? In the last six months, the only relationship I had was with my couch. We had three-ways with my television. Sometimes two guys named Ben and Jerry came around for an introvert gang bang.

"Well…" I trailed off, not having an answer, my gaze glued at a spot on the table as I fidgeted with my purse strap.

"Paisley."

I turned to him. "I've been spending a lot of quality time with myself."

His lips formed a thin line. "I was afraid you were going to say that. Is it because of Digby?"

My chest clenched as the hairs stood up on the back of my neck.

Digby.

"It's been almost a year since he moved. Do you keep in touch?"

I shrugged. "Occasionally."

If phone sex about a month ago and a midnight hookup four months ago on his way through town counted. After being together for almost three years, it still stunned me that we were over. He got an offer with the Dallas Cowboys' marketing team and two weeks later, he was gone.

Then again, I did nothing to follow him. We talked about it, he even proposed, but I couldn't commit to it…to him. A mindset that'd kept me down for a year. An almost perfect guy, one who loved me, and I let him go.

"There's someone out there for you, but you can't lock yourself inside all the time. Get out, enjoy the world. You only live once."

I leaned forward, wrapping my arms around his shoulders. "Thank you. I'll try."

A N HOUR LATER, OUR GROUP'S ATTENDANCE HIT THE unlucky number thirteen. Micah's voice was growing louder with each drink. His hands had already run Sandra off to hide behind Damon, who was in a surprisingly good mood and on his third beer. Dr. Mitchell was deep in conversation with Dr. Alma, as we affectionately called her. It was mainly due to the length of her hyphenated last name.

The glass in front of me was empty, putting me in desperate need of another if I was going to make it through another hour. Up at the bar, I found an empty seat in the now bustling establishment, and waited for the bartender to come my way.

When I had my new drink in hand, I didn't head back to the table. Instead, I sat, checking the time on my phone along with my social media notifications. Of which I had none. Where were all my friends?

Looking through my timeline, which was filled with tons of Valentine's Day pics from a few days before, there were updates from friends I hadn't seen in years.

Kristi Kallam: Counting down the days until spring break.
>.<

Teachers needed vacation, too.

Massy Reyes: Margarita time!!

Complete with a photo of a huge green filled glass the size of a fish bowl.

Marissa Wade: Loving this cool Arizona weather! Hike, here I come.

Cute selfie with the Arizona landscape behind her.

All three of them were friends of mine in school. After college, we split off to different parts of the country. Since then, most of our contact was via the Internet and the occasional birthday or holiday call or text.

I missed them, but moving apart was the sad drawback of growing up. I'd made a few friends around Cincinnati, but they weren't people I hung out with a lot. Add to that how my best friend was busy with two-month-old twins and that I had no man in my life, a homebody was born.

"Anyone sitting here?"

I looked up from my phone, and almost choked on the sip I just took as I saw the man before me. He was the cliché of tall, dark, and handsome—not the usual guy I attracted.

Not entirely true—Digby was tall, blond, and handsome.

"You." The word popped out of my mouth, proving I'd reached the happy drunk stage. Marcy did remind me earlier of my loose lips when drinking.

His blue eyes sparkled, and his mouth drew up into a smirk. The sharp angle of his jaw was accentuated by what appeared to be a few days' worth of stubble. His black suit was not off the rack, and his dark brown hair was longer and grab worthy.

"Simon."

He held out his hand, and I slipped mine in. It was rougher than I expected for a man in a tailored suit. Heat flooded my cheeks as I thought of him touching me all over. Rough, strong hands…

"Paisley."

He set his drink down, ordering another round for both of us, despite both of our glasses still being half full. Then again, they could be half empty, and he was just anticipating their imminent demise.

"What brings you here?" He took a sip of his vodka and tonic, lips pursed together as he swallowed.

The bob of his Adam's apple caught my eye, and a strong desire to lean forward and lick it took hold.

Months and months with nothing but silicone between my thighs, coupled with the booze and the front zip dress, and I was a tipsy hussy ready to spread my legs for him. Apparently, I wanted to jump the first real cock that showed the slightest bit of interest.

Which is exactly what gets you into trouble.

Then again, it could just be that he was very good looking and seemed interested in having a good time.

"Business. You?"

Another sip of my vodka and cranberry to quench my thirst. "Work party."

"Sounds…"

"Boring."

He chuckled. "The rowdy bunch in the corner?"

I peeked over, and sure enough, Micah was on the table doing a strip tease. I shook my head and turned back. Working with the dead, it was probably the first time any of them had lived in months. "I have no idea who those crazies are."

"I'm better company."

I quirked a brow at him and took another sip. "Awfully sure of yourself."

"I have a lot of self-confidence." He beamed at me.

And I had a lot of ways I was imagining mounting him on his bar stool. "Do you now? Cocky men are *not* attractive."

He shook his head. "There's a difference between cockiness and confidence."

"Enlighten me."

His finger traced the rim of his glass, his eyes locked on mine. "They both come from inside, but cockiness derives from a deep-seated need for attention to cover up insecurities and secure validation. I have no need for any of those."

I was stuck, transfixed or maybe hypnotized by him, unable to look away. "That's a pretty cocky statement." Even my words were stunted, low.

The man had me practically panting for him.

A bitch in heat.

Fuck me.

His tongue swiped across his lips as the corner of his mouth twitched up. "I suppose it is, but I assure you, there are no small parts of my anatomy I'm trying to compensate for."

"So, it comes from having a big head?"

Somebody shut me up!

A huge grin grew across his face. "Forward, aren't you? Talking about the size of my cock."

"Well, I meant the one on top of your neck. It is quite bulbous."

His brow crinkled. "I don't know how to take that."

"An observation."

Someone really needed to staple my lips shut. I was losing my best dick opportunity of the night.

"What is it that you do to make such an observation?" His smile dropped a little, no longer reaching his eyes or having that sexy edge.

"I'm a vampire."

His brows shot up, and he nodded. "Interesting, and a little macabre."

I wanted to slap myself. First guy in ages to flirt with me, and I was fubaring it. He was gone.

"Yep."

He leaned forward, surprising me, his interest seeming piqued by the near excitement in his expression. "I didn't realize being a vampire was a job."

I nodded. "Not very lucrative, though."

"Do you have other talents besides being a master sucker?"

The way he enunciated the last word coupled with the heavy lidded look he gave me had my pussy clenching.

My eyes widened.

And we're back.

"I…I…" I cleared my throat as my cheeks heated up. "What brings you to the great city of Cincinnati?"

He leaned back, but the sexy smirk thankfully stayed. "I travel a lot for work. For instance, I got off a plane from Chicago yesterday, and I'd been in Italy a few days before that."

"Italy? I've always wanted to go there."

"Can I persuade you to keep me company?" He reached out, fingers trailing up my forearm. "Or do you need to get back?"

"I don't know," I said with a glance to the table again.

He smirked. "You don't?"

I bit my lip and looked up at him from under my lashes. "I think it all depends on your method of persuasion." It was official at that sentence that I'd reached my limit: I'd just offered myself up.

"I know many ways." He leaned forward, his eyes on my lips before looking up. "I have words… I have touch." I drew in a ragged breath as his hand moved down the column of my neck. "Where would you like me to start? With my mouth or my body?"

"I can't have both?"

He chuckled as one hand moved to my waist, drawing me to him, while the other cupped my neck. When his lips touched mine, a jolt of pleasure zapped my clit, making it twitch. I let out a little moan as he slipped his tongue inside, stroking it against my own. Then, it wasn't just him holding me to his body, it was also my hands knotting in his suit, pulling me up and closer as the electric pulses danced in my veins.

I wanted him. Right there, on the bar stool.

I whimpered when he pulled back, my eyes heavy and cheeks hot.

His hips shifted, pushing his cock into my stomach.

"Can we try that again? Maybe somewhere with at least a little bit of privacy?" I asked, using every bit of strength in me to keep from climbing onto his lap.

He quirked his brow. "How much is a little bit?"

"At this point I don't care if it's in the men's restroom." There was no covering how breathy my voice was.

He smirked again and reached into his pocket, pulling out one of the hotel's key cards. "I'd like a little more time with you than a quickie in a stall, no matter how hot that sounds."

"Then how about we start there and work our way up?"

"Kinky." He leaned forward, his tongue swiping across my lips. "I like it."

Large hands wrapped around my waist and pulled me the rest of the way off the bar stool. He threw some bills down for our drinks and grabbed my hand.

I chanced a glance at my coworkers before sneaking out and into the hotel lobby. The heels of my boots clicked on the marble floor, Simon's long legs and large steps making it difficult to keep up.

Once we reached the elevator bay, he pressed the button and then pushed me against the wall. His fingers pulled at the zipper, teasing.

"Such a lewd dress," he said as he leaned down, licking the tops of my breasts, biting down with a moan.

"Lewd?" My body wouldn't stay still. The rough way he grabbed me, his bite. With the small taste he was giving me, he could easily turn out to be the fuck-beast I so desperately needed.

His fingers dug into my flesh as his hands moved around in a barely contained frenzy. "All I can think about is if you're wearing anything under it. How easy it would be to open it up and fuck the sexy body you're hiding."

I flung my arms around his shoulders and pulled his lips back down to mine.

How long had it been since I'd been called sexy by a man? Yeah, he was getting whatever he wanted, because I needed the memory to last.

The ping signaling the elevator's arrival didn't stop him. He bent over, coaxing my legs up and around his waist as he held on to my ass. Walking the few steps, he pressed me against the wall as he reached out to punch the button for his floor.

His teeth grabbed on to my bottom lip and pulled while his hips arched up, pressing his cock against my clit. There was no doubt in my mind my thong was soaked through. I was so turned on, I'd probably come if he stuffed me with his cock right there.

Fire in my veins heated, pulsing through me with each beat of my heart.

Either there was nobody in the halls, or we were completely oblivious to everything but each other as we exited and he took however many steps it was to his room. With each bounce came another hit to my clit, and I was whimpering, ready to meet his beast.

The moment we were inside his room he kicked the door shut. I still couldn't believe what I was doing with a stranger, but the chemistry between us was off the charts hot. Stranger or not, I needed him in the worst ways.

I bounced as he threw me down on the bed, letting out a small giggle. The excitement bubbled through me as he loomed over me.

He grabbed my breast, pinching the nipple between his fingers, exciting me more as he worked his way to the zipper. With each inch the zipper moved, revealing the skin beneath, his eyes darkened. He licked his lips as the split opened up, exposing my lacy bra. Groaning, his brow furrowed when he reached the bottom, viewing all of me.

I smiled up at him, letting him get a good look before I sat up. He didn't even seem to notice me working his belt open, but when his breathing sped up, I knew I had his full attention. I couldn't help running my palm against the defined dick straining his slacks as I opened his belt and popped open the button.

Yanking on one corner, the zipper slid down. I trailed my fingers along the elastic waistband of his briefs, earning a twitch from his cock. He stared down at me, my flitting glance catching the look of absolute primal desire focused on me.

Nothing like a sexy guy staring at you like you're the most desirable woman he'd ever seen.

I maneuvered the waistband over the bulge, teasing both of us as I exposed just the head and then each veiny, hard inch.

When was the last time I'd sucked a cock? Who knew, but I couldn't help salivating over the specimen in front of me. Above average length and girth with a slight, upward curve.

My pussy clenched in anticipation of what was going to happen, of the toe-curling pleasure I knew he could deliver.

I ran my tongue around the head, moving down the

underside of his shaft, wetting it before I wrapped my lips around and made my way down. His groans were encouraging as I worked to get as much of him in my mouth as possible before I began to choke.

Baby steps.

One of my hands wrapped around the base, stroking it as I bobbed up and down.

Turned out giving head was like riding a bike—a little intimidating at first, but once you got going, muscle memory kicked in.

"Enough," he said through heavy breaths.

I pulled back, twirling my tongue around the head as I pumped his shaft. "You don't want to come?"

"Oh, I do," he grabbed my wrist and pulled me back onto the bed, "but I want to come inside you first, then I can splatter you with my paint."

Fuck.

Charismatic, confident fucker with a panty wetting mouth. My hand slid down my abdomen, over my panties, and pressed against my clit as my legs fell open.

He slapped at my hand and I pulled it back, giving him a pout. All it did was make him smirk down at me.

"No touching yourself." Reaching down, he tore the thin fabric from my body and tossed it on the floor. "*I'm* going to make you come."

Fuck, yes, he was.

The bed dipped as he climbed on, settling between my thighs. He looked up, our eyes locking as his tongue flicked against my clit.

It felt like an electric charge pulsed through me, making my body jerk away from the intensity. His arms wrapped around my legs, holding me in place.

"Stay," he flicked his tongue out again, running it up my slit, "put."

I actually feared for my sanity, if I would have a mind when he was done. Driven crazy by the touch of a man.

A loud moan slipped from me as his mouth closed over my pussy, alternating between licking and sucking on my clit. The intense feeling made my pussy clench, dripping as it begged to be filled.

Yanking on my bra cups, I freed my breasts and my strained nipples. Light pinches and fluttering touches increased the euphoria pumping through me. My hips rose, writhed against his face, riding him, taking my orgasm from him. One he denied me as he sat up and moved to loom over me, cock in hand.

So fucking close. I glared at him, but that sly smirk was back on as he moved up, the tip of his dick trailing up, tapping against my skin until the hot head landed on my clit.

"Condom?" I asked just as his hand moved between us.

His eyes cleared for a brief second. "Shit. I don't have any."

My mind was all over the place, but important questions needed answered. "Clean?"

"Took a shower this morning," he said as he moved again to position himself.

I smacked my hand against his chest, and he chuckled.

"Don't laugh. This incredible feeling isn't worth some STD."

"Yes, I'm free of any and all diseases."

I twisted and reached down to the floor and pulled up my purse. Good thing I'd remembered to grab a few condoms for just in case.

After tearing one off and handing it to him, I set the rest on the bedside table. I had a sneaking suspicion we weren't going to be done after one round.

It was so hot watching him roll the condom on, inch by inch

by so many inches until it couldn't go any farther.

"Fuck, you're big."

He smirked at me, rocking his hips against my slit, making me shudder as he lubed up. I craned my neck up and he dipped down, hungry mouths meeting again. I rested my hands on his waist, helping me to lift my hips in time with his thrust.

So turned on I ached and burned, and every stroke against my clit gave me goose bumps.

"Let's see if it fits," I whispered with a smirk.

No words, no witty retort, just a possessive touch and a large cock forging a path into my underused pussy. The feeling was so intense my body shuddered and exploded. I shook beneath him, clamping down around him.

"Did you just come?" he asked, the surprise evident in his tone.

I whimpered and nodded as I convulsed in his arms.

"Damn, I'm good."

"There's that cockiness," I said through harsh breaths.

"Nope, you're just upping my already high confidence." He pulled out and slammed back in, then fisted my hair, tilting my head back as his teeth scraped against my neck. "Let's see if I can do it again."

There was no room to argue, no dispute, just a long keening from me as he slammed his cock into me. Fast, hard strokes to my still spasming pussy.

"Your pussy wants to come again. It's squeezing me so tight," he whispered against my ear.

"Fuck."

He pulled out and slammed back in. "What is it you think I'm doing?"

"Harder."

He smirked. "As you wish."

I asked for hard and he gave it, along with fast and pounding. Obliterating my pussy, blissed out and shaking as I came again.

A few more insanity making strokes before he let out a low groan, his hips jerking as he erupted.

Our breaths mingled, another kiss, soft and sensual as his strength gave out.

"Don't think I'm done," he said against my neck.

"No?" I asked, still trying to catch my breath.

He made a humming sound. "No. I'm going to make sure you can't walk out of this room."

Fuck. Me.

THREE HOURS OF SLEEP WAS NOT NEARLY ENOUGH BEFORE a ten-hour shift. My own fault for fucking a guy all night. I was paying for it in many ways. Walking was difficult, my thighs sore and weak, and there was a nonstop, pulsing ache in my pussy.

Fucking worth it.

"So, who was the guy you ran off with last night?" Sandra asked, surprising me when she leaned on the counter right next to me.

I blinked at her. "What?"

"Don't what me. I saw you sneak off with tall, dark, and handsome. His hands were all over you."

My mind wandered back to said hands. "He had great hands."

"So, you did do some in-depth examinations." She waggled her eyebrows, her brown eyes sparkling.

"He puts all other guys I've been with to shame."

Her eyes bulged. "Even Digby?"

I used to call my ex-boyfriend Digby my Norwegian pile driver. He was huge all over and known to bruise sensitive areas with how hard he pounded my pussy, but it was worth it.

However, his memory was being eclipsed by Simon, though I wasn't sure what about him made it better.

"Okay, he doesn't put Digby to shame, but he may top him."

"Damn." She blew out a breath and fanned herself. "You, me, wine. Thursday at my place and you are telling me every last detail. I think the men in my life just met a new standard."

I smiled at her and shook my head. "Wine sounds like an excellent idea."

"Perfect. I'll see you then." She waved as she pushed off and headed out the door.

With Sandra gone and Damon staring at me, I grabbed the top bin and began to process another vial. With one down, three more appeared, and I stepped up the pace. Plugging in my earbuds helped get me in the zone and I was off.

"Hey, Paisley, got a good one for you," Micah said as he walked up holding the basket containing a file and three vials of blood.

"Is it mutant?" I asked as I pulled out my earbuds and set them on the counter.

He laughed. "Better. John Doe."

I didn't often know patient names, even less about the person or how they died. They were all a series of barcodes attached to each vial.

I quirked my brow at Micah. "John Doe?"

"Yeah, Dr. Mitchell can't ID the guy. He's got no prints, no dental records, nothing."

"No prints?"

He shook his head. "Burned off."

"His fingertips are burned off? That's weird." So strange. It was the first I'd heard of it outside of Hollywood.

"Tell me about it. He showed up two days ago and there's not even a hint. Wonder if he's a spy or something."

I rolled my eyes as he headed back out the security door and down the hall. Micah's words came back to me, and a deep curiosity took over.

I loved a good mystery, after all.

Pushing against the floor, I rolled my chair over to a computer where I pulled up John Doe's electronic file, and clicked on the ME's report.

Almost everything about his physical aspects was average: height, weight, hair and eye color. Though his body composition noted an overly strong musculature. He was probably a fitness buff who spent a lot of time in the gym. Estimated age of late thirties to early forties. But, then there were the fingerprints, or finger smudges in his case.

His wounds consisted of a few scrapes on his knuckles along with bruising on his face and torso, indicating he'd been in some sort of fight. The killing blow was a single gunshot wound to the head from close proximity. The placement and angle suggested the oh-so-well-known, but rarely seen, execution-style.

I double clicked on his X-rays and stared in shock. I'd never trained in reading X-rays, but after looking at them for years, thanks to a combination of morbid curiosity and a constant need to know more, I'd learned to spot calluses: the signs of bone remodeling.

The extent of calluses on our Mr. Doe's skeleton was staggering. I'd seen the X-rays of jumpers who didn't have as many broken bones as this man had accumulated in his life.

Maybe Micah was right.

I wanted to laugh at the stupidity of that thought. A spy? In Cincinnati? Was he here to steal Skyline's chili recipe? Or find out why people were obsessed with goetta? Because I'd like to know the answer to that one.

Then again, GE Aviation was based here and they did have

government contracts…

Really, Paisley?

I shook my head and closed out the X-rays. There was one identifiable mark Dr. Mitchell found, so I pulled it up. When it opened, I squinted at the screen, trying to figure out what I was looking at and how Dr. Mitchell even noticed it.

Behind Mr. Mysterious's left ear, underneath the backside of the concha, in the crease where the ear and the skull meet, were three dots. Permanent markings on the skin, almost like freckles, but they were black.

I sat back and stared at the screen.

What a strange marking.

I'd heard about gangs having a three-dot tattoo, but those were mostly in a triangle and in a noticeable place. His was in an almost invisible place. Plus, besides the bodily damage he'd suffered over the years, nothing about him—tattoos, apparel, et cetera—suggested any gang relations. Christ, the man was wearing a suit when he was killed.

For the next few hours, I went about my job and obsessed about John Doe in the back of my mind. Who was he?

Later, close to my clock out time, when the tests were done—thanks to my curiosity moving it to the head of the class—I pulled up the results and shook my head.

The tests brought up a startling and confusing combination of drugs in John Doe's system. "This isn't right."

I printed off the results and walked over to where Damon was sitting.

"This can't be right, can it?" I asked, shoving the piece of paper in his face.

He scowled at me as he grabbed the paper and looked down at it. The annoyance on his face morphed into confusion.

"How are the other tests coming out?" he asked, his eyes

never leaving the page.

I shrugged. "Normal for this place."

"Do we need to recalibrate and rerun?"

"That's what I was wondering." I turned back to my station and looked at the stack of completed, all normal tests from before and after.

The telltale beep and click of the door's security flickered in the back of my mind.

"Holy shit." Damon's low curse was unusual, and my head popped up as I turned back and looked toward the door.

I barely had time to even comprehend who was standing there and why.

Time stopped.

The only thing I registered was the gun in a man's hand and each snap as it fired off. Precise shots from its silenced barrel that ended emerging screams.

In my peripheral, three of my lab mates fell to the ground. Five shots in all, but I was still standing, staring straight down the dark, life-ending barrel. I shifted my eyes to focus behind the gun to the man, to see my killer before I died, and my heart stopped.

Simon?

His expression was calm and serious—a man on a mission.

His finger lingered on the trigger, but then his arm relaxed to his side.

My heart raced, beating against my chest so fast it felt like it was trying to break out from my ribs. I couldn't think, couldn't move. Could only stare at him. Complete shock had hijacked my system.

He reached out and grabbed my arm, pulling me toward the door. "I need you."

Words that made my knees weak the day before made them weak again, but for a completely different reason. I stumbled, my feet seeming to have lost all memory of how to function. He was strong, and there was no resisting, even if I could.

As we moved through the door, I turned back and stared in wide-eyed horror.

The walls were dripping with red. Marcy, Damon, Murphy, Dr. Alma, and Ian were sprawled out on the floor. Their eyes were empty as blood pooled beneath them.

A scream built in my chest, but it wouldn't come out. The world fell from beneath me as I tried to understand, to process what was going on, that they were all dead.

Pain in my arm brought my attention back to the man who just last night was a dream come true. Now he seemed to be a thing made of nightmares.

I was still asleep. That had to be it. None of it was real.

"Open it."

I blinked up at him, then at the sign above the door—Morgue. The shock started to wear off, and I shook my head as I pulled back. "No."

He held his gun up again and pressed the still warm tip to my forehead. "Open it. Now."

I was going to die.

My life ending in a mess.

I didn't want to die. Not today. Not for a long time.

Why is this happening?

Tears began sliding down my cheeks as I prayed that it was empty, that all the bodies inside were dead. My hand shook as I reached out and slid my card through the reader, then entered in the six-digit code.

There was no pause in his stride as he entered, only a cool, deadly killer.

Meticulous.

Three snaps.

Cheryl.

Dr. Mitchell.

Micah.

They all slumped to the ground.

My stomach dropped. An explosion of screams was held in by the coiling suffocation around my chest. Squeezing. Choking.

He released me, and I fell back against the wall. Harsh, gulping breaths burned my lungs. The world spun, and my fingers dug into the wall for support.

Loud slams of the fridge doors opening and the ratcheting thumps of the drawers sliding out blasted in my ears. I flinched with each one. He wasted no time opening them all, exposing the bodies, disturbing the dead.

I wanted to scream at him to stop, but fear had me planted in place.

All of his focus was on whatever he was looking for, paying no attention to me. It was my chance to get away.

Run.

I reached out to the side with a trembling hand, using it to guide me to the exit. My feet shuffled in slow uncooperative steps, praying to any higher power that was listening to let me make it out alive.

With a sudden flex of his arm, the gun was pointed straight at me again, and I froze in terrified horror.

"Don't." He didn't even look my way.

I whimpered, my teeth chattering, frozen. "P-Please, Simon."

"Shut up."

When he opened one of the last doors and pulled back the sheet, his movements stopped. It was only a brief second, but it seemed he'd found what he was looking for.

"Three?"

He flipped up the earlobe of the man. I couldn't see, but that one action told me that was the body of John Doe.

For a few seconds the silence was deafening, then the calm demeanor slipped. A string of curses exploded from him, echoing off the tile walls. Then the calm was back as quickly as it had disappeared.

A beeping went off, and he walked straight forward, pointing his gun once again at my head.

"I have information about him you don't." My mind raced, my mouth spitting out words I wasn't sure I could back or would matter to him, but I'd say anything to buy more time.

"Tell me."

I shook my head, the only movement I seemed to be able to manage.

The beeping went off again. "Fuck." His lip curled up into a snarl, and he snatched my arm again.

His grip was severe, bruising. We practically ran down the hall, him walking briskly ahead of me and me being dragged along.

After multiple turns I realized we were headed to the parking garage.

"Simon?"

He looked back at me, his eyes narrowed to slits. "Stop calling me that."

"W-Why?"

He turned from me, scanning the garage. "Six."

My head tilted to the side and my brow scrunched. "Six?"

"My name. It's Six." He let go of my arm and reached into his pocket for keys as we neared a black sedan.

I continued to follow, knowing if I stopped, he'd shoot. "Why Six?"

Was he a secret agent or something? Like James Bond?

Scratch that. I probably didn't want to know. He had just murdered everyone I worked with. Innocent people.

He let out a frustrated sigh and pushed me into the side of the car. "Because I'm your motherfucking Satan. Now, get your ass in the damn car before I throw you in."

I stared at the car for a brief second, then slid in. The moment the door was closed, he had my wrists in his grip and was spinning a roll of duct tape around them, binding my hands.

He started the engine and pulled out, but not in the speeding rush I anticipated. Slow. The speed limit of the parking garage. Once we'd driven a few blocks in frightening silence, he pulled something from his pocket and pressed it.

A few seconds later an earsplitting explosion rocked us and everything around. I snapped forward, then slammed back into my seat as a shock wave hit. Smoke and flames reflected in the rearview mirror, emanating from the spot where my building resided—there was nothing remaining.

Everything was gone.

All the shock, the pain, the confusion, and the fear built up and I erupted. "What the fuck is going on?"

He was unfazed by my outburst, absorbed with the I-275 exit in front of him. "Better put your seatbelt on. I don't care if you live or die, but you may."

Hands bound, it was hard to maneuver the belt across my body, but after some tugging, it clicked in place.

The words of an ex of mine came back to haunt me as I stared down at the gray around my wrists: never get tied up.

It probably didn't matter because he could've killed me multiple times over, but I knew nothing good would come.

WE WERE TEN MILES UP THE ROAD, ALMOST TO THE I-74 exit, when Six's grip tightened on the wheel and his foot pressed on the gas. His gaze flickered to the mirrors, but when I looked, there were no red and blue lights like I expected. In fact, there was nothing but other cars.

He began weaving in and out of traffic, but even with everything, we still didn't stand out. The moment we passed the border into Indiana, he pulled into the inside lane and slammed on the gas, rocketing us forward. It was then I noticed a white sedan behind us doing the same.

We were being followed. Not by law enforcement, which probably meant it was someone as equally dangerous as him.

Six rolled down the windows as the other car gained on us. "Get down on the floor unless you want your bullet now." He grabbed his gun and a new clip, reloading it.

I frantically unlatched the seatbelt and slid to the carpet, tucking my body as far and deep into the space as I could. The wind whipped my hair around, and when I twisted and reached up to grab it, I brushed against his hand. His arm was outstretched, gun high. He pulled on the trigger in quick succession.

I covered my ears. Even with the silencer it was too loud,

being that close. The cool calm from before continued to surround him, but the surprise on his face was noticeable when the other car returned fire. I cringed and squeezed my eyes tight with each bullet that struck us. More than one made it through the layers of the door, missing me by inches.

A sudden movement knocked my head into the center console as the other car sideswiped us. I cried out and grabbed my forehead. Another couple of shots rang out, then tires squealed.

"Damn it." The engine revved again, and he closed up the windows. "Get up."

I pulled myself up, noting our speed had passed one hundred and the other car had disappeared.

Again, my heart was pounding, this time in sync with the bump on my head as I attempted to latch the belt again. My teeth chattered as tears flowed down my cheeks.

"Too much. This is too fucking much."

He pulled off on the first exit we came upon, somewhere in the middle of nowhere Indiana. "This has only begun."

Sobs burst from me in waves that rattled my core. It was all happening, not a dream. My coworkers, my friends, were dead. "Why? Why are you doing this? What is going on?"

His gaze never left the road. "None of that matters. You were in the wrong place at the wrong time."

"Why did you kill them all?" So many lives, gone.

"Collateral damage, just as you'll be." No emotion. A mechanical response.

Who is he?

"You don't have to kill me, just let me go. I swear I won't say anything." It was a feeble plea. One I wanted to believe would work, but after what I'd seen, I knew was a hopeless dream.

He shook his head. "Doesn't work like that. You have information, which is the only reason you're alive right now."

"So last night meant nothing?" I asked, more than willing to pimp out my body to live.

"Its purpose was pleasure. Nothing more," he said. His words cut right through me, adding to everything else, and made my stomach turn. "And you were excellent at giving it."

"Asshole. You knew you were going to kill me, and you fucked me," I said, tears spilling freely.

He took a sharp turn down a county road and the car accelerated, forcing me back into the seat. "Wrong. I didn't know until I lined up my gun to your head."

That didn't help.

It felt like every muscle was vibrating from being clenched so tight.

The car was tense, my hands still bound as I waited. So many questions flowed through my brain along with all of the what-ifs to go with the sheer, undeniable shock. There was a chance it could all be a dream, but the pain in my wrists squashed any further thoughts of my reality being any different.

"What do you know?" he asked, breaking the silence.

I shook my head. If I told him, there'd be no reason to keep me alive.

"I can get it out of you, but it's easier on you if you just tell me."

A tear spilled down my cheek, lip trembling. "I don't want to die." My voice, even forced, was barely above a whisper.

"Everybody dies."

I didn't know to take that as a generalization, or that everyone he came into contact with died.

He offered no words, no sense of remorse, and the quiet resumed.

We hit over three hours of painful silence, with the exception of my crying. I wanted to enjoy the scenery, but the situation wouldn't allow it. At least I would've had beautiful images as the last thing I saw instead of the gruesome ones from the lab.

In his haste, he saved me from seeing what he'd done to Marcy and the others, but from his precision...

Micah, Cheryl, and Dr. Mitchell... I let him in. I was the reason they were dead too.

No, that wasn't true. They would have died anyway.

But that fact didn't assuage the guilt, or free me of the vision of their lifeless, bleeding bodies on the morgue floor.

What horror was in store for me?

In the middle of nowhere, just into Tennessee, he pulled into a small-town motel. It was probably built in the '60s, with a dozen rooms attached to a floor-to-ceiling windowed circular main lobby area. There was a pool in the parking lot, but by the debris of lawn chairs and leaves, it hadn't been used in years.

"We'll stay here tonight." He stepped out of the car, locking the doors before dipping his head back in. "Try to run and you'll be dead in ten steps, and then I'll have to kill everyone here."

I nodded and stared after him.

When he returned, I shouldn't have been surprised to see an actual key in his hand versus a key card, but I was. The place was in such disrepair it was obvious its last update was probably in the '80s.

After parking closer to our room, aptly room 6, he slipped a knife through the tape binding me, then pulled my arms out of my lab coat, throwing it in the back. I rubbed at my wrists, flexing them and my arms before climbing out of the car. He grabbed on to my hand and I flinched, earning a glare and a more forceful taking of my hand.

Sticking the ancient brass key into the door, he pulled me in and flipped on the lights before closing up the curtains and locking the door.

The two double beds were dressed in gaudy floral print comforters and looked as old as the motel. Stains in the carpet, antenna on the ancient TV, and smoke residue coating the walls. The smell was noxious, stagnant, like the room hadn't been opened in a decade.

It was so bad, I stood five feet from anything with my hand over my mouth and nose.

Six threw his bag onto one of the beds, the springs squeaking as it bounced. "Do you need to go to the bathroom?" I nodded. He gestured his head to the small door at the back of the room. "Go."

Tentative steps moved me into the small, windowless room, and I shut the door. I looked around the tiny space as I pushed the sleeves of my undershirt up.

The bathroom was like the rest of the motel. The sink was stained from years of a constant drip and misuse. Dirty, cracked vinyl floors pulled away from the walls, and the once white tub was brown on the bottom, the surrounding tiles covered in mildew.

The whole thing was straight out of a horror movie. Then again, I was in the middle of one, so it didn't faze me too much after what had already happened.

I stared down at the toilet with its chipped seat and discolored bowl. Being my only option, I heaved a sigh and sat down. It wasn't like I really needed to be concerned with germs anyway.

My mind was quiet, still stunned. I was going through the motions, drifting in an ocean of uncertainty. How was I going to get out of this mess?

After washing my hands, ignoring my horrid reflection, I headed out to whatever was next. I stopped after a few feet, and stared.

Six stood next to a boxy-looking, wood-framed chair, the roll of duct tape in his hands. "Sit."

I shook my head and backed up.

His jaw flexed, making the muscles in his neck tighten. "Don't fucking mess with me right now. I have no problems making you, but it'll be easier on us both if you do as I say."

I looked down at the carpet and swallowed hard, then did as he requested. He immediately went to work securing my ankles to the legs of the chair and my wrists to the arms. He even went as far as taping just under my knee and at my elbow to the frame. Needless to say, I wasn't getting out of it on my own.

Another piece of duct tape was held out in front of me. "Can't have you screaming."

I pulled away from him, but it didn't help. He slapped the tape over my mouth, leaving me only my nose to breathe from.

"I'll be back." He let out a dark chuckle. "Don't go anywhere."

I cringed as the door slammed shut. There was the sound of him starting the car, and then nothing.

I scanned the dimly lit room, then looked down at myself. Taped up for who knew how long, all alone in the blistering silence.

My heart started to pound in my chest, my nostrils flaring with each labored breath. I struggled against the tape in a very futile effort to get free. Whimpers echoed in my throat, my face scrunching up as tears started to stream again.

Everyone was dead, except me, but I would be soon. Maybe his fast death was the better way to go, rather than experiencing the cruel torture of waiting, of being subjected to restraint.

Hope was slipping from me, as much as I clung to it.

Breathing became difficult. I couldn't get enough air, and it felt like I was going to suffocate. The more I thought about it, the worse it became.

Every shot echoed. The smell of the room.

Dead.

Everyone.

After a few minutes, the world went black.

RATTLING STIRRED ME, WAKING ME FROM MY SLUMBER. My eyes fluttered open as my head rose in time to see through the darkness a figure step through a door, locking it behind them. A flip of the switch, and I cringed against the harsh light.

After adjusting, I looked at the man, and everything came rushing back.

I guess in sleep I hoped to forget I was a captive taped to a chair.

Six walked to the bed, dumping half a dozen plastic bags.

"Did you just wake up?"

I scowled at him.

He chuckled, then stepped over, ripping the tape from my mouth.

"Ouch! Asshole, motherfucking hurt!" The sting of the tape taking hair was worse than a wax job.

"You'll be fine." He rummaged through the bags, pulling out a few boxes of hair dye.

"What's that for?" I asked, even though the answer was obvious.

"Are you going to tell me what you know?"

He pulled the gun out of his waistband. "Should I just shoot you now?"

"No."

He tore open one of the packages, emptying the contents before locating the instructions. "Then it's time for a change. Your hair is too unusual. We need to blend in."

"Oh, hell, no." I shook my head and glared at him. "I've never dyed my hair, and I'm not about to start now."

"You won't. I'll be doing it for you."

I cursed as I looked down at my restraints.

He disappeared into the bathroom, reappearing a few minutes later with his hair inches shorter than it had been and what I assumed was a bottle of dye for me. I whimpered as he began squirting the brown liquid onto my hair, scrunching it in with his glove covered hands. I cringed with each crinkle, my bottom lip jutting out.

The only good thing was if he was bothering to dye my hair, I was going to live a little longer. But how long would it really be before I got a bullet of my own?

After he was done, I was stuck waiting for him to get the chemical smelling shit off my hair while he showered.

A few minutes later, he walked out of the bathroom naked, running a towel over his hair. My mouth popped open as I stared at the chest and cock my tongue spent a lot of time getting to know not twenty-four hours prior.

Was I really thinking about that now? The clenching of my thighs, as best they could in their restraints, answered that question for me.

"You couldn't put on clothes?" I asked, embarrassed by my reactions.

Slut much, Paisley?

"What does it matter?" He moved the towel across his chest

and down his legs, making sure to shake his junk at me. "Besides, it's not like you haven't seen it before."

Yeah, but that was before I knew you were a murderer.

He opened up a leather bag he brought in with him and pulled out a knife. After slipping it out of its case, he stepped over to me and sliced at the tape. It hurt like a motherfucker when he yanked it off my arms, taking some fine hairs with it and making me regret I pulled my sleeves up, before doing the same to my legs.

Stiffness had taken over from so long in one position that it took me a minute to stand.

"Go wash that out," he said, then handed me a T-shirt. "Here."

I looked at him as I took it, noticing something was off.

"Your eyes…"

They were blue when I met him. I was sure of it. Bright blue, but no longer. Brown with flecks of gold and honey—an effect contacts couldn't replicate. His real eye color.

He didn't say anything, but it was another part of Simon that was a lie.

When I stripped my shirt off in the bathroom, I noticed a few spots and stared at them.

Looking down at my pants, there were more of the same small dots. Then more on my shoes, contrasting against the white.

Red dots.

Blood.

I stared down at them, all the fine droplets, my stomach rolling as their origin flashed through my mind. More tears fled from my eyes.

Everything was tainted.

I finished pulling off the rest of my clothes, suddenly happy for the T-shirt from the psychopath, and stepped into the disgusting shower. The moment the warm water hit my skin, tears streamed down my cheeks full force. There was no stopping the torrent flooding down my face or keeping the wailing cries in.

Every emotion poured out. So many feels, and no strength left to handle them.

The warmth helped to calm me some, to soothe me, but nothing could assuage the guilt or fear hanging over me. What was I going to do? How was I going to get away from him?

A fluke is the only thing that separated me from my coworkers, my friends. An ironic karma that stayed a bullet for a time.

When the water began to cool, I quickly shampooed my hair and made sure all the dye was off my eyebrows before I was forced to return to him.

I turned off the spray and grabbed a towel, drying my body before putting my panties back on along with the shirt he gave me. The bra stayed off, and I was too warm to put my scrub pants back on. Not to mention that I simply didn't want to put the blood of my friends and coworkers back on.

The mirror was steamed over, obscuring my reflection, but I wasn't sure I wanted to see the stranger, the ghost of me, anyway.

When I exited, Six was in a pair of jeans and nothing else, the play of light and shadows showing off his cut physique. The view reminded me of the night before and pissed me off that I was somehow still physically attracted to the son of a bitch who ruined my life.

I inched forward, setting my clothes on one of the beds. Staying silent seemed the best bet. I didn't have anything to say anyway. The surrealness seeped into my skin, causing a floating-like sensation to crawl around my body.

His back was to me as he rifled through one of the bags. My

gaze wandered around as I waited for whatever horror was next. I froze when I spotted the first sliver of an out I'd seen since he blasted into my life that day.

On the table sat his gun with the silencer still attached, along with a knife. It looked military, much larger than the average pocket knife, with the blade and handle being one piece. The tip curved up into a sharp point.

I couldn't take my eyes off it.

That piece of metal could free me.

The gun I could fuck up with, plus I didn't even know if it was still loaded with as many shots as he got off, but a knife? Anything goes.

I glanced over to Six. He was still facing away, giving me an opportunity. There wasn't much time, seconds, but it was enough.

I stepped forward and curled my fingers around the handle. As I turned, so did he, and I swung with every bit of strength I could.

His forearm shot out, blocking my attack, the blade tip slicing across his bicep. Before I could pull back and attempt another go, he grabbed hold of my wrist and twisted it, causing my fingers to open and the knife to fall down to the floor.

His lip twitched up into a snarl before he swung his arm out and connected with my face.

I landed hard on the ground, my head ringing as a pain began to throb at my cheek.

"What the fuck do you think you're doing?" His scream pierced through me, causing me to shake.

He stalked toward me, dead eyes watching as I scooted back until I hit the wall.

"Please…" My teeth started chattering as the fear took over.

"You want to live? Is that it?" he asked as he leaned down

and picked the knife up.

Hot tears streamed down my face as I forced the sobs back and nodded, my face screwed up. He stepped forward and squatted down in front of me, staring at me.

"You know…" he trailed off and turned the knife tip toward me. He brushed the back edge against my neck, running it lightly against my skin. "One tiny nick, right here." His cold eyes bored into me. "You'll be dead in seconds."

A knock on the door made his dangerous gaze narrow and the tip of the knife to press into my skin. "Not a peep."

He stood and walked toward the door, picking up his gun from the table on the way and slipping it into his waistband.

I sat, shaking, biting into my hand to keep quiet.

"Yes?" he asked whoever was on the other side of the door, the chain only allowing it to open a few inches.

"Hi, sorry to disturb you," a woman's voice said. "My name is Diane, and my husband and I are on his great backroads trip to the Appalachian trail and, well, our car broke down here of all places…" she let out a nervous laugh "…and we're staying in the room next door."

With each word his muscles tensed. "*And?*"

"And, well… Is everything all right? I heard a woman crying and screaming."

My eyes grew wide, and my heart started beating hard in my chest. Someone heard me. Maybe she could help me.

"Sorry, that was the TV," he said without missing a beat.

"Are you sure? It sounded so real."

My heart begged for her to believe the gut that lead her over, to call someone, to help me out of the nightmare I was in.

"Not all porn is girls begging for more."

"Oh," the woman said, but before she could say anything else, Six slammed the door and flipped the lock.

He remained where he was, listening. In the absolute silence I could hear her footsteps, her key jingling in the lock, the
creak of the door as it opened, then closed with a thud.

I'd been locked in fright, but when he turned back to me,
eyes in dangerous slits, an uncontrollable shaking took hold.

It only took him a few quick strides to get back over to me.
He squatted down and grabbed on to my hair and pulled, yanking my head back. I reached back, trying to get him to release,
my mind zapped blank by the pain.

"Stop," he hissed between his lock-jawed teeth. "You need
to shut the fuck up before I shut you up permanently."

I tried to snuff out the high-pitched sobs that squeaked out,
but there was no controlling my turbulent emotions and fear.

He shook me by the hair, then released me, standing up.

I didn't move. I couldn't. The shaking of my body was so
bad, the grimy floor and stained wall were my only friends.

Glued to the spot, I watched him move from one side of the
room to the other. Blood made fine trails down his arm, but he
didn't seem concerned with it. At one pass, he picked up a cell
phone from a black leather bag he'd pulled from the car.

Before he could do anything with it, there was another
knock, earning me a silencing glare as he headed back to the
door.

"Yes?" he asked through the small gap the chain gave.

"Hi, I'm staying next door and we've heard some strange
noises," a low male voice said. "Is everything okay?"

Saved. *He's going to save me.*

"I explained to your wife that it is just the TV."

Six tried to shut the door, but the man shoved his foot in
the gap.

"Can I look?" the man asked.

"No."

"Look, man, if you have nothing to hide, then what's the problem opening the door so I can see for myself? Then I can get my wife to shut up about it, and we won't bother you again."

I couldn't tell if it was just a line to gain a sympathetic edge, or if he really was annoyed with his wife's meddling.

"You want to see what I have in my room? Fine."

Six removed the chain and opened the door, grabbing on to the man's collar. He pulled him into the room and threw him on the floor. I let out a gasp, drawing his attention. He didn't look much older than me.

"Are you o—"

The silenced shot to the head cut him off, and I watched the light drain from his eyes as his body slumped onto the carpet. Thick, deep red pooled beneath him, and my stomach convulsed.

"Now you've seen."

A scream was trapped in my rolling stomach as I stared wide-eyed at the lifeless body of my savior.

Six opened the door, and I watched his shadow in the sliver of opening at the bottom of the curtain as he walked to the room next door. The slamming of what was probably his foot against the door sounded, a scream, a snap, then silence.

He walked back in and picked up the bags he'd purchased along with his duffle bag and anything else that we brought in. "Come on." He stared at me, waiting.

Tears slid down my cheeks. "What kind of monster are you?"

She tried to help me, and he killed her. He killed them both.

He stepped forward and yanked on my arm, pulling me up. "I'm *your* motherfucking monster. Get in the fucking car."

Once again, he gripped me tight, dragging me along with him.

"Why did you have to kill them?" I asked after I reluctantly slid into the car.

He grabbed on to my jaw, making me look at him. "You made me."

"What?"

"If you want to stay alive a little longer, if you want other people to stay alive, you will stop trying stupid shit. No trying to escape, no attempts to attack me, no talking to people. This is your life for the time being. Accept it."

He just expected me to accept that I was stuck with him for however long he felt like it? To not try to free myself?

Maybe he was more warped than I thought.

Somehow, some way, I was going to get free of him, but it was obvious I was going to have to wait for the perfect opportunity.

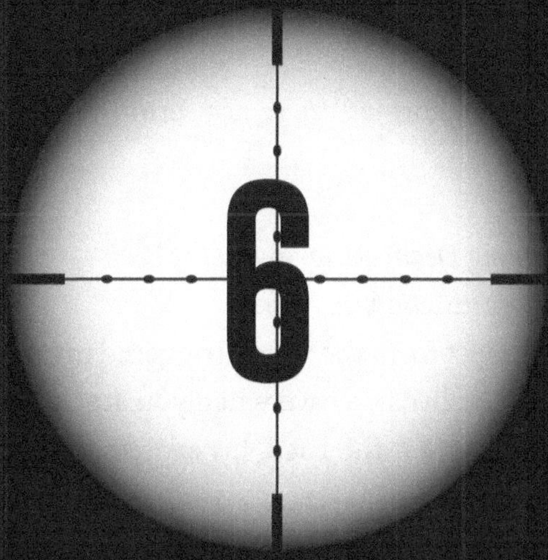

AWOKE TO THE CHANGE OF SPEED AND THE SUN SHINING IN my eyes. It took a moment for the sleep to leave and for me to once again remember all that had happened.

Alive, for the moment.

"Where are we?" I asked as I sat up. There was a sudden need to pee that took over, and a churn in my stomach. A quick glance down at the clock revealed it was just before 7 a.m.

"Outside Atlanta. We're going to stay here."

I nodded and noticed the anxiety in me was lower. Something in the night changed me. Inside, the turbulent seas had reduced to a yellow flag—as close to the Goldilocks zone as I was going to get in my situation. Add in to it that the urge to cry was missing.

I hadn't come to grips with what happened, but I did know crying wasn't going to help me. I was dealing with a deranged man who had no issue doing anything, including killing me.

The only thing to do was just as he said—accept the situation. If I didn't want more people to get hurt, or more precisely, killed, then I needed to have a level head and be smart about my actions.

A "Welcome" sign came up, and I read the name as we

passed by.

"Woodbury, Georgia? We're not seriously in Woodbury, are we?"

"Why?"

"*The Walking Dead*? Ring any bells?"

His brow scrunched up. "No."

His disconnect from the world triggered my sarcastic nature to say, "What? You live in a cave when you aren't killing people?"

His gaze never left the road, his expression neutral. "I'm always killing people."

I shook my head, trying dislodge info I really didn't want to know. If he didn't watch TV, he didn't know what he was driving into.

"It's one of the most popular shows on television."

"And?"

"And one of the big baddies ran the town of Woodbury, Georgia."

His foot slammed onto the brake, the force squeezing me against the seat belt and causing my bladder to nearly explode all over the seat. A horn blared as a car zoomed past us.

"Shit."

"What?"

"Give me a minute."

Less than a minute was all it took for him to slam his foot on the gas and swing a U-turn back the way we came.

"Okay…"

"Too many people."

"Oh, what, you think some dinky town with one shithole motel isn't going to remember the one new customer they've had in a month? That versus a town that is constantly revolving in population? Seriously, which one looks more suspicious?"

Shut the fuck up, you idiot!

Was I really arguing with my captor over where he stayed? Yes, I was.

He turned to look at me, and my eyes went wide.

But it wasn't just for the less suspicious avenue. The more people, the more chance I had to get away. Then again, also more people who could die in my escape attempt.

He didn't respond but kept driving. It took about forty-five minutes to arrive at the next town he picked, oddly or aptly named Woodland. Old, dilapidated, and empty were pretty good words to describe the decrepit main thoroughfare.

"Do you have an obsession with wood?" I asked as we pulled up to the barely standing Woodland Motel. The second *O* was dangling from the sign, barely attached, and the *L* was missing, only a shadow to show it was once there in the first place.

After putting the car in park, he reached into the back seat and threw some things on my lap. "Put those on." He got out of the car and leaned back in. "Stay."

I looked down at my shoes and scrub pants. The tiny bits of blood splatter stared back at me. There was no way I was putting them back on. I didn't want the reminder of all that happened on my body again. Besides, I *really* needed to pee, and another piece of clothing in my way was not going to help my predicament.

I threw them behind me and rubbed my hands against each other, trying to get their feel off me.

From the outside, the motel looked as bad if not worse than the last one, and just as seedy. Run down, not updated, slowly decaying with around ten rooms all in a row. Shingles were missing from the roof, the gutters bent and mangled. Paint chipped from nearly every piece of wood, while grass and weeds sprouted through the cracks of the sidewalk and even spots on the gravel parking lot.

Six stalked back to the car, a fiery ball of destructive

energy. At least, that was what he looked like to me.

"I told you to put your clothes on," he snarled at me as he pulled me from the car.

"There's no one around to see me half-naked anyway," I said as I tried to yank my arm away.

Futile attempt. I wasn't going anywhere, especially not without shoes. With what I noticed was an always watchful eye, Six pulled the bags from the back of the car. He handed me a few, light ones of course, and I slowly made my way across the gravel to the sidewalk while he unlocked the room—number 4 this time.

As soon as we were through the door, I tossed the bags onto the bed and flew to the bathroom.

I stepped in and flicked on the light, jumping back as a scream popped out and I nearly peed right there. "Shit!"

It was the first time I'd seen myself and the brown dye in full effect. The color really made my blue eyes pop, but my hair being anything other than my strawberry blonde had always been a rare Halloween occurrence and of my own volition. Forced upon me like that, and it was like I was someone else.

I turned to slam the door shut, but Six reached out and grabbed the edge.

"Door stays open," he said in an almost lifeless voice.

I heaved a sigh and stepped to the toilet, lifting the sides of the large T-shirt and hooking my thumbs in my panties. Just before I pulled them down I glanced toward the door and the psycho pervert watching me.

"Do you mind?"

His jaw ticked as he let go of the door and went to do whatever, leaving me to finally pee in peace.

With a thankfully emptied bladder, I looked around and was happy to find the bathroom to be a small improvement from the previous.

Small.

Minute.

Okay—they had better water, so it had less of an overall shade of gross brown. Still, years of lacking upkeep didn't do the tiny room any favors.

Hope sprang up in me for the briefest of moments when I noticed a window, but was shot down almost as fast. The window was tiny with obscure glass, but even if I was able to get it open enough to squeeze through, the shadow of metal bars on the exterior squashed any potential it held as an escape route.

"Oh, goodie," I said as I exited the bathroom and entered a near replica of the last room. Though the smell was improved, it shared a similar floral/geometric print on the bed and curtains, and stains on the floor. The peeling wallpaper was about the same, though this time one wall was clad in wood paneling.

Dresser with another rabbit eared TV, small table with two chairs, and to complete the out-of-time look, a rotary phone.

I hadn't seen one of those since my grandmother had one twenty years ago.

How the hell did he find these places? I didn't think they existed anymore.

"Dear *Syfy*, I've found a hole in space and time. Possibly *the* Lost Room or its cousin, room 11."

He turned to me. "What are you babbling about?"

I ignored him as something about the room was off. "Only one bed?"

"If you have a problem with it, I don't care."

My lips formed a thin line. "Right." Not like we hadn't shared a bed before. Only then, the hotel was much nicer and so was he.

I stood for a moment, taking in my new circle of hell and the fact that I'd be sleeping directly next to the psychopath. Which led me to the realization that he never slept the night before. It had to have been a six or seven hour drive from where we were.

As he rifled through his duffle, I looked him over. He didn't look tired, but maybe he was an insomniac. Maybe insomnia led to his psycho-ness.

Or maybe he was just psycho.

My focus moved to his face. The empty, black void of emotion. Was he really the same charismatic man who swept me off my feet?

Maybe he had split personality disorder. Simon was the sexy, charming personality, while Six was the killer. There could be other personalities, even good ones.

"In the chair."

My gaze snapped to his, and my shoulders slumped. "Oh, God, not again with the tape and the chair!"

He didn't budge. Instead, he pulled out his gun and motioned with it for me to sit.

Reluctantly, because what else was I going to do, I walked over and sat down. It was a similar type of chair as the day before, so once again he taped my forearm at the elbow, my wrists, my ankles, and my calves to the frame.

"Can you at least turn the TV on this time?"

He slapped a piece of tape over my mouth, made sure it was good and sealed, then grabbed hold of the chair to angle me toward the TV. Going over, he grabbed the remote and turned it on, then handed it to me.

"I'll be back."

I rolled my eyes and tried to talk. "Bwng fud."

He nodded, seeming to understand me, and walked out the door, locking it.

The TV sucked, big time. There were only half a dozen

channels, and most of them had terrible signal. The antenna the motel had was obviously shit, and I was left with a staticy mess of nothing but crappy daytime television.

Leaving it on some morning talk show, I contemplated my new surroundings and how I was going to make my way out of them.

One thing I could possibly manage was getting the tape off my mouth. While I highly doubted screaming was going to get me any help in the backwoods of Georgia where no one could hear me, I'd at least be more comfortable.

Using my shoulder, I rubbed against the corner of the tape, loosening the edge. It took some time, and some alternating of shoulders, but I eventually managed to work it off.

After that, I tried to see if the same was possible on my arms and legs, but that was quickly answered with a big fat no.

It didn't take long for boredom to become sleepiness and for the remote to slip from my fingers onto the floor when I began dozing in and out. Add in my lack of food or drink in nearly twenty-four hours, and I started getting drowsy loopiness.

When Six came back many hours later, I was ready to invoke my inner zombie and bite into him.

"Come here so I can eat your arm," I said as he walked into the room.

His brow quirked up as well as the corner of his lips, an almost smile making the sadist appear near human. Either he was amused by my comment, or the fact that I bested his tape over my mouth.

After setting a few brand new duffels on the bed, he produced a paper bag with the familiar golden arches and delicious smelling contents that had my stomach making the loudest grumbles I'd ever heard. He reached in and pulled out a few fries, and I opened my mouth like a baby bird.

Then he put the fries in his mouth while he looked at me.

The excitement in me drained, reformulating itself into anger. "Fucker."

"You're feisty today."

"Oh, you're talking to me like a human?"

Joking and sarcasm were my steady companion and defense mechanism. Without them, I didn't want to think about the broken, frightened girl I'd be. It was the strength I needed to get to the next minute.

He stared at me, then pulled more fries out, holding them in front of me. I gave him my best evil eye as I leaned forward. The farther I craned my neck, the more he retracted. The blood in my veins began to boil, and I was in no mood to play games.

"Assho—mmph!"

He shoved the fries in my mouth before I could finish the insult. However, my anger couldn't overcome the euphoria of food, of the taste of salt on my tongue, and I greedily chomped them down.

Once done, he held a bottle of water to my lips, tilting it back. Some of it spilled out of the corners of my mouth, but I didn't care and I moaned, gulping down half the bottle, chasing it as he pulled it back.

"You know, it would be easier if you'd just cut me loose."

"No. But I will cut the tape."

Oh, he's quick.

I hadn't even thought about the double meaning of my words.

Pulling out his trusty knife, the immortal words of Crocodile Dundee came to mind, but I had a feeling Six would not appreciate them. He kneeled down in front of me and slipped the tip under the edge just below my knee, slicing the sticky gray bindings. Once the other side was done, he pulled both sides at the same time. My eyes bugged out of my head and I cursed him and the woman that bore him due to the tape practically ripping my skin off.

Once he finished doing the same to my ankles, my freed legs stung, causing me to whimper.

"I told you to put your pants on," he said as he moved up to do the same to my arms.

I fucking hated to admit it, but he was right.

Every muscle was stiff and sore. He'd left me around eight, and I wondered how long I'd been stuck in one position as I turned to look at the clock.

"Jesus, you were gone for six fucking hours?" It was almost two thirty.

He didn't answer, which didn't surprise me. With each step over to the bed and the bag of food, I stretched, trying to get blood flow back to all my muscles.

It took five minutes, maybe less, to devour the two cheese-burgers and fries. For those few, brief minutes, I paid no atten-tion to Six or what he was doing. They were the best minutes since he'd burst into my lab.

I slumped back against the headboard and patted my full stomach. It was then I focused in on him and what he was do-ing. He'd set a few things on the bed, one of them being a set of large metal rings—two small, two medium, and one large.

I'd seen sets like it before. Digby and I made many trips to the local sex shops for some fun toys or movies. They were for restraints—wrists, ankles, neck—but the set Six found wasn't for the light fun I would've had with Digby.

Thick metal with what looked to be a built-in lock and a large gauge exterior ring.

Suddenly, the food wasn't sitting very well.

There was a multitude of other things, one being a bundle of wire.

"What is all that for?" I asked, though I already had an idea.

"We might be here for a while."

I nodded. Good news was I was going to be alive longer. Bad news was instead of tape, it looked like I was going to be hog-tied or worse. The key was not to panic. Keep the yellow flag flying, no red.

It took him over an hour to complete, but once done, there was a long wire connecting the legs of the bed to the base of the toilet. Attached to that was about four more feet, and at the end of that, one of the ankle restraints.

He grabbed hold of my right ankle and dragged me to the edge of the bed. Then cool metal wrapped around my bare ankle. The lock was set and he pulled out the key, stuffing it into his pocket.

I guess I should have been happy he didn't strap me down to the bed or something. A little bit of freedom was better than taped to a chair.

The long wire had a little bit of give, allowing me to lie in the middle of the bed without tugging, but not allowing me to get to the door or phone. If the phone was still there, that was. He ripped it out of the wall and took it outside. The bed and bathroom were the only areas I had access to.

Six turned on the TV and being that it was after five, found nothing but news on the limited channels.

All the water I'd caught up on wanted out, so I tried out my bound freedom and went to the bathroom. My head fell into my hands as I resigned myself to my purgatory, wondering what life was like on the outside. For the first time, my thoughts drifted to the aftermath.

Would they find bodies, or just pieces? Then identifying

them and contacting next of kin. All the husbands and wives, parents, siblings, children…everyone in their lives. The emotional devastation.

It wasn't just the people I worked with. In the explosion, he probably killed everyone in the building.

What about mine? Would my parents find out from a knock on their door? I wanted to call them, but at the same time, I didn't. At that moment, I was being held against my will with little chance of escape. I would tell them how much I loved them. Thank them for everything they'd done for me all my life.

Then who? Digby? Right then, I kicked myself for not going with him. If I had, I wouldn't have tears rolling down my face, thinking of how my mom would take the news of my death.

After finishing up and wiping the tears from my cheeks, I made my way out. Six was standing at the foot of the bed, eyes glued to the TV.

I glanced over, my eyes going wide as a picture of the motel we'd been at flashed on the screen along with the headline "Couple found dead in small-town motel."

Something didn't sit right. We were far away in another state. Why would we see that report where we were? Then it hit me. It wasn't a local news station—it was national.

But why would that make national news? Murders happened all the time around the country.

"Fingerprints were found at the grisly crime scene of the small motel just inside the Tennessee border, identifying twenty-eight-year-old Paisley Warren, a laboratory technician from the Hamilton County Office of the Chief Medical Examiner in Cincinnati, Ohio."

Oh… Shit! A picture of me, next to the building I spent five days a week in, filled the screen as the newscaster's voice continued.

"The same building in which she was thought to have perished in the day before when an unknown explosion destroyed the building. The cause of the explosion is under investigation, but police are not ruling out foul play and are listing Warren as a person of interest in both cases. If you have any information or see Paisley Warren, please contact your local police department."

I stared at the screen in complete and total horror.

Kidnapped.

Hostage.

And *I* was the number one suspect for the crimes my captor committed.

"There are others after you now. Not just the police," he said next to me, then he sighed. "This's going to make things harder."

I turned to him. "Harder?" My arm swung back then forward, connecting with his chest. "I hate you! I hate you!" I pounded my fists against him. "They think I killed them! Why didn't you just kill me? Bastard!"

A few hits was all I got in before he took hold of my wrists, stopping me. "Do you want to die?"

I struggled against his grip, wanting to bash his skull in and get away. "No, but if I'm going to die, I'd rather it be by anyone but you! I was actually happy that night. I thought you were something real, but you're just a lunatic murderer!"

His lip curled up into a snarl. He pulled my arm high while his other hand grabbed the back of my neck, pulling me to him. When his lips pressed against mine, tongue slipping across, forcing it deeper, I thought I could hold my own. I thought I'd be disgusted.

I was wrong.

Just like that night that seemed like a lifetime ago versus less than forty-eight hours, I melted into him. All the hatred for him disappeared as our bodies mashed together. A moan crawled its way out of me, and as soon as the vibration hit him, he stopped.

His breath was harsh when he stepped back. Our eyes met, and the force of his glare made me flinch. He stepped forward and pushed against my chest, sending me falling onto the bed.

He stood over me, and the blood that pumped furiously through my veins fell from my face. He pulled his shirt up and over his head, tossing it to the ground, before crawling onto the bed.

I drew in a shaky breath, pushing back as he forced my legs open and caged me against the bed with his arms. My eyes were wide as I reached up and placed my palms on his chest.

"I've been pretty fucking nice to you, Paisley, wouldn't you agree?"

"Y-Yes," I managed to stutter out between my shaking lips.

He reached between us, his hand skimming across my stomach until he reached my panties. Grabbing them and twisting, he pulled them until they tore away from me.

"Then I'll make you hate me even more. You're nothing but a fucking beader. I'm going to use you, fuck you, and there's nothing you can do about it."

I whimpered, my body shaking as he shifted his weight, popping open his jeans. My body tensed and I tried to crawl back, but he held my hip down on the mattress with the force of his weight.

The tip pressed against me, bare, but I didn't care about a condom any longer. I was going to die, so what did it matter?

He grunted when he thrust his hips forward, pressing his cock into me.

I gasped, my mind going blank, moaning when he pulled out and pushed all the way back in. Everything that happened evaporated, except my body remembering his.

And he felt even better bare. Skin-to-skin delicious friction.

Every logical thought said to be appalled and frightened. To scream and curse at him. To tell him no and push against him. Something, anything, that indicated I didn't want what he was doing.

Instead, my heels pressed into the mattress as my hips rocked up to meet his.

I was scared. I was turned on. Every emotion in me was on the fritz to the point I didn't know *what* to feel. Confusion laced with desire and an edge of fear topped off with a gorgeous body slamming a big cock into me.

"Your pussy is squeezing my cock. You aren't supposed to be enjoying this." He hissed into my ear as he grabbed on to my throat. His breath was hot against my neck. "Then again, I'm sure your body remembers the other night. I bet you felt me all day long." He snickered. The lack of air increased the intensity of everything I was feeling, my pussy clenching down tighter around him. "Have you been horny, waiting for me to press my body against you, shove my cock in your pussy?"

My back arched, and I whimpered.

"Tell me, Paisley, do you like my cock in you?" He relaxed his grip on my neck.

I drew in a shuddering breath, my eyes fluttering. "Yes."

"Are you about to come? Too bad." His voice was strained at the end, muscles coiled tight as his hips jerked with so much force he had to grab onto my shoulders to keep me still, his cock twitching with each spurt inside me.

I wanted to cry, the conflicting emotions in me tearing me up from the inside. He was trying to rape me, and I'd been so close to coming. I wanted to come. It was the only pleasure I was going to get before I died. Why did he have to deny me?

He pulled out, gaze locked on my pussy, which was

practically begging his cock to come back in for another round. Reaching down, he grabbed my hair and twisted my body around.

"Clean me up."

It wasn't a request.

The juice covered tip of his cock hovered above my lips. One hand still in my hair, he used the other to angle his dick down and between my lips.

Jizz and my own juices covered the hot head and slipped down into my mouth as my tongue worked circles around his still hard cock.

He pushed his hips forward, forcing past my gag reflex. "Relax, baby. I've been down your throat before, you can do it again."

My gag reflex kicked in, my throat trying to evict his finally-starting-to-soften dick. Little moans from him turned me on, to my own self-disgust. A little slap to my clit, and I moaned around him.

His fingers untangled from my hair as he pulled out and stuffed his dick back in his pants.

"Do you often try to rape women?" I asked, unmoving from my position as I regained my breath.

He stared down at me with a cool gaze. "No. All I have to do is find the nearest bar and look for the most desperate and available one."

Desperate? Oh, God. Is that how I appeared?

Fluid leaked out, the feel of his come slipping down my skin to the bed. "Why bareback?"

"You're going to be dead soon, so what does it matter?"

I sprang from the bed and moved into the bathroom in an attempt to get away from him and get the rest of his come out of me.

When had I become the desperate woman men preyed after? Fuck!

On my way back to the bed, my shackles rattling as I weaved around trying not to trip on the wire, I picked up the bottle of water I'd been sucking on before I was sucking on him. What I wouldn't do for something stronger, or at least a Sprite.

I refused to look at him, pissed at what he'd gotten me in to.

Wanted. I was *wanted*.

Granted, it was for questioning, but that was just the formal description for a suspect. After all, the evidence pointed to me.

Then again, Six did bleed on the floor after I cut him.

I glanced over to where he was sitting, looking at something on his phone. Wrapped around his left bicep was gauze, covering the slice I'd managed to land.

"Won't they find your blood and fingerprints?"

He looked up from his phone, his expression blank. "Doesn't matter."

My brow scrunched up. "Why?"

"Because they'll never be able to match them."

It didn't make sense. They had to have his blood on file. "You have to have left some evidence of you in some other crime scene."

He picked up his gun from the table and pointed it in my direction. "Go to sleep."

I gave him a little huff before slipping under the sheet. There was going to be a period of adjustment as I wasn't used to sleeping without panties on and I felt exposed.

Shutting off the bedside light, I turned onto my side and stared at the wallpaper. There was a small rip, throwing the pattern off, bugging me. In fact, none of the seams were hiding. They all seemed to be popping out, frayed.

The bed dipped, and I held my breath as Six worked his way

under the covers beside me. My only solace was that he wasn't touching me.

But that brief moment was ruined when his arm wrapped around my waist and he pulled me flush with his chest.

I froze, eyes wide. "What are you doing?"

"Making sure you don't go anywhere." His breath was hot waves against my neck.

He was warm, and I wasn't afraid. I felt oddly safe in his arms. There was a comfort I wasn't supposed to feel, but I did.

Maybe sleeping with a killer was the safest place to be.

GRUNTING AND SOME CURSES GREETED ME IN THE MORNING as I fought to either wake or sleep. The pain in my side from a rogue spring told me I wanted to go back to sleep. My back was sore. The shittastic mattress was the most uncomfortable thing I'd ever slept on. But I was no longer pinned down by a body.

He was the one making all the noise. I groaned and sat up. There was twisting and muscles flexing and my captor looking way too hot as he fought with whatever inanimate object was giving him trouble.

I yawned and scratched at my head. My hair had to be a mess—he kept twisting it in the night as I moved around to get it away from him. It was a chore to open my eyes and look at him. Every part of me was stiff.

He didn't pay any attention to me. I made a huffing noise as I threw the covers back and made my way to the bathroom. I used my fingers to comb through my hair to get the knots out and straighten the mess out some, but the only thing it seemed to be doing was breaking and freaking me out that my reflection was almost unrecognizable to myself.

A few minutes later, I was back to my spot on the bed,

wishing I had a toothbrush. My teeth felt like there was fuzz growing on them. Maybe some face wash as well. Lip balm would be awesome and some lotion.

Couldn't a captive get some toiletries? Basic necessities so I didn't look like a zombie apocalypse survivor?

"Tell me what you know," Six said, his forearms resting on his thighs.

I looked over to him, surprised by his sudden outburst. He sat in the chair he'd taped me to the day before while I was still tethered to the bed. Hell, he'd spent the night curled around me. Couldn't a girl get a "good morning" at least?

"That's a long list." I lay down and propped myself up on my elbow.

His gaze narrowed. "About John Doe."

"Which one?" I asked, just to be a bitch.

His lip curled up into a snarl, and he stood and closed the space between us. Reaching out, he fisted my hair, tilting my head back. I hissed, teeth clenched as my eyes watered from the pain.

"You will tell me what you know," he growled out.

I met his hard gaze. "So you can kill me?"

"You wouldn't be the first corpse I left tied up in a hotel room."

He pulled on my hair as he let go, making me fall back onto the bed. I watched as he moved back, threw his T-shirt on, and slipped on his shoes as he grabbed his keys. Without a word to me, he walked out of the room. The sound of a car engine roared to life, wheels kicking up gravel, and he was gone.

Stuck alone again in a room in the middle of nowhere.

Unlike the last time, I had freedom and the possibility of escape. That small speck of hope had me sitting straight up and taking a much closer look at my restraints.

First, I inspected the cuff around my ankle and the wire it was attached to. There was no getting it off with my bare hands, and the key was still in his pocket or hidden away by then. My gaze bounced around the room in search of the duffle bags which held the tools he'd used to put my leash together.

I stood and took a few steps around the bed, then stopped. My right leg pulled at the wire creating a wide V, but that was the end. The bags sat against the far wall, next to the door, and out of my reach by a good six feet or more. He was far too acute to leave me near anything to aid in my escape.

My own Machiavellian mind moved outside the box for a MacGyver solution.

One end was secure around the basin of the toilet, which was actually very well installed and unmovable, even if I was able to get the loop of wire around the basin. Of course. He'd even gone as far as putting a stopper of some sort so that there was no slack in the loop.

The other end was not simply tied around one leg of the bed as I thought. No, that would have been a struggle, but a simple lift of the bed. He knotted it around each leg.

He was a busy boy while I was in the shower the day before.

Sitting down on the floor, I pulled at the wire in an attempt to get the bed to move, but it wouldn't budge.

Lying down on the bed, I peered over the opposite edge and groaned.

Not only had he knotted it up, he had screwed it into the floor with a pretty hefty-looking bracket. Which explained the sound I'd heard.

"Fuck."

I flopped onto my back and stared up at the ceiling in momentary defeat.

Lead wire was out.

Cuff attached to ankle? There was a small possibility I could get it unlocked if I could find something, like a bobby pin.

That is, if bobby pins actually worked and weren't a Hollywood fabrication.

I sat up and inspected the lock. It was tiny and possibly took a key that wasn't very intricate, kind of like a suitcase key. Through the large O-ring was the wire, clamped in a loop by a *C* like piece of metal. If there were some way to open that up, I could get the wire out and be free.

The hunt for an unconventional tool began.

On the nightstand there was nothing of use—a lamp and the standard bible in the drawer that used to be all the rage. No loose screws on anything I could reach. Not even the knob would come off the drawer.

In the bathroom there were the few toiletries, but otherwise just the sink, mirror, toilet, and shower. Still, I scoured every inch. There had to be *something* to help me. The sparsity of the room drove me crazy.

I stood and stared at my reflection, still stunned by the brunette woman who looked back. Something flew by the window and reflected in the mirror, drawing my eye. That was when I saw it—a nail.

The round head only stood about a quarter of an inch off the wood trim it was hammered into, but it was enough to grab on to. Sharp edges dug into my skin as I tightened my fingers around it, then they slipped off, scraping against my skin.

I hissed and brought my finger up to my mouth, trying to suck the pain away. Like that was going to work.

Picking up a towel sitting on the sink, I wrapped it around the nail head and grabbed on. It took a lot of wiggling, jiggling, and cursing, but after a few minutes it released and slid right out.

"Yes!"

Moving back to the bed, I sat down and arranged the cuff to get better access to the clamp. There wasn't much of a gap to work with, the pointed tip barely able to slip in. A little bit of leverage and a lot of force sent my hand flying and made the cuff twist.

"Shit."

I moved the cuff back around and held it tight while I attempted to pry the thick fastener open. Each jab and twist usually ended in a swift loss of grip and the nail to slip. With nothing else to do, all of my attention was on the task of getting it open.

The small gap becoming even minutely larger kept me going, kept me from giving up and finding something else. Because without that movement, that small sliver of hope, there wasn't much else but giving up. And I wasn't about to give up.

I was going to live. For as long as I could, I wasn't going to stop living.

Another sliver of hope was housekeeping. They had to come around at some point, right? That was if this place had any sort of maid service. It was probably the one person who manned the front desk, but even just coming to check if we needed towels would help.

Six probably told them we didn't want to be disturbed.

Hope that one of the staff would come by was small, as small as my traction with the nail, but still there as a possibility.

After some time digging, I tried to get one of the wires through. There was still a ways to go as the gap was only half the width of the cable.

A little bit wider. Just a little more, I chanted to myself.

The sound of a car on gravel made me freeze. All movement, even breath stopped as I listened. When a car door slammed, my heart began racing as I frantically searched for a place to hide my tool. The nearest place was the nightstand, so I tossed it in the drawer before positioning myself on the bed.

I looked at the clock to see how long he was gone, and was stunned. Had four hours really passed since he left?

Six entered a split second later, locking the door behind him, then threw a bag next to me on the bed and motioned for me to open it. Inside, I found some new panties, women's T-shirts, and even a pair of jeans and flats. He'd done something with my old clothes, with the exception of my bra.

And the other bag contained a pack of toiletries.

"Wow. Thanks, I guess." I was really happy to have new panties, since he destroyed the only pair I had and I'd been commando all day in nothing but the shirt he gave me. And ecstatic for the toiletries, but I didn't want to admit that to him. It was the little things in my situation that brightened the grime of my surroundings.

I yanked off the dirty shirt of his I'd been wearing for two days, not caring that I was naked in front of him anymore. Toiletries in hand, I felt his eyes on me with each step I took toward the bathroom.

It was a basic hygiene kit with travel sizes and a single blade disposable razor, but a huge improvement and even included much needed lip balm.

Cherry flavored, balm. My favorite.

Assessing the situation, I glanced from the shower to my cuff. The logistics of my predicament were about to make for an interesting shower dance.

There wasn't enough slack to put my foot down into the tub, and the shower head was on the wrong wall to hit the front of my body. With some tricky maneuvering and bending and holding on for dear life, I scrubbed down with the horrible soap the motel provided. At least washing my hair was easy.

Once out, I did a quick brush of my teeth and towel off of

my body and hair.

"You could have made it a little easier to take a shower."

"You could have asked and I would have unlocked you."

I blinked at his expressionless face.

Well…shit.

"Touché."

With that, he stood and walked over while I pulled one of the bags closer.

"What are you?" I asked as I busted open the six-pack of generic panties. Beggars couldn't be choosers. Silver lining and all.

He mulled over my question as he unlocked the metal surrounding my ankle, allowing me to pull on my new bikini cut panties. His eyes never left my thighs or what was between them. "A killer."

"I know that." The new T-shirts only went to my waist, leaving me less dressed than I was before. Oh, well. I'd already lost a lot of modesty. What did it matter anyway?

He licked his lips and adjusted his hardening cock. Killers also seemed to be horny motherfuckers. Then again, I had just shown him all my goods and done a little striptease of sorts.

"You asked me what I was."

"You're not one to give up information, are you?" I asked as I stretched my momentarily free leg.

"No. Information is power. Therefore, I don't talk about myself to a stranger at a bar."

My mouth popped open. "A jab? Wow. You know that's what normal people do? Part of that whole getting-to-know-you thing."

"I don't want to get to know you, and I sure as hell don't want you to know me." He opened the cuff and snapped it back on, clicking the lock in place. All movement stopped, his gaze focused on the cuff.

I froze and looked down, taking in all the little lines the nail had dug into the metal.

Shit.

He reached forward, grabbed on to my neck, and slammed me face down on the bed. He pushed my head against the mattress, his body climbing over mine, caging me in place.

"Maybe I should have used all of the restraints and tied them to the bed in one continuous chain. That way you couldn't move at all," he growled into my ear. I whimpered and sniffed from pain. "I gave you room to move. I thought we had an agreement."

"You really expect me or any other sane human being to just stay here? I want to go home, you asshole!"

"You can't. You're just another dead girl."

He was straddling my hips, the bulge of his cock pressing against my butt cheeks.

"I was fucking nice to you again, giving you room to move. Guess it's back to being mean."

With one hand he yanked on the brand new panties I'd just put on. The other hand was still pushing against my neck, but that didn't slow down the popping of his button or the sound of his zipper sliding down.

How was that damn zipper one of the most erotic sounds I'd ever heard? The amp up of anticipation. The knowledge of my ability to move seemed to have left me along with my brain.

I should have been struggling against him. Instead I was pliant to his will, held by only one hand on my neck.

"Fucknugget." The one word I could come up with as his cock found the opening to my pussy and he forced it in with a thrust of his hips.

"I never knew a hostage could have such advantages." He let go of me, instead grabbing on to my wrists as he rotated his hips, pushing and pulling, rubbing against my sensitive walls. His teeth nipped against my neck.

Once again, the sane response was missing. Repulsion was replaced with what felt like jolts of electricity through my veins and the need for more.

"Rape is an advantage?" I asked, trying to sound offended by what he was doing.

But my body betrayed me, and I couldn't stop the moan that left me. The fucker snickered as he pulled out and pushed back in.

"You haven't told me to stop."

My eyes fluttered as he continued to hit a spot that spurred on the same jolts of electricity with each pass. "Doesn't mean I want it."

He sped up his pace, slamming against my ass. "Are you sure about that? Your pussy is awfully wet."

Fuck. He was right. I was still turned on from the day before. Being used as a fuck hole to a killer I couldn't get away from wasn't as appalling as it should have been.

Maybe because we'd already had sex. A lot of very good sex, for hours. Maybe I was developing Stockholm Syndrome.

The latter I doubted, simply because I continued to be scared of and hate the man. Was some good, rough sex before I died such a bad thing to enjoy? There was a lot of certainty that he was going to kill me if I couldn't escape—was it really so bad to *not* be absolutely miserable before I died?

Was I supposed to be nothing but a helpless pool of woman, cowering from him, giving him every bit of power out of fear for what I already knew he was going to do?

No. That was the one thing I had control of in a situation out of my control. It was my choice to give up, and I wasn't going to do it.

But I was going to give in to the way his body felt against mine. To the pleasure of a man.

Harsh breath against my neck in time with his thrusts. A lot of his weight was balanced on the hand on my neck, and it pushed me further into the bed.

Even his angry fuck had my pussy clenching around him. Trying to assert himself over me with his strength only made my eyes fluttered every time he bottomed out.

There was no sound, no warning as he slammed against me, jerking as his balls emptied his come deep inside me.

Denied an orgasm again.

"Your life is mine," he hissed into my ear. "There are consequences for disobedience. Remember that, because the next time, I won't be half as nice."

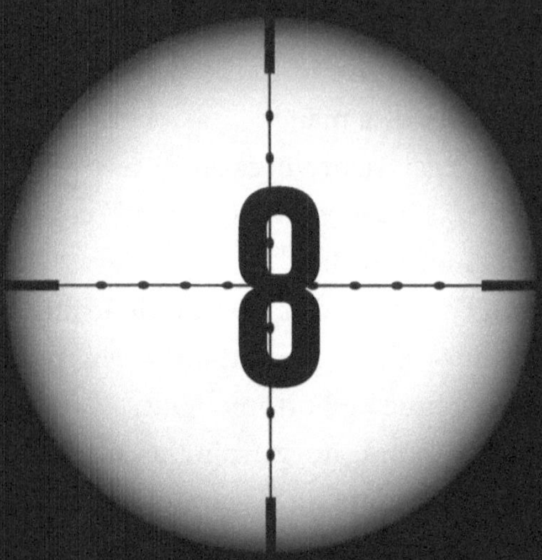

I HUMMED A TUNE. AN ANNOYING ONE.

All on purpose.

What else was I going to do? Sarcasm was my nature. Bating the beast my fun. There was no stopping who I was, and that alone was bound to get me killed sooner rather than the never I dreamed of.

We'd been at the same motel for three days. The only time I'd gotten fresh air was when Six opened the door in his comings and goings, leaving me chained to the bed of this shithole.

And it really was a shithole. The longer I was there, the more I saw. Good thing I wasn't a germaphobe, because I didn't want to overthink what could be lurking in the bed I was lying on.

Over the prior seventy-two hours, I'd become fully immersed in my new reality. Accepting my situation and all. The fact that I was going to die much sooner than later only spurred on my whole let-it-go attitude.

And there was a vision of Elsa from *Frozen* in her blue gown singing in the snow.

It wasn't that I hadn't tried to escape, but the sad news was he knew what he was doing. He engineered the fuck out of my restraints, giving me another clue to my executioner's intelligence.

"Shut it," Six grumbled, the sound muffled by his clenched teeth. "You're getting on my last nerve."

I spun onto my stomach and propped up on my forearms. "Then let me go." For some reason, he had neither forced me to tell what I knew—which I was certain he could easily torture out of me—or killed me. If he was keeping me around for something other than a fuck, it was lost to me.

He shook his head, eyes still locked on the screen of his super-secret laptop. "Sorry, sweets. You know your only way out is when I kill you."

I swung my legs behind me, the cuff on my ankle pulling against the leader cable of the trolley system I was attached to, slapping the cable across my hip. "I prefer option B—me walking out of here."

"You should be thankful to me for every moment you're breathing. Besides, do you really think you can return to your old life?"

I shrugged. "No, but any life is better than death."

That caught his attention, and he turned to me. "Are you sure about that?"

I popped up onto my knees. "Are you actually engaging me in a philosophical discussion?"

His eyes narrowed, sending a chill down my spine. Every time he gave me that look, I wondered if I'd finally pushed him too far. Always rattling his cage, trying to incite him. Playing with his fire, stoking his anger, all in the name of conversation to stem my boredom.

"I will shut you up if you don't stop."

"By throwing some duct tape over my mouth again?" I smirked up at him.

A dare.

A tempt.

One I knew he'd take.

He stormed over and reached out, fisting my hair and tilting my head back, making me look up at him. "You know exactly how—by shoving my cock down your throat." His eyes grew darker as his thumb swiped across my bottom lip, his tongue slipping out to wet his own. "Actually, that's not a bad idea."

His lips crashed to mine, forcing my mouth open and letting his tongue in with mine. I arched into him, fisting my hand in his shirt collar, drawing him closer.

His reaction was exactly what I was aiming for. After all, I figured I'd reached the mentally broken stage of acceptance of my situation.

Not that it mattered. As much as I hated him for ruining my life, I couldn't stop my attraction for him. Nothing he did seemed to be able to erase the version of him I met that first night, or how fucking perfect he felt inside me.

I wanted pleasure, needed it to keep me company while I waited to die, and my body willingly took it any way Six would give it.

He pulled back, leaving me a heavy lidded, flushed, panting mess. His lip twitched, then his grip on my hair tightened, forcing my head back and down to the bed.

"Ow!" I hissed and reached back.

The pain whited out my brain for a moment. When I managed to open my eyes, his dick was the first thing to greet me. He slapped the head against my lip, then brushed it against my cheek. The silky hot skin on his cock was as alluring as his perfect body.

"Open."

My pussy twitched at his tone. I barely had my lips parted

when he pushed my head down, shoving his cock in, making me gag. He pulled out and pushed back in with no regard for me.

He wasn't gentle.

"You are nothing but a come dump until I have no use of you anymore," he said as he used my mouth, growing harder by the second. "Take my cock." His hand was harsh on the back of my head, hips tilting forward, pushing his cock down my throat.

I continued to gag, tears welling in my eyes. Pushing against his legs did nothing, and my lungs began to burn.

A few more thrusts and he pulled out, letting me catch my breath as he let the head rest against my lips.

"Your cheeks are red. Are you wet?"

"I couldn't breathe, asshole." My voice was raspy.

Using my hair again, he pulled me up to my knees and leaned down close to my ear. "People are animals, too." My eyes widened as his hand moved down my abdomen and cupped my pussy. "I can smell your arousal, so thick I can almost drink it." He leaned down and bit my nipple through my shirt.

I cried out and looked away from him, keeping the tears in, the embarrassment. When his fingers worked the fabric to the side and slipped across my clit, I jumped, a shuddering moan tearing its way from me. He pushed two fingers into my pussy, and I screamed as I reached out to grab his arm. My hips rose up, riding his fingers.

My thighs trembled as my head fell to his shoulder, my muscles tensing.

Then he was gone. He smirked at me as he pulled his zipper up and went back to sitting at the table and his laptop.

Tease.

After a few times of him working me over just to stop, I realized it was a control thing. Keeping me turned on meant keeping me wanting him, even if it was just to scratch the itch he created.

The next day, Six had an arsenal sprawled out on the small faux-wood chipped laminate table. I knew some of them, including what seemed to be his favorite—he had three of them after all—assorted knives, rifles, silencers, and I swear there was an ice pick. All of that in one of his multiple bags.

"How does someone become…like you?" I asked after over an hour of watching him.

His eyes flickered up at me and he leaned back in the chair, acknowledging my existence for the first time since he'd returned with breakfast two hours earlier. "A killer?"

My head bobbed around. "Yeah, I guess. I'm just trying to figure out how you ended up in your…profession? I mean, do you make money killing people?"

A small chuckle left his lips as he adjusted his seat and resumed cleaning the gun. "There are many things you need to know to become a proficient killer, but the military can be a good starting point."

Was he talking to me about himself? "Was it?" I asked, testing the waters.

He glanced at me sideways, probably deciding if he wanted to divulge any personal information, especially after he told me he didn't do that. "Yes. I trained my body, perfecting the art of war in any form I could until doing them was instinct. Then there's my…moral defect."

"Moral defect?"

"Anyone can be a killer, whether they believe it or not. Self-preservation is extremely strong in humans, as is protection of family and loved ones. If, say, someone shoved a gun in your face…" his lip quirked up as his analogy hit home "…what would you do?"

"Anything I could to stay alive." Because that was precisely what I was doing.

"Even if it meant killing them?"

I pursed my lips and tilted my head to the side. "If they were trying to kill me, yes."

"And when you looked down at their body, bleeding and lifeless, how would you feel?"

My stomach dropped at the image he painted. No matter what, the body was a person with family and friends that would never see them again. "Guilty."

He pointed his finger toward me. "That's the difference between everyone else and me. I have no guilt."

"You're a sociopath."

"And more. The added defect in not seeing that killing is bad. My brain knows it is, but I don't care. One less *creature* roaming the earth. Thinning out the herd."

My brow scrunched up. "That's really how you view people?"

He stared straight into my eyes. "Yes."

His attention moved back down to the gun, and I took the time to study him as I thought over what he said. It was true. Even me, who never hurt anyone, could kill under the right circumstance. Six's view meant he held no value in the human life, and it was disturbing to think there were people out there that thought the same.

Not that it surprised me, really. I'd worked for the medical examiner for years and saw firsthand what people were capable of doing to one another. Someone had to be the first sociopath. There wouldn't be a diagnosis, an entire field of study on the disorder, if it weren't really a problem.

I scooted to the edge of the bed and leaned forward. He didn't pay me any attention that I saw, but I knew he was acutely aware of me, just like everything else around him. If there was a fly in the room, I was certain he knew exactly where it was.

"Have you ever been in love?"

There was a slight pause in his movements, and he sighed. "Why are you so nosy? Can't you sit on the bed crying like a good fucking captive?"

I pursed my lips. "Would it make you feel better?"

"If I was normal, I would say seeing you cry would assuage me in some way. No—you like this is more…unnerving."

My head quirked to the side, curiosity getting the better of me. "I unnerve you?"

He slammed one of the guns on the table then turned toward me, his eyes narrowed. "You make my trigger finger twitchy."

I pulled my legs up and rested my chin on my knees. "Go ahead. It's exhausting mentally and physically waiting for you to decide when you're finally going to kill me."

He picked up one of the guns in front of him and stood, walking the few steps over to me. The cold steel of the barrel end pressed to my forehead. Instead of panic or fear, instead of my body tensing, waiting for the shot, relief flooded. A half-inch move of his finger, and the nightmare my life had become would be over.

His lip curled up in a snarl. "I'll kill you when I'm ready, and not before I'm done with you. Now, shut up."

He pushed the gun forward, tipping me until I fell back onto the bed.

Laid out, I stared up at the ceiling, contemplating if I wished he'd pulled the trigger or not.

A few hours later, I'd finally tallied up the number of water spots and determined that the shit motel was in desperate need of a new roof before the current one collapsed. Not that it would be any great loss. Who would come to such a small dead town and rent a room besides a psycho anyway?

"Bored," I said as I lay on my side and stared at him.

The gun in front of him had his complete attention. "Not my problem."

How long did it take to clean a damn gun?

"Yes, it is. You're the one who kidnapped me and dragged me to a place with no Internet or even a damn book to read while you polish your weapons. Seriously, how much do you have to do that?" I looked over to him, but he ignored me. His movements were skilled, practiced, and I watched in warped captivation of his deadly collection.

"Watch TV then."

I grimaced. "Ugh. There's no cable, and all that's on is day-time shows that make me gag." I rolled onto my back and stared up, counting the water stains on the ceiling for the umpteenth time. At the snail's pace rate of nowhere we were moving, I was going to go crazy. "You never did answer me. Have you ever been in love? And with a person, not your weapons."

"Love creates weakness."

His answer surprised me, and not just the implication, but that he responded. Obviously, love was not for cold-blooded killers.

"Aren't you ever lonely?"

He chuckled, dark and deep. "All I need a woman for is the

companionship of her pussy with my dick."

"Which am I then? Captive or companion?"

His jaw flexed, and he stormed over to me. The anger in his eyes made me flinch—I'd really pissed him off. Flight kicked in and I tried to crawl back up the bed away from him, but it was futile.

He grabbed hold of my throat and pulled me up, bringing my face even with his. It hurt, his grip tight, making it difficult to breathe. I dug my nails into his hand on instinct to get him to release, but pain didn't seem to register much to him.

The hand on my neck squeezed tighter. "Shut the fuck up or your throat will be polishing *my* weapon!"

He shoved me down on the bed, releasing my neck. My throat was on fire as I drew in a fresh breath, coughing at my attempt to get oxygen back in my system.

It seemed talking was not on his list of things he liked to do. I'd barely said anything, and he'd gone off. Then again, I asked questions and annoyed him on purpose. It was no wonder he was angry.

I stopped talking then and instead studied him. The quintessential handsome man—strong jaw complete with sharp jawline, straight nose—though I was certain his had to have been broken more than once—and intense dark eyes. Add to that an athletic physique and there really wasn't much room to wonder why I was so physically attracted to him.

Granted, his actions should have overwritten that attraction, but for some reason, they didn't.

I was one fucked-up person. I had to be, right? To *want* sex with a man who killed my friends and kidnapped me.

Eventually I stopped staring at him, but didn't move, only let my vision unfocus.

"What?" he huffed some time later.

"What, what?" I asked as I sat up, bringing my attention

back to him.

"Your staring is getting annoying."

I wanted to laugh. My gaze was aimed at him, but I'd long stopped looking at him.

"Why didn't they find your fingerprints at the motel?" The thought had nagged in the back of my mind since we saw the news report, and what a perfect segue.

He walked over and held his hand out in front of me. Angling it in the light, I understood—just like John Doe, Six had no fingerprints.

"You knew him," I said, not even bothering to ask. His reaction told me that. "That's why I'm still alive. You want to know why he's dead."

He pulled his hand back and returned to the chair. "A bullet to the head killed him, but you are the only one who knows why a bullet was able to get there."

I quirked my brow. "You and him are the only two to make that kind of shot? It was execution style, that's how."

Six shook his head. "Not possible."

"Why? You're so badass that you can't be beaten, is that it?"

"I was sent to clean his discovery and all evidence. Once I saw who it was and how he died… It was a message."

"What did the cranial hole tell you?" I wanted to roll my eyes, my sarcasm leaking out a little more than I intended.

But Six became more distant as he stared out the slit in the curtains. "Time's up."

My brow scrunched up. "Like your time is up? You're the next one to end up on a slab? How do you know?"

He didn't answer. Apparently, I'd hit the too-much-information level.

From his tone, I did decipher one thing—I might not be the only one in the room waiting on a bullet to the brain.

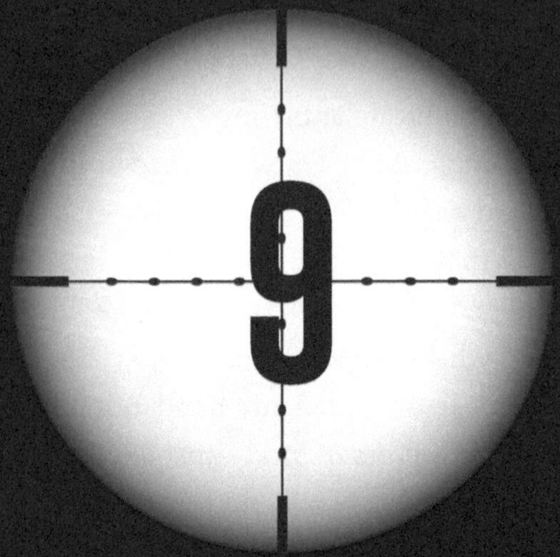

TATS:

10 – days held captive by a killer

9 – days in shithole motel

7 – times I pissed my captor off

5 – times a gun was pointed at me

12 – times his cock was in me in some way

7 – number of orgasms (fucker stopped 5 others)

2 – escape attempts (discontinued after day 3)

11 – times his hands were around my neck (4 orgasms obtained, seemed I liked a little breath play)

19 – number of times I ate fast food. Always good, but I was ready to be done with it for a while.

24 – visible weapons of assortment

1 – pair of clean underwear left

428 – times I was pissed at myself for being physically attracted to the psycho

"Here," Six said as he walked through the door, following another of his disappearances, and threw an envelope at me.

For the past eight days he'd left for hours each day. Usually he came back with food of some sort. I had no idea where he went or what he did, but I'd fallen victim to the strange routine.

The morning began with him already awake and doing whatever it was that he did on his computer. Breakfast was a granola bar and a bottle of water, and then he was out. Which left me alone and bored. I usually took an awkward shower and tried to keep my mind occupied—a hard thing to do by day five.

That was the day he came back with three books. I didn't give a shit what they were. It was stimulation.

Conversation was stilted, his refusal to answer questions or engage was infuriating. Sarcasm was at a high, continuing to get me into trouble.

The one thing that made me feel alive, that I craved, was sex. It broke down barriers, quelled tension, and provided a release we both needed.

It changed our dynamic. His frightening demeanor morphed from terrifying to menacing. I knew the underlying deadly killer, but the atmosphere had relaxed.

Each day was a stepping stone to the normalcy that led to him taking me with him. Even the news had stopped blasting my photo everywhere. In fact, we'd barely seen anything on the explosion in days.

There was a huge difference for that day—we were leaving. Finally vacating the dump that had been an odd home.

I didn't bother to ask what it was in the package and went right to opening it, sliding my finger under the edge. There was a strange trust I'd developed for my killer. Probably because I knew when he killed me, it was going to be a bullet and nothing else.

My brow scrunched as the items tumbled out: driver's license, passport, various credit and shopper's cards, and a small wad of cash. The picture on the license and the passport were the ones he'd taken earlier that morning. He dyed both of our hair blond a few days before, changing our appearance yet again, but for the photo, he had me put in brown contacts.

Even more off than the picture was the name attached to the strange woman.

"Lacey?"

"Your new name."

My brow scrunched. "Why Lacey?"

He took out a wallet and began changing out similar documents. "It's like a mondegreen or homophone of Paisley."

"A what?" I swore he was making words up. Were they even English?

"When I say Paisley, what stands out most?"

I thought about the way he said my name and the last sound, the last syllable, stood out. "*E.*"

"And Lacey?"

"*E* again."

He began stuffing things into a bag. "I'll get a realistic response out of you with a name that has that same strong *E* sound."

I nodded, finally understanding. It happened all the time, hearing the end of a word and thinking someone was calling my name. "Are you going to be Simon again?"

"Sean." He held out his passport, and I blinked.

"Wait, Collins?" I looked back to my own new form of identification. "Why do we have the same last name?"

"Because you're my wife."

"What?" My eyes widened as I stared up at him. Married?

He held up a marriage license: Lacey Anne Moran and Sean Thomas Collins.

"It should be easy, especially physically. I've lost count of how many times we've had sex," he said with a smirk.

I shook my head. "No you haven't."

His lip twitched. "No. I haven't."

"So, what now?" My first venture out in almost two weeks.

"Now, we go shopping. You need to look like we're going on vacation."

I looked back down to the papers. "Why are you taking me with you?"

His expression dropped as his jaw ticked. "I need to find another agent, and seeing as I've been targeted, I need a cover."

"Traveling with a wife versus traveling as a single man." It made sense. "Is that why you haven't forced me to tell you?" He easily could have.

He nodded and headed over to my lead wire. "Look at me." Our eyes met as his tone changed. "Are you going to try anything stupid?"

A ripple of fear raced down my spine, and I covered it up with a roll of my eyes and my sarcastic mouth. "Thanks to you, I'm wanted. Add in that you've warned me enough about how you're going to kill me, or if I try anything you'll kill me, or that I know you have a bullet for me to eat. I think I'm good."

"Say it." He held the key above the lock, waiting.

I sighed. "I'm not going to try and get away, asshole. No fucking point, anyway."

"Because I'll kill you," he said, making sure he stressed again how this game was ending.

I folded my arms in front of me. "You're a broken record, you know that?"

"Making sure you know what the stakes are."

I help up one hand. "Death." Then held up the other. "Kinky sex with some adventure, then death."

He pulled his gun from his waistband and held it up. "And which is it?"

I rolled my eyes. "You're a moron." His finger moved to the

trigger. "You really need me to tell you I want kinky sex before I die?"

His lip twitched into a smirk. "Yeah." He lowered the gun and put it back.

"Ass," I said under my breath as he undid the hunk of metal.

There was nothing like the feeling of no longer being attached to that damn wire. I rolled my ankle first, then my leg, moving everything around unhindered. There were marks and bruises, but all in all, everything was okay, just a little stiff.

My good mood was dampened by a pair of jeans being thrown at my face.

"Get dressed."

Buzzkill.

Still, excitement moved through me—I was leaving the shithole. Granted, the scenery may change, but my companion would not. I believed his promises. I knew by his physical presence, the strength he'd used on me, that he could kill me with his bare hands.

Stripping my clothes off in front of Six was no longer embarrassing. Amazing what a few weeks being chained to a bed and fucked will do. For the first time in over a week I slipped on my bra, new jeans, and the flats he bought.

"Contacts," he said, stopping my beeline to the door.

I stopped in my tracks. "What?"

"The contacts." He held a small bag out to me.

"Why?"

He sighed, his jaw clenching. "Because your eyes stand out almost as much as your hair did."

"Isn't there stuff like facial recognition software everywhere now?" I asked as I snatched the bag from him and moved to the bathroom.

I hated putting in contacts. There was a reason I had laser

eye correction surgery the moment I could.

Once done, I picked up everything and walked toward the door where Six was waiting.

We loaded into a different car than we arrived in, and I had no idea when he changed or if it was even the first one in the time we'd been there. It was an upgrade from the shitty one he'd stolen, though.

"Where'd you heist this one from?" I asked as we exited the motel parking lot. I half expected the place to go up in flames in the rearview mirror, but it didn't happen. Surprising, since my lead cable was still there.

"Doesn't matter."

"How are you so confident in your actions?"

"Because it's my job."

Ah-ha. His *job*. A one word confirmation of something I'd suspected.

"Gun for hire or secret agent man?"

Silence.

I thought maybe I'd get some reaction from him, but instead an eerie calm fell over him and his fingers were clenched tight around the steering wheel.

He let go of one small piece of information about himself. It was a start.

It took about an hour for us to reach a mall, and we headed into Macy's hand in hand. He did let go once shopping commenced, but his watchful eye was always on me and he remained within a ten- or twenty-foot radius of me.

Not exactly sure what I was looking for, I started pulling

items I liked from the racks. As I headed to the dressing room, Six was steps behind, a handful of items in his arms.

There was quite a difference in colors we picked. Everything Six had was neutral—grays and blacks—and devoid of any pattern, while I had colorful prints and stripes along with some plain pieces.

We entered one of the larger dressing rooms and I began trying clothes on, the lust in his eyes growing heavier with each time I stripped.

I flipped over the tag of a dress Six handed me. "Two hundred dollars?" I balked at the price for what was nothing more than a simple sweater dress.

The last dress I bought for that much was for my friend Alison's wedding two years ago.

"Money isn't an option."

"What does that mean?"

"It means, don't worry about price. We need to buy everything you would pack in a suitcase."

For the next three hours we worked our way around the different departments. By the end, I had enough clothes for about seven days, a few different styles of shoes, undergarments, purse with accompanying wallet, costume jewelry as well as some real pieces Six picked out, and a hard sided suitcase to put it all in. There was even a full cosmetics bag, and the clerk had done my makeup.

Six was so involved in the process, he had a hand in choosing a lot of my clothes and shoes. He even picked out a few undergarments he was partial to, adjusting his cock as he held them up in front of me. The man had no shame in letting me know when he wanted to fuck, which seemed to be always.

In the ten days I'd known him, the guy shopping with me was vastly different from the captor who chained me up. The way he acted like an eccentric man spoiling a socialite woman, although I was anything but, was a huge contrast to the gun-toting killer who smacked me around more than once when I got out of line.

Either he was a really good actor, or he really did have multiple personalities. Jury was still out.

After looking at myself in the mirror, however, I felt the same. In a few short hours, a lot of money, and some makeup, I was transformed into a high-class suburban housewife, but I didn't feel the part.

Six also purchased his own set of items. The amount of clothes he'd had all week wasn't much more than the basics I had been wearing.

"Why are we getting so much?" I asked as he swiped a credit card for the fourth purchase, making our total well over four grand, if not more.

"Baby, they lost our luggage." He played up our cover well, but I had a feeling this was not his first time at the rodeo.

Once done, we returned to the car to drop off our purchases. I thought we were done, but Six drove around the parking lot to another store.

Next was Nordstrom's, it seemed. I'd never stepped foot in one before, and I suddenly felt very out of place.

"These dresses are made for the super skinny," I whispered. It was for the looked-like-a-runway-model kind of place. Not to mention what was sure to be a hefty price tag.

"You're curvy in all the right places," he said, wetting his lips and giving me a little groan as he squeezed my ass.

Fucking brain stopped and my pussy got wet. Why did that turn me on? I was a motherfucking *hostage*.

The situation was too weird, too strange to even compute. Sane people would be flagging clerks down, slipping between clothing racks and hightailing it away from him. Instead, I was standing in a department store acting like his wife with a wet spot in my underwear.

All the psych evaluations I did to get my job were suddenly moot and obviously a failure if the mindset I was in seeped through.

"Why are we here? Didn't we get enough?" I asked as he pulled me through the store.

Once again, he didn't say anything, but when we stopped in front of a case holding some heels, my mouth dropped open.

"Those are Christian Louboutins," I said with wide eyes and possibly some drool.

"And?"

"And they cost a lot."

"Who the fuck cares?" He leaned forward, the soft edge leaving his eyes. "I want to fuck you wearing nothing but those." He pointed to a pair of patent black peep-toe platform heels.

Seemed we had begun bartering shoes for sex.

I needed to add Louboutins to my bucket list and check them off. Sex for those shoes? Yes, please!

Who the hell was I kidding? The man didn't need to buy me anything to fuck me. He had the strength to take what he wanted, and I'd become a willing participant in his depraved acrobatics.

"You need a few expensive pieces."

"I do?"

"None of what we bought screamed 'I have more money than sense.' You need a dress, shoes, and a purse somewhere in the five mark."

"Hundred?"

He shook his head. "Thousand." My mouth dropped open. "I also need a tailored suit of equal expense."

"How much time do we have to do all that?"

His lip twitched up into a smirk. "Luckily, I already have such a suit. Now to find you something sexy."

An hour later, I had a month's salary worth of a dress, shoes, and a purse and we were headed out the door.

"Ah, one last thing." He grabbed my hand and slipped a ring onto my left ring finger.

A gasp left me as I looked down at the bridal set and the huge solitaire diamond. The set was beautiful. "Is this real?"

"For thirty thousand, it better be."

"What?" I stared down at my hand and the equivalent of four months' salary.

"It's two carats."

"How?" And why in the hell was I getting emotional over the fake relationship the ring represented? I knew the real Six, and not the actor in front of me.

He shrugged and smiled. "I have a lot of money and no overhead."

"All for a woman you're going to kill?"

"Authenticity. Besides, when am I going to be a married man again? And don't women like shopping sprees?"

I nodded, still dumbfounded. "I'm adding this to my bucket list. I don't give a fuck that it's fake."

"The shopping or the marriage?"

"All of the above." I stared down at the way light reflected off the precision cuts. "But it will be nice to be married before I die, even if there was no wedding or love… Though love would've been great to have…at the end."

Before we left the mall, I ended up changing into the sweater dress with some leggings and the knee-high boots we purchased, adding in a belt to give the charcoal gray plain dress a little flare. But not too much. Six had already pressed for neutral colors.

Even he was wearing jeans and a gray T-shirt with a sports jacket.

"We match," I said as we stood in front of the dressing room mirror. Same colored clothing to go with our matching blond hair and brown eyes. "We look more like twins than lovers like this."

He pursed his lips. "I've got some other colors of contacts in the car."

"What color does your passport say?"

"Blue."

"And you didn't put them in before we left?" I asked him. He'd been so adamant about mine, I was surprised he forgot.

"I'm a constant chameleon with three other sets of identities on me. You are the one whose face has been blasted everywhere for the past week."

Somewhere there had to be a karma chameleon to bite his constant chameleon status in the ass.

10

M Y HANDS SHOOK THE ENTIRE WAY TO THE AIRPORT. I never took drama in high school. Besides faking an occasional orgasm with a boyfriend, I'd never delved into acting at all. Now, I was about to enter an airport with a killer, who'd had me chained in a motel for a week, and pose as his wife.

Shopping was different. Shopping I had fun with, especially when there was no limit. Going through a security checkpoint and customs with falsified documentation scared me in more ways than I could keep track of.

There was nothing gentle, loving, or affectionate in Six's touch. Then again, he fooled me the night I met him. Maybe if he acted like that, I could channel the me from that night and a dream of what that version of him and I could've morphed into.

My mind wandered back to that night, to his smile. Since meeting Six, the only smile I was graced with was a condescending one or a menacing one when he had his cock in hand. When he was Simon, he was smooth, personable, and flirtatious.

He was the kind of man I would've dated, explored a relationship with. Even taken him to meet my parents and maybe one day married.

"Calm yourself. If you fuck this up, just remember I don't need a gun to kill you, and a crowded airport won't stop me."

All of the fuzzy thoughts and feelings vanished, and I sighed. Dream dead.

"I was getting in the zone. Did you need to ruin it by once again reminding me of the coming bullet to my brainpan?"

His brow scrunched, and he shot me an icy glare.

I threw my hand up in his face. "Shut up. I don't fucking care about your retort. You're going to kill me, blah, blah, blah. I know." The light turned red, and the moment the car was stopped he turned in his seat. "Don't fucking look at me that way. You're the one who didn't kill me and is now jet setting me to fuck knows where. You want me act like a bubbly blonde, loving wife? Give me some motherfucking inspiration."

Anxiety took over, my heart hammering in my chest, and I felt like I was about to have a panic attack. How was I supposed to be convincing with him reminding me he was going to snuff out my existence?

"Like what?"

I threw my arms up in the air in exasperation as I tried to find the words. "Kiss me. Kiss me like you want to eat me whole, suck out my essence." Passion, desire, something to inspire our fake marriage. "Like if you don't kiss me as if the world is about to end, you'll explode. Take the breath from me, and when you're done, give me a sexy smile and take my hand."

He stared at me, probably wondering if his captive had lost her mind, then righted his posture and hit the gas.

"I'm not a character from a romance novel."

"Thanks for that, Captain Obvious, but could you maybe act like it for one minute? Just one fucking minute before I have to hang on your arm like a trophy?"

I crossed my arms and sat back with a huff, my jaw

clenching. Couldn't a girl ask for some romance from her fake husband-slash-captor? Bring back the guy I was shopping with, because he was better than the jerk behind the wheel.

We pulled into the airport area, and my leg began to bounce. My brow scrunched a bit when he didn't follow the signs for long-term parking, and instead went to the short-term garage.

"Why are we parking here?"

He sighed. "Stolen cars take longer to notice here."

"Really?" With all the cameras around I would think they would notice. Then again, he could be feeding me a line of bullshit.

As he turned the car off, he left the keys and climbed out. The trunk popped and suitcases were pulled out while I just sat there, trying to calm down.

Breathe in. Breathe out.

In.

Out.

I climbed out of the car and shut the door all while continuing to take deep breaths.

Six wheeled the suitcases over and stood in front of me. He reached out and cupped my face before leaning down and pressing his lips to mine. Light at first, testing the waters or himself, I wasn't sure.

Then it was gone.

His lips smashed against mine, our teeth hitting. The force pressed me against the side of the car, his lips prying mine open as his fingers dug into my flesh, pulling me closer. His tongue swiped across mine as he devoured my mouth.

Mind blowing didn't cover the intensity of his touch or the need of his hard cock pressing against me.

I grabbed on to his hair, fisting it as I tried to pull him closer. I wanted to suck his tongue, eat his mouth like it was a last meal, because if things went south that kiss really would be it.

When he let go, his eyes were dark orbs, his hips rocking in small movements.

"Good enough?" he asked, his voice low and grumbling.

I stared up at him, boneless and more turned on than I'd ever been in my life, and shook my head. "I think I need more."

His fingers flexed, digging into my skin. "Any more and I'll have my cock shoved up your cunt right here."

"I'm down."

"Fucking kinky woman," he whispered under his breath. "We have a flight to catch." He stepped back and grabbed hold of our suitcases.

I bent over to pick my purse up from the ground and jumped when an arm encircled my waist. His lips attacked my neck, sucking and nipping a trail up to my ear. I craned my neck, giving him room as I leaned back into him.

"I may have to induct you into the mile-high club. Not sure I can last the entire flight after that."

Motherfucking inspiration.

After getting our tickets and handing over our luggage, we headed to the much dreaded security checkpoint. So far was so good, but the real test was thirty people in front of me.

The entire time we were in the security line my palms sweated. Would they be able to detect my fake passport? If so, what then? Would Six break my neck right there so I couldn't talk?

Ten feet, then five, then I wondered if I'd reached my last moment when I passed the TSA agent my passport.

He glanced from the picture to me, doing the same for Six's. My heart slammed against my chest in a furious beat. He shined a light onto them before making some scribbles on our tickets, then handed them back.

I stared at the documents in my hand in shock, Six guiding me to the X-ray machines and body scanners.

"Fucking hate this part," he said with a groan.

I'm sure he did—he was bare of all his beloved weapons. He packed his arsenal away in a "safe place," putting only one gun and one knife into his checked luggage.

There was nothing that stood out in our carry-ons or our bodies, and after putting our shoes back on, we headed to our gate.

The jitters still had me, my hand holding my passport shaking.

Six picked up the pace and grabbed hold of my hand to make sure I kept up.

I had no doubts that he could kill me, even without his beloved gun, but I wasn't about to test him. His jaw ticked, eyes scanning, agitation almost pouring out of him.

He found a bank of empty seats near our gate and he sat down, expecting me to follow.

So, I did. Right onto his lap.

I wrapped my arms around his shoulders. Everything about him was stiff, which I found odd due to how relaxed and how good of an actor I'd seen him be. What changed from two hours ago when we were shopping?

I dipped my head in the crook of his neck and nipped, which received no reaction.

"You suck at this. No one is going to believe us if you don't relax."

He let out a hard breath, moving one hand to my back while the other trailed up my leg to settle on my thigh.

"I'm not used to doing this with a novice. Having to make sure you don't try anything."

"And you hate being without your gun," I said. When he nodded, I knew where a lot of his anxiety came from. "You were doing great earlier when we were shopping. The only novice here is you."

His gaze snapped to me, eyes hard. "What's that supposed to mean?"

"It means, you've either never been in a relationship, or it's been so long you've forgotten how it goes. If we're supposed to be in love, you have to be affectionate." I leaned back, finding his eyes, still confused by the color blue staring back at me, trying to see if he understood. "Kiss me." My voice was loud enough that time so that those around us would hear. I even played it up with a pout and batted my eyes lashes. I then made patterns with my fingers on his chest. "He was only looking at me, baby. You get so jealous."

He leaned forward in a rush, his lips meeting mine, and that wonderful humming feeling moved through me. The kiss was softer than the passion filled one of the parking garage but somehow still intense and full of unknown promises.

We continued to kiss, light and playful. Delightfully teasing as we tasted each other. A whole other man had me in his arms. Sensual and needy.

He stopped, his forehead resting against mine. "Fuck, Lacey, I want to shove you against that wall and fuck you so hard everyone in this airport will hear you screaming."

Lacey?

The heat in my blood cooled off.

Everything was a mass of confusion and a maze of emotions.

Lacey wasn't my name, but I realized he would never call me Paisley again.

Paisley was his captive while Lacey was his companion. Both the same and both marked for death.

Eight hours on a plane with a killer. Nothing to be worried about.

Right?

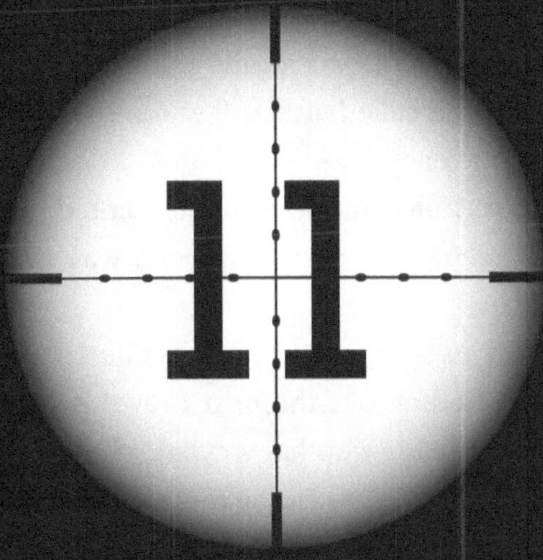

COULDN'T STOP STARING UP AT THE HUGE STEEL STRUCTURE. It was larger than I ever dreamed. The one-third scale version at Kings Island couldn't compare to the real thing—*the* Eiffel Tower.

My kidnapper had taken me over four thousand miles from home. Not only that, I was staring out our hotel window right at the magnificent Paris icon.

No dive motel. It probably cost over a grand per night. The view alone was worth that, and the hotel was pretty swanky as well. There was a four-poster bed with lavish and plush bedding. No springs in my side there.

Near the window was a sofa and chairs with a few side tables, giving me the perfect lookout over the city. Just past the sitting area was a desk and chair, which Six turned around so he was always looking out over the room and keeping tabs on me.

"I'm surprised we're not in some back-alley special," I said, still stunned, as I sat in the chair and continued to scan the skyline.

He said nothing, but that was usual Six style. It was like talking to an old dog with selective hearing. They couldn't hear you calling their name, but they sure as hell heard the piece of food drop onto the floor two rooms and thirty feet away.

"Come on," he called after a few minutes. "We don't have much time to get ready."

He could've killed me then if he wanted, and I wouldn't have minded. Seeing any part of Europe was another item off my bucket list.

We arrived two days prior, and while I was getting over jet lag, Six was finding out the next move. It seemed we were pressed to get ready for who knew what.

Walking to him, I noticed he'd pulled out the insanely expensive designer-I-couldn't-pronounce bandage dress along with the Louboutins.

"Look at me."

I did as he asked.

"I can dress you up, but if you can't play the part, you're just an average woman in expensive wrappings."

Ouch.

"What part am I to play for you today, Master?" I asked in a sweet, high tone.

His eyes narrowed into a glare. "Money infused arm candy."

"Are you my sugar daddy?" I smirked.

His jaw ticked. "Shut the fuck up. I don't have time to shove my cock down that obnoxious mouth of yours."

Ah, there was my murderous charmer.

"Am I going for high-class whore or bitchy socialite?" There was a distinction, after all. And if I was to play the part, it was an important detail.

"High-class socialite whore who knows to be fucking quiet and not say a word. Look fuckable. Draw attention away from me."

Wearing the outfit laying in front of me, there was no doubt I was going to draw attention. The short, skintight dress aptly resembled a cage, thanks to the shapes the black bandage sections formed over the cream and white geometric print. Add the black patent leather peep toe Louboutins and it was a combination to call all men.

Hopefully I could pull the look off. I was a scrubs girl. It was what I wore daily. Dressing up was a rare occasion, and never anything as expensive as what laid before me.

Before changing though, I clipped my hair up and took a quick shower. There was no way I was putting that dress on without one.

I toweled my skin dry, then threw the towel onto the bed. From inside my suitcase I pulled out a sexy set of lingerie that he'd picked out and were probably best for the dress. Before I could attempt to put them on, Six grabbed them from me and shoved the dress at me.

"No."

I glanced down at the dress in front of me. "No? What do you mean?"

He threw the items back in my suitcase and stepped in front of me. Reaching out, he slipped his fingers across my slit, making me shiver.

"Nothing underneath," he said as he dipped his fingers into my pussy.

He let out a small groan and licked his lips as he slowly pumped his fingers in and out. My mouth dropped open, and my hips rode his fingers as I stared into his eyes.

Commando would get rid of panty lines, but I had a feeling that wasn't why Six had taken them from me.

"No bra? My boobs aren't as perky as they used to be."

His other hand reached out and grabbed on to my tit hard, squeezing it. I hissed from the pain and tried to pull back. Being a B-cup, there wasn't a whole heck of a lot for him to grab, but it seemed enough for him to keep me where I was. That and the other hand that was still working my pussy.

"You need to stop fucking distracting me."

"You're the one who told me to strip." My voice came out breathy and needy.

In an almost violent spin, he released me and stormed off to the bathroom for his own shower. My legs went weak, and I sat down on the bed to calm down.

I hated the man, despised what he'd done to my life, yet I wanted nothing more than his body on mine, his cock inside me.

The duality raging inside me had me not knowing which side was up and hanging on for dear life.

"I shouldn't have to rub one out with you so close," Six said an hour later as we headed out the door.

"You could have fucked me. We both wanted it." I stopped denying I wanted him a week prior. It just made life easier, especially with the difficulty my life had become. One less thing to fret about.

"We didn't have time." The elevator stopped one floor down and two good looking men in tailored suits stepped on, causing Six to pull me closer. "But later, I'm going to fucking tear your pussy apart."

A shudder ran through me, my pussy clenching at the thought. The comment even earned a glance from the two men, whose gazes lingered on my body before they turned back around.

The part I couldn't understand was why did sex sound so

good coming from the man who was going to kill me?

Probably because Six was really good at sex. The only good thing in my complicated existence.

The two men exited the elevator first, giving me another passing glance, which I had to admit excited me a little bit.

"Why dress me up in the first place?" I asked as we slid into the car we picked up upon arrival, that I wasn't sure I wanted to know where it came from. It fell into his more-money-than-common-sense spending. "You could have just kept me locked up, as usual."

"Just keep your mouth shut when we get there."

I rolled my eyes. The man couldn't answer most questions, and I never knew what he was thinking about. With the exception of sex. He had so many tells for that.

My gaze gobbled up each and every building and monument we passed. Paris was beautiful and historic, and it made me wish even more that I'd traveled while in college.

We stopped in front of a rather large building with columns, the door up a flight of stone steps. Those were going to be a bitch in the heels I was wearing.

"Play your part well, and I'll let you come multiple times," he said as he held out his arm for me to grab on to.

I nodded and wrapped my arm in his, my heart hammering in my chest. By force of will, I tilted my head back and forced my muscles to relax and tightened back up in what I hoped resembled a confident posture.

My first step ended in a bit of a wobble, due to nerves or the uneven surface. I wasn't quite sure which, but with luck, Six's arm, and good balance, I remained standing.

"Don't fucking fall. I'm not picking your ass up," he said between clenched teeth.

Chivalry dead? I was beginning to think so. Then again, he

probably exhibited manners only when the situation warranted them.

We stepped through two huge, thick wooden doors that had to be at least twelve feet high. Elegant crystal chandeliers hung from the ceiling, and the floors were made of marble with intricate inlaid patterns. Enormous antique mirrors with golden frames hung from the twenty-foot-high walls. Elaborate décor and accessories enhanced the air of aristocracy of the large lobby.

It was a stunning tribute to the craftsmen who created them.

A man stepped up to us about twenty feet in. He appeared to be an employee and not the caliber of clientele the establishment catered to. With a wary smile, he spoke what I was pretty sure was a welcoming greeting and not a *Pretty Woman* you-can't-shop-here attitude.

While I may have been a perfect Vivian replica in this case, Six was no Edward, though he could play the part well. Vivian got paid, not killed, and ended up with her prince, while I was going to end up six feet under.

Six responded in words I didn't understand. Gibberish to my ears. I took a few years of Spanish in school, a language I'd long forgotten, minus how to order a good margarita at my local Mexican restaurant.

Welcome to France!

The man bowed and stepped back, opening his arm out, gesturing for us to proceed. Whatever he said must have been pretty good, because the wary smile was dropped in favor of a more reverent attitude.

My stilettos clicked against the marble floors, hips sashaying as I played my part of arm candy. Amazing how I always thought of myself as pretty average, maybe a bit above, but linked with Six, I felt like the sexiest woman in the room.

Maybe it was the blonde hair or the makeup. Could've been

the two-thousand-dollar dress I was wearing, or thousand-dollar Christian Louboutin peep-toes, or even the nine-hundred-dollar clutch. Whatever it was, I didn't feel like myself.

I wasn't Paisley anymore—I really was Lacey.

With my head high, I acted as well as any Oscar-winning actress.

Pretentious as anyone else in the room. Elite and selfish, caring for nothing but the man on my arm and what he could buy me.

Another suit wearing man stepped in front of us, cutting off the direction we were headed. "Excuse me, sir, can I help you?"

English!

Six arched a brow at him. "The only assistance I require is for you to remove yourself from my path and point me toward Samuel Winston."

Damn, he could play just about any part. And the Oscar goes to Six.

"May I ask your name?"

"Sean Collins."

He disappeared through a set of elaborately carved wooden doors and reappeared almost immediately, ushering us forth. As we stepped into the room, I was once again struck with awe. Tall ceilings, massive fireplace, lush décor, and occupied by only two people.

A snotty looking blonde sat on a chair while a *Fifty Shades of Grey* like man stood in front of the fireplace.

"Mr. Winston, a Mr. Collins for you."

"Thank you, William." His voice was deep, and held an air of authority.

The only thing that ran through my head was the conversation Six and I had on the first day we met.

Cocky. Mr. Christian Grey wannabe was cocky, arrogant,

and probably an asshole as well.

When he turned, I almost stepped back. Black hair, seemingly glowing green eyes, and an aura of power. With the fire roaring behind him, he resembled the devil.

As soon as the door closed, the blonde stood. It was amazing the similarity of presence they projected. When I turned to look at Six, I pulled back. The air around him had changed as well, almost matching theirs, only his lacked the cocky edge.

There was almost a competition going on, and it was blatantly obvious who was the oddball—me.

"Six, it's been a while," the devil said as he stepped forward, angling toward the blonde.

She smirked at the devil as he continued his approach. "Maybe for you. I was with him a month ago." She gave Six a wink. "Under the name of Evan Arden, wasn't it?"

"Nine." He nodded to the man, then turned to the woman. "One."

Nine? One? Six?

"Huh." The noise escaped and seemed to draw their attention to me.

If they were anything like Six, they knew I was there, but just ignored me. I wasn't worth their gaze.

The blonde's face soured. "Are you sure you want to discuss business in front of your toy?"

Six shrugged. "Just meat."

A smirk grew on the blonde's face. "True."

Great. After two weeks of being with the psycho and being "married" to him, I was still just cattle.

Moo.

"Did we miss orders?" Nine asked.

"Three is dead." Six wasted no time getting to the point.

Three?

Things started to make more sense and less sense in that moment. Three was the word that Six spoke when he saw the body on the slab right before he kidnapped me and blew up my work.

There was no startled gasp or change in their expression. No one seemed upset. What appeared to be another of their rank was dead, and they were unfeeling, unconcerned.

They really were monsters, and I was trapped in a room with three of them.

Nine quirked a brow. "You think it means something."

"A Cleaner sent to clean up another Cleaner? To erase any evidence of us?"

The way he said Cleaner threw me off. It was spoken as if it was a title and not a housekeeping position.

"That's to be expected," Nine said as he walked over to a cart that held a decanter. He pulled out the stopper and poured some of the amber liquid into a glass. "They don't acknowledge our existence in any way."

"They don't want any blood on their pristine, white hands," One added.

"Then someone tried to erase me," Six said.

That got their attention.

Nine had raised the glass to his lips, but he lowered it. "Cleaning house?"

One's eyes were wide. "Have you talked to Jason?"

Six nodded. "Even he didn't know who the job was."

"We still have an assignment," Nine said after a swig, finishing off the drink. "Thank you for letting us know."

Six's brow furrowed. "That's it?"

Nine looked to One, then back to Six. "It's the job. It's what we do. We don't ask questions."

Six shook his head. "Five years of doing their dirty work. I will not be taken down by a lesser man."

Nine's demeanor seemed to soften. "We have a few weeks left here. Once completed, we'll contact Jason for a meeting."

That seemed to satiate Six enough, but I couldn't help wondering if that meant a few more weeks left in my life.

"Watch your back," Six said as we turned back to the door.

"Wait," One called out.

Six turned us as One sauntered over. When she reached us, she put one hand on Six's chest and pushed her body against his, then pressed her red lips to his. The hand on his chest moved up to his jaw, her fingers resting as their lips parted and tongues swirled together.

For some reason my eye twitched and I felt the need to vomit.

She pulled back, her eyes moving to me as her lips twitched up into a smirk before she looked back to him.

"Stay safe."

"**S**O, YOU SPEAK FRENCH," I SAID ONCE WE WERE OUT of the gorgeous building and the untouchable beings inside. It was like Mount Olympus in there.

No response, like usual.

"Any others?" Annoyance seeped in. Was it so fucking hard to answer a few simple questions?

"About seven."

"Wow. Talented tongue."

He turned and smirked at me. "I thought I proved that the first night."

Fuck.

Yes, he did.

"You've slept with her." The words were out before I could retract them. His dismissive attitude grated on me.

He turned to me. "You picked that up from a kiss?" He pulled out a handkerchief from his pocket and wiped his lips.

I rolled my eyes. "Sometimes you are just a regular guy."

"What does that mean?" he asked, his brow scrunching.

"That means, duh, asshole. Pretty obvious when she gave your junk a little squeeze at the end there."

The valets opened the car doors and we both slipped in, Six

tipping the driver as we did.

My arms crossed over my chest, and I stared out the front window. The vision of her pressing her overly painted lips to his made my stomach turn. There was something about her that rubbed me wrong. I couldn't put my finger on it, but I did know one thing—the bitch baited me.

"Why does it seem like it bothers you that I've had sex with her?"

I turned to him and blinked. At least he wasn't trying to deny it. Why did it? Was it because he'd fucked another woman and not killed her? Or was it because she threw it in my face while she tongue banged him in front of me?

"It doesn't."

"Good, then you can stop acting like a pissy brat."

My jaw dropped and my arms relaxed. Fine. "What now, Master?"

He glared at me and put his foot to the gas. "Now I'm going to bend you over, lift your dress just over your ass, and fuck your pussy. The question is…in public or over the desk in our room?"

He'd just kissed a woman in front of me and was talking about not only kissing me with that red shade still slightly visible, but fucking me too.

"Did she turn you on that much?"

"Lacey," he growled in warning. "I'm going to shove my dick in you because you fucking made it hard the second you put on that dress. Knowing you're bare underneath…" He reached down and palmed the bulge in his pants. "I almost bent you over in that room and fucked you right in front of them."

In front of them? In front of *her*?

One fucking point to Paisley, zero for blonde bitch.

"Public." The whispered word shot out of my mouth before I could stop it. Pussy clenching at just the idea. That would show blondie.

"That's what I thought you'd say."

His hand moved to my leg, slipping between my thighs and up under my short dress. I sucked in a breath when his fingertips grazed my clit and sunk further down. There was no stopping my hips from rising, drawing his fingers in and deeper. Positioning him right where I wanted him.

"What the fuck is so addictive about this pussy that it drives me crazy?" he asked as his fingers slipped inside, the palm of his hand pressing against my clit.

"The obnoxious mouth that comes with it?"

He let out a low chuckle, his hand curling and drawing my hips off the seat.

Sadly, it was then we pulled back up to the hotel and he removed his hand, making me whimper.

If I didn't watch it, I was bound to become addicted to him. Which, considering he was going to kill me, was a very bad idea.

His arm was around my waist as we walked toward the elevator. My heart sunk, adrenaline waning. Fun times were not going to be in public. I wasn't an exhibitionist or anything, but the thought of someone watching drove me wild.

There were a few people waiting, and an older woman gave me a curt smile. It wasn't like I had my tits hanging out or anything, but my guess was the length of it was too short for her taste.

When the elevator arrived, I stepped forward, but he pulled me back. "Wait."

As the doors closed, there was a ping as the elevator behind us opened up. A few people unloaded, then we stepped on.

Before the doors were even shut he turned me around and pushed on my back, bending me over as he pressed his hips against me.

His fingers tangled into my hair and pulled my head up while he held my back down, forcing it to arch.

Leaning over me, his teeth nipped at my neck. "I've been waiting to fuck you in those shoes since I bought them."

He let go of my hair, and I put my hands up against the wall for balance. At that angle, I felt the air move around my almost exposed pussy. The hem of my dress moved up until I felt his hand passing over my ass, his fingers rubbing against my slit and hitting my clit.

A sharp sting on my left cheek made me hiss, then I felt his consuming desire when his fingers dug into my flesh.

He reached out and hit a few buttons. The elevator gave a jolt, causing my hips to sway and bump into the hot head of his cock.

The man got it out fast and began running it against my wet opening before slipping in.

My mouth popped open, spine tingling.

Nothing beat the first thrust.

"Fuck, yes," he hissed as he rotated his hips, moving in and out.

The elevator slowed down and stopped on the first button he hit. My heart stopped as the doors slid open, muscles tensing, but there was nobody waiting.

They slid closed again and Six fisted my hair again, pulling my head back and changing the angle he was hitting inside.

A low moan crawled out of me as my eyes fluttered. My calves burned from the shoes and the position I was in, but I didn't care.

My killer's cock was in me along with the thrill of people seeing me get off on it.

It was official—I was sick and twisted.

The doors opened, and I recognized the two men we'd run

into earlier as they stared at us with the most hilarious stunned expressions. Much to my surprise, they stepped on, unable to take their eyes off Six's cock slamming into me.

His fingers dug deeper into my hip and he sped up. A shattering whimper slipped from my open mouth, and I clenched down on him.

"That's it, baby, milk my cock."

Fuck. Me.

The words were out of place for Six. He was playing the roll and showing off to the men in front of us.

They were watching me get fucked. Two good looking guys stared at me like they wished they were him.

Incomprehensible sounds forced their way out of me with each thrust. There was no way to hold them in, even if I wanted to. His body drew them from mine. A song of pleasure that spurred him on.

Every muscle was tight, all my nerves vibrating as he played my body. No sound came out, then a wailing scream as I broke, convulsing as I came.

There was no reprieve for me. He was still hard.

The elevator stopped on another floor and I froze, but once again, nobody was there. Our onlookers continued to watch, one of them running his hand along the hard-on tenting his pants.

Six's arm flexed, pulling my head back farther, bending me until I was staring up at the ceiling. My legs shook as he slammed into me. A few hard thrusts, and a low groan vibrated in his chest as his hips flexed forward. I felt him twitch inside, letting out each spurt of come.

He stayed buried deep before letting go of my hair and pulling out. A little smack to my ass before pulling my dress down right as the elevator pinged for the next stop. Six finished tucking his dick back in and grabbed on to my waist, bringing me to him. He pressed his lips to mine, devouring my mouth just as the doors opened.

"Gentlemen," he said, nodding to our onlookers as he pushed between them.

Hot, wet come began to slide down my thigh as we walked, dripping down to the floor. A string of groans and curses came from the elevator as the doors closed.

"Did I just become fapping material?"

One of Six's brows lifted, as did the opposite corner of his mouth, as he looked down at me. "Yes. That is a definite yes."

Sometimes, Six wasn't that bad of a guy.

We didn't leave Paris right away like I thought, but it seemed Six liked to lay low until he got his next move together. My guess was he also wanted to stick around just in case. Instead of moving on, we'd spent three days held up in the hotel room while he talked to contacts.

They used a bunch of super spy slang or killer code, so I couldn't understand half of what he said.

A lot of the rest of his time was spent working out in the room, probably to tease me.

Not that I minded being there, because it was a *huge* step up from the previous hotels, but I would have loved to see more of the city. The Louvre, Notre Dame, Versailles, along with so many other landmarks and quintessential Parisian architecture. It was a shame to be in such a city and not able to fully take it in.

So I sat there, studying the Eiffel Tower and the buildings around it along with the Seine, and watching people walk around with a freedom I once took for granted. A freedom I would never have again.

Where did being a homebody and workaholic get me? Stuck in one hotel room after the other for what was going to be the rest of my life.

At least I was allowed to indulge in some Parisian cuisine and, an order unbeknownst to my captor, wine. Gotta love room service.

"Are you going to drink that whole bottle yourself?" he asked, looking up from his laptop as I poured my fourth glass.

I stared at him as the last few drops from the bottle landed in my glass. "Yep." Tipping the glass back I made sure to down the entire thing while he watched.

It burned, but I couldn't help but love the flash of anger in his eyes. Somehow, some way, I got to the son of a bitch. Probably more than anyone else. I could annoy the fuck out of him, make him lash out.

Sometimes the result was painful, other times pleasurable, but nevertheless, I got a rise, and nothing made me feel as alive as taunting Six.

Who was the fucked up one again? I was beginning to think it was me. Rational humans didn't react in such a destructive manner. Maybe it was due to my impending death. What did I have to lose that wasn't already slated for demolition?

Self-respect was long gone. Anger and fear did nothing to help. I accepted. I kept living.

I did whatever the fuck I could get away with.

Getting up from the sofa I'd been occupying for hours, I made a curvy path to the phone.

Time for another bottle.

The stupid phone was across the room, and I had a hard time figuring out the little symbols. I hit the most likely key and let it ring.

"Room service."

Jackpot.

"Hi, can I get another bottle of Cabernet?"

"Lacey!"

I shivered, then pulled the phone away from my ear and turned to Six, holding my finger up to my lips. "Shh, I'm talking to room service." Returning my attention back to the call, I couldn't help give a little giggle.

"We will get that right up to you, madam," the attendant said.

"Thanks." I put the phone back on the receiver. "It'll be here soon."

When I turned around, I could almost feel his anger from ten feet away. His eyes were dark, and he was beyond pissed. Somehow, probably due to being a bit drunk from the wine, I wasn't scared at all.

I couldn't stop the smile that spread on my face as I walked back over to my sofa perch by the window.

A loud bang stopped my weaving. Six stood so fast the chair fell over, and he stomped toward me. My whole body heated, the thrill sending chills down my spine.

The smile never left my face as he fisted my hair, bending my head back to look at his furious face.

"Look, it's the big, bad wolf." Another giggle slipped out, but he didn't laugh with me.

His jaw ticked, and his lip twitched up into a snarl. "Mean it is, because you need to fucking learn a lesson."

He yanked on my hair, making me cry out in pain as he led me across the room to one of his bags and fished out another damn roll of duct tape.

I poked the bear one too many times, and I had a feeling I was about to pay dearly for it.

We moved to the bed and he let go, shoving me down. I lay

there as he spun me around, positioned me where he wanted, then grabbed hold of one wrist. First, he wound the tape around my wrist, then drew it around the bedpost, then spun it around my wrist again in the opposite direction, making sure to loop the strands together.

My heart started pounding, and adrenaline kicked in. A growing fear began to circulate through my veins when he pulled my head just over the edge, then reached for my other hand.

I moved it away from his grip, trying to keep it away, rolling onto my side, but he was faster and stronger. He repeated the same movements, my arms spread wide. When he walked away I tugged at them, but there wasn't much wiggle room.

He fisted the shirt I was wearing, which was one of his dress shirts, and tore it open, sending buttons flying everywhere. My nipples hardened from the cool air, and when I looked down, he yanked my panties over my hips before throwing them onto the floor.

I couldn't help but rub my thighs together. My tipsy mind could only come up with cock-in-pussy scenarios, and my tight nipples only encouraged those thoughts.

I whimpered when he pulled one of my legs away and began to tape it to the bedpost just as he had my arms. Soon I was immobile—every limb was attached to a bedpost, and I was completely naked.

There was an excited buzz running through me, my pussy growing wet in anticipation. Angry, rough sex was the best.

From upside down I watched him undo his belt, then pull it through each loop of his jeans. I licked my lips, the excitement kicking up. But that soon began to fade as he kept it in his hand and folded it over.

Stepping closer, he popped the button and dropped the zipper, shuffling both his jeans and boxer briefs down his hips.

"I think you need a reminder of the stakes, because you've been acting like you can do and say anything and I'll do nothing." His cock popped out and smacked against my forehead. "That," he tapped it a few times, "is where I'm going to put a bullet and snuff out your life."

I giggled again and angled my head, flicking my tongue against the head of his dick.

Then screamed after a snap filled my ears before pain radiated just above my hip. Tears sprung to my eyes, and I wanted to turn onto my side but was trapped on my back.

"What the fuck?" My brain cleared, the fuzz the wine created disappearing with the surprising pain.

"Don't speak," he said through clenched teeth, slapping his belt down again, this time landing on my pussy and clit.

With the hit, there was an odd spark of pleasure mixed in, lessening the intensity. But it didn't stop the whimper of pain.

He tapped on my mouth with his cock and pressed it between my parted lips. "Open."

With a flex of his hips he shoved his cock all the way to the back of my mouth, making me gag as he hit the entrance to my throat. The leather snapped against my thigh and I screamed, but it was muffled with my mouth full.

"I'm the fucking king, you are the pawn. Do you understand, Lacey? This game you're playing ends the same way no matter what."

I cried out, muscles tensing, back arching as he landed another strike to my stomach, sobbing and choking around his cock as his belt bit into my skin.

Each spot he hit burned.

"Come in."

Come in?

I hadn't heard the knock on the door, but I did catch, "Good afternoon, sir. I have the…" The next words were gibberish and French sounding.

However, even if I did know any French, I doubted I'd be able to understand him in my predicament.

Some stranger had just seen me completely naked and completely helpless as a man force-fed me his dick.

Mortification set in, especially when Six directed him on where to put the bottle I'd ordered.

"Set it over there."

A few thrusts gagged me, and there was a slam, then another smack to my pussy.

"Whining and crying just makes me want to do it harder."

He was breathing harder, and I prayed he was close to coming, to ending the torture. Saliva and slime slid down my face as he abused my mouth. I couldn't do anything but take it.

I couldn't see, but there was a sound I couldn't identify, then the hand that had been dealing the damage was squeezing my tit, followed by his other hand.

At least he stopped whipping me, but I was barely getting any air as he crammed his cock, forcing it as far into my throat as he could.

"You like to show off, like to argue. I'm your ruler. You want to keep breathing, you will do exactly as I say."

He pulled out and I gulped air, filling my lungs. Grabbing hold of my hair, he lifted my head just as hot beads of come landed on my cheeks, lips, hair, forehead, nose. Basically, the entirety of my face with a few drops from the first spurt landing on my chest.

Every part of him receded, leaving me lying there in complete humiliation.

"Are you still so sure that any life is better than death?"

Tears streamed down the side of my face, and I chocked on

my own restricted sobs.

He stuffed his dick back in his jeans. "Fucking stay."

Where was I going to go?

I was covered in semen, spit, and tears. Left abandoned. Strapped down to a bed.

The come on my face cooled while the welts on my body ached.

Six was not a nice guy. Six was a monster.

Four hours I laid there with multiple fluids drying on my face. I was freezing cold, needed to pee, but at least the pain had subsided. I had a feeling the last one would change when I was able to move again.

Four hours of reflection, of suffering the humiliation and pain and fear. How had I found pleasure in the man before?

I gave in to the hopelessness after the first hour. That was when the depression set in.

Damsels in distress were only in fairy tales and romance books. While I may have fit the bill of a damsel and distress, Six was no prince.

I wasn't in a love story.

I was in a death story.

There would be no one swooping in to save the day. No Superman to fly me away.

I'd accepted my fate, and maybe become a little too cavalier in what I believed I could get away with.

But it wasn't in my nature to be the crying, wimpy, pathetic captive, even though I did have tons of dried tears on my face.

I also hadn't truly faced his anger before. He'd lashed out

plenty of times—grabbing on to my neck, pulling my hair, the rare smack to the face when I made an escape attempt.

For the first time in weeks, since I had accepted my situation, I was afraid. Not of dying, not of the pain or even he who dealt it, but of the feelings that consumed me, the feelings I'd locked away.

Sarcasm was my security blanket. I used my obnoxious mouth to deflect and cover up. Making people laugh hid the insecurities that ate at me.

Lacey was a role. A chance to be someone else. But I missed the orangish tint of my hair. My couch and blanket with the TV on, binging on Netflix, curled into Digby's side.

And that was the hardest thing in all of it, the sliding door. How different would my life be in that moment if I'd gone with Digby? Saddened as I watched the destruction of my former place of employment, and my friends inside, but I would've been alive and would've worked past those feelings. I wouldn't have wallowed in depression over the last year, but I also wasn't sure if I'd have been happy.

While the grass definitely was looking pretty green in that alternate world, because I wasn't waiting for the chopping block, it was a vision built on a lie. I'd be safe and normal and not going to die before my time. There were reasons I didn't go with him, fights we had about it. The yelling and screaming and crying. As perfect as we seemed, we were far from it.

When he asked me to marry him and the word *no* came out, we were both in shock.

I loved him. We had so much fun together, and the sex was amazing.

It wasn't like I was afraid of commitment, just afraid of committing to him. Because I knew he loved me more than I loved him. Because as great and perfect and wonderful as he was, at least to me, there were also things that made us incompatible.

So when I told everyone and they asked what happened, all I could say was, "I don't know." A feeling I couldn't put into words, an explanation I couldn't give.

Which only added to my reclusive behavior of the past year.

My life may have boring and unfulfilling of late, but it was mine, not the sham I was living. The half death as an alternate personality.

"Are you ready to behave?" Six asked, twirling his knife between his fingers as he walked toward me.

I tilted my head to look back at him. There was utter defeat in my expression, I could just tell. A tear slipped from my eye.

One side of my mouth twitched up as my lips trembled. "Nah."

Tiny word, big reaction. His muscles tensed, jaw so tight I thought his teeth might crack, and there was a furious fire in his eyes.

"I'll play the game, play by your rules, but I don't behave."

He stared down at me, our eyes locked as he gauged my answer, then his arm swung out and I turned my head, flinching from the action. Instead of the pain from a knife slicing through me, there was pain of muscles relaxing that had been pulled taut for too long.

"Get yourself the rest of the way."

I looked back to him, watching as he spun and headed back to working on his laptop.

Stretching my fingers, I held my hand in front of me, twisting and twirling, getting movement back in the stiff joints. I reached over, cringing as I twisted in order to get to my other wrist and work the tape off.

The remnants of his anger marred my skin. They were visible in the form of precise, edged welts his belt had created and blossoming bruises of varying shades. Every movement agitated them, causing whimpers of pain to slip from my lips as I twisted further, my nails picking at the edge of a substance I was beginning to have loathing for.

It wasn't an overly complicated pattern. Yet it was difficult to unravel thanks in great part to my legs still being bound.

A few lost hairs on my arm, and I collapsed back down on my back. With my freed hand, I worked on removing the remainder of tape still around my other wrist.

After that was done, I threw the scraps on the floor and silently cursed out the creator of duct tape.

When I had my legs freed, I moved them around just as I had my arms. Ligaments and muscles burned, not to mention the welts. I slid off the bed and took ginger steps toward the bathroom. There was no energy or desire to move faster, with the exception of a full bladder. Just the need to wash my face and maybe soak in the tub.

I felt Six's gaze on me as I passed him, but I refused to even look his way.

Upon entering the bathroom, I cringed at my reflection. My skin was marked with angry red splotches, making me look polka dotted. Nothing he did was permanent, lasting, but he made sure to make it hurt and remind me who was in control.

As if I had any doubt.

I turned on the water to the large jetted tub and threw in some of the bath salts on my way to the toilet. My hair was in knots and on the crusty side, and I noticed then that there was not only some muscle pain in my jaw, but the back of my mouth and throat were also a bit sore.

Bastard.

Fucking asshole.

I washed my face off as I waited for the tub to fill, scouring the skin to get all of his jizz off.

Facials were good and fun and sexy with someone you loved. With the random jackass kidnapper, definitely not.

Emotionally drained, physically pained, I was left wondering why I enjoyed him before. The elevator had been hot. In fact, most every other time had been pleasure filled.

He liked to dominate, to be in control, and that translated into passion and need for my body. But what he did that night was for pure humiliation, to put me in my place.

It worked to a point. I was humiliated.

Frothy bubbles formed a layer on top of the filled tub. The warmth burned my cold skin as I slipped my legs in, but soon morphed into a soothing heat.

I hissed each time the water hit one of the welts, my hands shaking as I sunk down. All the way down I went until the water consumed me, then back up, leaning against the side of the tub.

I was going to die. Not later, not of old age. I was going to die—shot in the head—my body dumped possibly somewhere no one would ever find. My family would never know what happened to me.

Just another slain beast. Used and thrown away.

Tears welled in my eyes, my face scrunching up as small sobs shook me. I reached up, my hands covering my mouth in an effort to muffle the sound, to muffle the pain not only from him, but from my own ears.

Maybe I hadn't really accepted the situation until then. My fate. Maybe I lied to myself. Maybe I buried it all away in order to endure, to live just a little bit longer.

Some things were pretty certain—Six was ruthless, and I would die by his hand.

"**A**RE YOU FINISHED?" SIX ASKED AS HE REACHED across the coffee table.

I looked up at him as I took another sip of my wine. Glancing down at my plate, there was still half a chicken breast and some cheese and baguette, but I nodded anyway and turned toward the window just in time to see the Eiffel Tower start twinkling in the moonlight.

It was late, and I was hoping the wine, which Six ordered, would make it easier to fall asleep. Five days had passed, and I had become very blasé.

My spark was gone, or at least hiding. Depression was overpowering everything, and I had no will to do anything. Even sleep eluded me as my mind whirled about *nothing*. I stared up at the ceiling, blank, unresponsive in the night.

It wasn't me. *I* wasn't me.

Cracked and broken as I tried not to cry, thinking about everything that was wrong. Accepting that I was already dead inside. Being on my period didn't help, nor the trip with him to a pharmacy, the hormonal shift making my depression worse.

Purple and yellow still covered my skin, but ever so slowly waned away.

Six's eyes were on me, as they had been for days. I hardly spoke, just stared out the window as he stared at me.

Sex wasn't the same. I wasn't the same. The whole fucked-up situation wasn't the same, and I desperately wanted to brighten up, to sass him back like usual, but I just didn't have the energy for it.

Cabin fever made my skin itch, and hours on the clock ticked by in slow, repetitive succession.

Purgatory. Trapped in an endless cycle of rinse, repeat boredom.

Unlike the last hotel, Six never left. All business was conducted on either his laptop or phone. There seemed to be a lot of waiting in the killing game.

Once the last sip was gone from my glass, I set it down and stood up, stripping off my lounge pants and sweatshirt on my way to the bed. I burrowed under the covers and shortly thereafter, Six did the same. His right arm became my pillow, as it was every night, while his left wrapped around my waist, pulling me to him.

Stiff, on edge muscles soon relaxed as I settled against his body. Every night, no matter how angry or hurt, it happened—I melted into him. Even *that* night, after his show of power.

Maybe because encased in him, I knew I was safe. The safest place to be was wrapped in the arms of the scariest monster, right?

"We're leaving in two days," he said, his lips brushing against my neck.

I didn't respond right away as the news took me by surprise. There'd been no indication. "Where are we going?"

"Miami. Jason thinks Five might be there."

"Who's Jason?" Nine said the same name when we went to talk to him.

"My handler."

Somehow, that one word made me chuckle inside. It sparked the usual me. "Handler? What's a handler? Does he handle you? Is that like fondling?"

Silence. His usual non-response.

When I decided he wasn't going to answer, I took a deep breath, closed my eyes, and attempted to drift off. It was working. I was almost there when he spoke, startling me back awake.

"He's my liaison with Home. He doles out the assignments to each Cleaner."

I'd heard the title Cleaner that time as well, but what was Home?

"What's a Cleaner?" I asked, hoping he'd continue opening up.

"The boogeymen who take care of things nobody else wants to know about."

Six definitely fit that name. "A Killing Corps."

"Precisely."

He wasn't just a monster for monster's sake. He was part of an organization that paid him and others to kill people.

Pushing my luck, I asked the question that was now the elephant in the room. "Who do you work for? Who is Home?"

He sighed. "Go to sleep."

It was too much to hope for that I might unravel the mystery of my executioner a little bit more. I guess I should have been thankful to the little bit I was privy to.

Instead of counting sheep, I counted down to the next flight, the next destination.

Two days. Less than forty-eight hours. Roughly thirty until we left the hotel. A nine-hour flight, followed by a possible two-hour connection and in three days, I'd be back on American soil.

Eight days in Paris, and I barely saw anything besides the

interior of a beautiful hotel room.

Maybe there was a chance I could get away.

I said I'd play by his rules, but I refused to give up on living, on the small sliver of hope that I would make it through to a life past Six and his bullet.

"Welcome to Miami," I said as I stepped out into the hot, humid air of southern Florida. Ah, heat, how I'd missed it.

Almost an entire month had passed since Six tore me away from my life. One month I'd spent living with an extremely hot, extremely deadly hit man. One month where I'd spent days on end staring at the walls of hotel rooms.

It was a long flight from Paris to Atlanta after our near two-week trip, then a short hop down to Miami. Hard to admit, but I was actually glad we'd soon be seeing a hotel room. I really needed a nap.

There was a car waiting for us in long-term parking, and I pursed my lips as I looked at the black sedan.

"How in the hell is this waiting?" I asked.

Six had already started to load our bags into the trunk and didn't respond, while I stared at the handle. How long had it been baking in the Florida sun? The car was bound to be stifling if I could even get it open.

Wrapping my fingers in my shirt, I squatted down and pulled on the lever. The door popped open and I caught it with my foot, prying it open.

Even hotter air flowed from the vented interior. There wasn't a thing inside that wasn't going to burn me.

Suddenly the car started, making me jump back. A low

chuckle made my head turn to the back of the car where Six was loading in the last suitcase with a smirk on his face.

"You think you're funny, huh?" Remote start gag equals not funny.

"No."

"But you thought that was funny."

"Yes."

I rolled my eyes, not that he could see behind my sunglasses, and reached down to feel the air coming from the vents. It was warm, but began to cool. Soon, cold air was pumping out at top speed and I braved the leather interior.

Thankfully, I was wearing jeans, so no dreaded thigh burn, but I could still feel the heat of the leather through them. The burn zapped my arms, though—the armrests were definite no-gos.

Six slid into the driver's seat and put the key in the ignition, then shut his door. He sat back and did nothing, touched nothing.

"Are we waiting on something?" I asked after a few minutes. "The car will cool down faster once it gets moving."

"I'm waiting until a silver sedan two rows over and three back leaves."

Once again I was reminded that Six always knew his surroundings.

"Did you scare me on purpose?"

He smirked and glanced up at the rearview mirror. "Haven't you realized by now that everything I do has a purpose?"

I thought on that, my mind wandering back. I was a wild-card dropped on him, but from the moment we were out of the city, there was a reason for everything he did. Even the harsh things he'd done to me served a purpose. Reminders that my life was in his hands, and if I wanted more time above the ground, I had to get in line with the program.

A flash from the mirror caught my eye, and I watched the silver sedan head for the exit, whooshing past us.

"So, secret spy guy, what made that driver suspicious?" I asked as we both turned.

"He was sitting at arrivals with a carry-on. When we passed, he followed."

At the exit, the driver paid, then zoomed away down the street.

"He could have just been resting or tying his shoe."

"Slim possibility."

Paranoid much? "Is it really so slim? His car was in the parking lot."

"So was this one. Waiting for us."

Touché. Which reminded me…

"You didn't answer—how was it waiting for us?"

He picked up the keys from a car rental counter, but didn't fill out any paperwork.

Silence.

Damn it. I hated when he pulled his no answer crap.

There was a week's worth of a fee for the parking lot, and we were off. I didn't know where in Miami we were headed, but I hoped there would be a view of the ocean. We weren't on the interstate long when blue showed up at the horizon.

My eyes grew wide as the interstate turned into a bridge and the ocean finally came into view. The sign read Miami Beach. It'd been years since I'd been to the beach, since college. Before then, I used to travel to Sanibel Island with my parents every year, sometimes twice a year.

Granted, I knew that there was a high likelihood no beach lounging would be going on, but there was still the warm, salty breeze and sun that always seemed to melt everything away. And that was something I was in desperate need of.

I made a little whimper, then chanced a tentative peek in Six's direction. "I will fuck you so hard, squeeze your cock so tight, let you do whatever you want to me, if you will just let me have a few hours to sun on the beach and play in the waves."

I couldn't take my eyes off it. Right out the front window, in the not too far distance, was the ocean for as far as the eye could see.

Maybe I could swim to freedom. Wonder how many people try to get into Cuba…

"I already get to fuck you whenever and however I want. Where's the incentive?"

"You can fuck my ass without complaint."

The corner of his lip drew up, and his eyes glanced toward me. "Hmm, that's an intriguing proposition."

We made a left, and I lost sight of the beach as we headed down another out-of-time experience. There were a lot of art deco buildings. After about a mile and a half, we turned into a huge parking garage and found a spot in the shade.

"Okay…"

Six moved to the trunk and unloaded our bags.

"Where is this place?" I asked, suitcase in tow.

"Up ahead."

There was a back alley between buildings and if I hadn't been with Six it would be giving me a wiggy vibe. The drug deal going down might have been one reason for that uneasy feeling.

Down another shorter alley and we were back on the street with Six holding open a door for me. There was some parking out front, but not much.

If the lobby was any indicator of the rest of the hotel, I sensed a repeat of our previous US stays, and the direct opposite of our Parisian one.

A couple hundred bucks in cash handed over in exchange for another outdated brass key. We passed by an in-house restaurant that had a health inspector notice on the window. Great indicator there.

The elevator was closed for repairs, so we huffed it up the flight of stairs to a stained door and salt worn doorknob.

The inside of the room was just as disgusting as I imagined. It was actually worse than the hotel outside Atlanta, and I didn't think there was a worse.

Everything was out of date with exception of the television. Stains on the chairs and carpet, even a few on the bedding. Cracked and popped tile flooring.

Icing on the cake was the smell—dank, vomit-like, stuffy, with a hint of sea air. By far the worst.

Why was there no upkeep or maintenance? And how did a place like that stay in business in such a hotel saturated area?

"How do you find these shitty places? Is there a shitholehotels.com or something?

He chuckled.

A fucking chuckle.

Six voiced amusement.

My mouth popped open as I stared at him as he worked to locate something in one of his bags. He didn't look my way, just continued what he was doing.

"Why do you always have duct tape on you?" I asked after he pulled it out and set it aside.

He continued to shuffle through the bag. "If I need to tie someone up or fix something. Duct tape does it all."

"Why not rope when tying up hostages?"

He gave me the side eye. "Not as easy to work with or as fast."

Fair point. It would have taken a lot of time, experience, and rope to tie me up in the ways he had. Duct tape was more compact and only took a few seconds to bind hands or feet.

"So, what's next?"

"Food."

I nodded. "Food is good."

We headed out the front door and walked down the street. The art deco buildings had me sighing. Such beautiful lines. I didn't know why I liked the style so much, maybe it was something to do with the lines. They almost seemed romantic.

They were sexy and appealing, much like the man beside me who was getting major looks from some of the bikini clad chicks coming in from the beach.

If only they knew.

Yes, he was good at sex, but being a death row hostage wasn't fun. One did not make up for the other.

We found a Mediterranean eatery and popped in. Chicken kabobs were a favorite, and I was happy to get some hummus and falafel. Best meal since we'd left Paris.

On the way back, I couldn't help but window shop, spotting a cute bikini and causing us to stop. "So pretty."

Six didn't seem to be in a hurry. There was no pressing matter, so he indulged me. Perhaps he was thinking on my earlier request, perhaps he was just a pervert, but when we stepped in, he grabbed a basket.

We were only at the first rack when I spotted a cute striped strapless set. There was also pretty geometric prints, beautiful floral prints, and plain colors.

Like weeks before, Six helped me shop. He picked out wildly varying suits and threw them in the basket. By the time we reached a dozen, I cut him off.

"I think that's enough for now," I said, smiling at him.

He quirked his brow and we headed to the dressing room.

What I thought was going to be a one person show he decided was going to be a team effort.

"There's not enough room," I said as I tried to close the curtain, my eyes glancing behind him to the girl working the counter who was eyeing his ass. "You won't fit."

The corner of his lip pulled up as he stepped forward, pushing me back into the room. "Oh, I've proven many times that I do fit."

Fucking double meaning bastard.

The room was really tiny, but after closing the curtain—the only divider between the fitting room and the store floor—he took a seat on the chair in the corner.

Reaching into the basket, he picked one of the bikinis up and handed it to me.

Over weeks I'd gotten used to changing in front of him, of being in my birthday suit often, but there was something about the intimacy of the small room that made me almost shy. Taking off my shirt didn't have the fluidity as it did in the hotel room. It was awkward, making me feel a bit awkward, especially with him staring at me.

Shirt and shorts off, I reached behind me to unclasp my bra, turning away from his unwavering gaze. Strange that after all that had happened, him staring at me was unnerving.

"Why don't you take your panties off?" he asked after I'd gotten the top on and was pulling the bottom up my legs.

My brow furrowed as I worked the bottom over my hips. "You don't take them off to try on swimsuits. That's just gross."

"Why?"

"If I'm trying on and decide I don't like it that means my pussy has touched it for the next person as well as all those before me. Ick." I made a gagging motion before something clicked and I turned to glare at him. "You just want me to be completely naked."

No reaction.

Fucker was king of the poker face, but he couldn't hide the heaviness of his gaze.

"You are such a perverted cock monster."

A quick look in the mirror, and the bikini was out. Unflattering and without my normal hair color, a bad tone for me.

I hung it back up and grabbed another one from the basket, ignoring him. Instead, he had other ideas. Reaching, he grabbed onto my hips and pulled me to stand between his legs. I jumped as his tongue ran up my abdomen, his teeth nipping the underside of my breast.

"I do believe someone said she'd be willing to do just about anything to have a little beach time."

I leaned back and squinted my eyes. "What's going on in the fucked-up brain of yours?"

The skin beneath his hands burned as he moved them around my hips to my ass, sliding his fingertips under the edge of my panties and grabbing both cheeks. A low groan rumbled from his chest as he twisted his fingers around the waistband and tugged. The jerking made me almost lose my balance, and I leaned into his chest, my hands on his shoulders.

"I want you," he yanked again, both sides over my hips and sliding down my thighs, catching on the tops of my calves, "to fuck yourself on my cock."

My heart hammered in my chest, beating wildly at what he was asking. He coaxed one leg up, then the other until I was straddling him. Reaching between us, he opened up his jeans and pulled out his cock and balls.

"Right here." He stroked his hard length. "Right now."

Fuck. Me.

My tongue peeked out, wetting my lips as I stared down at the one thing about him I really liked. As he scooted down the chair, adjusting, he pulled me closer, one arm wrapping around me while the other positioned the head of his cock.

"Ride me. Make me come and you'll get it," he said as he wet the tip against my aching slit.

I nodded and dropped my hips, taking him all in one shot.

Mind wiping, skin tingling, body shuddering ripped through me as well as a low moan. By the smirk on his face, I'd just shown off a very erotic display.

"Just sitting on my dick isn't going to do it."

I smacked his chest. "Just give me a sec. You're kinda big."

The room was so small, there was no room to put my feet on the floor that would let me be able to bounce on his lap. Looking behind me, I decided it was time I learned a new trick and bent one leg, pulling my foot up so that my ankle rested on his thigh. As I repeated on the other side, he groaned, head falling back.

Apparently, all my moving around squeezed him in all the right ways.

Forearms resting on his shoulder, gripping the edge of the chair, I pushed against his legs and slid up, then back down his length. It was difficult with the angle, but I eventually worked into a good rhythm.

By the glassed over look on his face, I'd say a very good rhythm.

Even though he said he wanted me to *make* him come, his hands soon found their way from my thigh to my hips, then my ass, helping to guide me. After that, it seemed I wasn't going fast or hard enough for him and he thrust up into me.

"Stop."

His eyes cleared for a split second and his face morphed

from blissed out to confused to glaring.

"If you do some of the work, I won't get my beach day," I said, stating my argument.

He shook his head. "You're going to get it. Now get my fucking come into your pussy."

All of my focus was on milking his dick, trying to get him to come, that my own pleasure and breathy moans were a secondary thought. I had no idea how loud we were being. No concept on if the clerks could hear our skin slapping together or the obscene sounds we were making.

With as hardcore dominant and take charge as Six was, he really seemed to be enjoying my efforts.

His head tipped back, fingers dug into my ass, and his thrusts picked up in slamming intensity.

Each time he bottomed out sent a ripple of what felt like an electric spark through me, lighting up my skin.

His hands stopped my movements and his eyes locked with mine. The control was back to him, and I watched his dark eyes empty as he thrust up and slammed my body down. He jerked beneath me and inside me as his cock fired off stream after stream.

There was something primal about going bare, about feeling him fill me. It wasn't something I'd experienced much in my life and as I stared at his face and his slack jaw, I couldn't help leaning forward and licking his lips.

He craned his head up, mashing our lips together, tongues languidly touching in slow, steady kisses.

It was the kind of experience that made me forget who I was and who he was and how we got where we were. Made me forget what he'd done. It was a false feeling of sexual comfort, but I'd take it.

Untangling my legs was a bit difficult as they'd gotten stiff, but when I managed to stand, he slipped out, along with a gush of warm, wet pearly white come. I glanced down, staring at the puddle on his abdomen and knowing there was still more deeper in.

He didn't say a word, just stuffed his soaked cock away and buttoned up his jeans. At least we were only a block or two from the hotel.

My pussy was wet with an aching tingle as I found my panties and pulled them back on. He left me on the edge, and I wanted to jump him.

Looking down at the basket of bikinis, I pursed my lips. "Hmm, I only got to try on one."

He leaned over and rifled through, holding each one up to me before throwing it down. About halfway through he kept one and sat back.

"This one."

I shrugged, and picked my bra off the floor along with the rest of my clothes and put them back on.

In the end, the bikini didn't really matter. Whichever one he picked would be fine. After all, he was paying for it *and* letting me wear it on the beach.

At least he picked one of the prints I liked the most—a stripe with geometric shapes that resembled a kaleidoscope of colors.

I made Six walk through the curtain first, and I trailed behind. There were a few new customers in the store and some of them turned to stare at us.

We were heard.

I tried not to be embarrassed, but when I caught the nasty glare of the clerk at the register, heat flooded my cheeks.

On our way to the register, I weaved through the racks, picking up a pair of shorts, a tanktop, and flip flops. He said I was going to get my beach day, so I topped it off with a towel, sunscreen, and a beach bag.

I couldn't stop smiling. For the first time in a month, I was going to do something *I* wanted to do. Something I enjoyed. I was going to savor the fuck out of whatever beach time he gave me.

It may have just been fulfilling a dying woman's wish, but I didn't care. I had a date with the ocean.

SIX LET ME HAVE THE NEXT AFTERNOON ON THE BEACH. Warm sun and sand, salty waters, the whole shebang. Though I had to admit it wasn't as much fun by myself, even with the rented chairs and umbrella complete with a waiter that brought me a Six-approved fruity drink.

Six was simply a guardian, making sure I didn't pursue my swim to Cuba idea or get carried away by one of the meatheads tanning his over-muscled, over-tanned skin. Glued to his phone, he only left the lounger to get his feet wet in the waves. He even brought his gun with us, stuffed in the beach bag and under his chair.

Digby and I had talked multiple times about going to Miami for vacation, but it never happened.

"Your burn faded," Six said the next morning.

I turned in front of the mirror to get a look at my back and shoulders. Sure enough, the color had evened out. Though, no matter how tan I got, I still looked burned.

By evening, pink had begun to blossom on my skin. Even applying SPF 50 every few hours wasn't enough to protect my pale skin from the intense Miami sun.

It didn't hurt. I'd been burned so many times in my life that mild burns didn't even phase me. I let out a small laugh, remembering the time my olive skinned friend got her first burn. It was mild, and she was a big baby about it.

I spun back around and was about to say something when a giant cockroach flew in front of my face. I let out a scream, swatting at the air and moving back.

"I *hate* this place!"

Even Six's lips turned down in disgust as he hunted the motherfucker down. It was the worst of all of the motels. Old and dilapidated, outdated—sure, I could handle that. Disgusting, dirty, probably hadn't been cleaned in months, and infested with bugs was too much. Why wasn't the place shut down?

"At least they shut down the restaurant. I can't imagine how bad that place would be," I said as I shivered in disgust. "Today's special is our *Joe's Apartment* burger, topped off with locally cultivated roaches. So local, they come from our own walls."

Six picked up his gun and stuffed it under his shirt in his waistband. "Let's go get some food."

I stared at him. "Do you have a sense of humor?"

"Maybe."

I rolled my eyes and followed him out the door. "How can you even think about food after that?"

"It's a bug."

I stuck my tongue out with a gagging noise. "A nasty-ass bug."

"I've eaten worse."

I stopped in my tracks. "Eew. I've kissed that mouth."

He started down the stairs and turned back to me. "Sometimes you do whatever you have to in order to survive."

Damn if I didn't know that. "Story of my fucking life."

He didn't respond. In fact, I was lucky to have gotten that far.

After a yummy lunch at a diner a few blocks down, Six didn't head back to the hotel.

"Where are we going?" I asked, confused to be going in the opposite direction of the disgusting place we slept.

Then again, it might have been good we weren't going back right away—I liked what I had for lunch and wanted to keep it down.

"To meet someone."

"About something? Then we'll go somewhere?" I asked in a chipper voice, earning a glare for my fun.

After a few blocks, he turned down an alley and we popped out on the beach. I sighed as I stared out at the waves. The day before had been so much fun, and I wanted nothing more than to run back into the surf.

We stepped onto the beach walk that ran in front of a bunch of hotels. It seemed a weird route and an even stranger way to go to meet someone, but what did I really know about the way he operated? Hell, I didn't even know sociopathic killers operated a certain way.

Keeping up with Six's long strides was difficult, and I'd fallen a few feet behind him when a familiar laugh hit my ears. Looking back out onto the beach, there was a toned body I knew all too well, with a smile that used to make my day better.

Chiseled features and blue eyes. Tall, blond, and built—my Norwegian pile driver.

Digby.

I stared out at the man who I'd wished for a month now that I'd gone with so I wouldn't be in the hell I was in, as he laughed on the beach, talking with another woman. They looked like strangers, but flirting strangers.

A tear slipped down my cheek as I stared. He wasn't thirty feet from me.

Why? Of all the places and all of the times, was he exactly where I was? He had to be on vacation, but what were the odds I'd run into him?

I wanted to run to him, but the looming terror a few yards ahead of me kept me locked in place. There was no tearing my gaze away, no matter how much I told myself to. Because I knew what would happen if he looked up and recognized me, despite my blonde hair. But I couldn't look away, because my past *was* staring at me in disbelief.

It was a gut punch. Crushing my entire being with the weight of his recognition.

And I had to run.

Six was ahead of me on the beach walk. If Digby caught up to me, if Six saw…

"Paisley?"

I froze at the name I hadn't heard in a month. The pain twisted in my chest, propelling the frantic need to get as far from him as possible. I promptly dashed through some palm trees and up some stairs that led to a pool deck. There were a ton of people, and I hoped to lose him in the swarm.

I'd deal with the repercussion of leaving Six's side later.

He called after me again as I worked my way through the crowd. If Six knew… If Six saw…

Digby.

I couldn't stand it. Couldn't forgive him.

Couldn't forgive myself.

What cruel twist of fate would put him in Six's path?

My eyes were wet, blurring my vision. With a set of exterior doors in sight, just through the hotel's lobby, I breathed a sigh as I spotted the road to our hotel.

It was short lived though, because a strong arm grabbed on to me, stopping my getaway.

"Paisley?"

No.

No.

No, no, no!

I couldn't turn, couldn't look at him. Just froze. My mind spun, trying to figure out what to do.

"Let me go," I said, yanking on my arm.

"It's you, isn't it?"

I shook my head. "No."

There was no stopping him from turning me around, no matter how much I resisted. He was almost a foot taller than me and twice my weight—there was nothing I could do. But I refused to look up. I couldn't. If I showed interest, he would see. Six would come.

I cursed the heavens and prayed to hell that the devil wouldn't take away the angel before me.

"Please." With the warm hand I knew so well, he tipped my chin up.

His blue eyes were as soft and caring as I remembered. I wanted to get lost in them and have them take me back to another time.

My face scrunched up as I held in a sob, shaking my head back and forth. "Let me go. Please, you have to let me go."

"What's wrong? What's going on?"

Over the side of his arm I saw the figure I dreaded the most headed our way. My eyes popped wide as my breath sped up.

"Please, Digby. Please, if you ever loved me, let me go." My bottom lip trembled, tears flowing down my face.

"Pais, calm down."

"He'll kill you," I said with a hiss.

"You didn't do it, did you?" It wasn't really a question, but more of an affirmation to himself of what happened.

I nodded. "I didn't do any of it." My whole body shook as I glanced frantically around. "If he sees you—"

I didn't get to finish as he leaned down. Soft lips I'd almost forgotten pressed against mine. Strong arms that held me with care and a possessive desire slipped around my waist.

"I thought you were dead." Tears trailed down his cheeks as his forehead rested on mine.

"You have to leave here. Go home. Please."

"I'll get you out of here."

I shook my head. "No. You can't."

Confusion swirled in his eyes. His thumb swiped against my cheek. "Let me help."

"Then leave and forget you saw me. *Leave.* Today."

"I'll get the cops."

I shook my head. "You can't. He'll kill me. You can't tell anyone. If you say anything, if you alert the police, he *will* kill me. He *will* know. *Trust me.*"

His eyes switched focus between each of mine. Utter pain and devastation etched in the growing fine lines of his face at my words.

"Please, Digby. Don't do anything. He'll come after you, and I want you to live. I need you to live."

He scrunched his brow and gritted his teeth. "I want to help you."

"Then give me a last kiss and run for your life." I ran my hand up his chest to his face to wipe his tears while my own continued. "Give me some time. I'll contact you. Just… Don't die for me." My chest constricted, each second the panic growing. "Promise me you won't do anything."

He nodded in agreement. "I won't. Find a way. I'll wait." His lips pressed against mine again. "I still love you, Pais."

"I should have gone with you," I whispered through my

tears. "Now kiss me goodbye…one last time."

Lips, tongues, mouths devouring. I could taste the salt of our tears on our lips. Feel the desperation of his body against mine, like he was trying to fold me into his. To keep me safe.

But there was no keeping me safe from an assassin.

One last tongue battle, one last feeling of his lips against mine. One last time feeling loved and cherished.

One last goodbye.

It took every bit of strength in me to pull away, to leave him.

Digby was the chance I'd been waiting for to escape, but there was no way I was going to risk his life in order to save mine. Even if I was ever able to get away from Six, there was already no way to go back.

Digby was a past that would never be my future, even if a part of me still loved him.

My future was written in blood and bathed in black.

Only a few steps later was when I intersected with Six. His jaw was tight, eyes empty as he looked down at my face. I was a mess, and there was no hiding it from him. He glanced behind me, and I didn't dare to do the same.

"Let's go." He grabbed my hand and yanked me away from Digby.

For the two-block trek back to the hotel, anger rolled off Six's back, creating a tension that had people inadvertently steering clear.

The moment we were back in the room, he was stuffing things in suitcases.

"Get moving."

"We're leaving?" I asked. We'd just been on our way to meet a contact.

His spine straightened and he turned, a cold, hard glare meeting my gaze. "Who was he?"

I shook my head. "No one."

He picked up his gun and cocked it before slipping it into his waistband.

"No!" I blocked his path do the door.

"He knows you. He saw you."

"He didn't."

His hand gripped my neck, then he pushed me against the wall, baring his teeth. "Who is he, Lacey?" His hand tightened as he lifted me off the ground by my neck. "He was fucking kissing you. Holding you. In an intimate way," he seethed. "You were crying. He *knew* you. What did you tell him?"

"He's my ex-boyfriend," I managed to choke out.

His breath was heavy when he added through clenched teeth, "No, he's a dead man." He released me, sending me crashing down to the floor.

I scrambled to my knees, grabbing at his legs. "Please don't!"

He pulled out his gun and pressed the tip into my forehead. "Putting please before don't isn't going to change my mind. Pleasantries aren't for killers, remember?"

"You don't need to worry about him."

"What part of 'he saw you' don't you fucking understand?"

"He won't say or do anything." Please, not Digby. Don't kill him.

"You're right, because dead men don't talk."

He grabbed my hair, fisting it hard and pulling me back up to my feet. The pain was blinding, and it felt like he was about to tear my hair out. He leaned down, his teeth scraping against my neck before he bit down just below my ear. There was no pleasure, only pain. His whole body was tense, vibrating with a destructive energy. His other hand roughly kneaded my breast before he let go with so much force I stumbled back down to the floor.

Facing the anger of a killer wasn't something I'd wanted to do in Paris, but I would do it to protect Digby.

He put the gun up on the table and picked up his knife. Kneeling between my legs, he grabbed onto the front of my shirt and sliced it open in one swift move.

My teeth chattered and I scooted back, only to have him draw me closer, prying my thighs open and slamming them to the floor. I wasn't used to this side of him. It was worse than Paris.

He was out of control.

I didn't know what was going on because it was more than just the possibility of Digby talking. The wild look in his eyes as he tore my shorts down, staring at my almost naked body with an aura of domination.

Maybe he saw me as out of control again and needed to assert his control over me. I really didn't want another belt lashing.

The cool blade of his knife slid up my thigh and I froze, waiting to see where he was headed. The tip slipped under the edge of my panties and with a quick flip of his wrist, cut right through. He cut the other side, then pulled the scrap of clothing away from me.

Nostrils flared as he took deep breaths while he continued to run the tip of the knife around my skin.

"You are *my* wife in this life."

His anger shifted, lust clouding his still turbulent eyes. I couldn't do anything but lie there and pray that him being distracted provided enough time for Digby to leave.

The knife was tossed to the side as he opened up his jeans and pulled his cock out. No prep, just a lick to his hand to wet the tip before shoving it in. It wasn't painful, but it wasn't exactly comfortable as he worked his way into my dry pussy.

I tried to retreat, but he gripped my neck with one hand and pinned my hips with the other.

Grunting and groaning, it only took a few strokes of his cock for my body to react and my pussy to start practically squirting all over the place. The lube served for each thrust of his hips to grind me harder into the floor.

His hand tightened around my neck as his hips slammed into me. Cold eyes stared into mine. "Are you trying to piss me off?"

My mind began to go blank from the rough fucking I was getting. I was nothing but a fuck doll. Used. Abused. Fucked out of anger and control.

Each thrust in was harder than the last as he fucked his possession into my pussy.

Was that what it was about? It was different than before. Was Six jealous?

My eyes rolled back as my walls clenched around him. I couldn't think, could hardly breathe, but as my thighs squeezed his hips, I cracked, coming in convulsing waves.

Somehow, he sped up his assault, fucking me harder and faster. Destroying my pussy for anyone else.

His fingers clamped down around my neck as his hips jerked, and he let out a roar I'd never heard before.

The fluttering of my pussy could still be felt as I struggled for breath and my vision blurred into nothingness.

THERE WAS A CONSTANT HUMMING AND AN OCCASIONAL bump, but I couldn't see anything. My eyes were glued shut as I slowly woke up.

Based on the ache in my neck and throat that was blossoming into my consciousness, I probably didn't want to see. As my eyes fluttered open, there was another bump and the humming grew louder, but I couldn't make out what was in front of me.

I was sagged to the side, and as my eyes opened I sat up, cracking my neck and shoulders in the process. It was then my brain aligned with my vision and I saw that we were in the car, driving down some highway.

"Whe—" I reached up and cupped my throat. It was raw, making it hard to talk, and it hurt. "Where are we?" I managed to get out, but it was dry sounding and scratchy, lower than normal.

I glanced to Six, but he didn't say anything. He didn't even look at me, just stared straight ahead. It even hurt to swallow, so I pulled down the vanity mirror to check my tonsils. I really hoped I wasn't coming down with something.

The reflection that greeted me was not pretty. My hair was a rat's nest, and my eyes were bloodshot from crying. How long had I been out?

I rubbed my throat again, then moved my hand. My mouth popped open as I stared at the bruises that covered my skin.

An almost perfect shadow of a hand.

Oh.

"Were you trying to kill me?"

He stayed silent, but the hand he had on the wheel flexed, tightening.

"How close did you get?"

His lip curled up. "Don't even fucking tempt me right now."

"Why did you stop?"

He didn't say anything more, but continued brooding in his probably violent fantasies. So we drove. After a while, I realized I had to have been out for at least four hours. Based on the direction of the sun, we were headed north

Six was an asshole, a bastard in a god's body, and I hated him. So, why didn't I just run? Why didn't I grab Digby's hand and *run*? He was going to kill me anyway, so why put it off any longer? Why was I letting him drag me all over the planet and letting him fuck me whenever and however he wanted?

The last one was easy, because as much as I despised him and the situation he put me in, I craved his body all over mine. Rough, raw, and as abrasive as his personality.

That, and one of the last people I wanted him to kill was Digby.

The lessons were well learned—had been burned into my flesh. The marks would fade, just as the belt welts had.

I may have been snarky with a penchant for annoying, but Six...

He was Alpha and Omega.

He was Six.

He was the most dangerous game.

I stayed silent, which was best for my damaged throat.

He had lost complete control of himself. I'd seen him angry, I'd seen him kill, but I'd never seen him lose his cool. Even in Paris when he put me in my victim place, he was dialed in.

More hours passed and the sun set in strained silence. Signs for Atlanta streamed by, and at nearly ten at night we pulled into a motel.

In Woodland.

"You've got to be fucking kidding me!" I croaked as I stared at the dilapidated shitstain motel in the middle of BFE. The one that probably still held the lead wire that he kept me chained to for almost two weeks.

He didn't respond, didn't even look my way as he exited the car and walked into the lobby.

Odd. Six *always* gave me a warning.

Sure enough, he walked straight from the lobby to room 4 and unlocked it.

I stared through the window as he began unloading the trunk.

I was free of the nightmare inside and really didn't want to go back. Was it my punishment for Digby? Since we'd left weeks before, he'd granted me certain freedoms. I'd been allowed outdoors with him, to dress like a normal human being, and to sleep without being bound to a damn bed. I dreaded that those luxuries would be taken away.

I blew out a breath, then climbed out of the car. My hands shook as I made my way to the door. Tears filled my eyes as I peered in and, sure enough, the wire remained.

My breath sped up as tears welled in my eyes. The shaking in my hand spread through my whole body, making it to my bottom lip as cold, angry eyes stared at me.

A tear slipped down my cheek as I shut the door and slowly

stepped toward him.

He grabbed hold of my chin, tilting my eyes up to meet his, jaw set as his lip curled up.

"Here's how things are going to go." He held up a small key in front of me—the key to the ankle cuff. "That guy is alive, *for now.*"

He reached down and opened up the cuff, and I held my leg out for him to click the cuff around my ankle.

Hostage again. Freedoms gone.

He took hold of my chin again. "So you understand, you make one tiny move out of line again and he's dead. I will hunt him down and I will shove my knife into his gut, letting his entrails spill out in front of him as I dig it upward right into his heart."

Another tear slipped down as I swallowed and nodded. Digby wouldn't die because of me. Nobody would.

His gaze slipped from mine, watching the tear trail down my cheek before leaning forward and licking it up. A small gasp jumped from me and as he pulled back, his hand moving along my jaw, his thumb inadvertently swiping another one away.

My brow furrowed as his eyes lost their intense edge. He pressed his lips to mine, and it was unlike anything he'd done before. Soft, quick, then he stepped back. His muscles tensed again as he faced away from me, moving on to some task.

I stared after him, confused, watching the muscles in his back and shoulders contract as he pulled items out of his duffle bag.

My tongue peeked out, wetting my lips, tasting his. I sat down on the bed.

Somehow, things were different. But I didn't know if that was different good or different bad.

All I knew was I was back to being trapped. Chained down.

Back to the beginning, with one very significant change—I knew the game.

All I had to do was play by his rules, and I'd stay on the board a little longer.

I was going to live to the fullest and when he took me down, I wanted it to be in a blaze of glory, not a pig to slaughter.

The next morning, I woke to hot breath on my neck. Six's arm was dead weight, and it was hard to get out of his death grip.

After some fancy maneuvering, I stood and I looked down at him. There was no indication that he was awake, which was weird. He was always awake before me, and anytime I moved usually stirred him.

The cuff around my ankle pulled as I made my way to the bathroom. My reflection was a mess, and I stared in shock at my horror-movie-like appearance.

The handprint bruise was much more evident, but the freakiest part was my eyes. When I'd glanced at the vanity mirror when we were driving I thought my eyes were red from crying the day before, but that wasn't the case. Blood red stained the white of my eyes, the left worse than the right.

"Shit!"

There was a rumble and crash, followed by the cocking of a gun and stomping of feet before Six appeared behind me. His eyes were wide, breath hard as his head swung from side to side.

"Wow. That was some kind of spaztastic."

"What?" He shook his head and ran a hand across his face and scrunched his brow. "How?"

"Look what you fucking did," I said, ignoring his confusion

and turned around. With my finger I pointed to my eyes. "You fucking broke my blood vessels. I look like I should be in some slasher flick."

He blinked at me. "It'll go away in a week or two."

Of course he knew that.

I slapped his chest. "That's not the point! I look like a freak."

The furrow in his brow deepened. "Did you really get up without me noticing?"

Oh, I wasn't the only one who noticed that.

I nodded and he pushed past me, opening his toiletries case and pulling out his toothbrush. Without a word, he frantically brushed his teeth, and once done, pushed past me as he hurried to throw on some clothes.

He glanced down at my ankle, then threw all of the bags into the farthest corner. There wasn't a word said as he stepped out of the room, the door slamming behind him. A minute later the car fired up, and the tires crunched on the gravel.

I was left standing, staring at the door. "What the fuck?"

Shaking my head, I turned back into the bathroom. After running a brush through my hair, I tossed it up in a loose bun, then washed my face and brushed my teeth. Deodorant, lotion, body spray, and I was set.

Left waiting.

Again.

I should have reveled in my first free period without him in over two weeks, but instead I was stuck contemplating his strange behavior.

Changing my clothes would have been nice, but he threw my suitcase in the corner with the others and one leg was unavailable at the moment.

My book was also in there.

Some lawyer forbidden romance with lots of sex.

I was alone, hungry, and with no idea when Six would be back.

Yes, things had been weird since I woke up in a car the day before, but why? I understood his anger and reprimanding me, even locking me up again, but the other stuff left me scratching my head.

I couldn't even hazard a guess on what was going through him because he always kept himself closed off.

Luckily I had access to my water bottle and the TV remote, but as I switched it on and flipped through the limited channels, I found myself hating the shithole once again.

It took four hours of talk shows along with some soaps for Six to return. The tires on gravel stopped my heart for a beat, then I heard the slam of the car door. I stared at the door, watching as it opened and he stepped in.

The strange man of the morning was gone, replaced with the normal cool, collected version.

He threw a bag onto the bed as he walked over.

"What goodies do we have today?" I asked.

The bag had no markings, but inside was a wrapped deli sandwich and some chips. I licked my lips and smiled up at him. The tick of his jaw caught my eye just before he held out a can of Coke.

I grabbed his wrist and pulled him forward onto the bed where I moved up to my knees and wrapped my arms around his shoulders. A quick squeeze before pulling back and, just to confuse him, I placed a light kiss on his lips before I settled back down on the bed.

Turnabout being fair play and all.

"What was the hurry about this morning?" I asked as I unwrapped the sandwich.

He had to have driven far, because I doubted the tiny town we were in carried a delicatessen housing dark rye bread. There was turkey, Swiss, lettuce, mayo, pickles, tomato, and sprouts. Definitely not local.

I opened my mouth and ripped a bite out of the sandwich like a starving animal.

He didn't respond, but I didn't expect him to. Instead, he startled me with a subject he hadn't broached in quite some time.

"I need you to tell me what you know about Three."

My chewing slowed, and I took a hard swallow. "Can I eat before we do this?"

"Tell me."

I shook my head and put the sandwich down as a vice wrapped around my chest.

"Lacey, fucking tell me."

Tears filled my eyes as I screamed out, "I'm not ready to die!"

He sat down, his elbows resting on his knees as he leaned forward. "I am going to kill you. I am going to shoot you in the head. Quick, clean, painless. But it's not going to be right now. I need you, and not just for the secret information you're keeping from me."

"To fuck?"

He smirked. "There is that. If someone is out to erase the Cleaners, you make a great cover."

I laughed. "So, I'm only around to help keep you alive, and you're still going to kill me?"

"Yes."

I jumped up from the bed. "Why? I want to fucking live too,

you asshole!"

He stood back up and walked around the bed to me. "Do you think I care about that?"

"No. You just think about your desire to live. Well, Mr. Killer, what the fuck is so important in your life?"

"It's mine, and I've worked damn hard to keep it."

I threw my hands up in the air. "All you do is *take* life! You aren't a harbinger of death, no higher cause, you're just a fucked-up psychopath!"

His lip curled up as he stepped forward, his hand closing around my neck as he slammed me down onto the bed. My head was tilted back as I looked up into his eyes, to the snarl of his lip.

"Do you really want to go down this path again?"

I dug my nails into his arm and glared at him. "You know what I *want* to do, but since that isn't going to happen and I'm not going to tell you *anything*, why don't you let me stuff myself with the sandwich and then you can stuff me with your cock."

He blinked at me, his expression sliding back into neutral as his hand relaxed. Those brown eyes of his studied me for minute, as I studied them. I'd never really noticed the multitude of shades. Amber, chocolate, flecks of gold, and in the center a rust-like color.

"Why would the death of one of the Killing Corps demand a cleaning?" I asked, staring deep into his eyes.

The ticking of the intricate clockworks of his brain could almost be seen as he thought about not only answering the question, but how much to give away if he did.

"We're the sadistic children even the CIA doesn't want to admit are theirs. Nothing to tie us to them so they can have full deniability."

My heart stopped, and I froze.

CIA?

Central Intelligence Agency?

Fuck. Everything began to make more and more sense. At the same time, I felt sick. A government agent had kidnapped me and was going to kill me.

He pulled back, and I sat up. "So, you're not just some delusional psychopathic killer, huh?"

He shook his head. "I get paid to kill people the CIA wants to disappear."

"What about bystanders?"

"Casualties of war."

Oh.

Wrong place, wrong time. Just another person caught in the crossfire.

The brass bullet from Six's gun was going to make me disappear. Just another casualty in a war silently raging in the shadows.

A DAY LATER, SIX RELEASED THE CUFF AROUND MY ANKLE. Seemed we'd come to a sort of agreement—I wouldn't try to run, and he wouldn't kill me the moment I stepped out of line.

For three days I had freedom from the wire. It also meant wherever he went, so did I. Like a shadow, or a woman from the 1950s.

"What's the plan today?" I asked as I toweled off my hair, fresh from the shower.

Six was pulling jeans up his legs and stopped.

I looked down, confused, then smirked as I tugged one edge of the towel around my body to the side, exposing my hip.

His tongue slipped across his lips. "Are you teasing me for a reason?"

I shook my head. "You're the one staring."

He stepped forward, buttoning his jeans as he walked. Reaching out, he brushed the other edge of the towel away and cupped my pussy. He leaned down, lips running up the column of my neck and spreading a heat through me.

His fingers pressed against my clit, and I reached out to grab on to his arms.

"When we get back…" A harsh breath brushed against my neck. "I think it's about time for an all-night fuck fest."

I felt the heat rise to my cheeks, and a lust fueled excitement coursed through me.

Stepping back, he returned to getting dressed, leaving me hot and bothered.

In it all, I realized one thing—I was seriously fucked up.

After everything, all he'd done to me, that physical chemistry from the first day we met still lingered. His cruel treatment and the inevitable role he would play in my life hadn't diminished my desire for him, like it should have in any sane minded person.

Then again, I was a woman with one foot in the grave. Hating him only added strife to the situation. I was a roll-with-the-punches kinda girl, and that had paid off thus far. But I also knew I wasn't the woman I was almost five weeks prior.

Even after the time we'd spent together, he continued to be sexy, mysterious, and alluring. Dark things that attracted me, for better or worse.

Being a real secret agent also added to the appeal.

It was chilly out, so I put on jeans, my boots, a T-shirt, and the leather jacket Six picked up the other day. The jacket almost matched his. If he put in his blue contacts or I put in my brown, we would look like a matchy-matchy couple again or twins.

I threw my hair up into a ponytail, stuffed my lip balm in my pocket, and then picked up a bottle of water before heading for the door to a waiting Six.

We loaded into the car and peeled out as good as one can on gravel.

"Where are we going?" I asked as I pulled on my sunglasses.

"Atlanta."

It was going to be about an hour and a half drive to get to

Atlanta, depending on traffic.

"Why?"

"Why do you ask so many questions?"

I shrugged. "Curiosity. I like to know things."

"I'm meeting Jason."

"Jason the handler, Jason?" I asked, surprised that I'd be going along. He turned to glare at me, and I held my hands up. "Just trying to clarify. Do you know how many people have the name Jason? I'm also just surprised you're meeting him in person."

"It's necessary right now."

My mind started spinning with visions of what Jason looked like. To me, he was a faceless person Six talked to. He might as well have been a computer for all I knew.

Reaching out, I pressed the power button to the radio and fiddled around until I found a good station. Six didn't stop me and didn't seem to mind my pop/rock choice. I bopped around in my seat to the songs, some familiar, some new, and hummed to a few.

It was nice, relaxing.

Normal.

It was as normal as we could get. Two people driving down the road, music playing, and looking out the window with a smile as I actually got to enjoy the scenery. It was beautiful, wooded, and I half expected to see a zombie lurking in the woods or on the side of the road.

That might be one of the things that pissed me off the most since my capture—I was missing *The Walking Dead*.

I reached over and smacked Six's arm.

His head snapped to me with a very much what the fuck look that made me laugh.

"What are you doing?"

"Reprimanding you." I gave him another light whack.

He looked down at his arm, his brow quirking up. "For?"

"Kidnapping me."

He shook his head. "It's been five weeks. Get over it."

"No. You've made me miss my show! I only watch one show religiously. Everything else is on Netflix."

"What is Netflix?"

I stared at him open mouthed. "Seriously? It wouldn't hurt you to take a break and merge into the world for a little while. You're like a hermit."

He gave a chuckle. "One said the same thing."

I groaned. "I don't want to know about your sexcapades with her."

He made a *hmph* sound, and the corner of his mouth twitched. What I wouldn't give to know what he was thinking. What amused him?

Was it my…jealousy? No, that couldn't be the right word, but that was a bit what it felt like when talking about that cunt rag.

Not ten minutes with her and I wanted to scratch her eyes out, which was weird. I was a laid back person, but she rubbed me wrong from the moment we walked in. Then her little show that she was on his dick first…

Once again, I was asking myself why I cared. He was a sadistic bastard killer. What was there to like?

I threw my head back into the headrest. There was nothing redeeming about him, but there was something between us. I couldn't doubt that. As much as I didn't want it, as disgusting as it should have been, I'd developed some sort of liking for the man.

Fuck me.

Walking down the streets of Atlanta hand in hand was a bit strange. Good strange or bad strange, I wasn't sure. There were plenty of times he'd held my hand before, but it'd been with an iron grip compared to the more relaxed one he had.

It was midday on a Friday at noon, the streets bustling with people. We ducked into a small coffee shop and walked to an alcove in the back.

There was a man sitting with his face in his phone, but Six stopped in front of the table and waited.

He looked up and gave us a smile that lit up his face.

"Hey."

"Hey, Jason," Six said.

Jason?

The man before us was not what I was expecting. Truth was, during the drive I'd painted a picture in my mind. I expected a pudgy guy with a friendly face and glasses who spent all of his time locked up in a dark, soundproofed room. He'd be pale as the only light he saw was from the computer monitors he stared at daily.

"You're early, Six." He stood and held out his hand.

Jason, handler to the CIA's secret assassin squad, was the opposite of that. First, he was black. Second, he was gorgeous— tall, lean, with bright eyes and a brilliant smile. He stood out.

I should have known not to cliché him based on Hollywood.

"Do I do late?"

Jason motioned for us to sit opposite of him.

"What's going on?" Six asked as we sat, not wasting any time getting to the point.

Jason's smile faded. "I don't know. Home has gone silent, and I lost contact with Eight two days ago. How were Nine and One?"

"Fine when I left a few weeks ago."

Jason nodded. "They got the last assignment I received. There normally isn't this much time in between." His head rocked back and forth. "Man, I don't like this."

"Are you keeping on the move?" Six asked as he leaned forward, resting his forearms on the table.

Jason nodded. "Always. But since Three, I'm laying lower than normal."

"Do you think there's something going on at Home?" Six glanced behind him, then back to Jason.

"Your guess is as good as mine at this point."

Six craned his head around to the door. "Where was Eight last?"

"Indianapolis."

"I'll head there, see if I can find him."

We'd be so close to home. There'd be a chance someone might recognize me.

"I'll send you the last update." His gaze flickered over to me. "Are you keeping your cat?"

Six nodded after another glance behind him. "For now."

"You know how Home doesn't like pets."

Pets? Sure, why not. I'd been cattle and a toy already.

"I still need her."

Jason shook his head. "A beader. You're carrying around a goddamn beader. Out of everyone, you were the last I expected."

My brow furrowed. What was a beader?

Six's jaw clenched. "I have my reasons."

Jason's lips formed a thin line. "She may be the best cover you ever had, but I've done what I can—her face is still everywhere."

"What does that mean?" I asked.

Jason finally turned to me, the kind face when we came in long gone. "It means you're still a person of interest in what happened. And if there really is something going down, it won't take long to associate you with him, and they'll stop looking for him and start looking for you."

My brow furrowed. "Why me?"

"Because you're the loose cannon," Six said. "I'm trained to be invisible, and you're part of the herd."

"How are they going to pick me out of all the norms?" My voice skidded on the edge of serious and annoyance at once again being nothing but a beast to slaughter.

"Shadow," Jason said.

"What?"

Six sighed and threw another look over his shoulder. "Shadow. A trick of the eyes. We stand out because you're trying to blend in."

"But I thought I was part of the herd? How does that stand out?"

"You *were* part of the herd," Jason said, stressing the past tense. "Being with him, you've inadvertently changed your behavior, making you try to be your new identity."

I turned to Six. "Which makes me bad for you and you should just let me go."

Six's jaw clenched and he pulled me close to his side. When he reached into his waistband, I froze. He pulled out one of the guns he was hiding and pressed it against my chest.

My heart stopped for more than a beat as my eyes widened. Everything in me froze.

His lips rested against my ear as I stared at Jason, who only looked annoyed and shook his head. "Don't fucking test me. I will send a bullet straight through your fucking chest without blinking or thinking twice. If you even think you've gained some power over me, think again."

Six sat back, stowing his gun and continued talking, leaving me a shaking mess.

Asshole.

I hadn't broken any rules or stepped over any lines.

It was a play, I knew it was. A show for Jason.

"I'm pretty sure there are crews around, so watch your back."

Six nodded. "They are. I think that's who tried to take me out as I left Cincinnati."

"It doesn't bode well for the Cleaners." Jason slipped his hand palm down across the table and Six reached out and set his hand on top. "I hope we meet again."

"Three was the first," Six said as he stood. "I then became the second target, but I won that battle."

One of Jason's brows rose. "You think it's war?"

"Whatever's going on hasn't stopped." Six held out his hand. "There will be more. We need everyone together before they wipe us all out."

Jason nodded and shook his hand. "I'll find them all."

With a curt nod, Six took my hand and we walked out the front door.

Each step away my mind swirled with the conversation. Dissecting words used, emphasis on some while others were skimmed over. The covert exchange on the table. Even the time we were there—ten minutes.

By the time we were back in the car, the cryptic words and unknown definitions revealed little.

"What's a beader?" I asked once we were a few miles down the road.

His jaw ticked before answering, "Just about anything."

"The way Jason said it, sounded like it meant something."

He seemed reluctant to answer, but I was happy he was. My questions were pretty innocuous. "You're an object that I had a bead on, thus making you what we call a beader."

"Bead?"

"Gun lined up, had you in my sights."

And he did. Gun lined up right to my forehead.

Over a dozen times he failed to pull the trigger.

Before leaving Atlanta, we stopped by the building where Six had stashed his weapons before heading back to the motel.

"Why isn't there an elevator?" I asked after the third of six flights of stairs.

Always with the number six.

When we approached the door, he fished in his pocket for something, producing a key.

Which led to the question of, "What happens if you lose your key?"

His lip twitched up in a smirk, and the lightbulb turned on.

Jason.

That was what he slipped him.

The apartment was in a run-down part of town. A small studio apartment. Sparse, a lived- in feeling, but I doubted any-one lived there. Perhaps he stayed there from time to time, but it was definitely not a home.

There was a mattress on the floor, a table and chairs, dresser, and dirty dishes in the sink.

Dirty dishes that hadn't been there the last time. Interesting.

Secret panels in the wall hid what I was certain to be count-less weapons, along with who knew what else.

I supposed he had to have a good centralized location to hold things he needed. Maybe it was the closest thing he had to a home.

It was a quick in and out, bag in hand, and we were out the door.

Next was the hour back to the motel, then a nearly eight-hour trek up to Indianapolis. I was buzzing with excitement to be so close to home, but I also had to remind myself of the stakes, or the rules.

We'd been driving for about four hours when his phone rang. By the tone and the sudden deceleration of the car, we weren't going to Indianapolis any longer.

"Change of plans," he said, turning the wheel for a sudden U-turn.

"What?"

"Jason set up a meet in Nashville."

"What about Eight?"

Six was silent, but not the normal silence I usually got. "Eight is dead."

WHEN SIX GOT THE CALL FROM JASON, WE WEREN'T too far past Nashville so it was an easy flip around.

The motel we pulled up to was an improvement over the usual shitholes Six stayed at. The upkeep was going on, and it didn't look like meth heads were around. The two-story building was older, but the white paint was in good condition, the roof jet black, and the asphalt had a recent layer added.

"Nice motel. I was really starting to get afraid of what STDs I was going to pick up in the cesspools you like," I said as Six pulled into a parking spot.

He threw the car into park and pulled out the key. "Doesn't matter if you're dead."

"Yeah, I know, but you would get it too with all the times your cock is inside me."

The muscle in his jaw ticked. "True."

His mood soured after the news of Eight. Pointing that out to him only seemed to incite his grumpy mood. We both got out of the car and moved to the trunk.

"You get mad when I look at things differently, don't you."

"Yes."

"Why?" I asked as he handed me my suitcase.

He pulled out his own, then locked eyes with me. "Because, every single fucking time you do it, you point out a weakness in me."

That surprised me. "Ouch. Wounded pride."

He looked around before pulling out the weapons bag, slamming the trunk lid when done. "Weakness will get you killed in this business."

"Like your friend?" The parking lot was empty, so I kept on with my questioning as we made our way up to the second story.

"Three wasn't a friend."

"Then why were you so upset when you saw him?" When we reached the top, he turned back to me. "I may have been practically pissing myself scared at the time, but I noticed the change."

He didn't respond, and continued walking.

We stopped a few rooms down. A few taps in a distinct pattern, and the door creaked open. A warm, broad smile ushered us in.

"Jason said you'd be here soon. What a delightful surprise," the man said. He was younger than Six, and I was pretty sure in the first five seconds he was batting for the other team.

"Five."

Five? Another agent.

It was odd how the ones I'd met were eerily the same, but vastly different at the same time.

Five had a short cut of his brown hair, but bright blue eyes to go with his oddly bright personality. He was taller like Six and Nine, even Three, all fitting in the 5'10" to 6'2" range.

Five stared at me. His eyes were wide, mouth open almost as if he was in awe. "What a pretty cat."

"Meow, jerk."

His mouth promptly shut and he gave me a slight smile,

which had to be the warmest regard I'd received from one of Six's brethren.

"Sorry, it's just that we work alone and if what I've heard is correct, you two have been glued together for quite some time." His gaze wandered over to Six, who met him with a glare.

Six crossed his arms in front of him. "Jason needs to keep his mouth shut."

"Not about why you have this strumpet with you, though. What's your theory?"

"What was your last job?" Six asked, his jaw ticking.

Five sighed. "Eight. He's dead."

"So is Three."

Five's eyes popped. Finally someone showed a little more surprise about a death. "Damn. We're down two?" Six nodded. "Any ideas?"

"A few, but all speculation. Whatever's going on, it has Jason hiding."

Five pursed his lips. "Three was the first."

"First what?" I asked

Five turned to me. "The first of us to die."

"Ever?" I'd never thought about one of them dying.

"We've only been sanctioned for five years."

Six glared at him. At least Five was talking. It was nice to know things sometimes.

"That's a long time and a lot of bullets not finding their targets."

"Firefights are unusual," Six said, annoyed at the conversation.

"The bullet hole scars in your skin say different."

He looked down at his covered chest. "Most of those are from my Army days." He turned back to Five. "When did you get your assignment?"

Five scratched his jaw. "I was in Texas last week finishing up a four-month stint when Jason called."

"He didn't know the job, did he?"

"No." Five shook his head. "How long have you had your little pet?"

Six glanced to me. "I picked her up when I was cleaning Three."

"That was how long ago?" Five moved to stand next to Six, his fingers lacing in front of him. "If I didn't know you better, I'd say you had feelings for the girl."

Six's gaze narrowed. "But you do know me, or at least what I am."

"One of the true sociopaths of our little ragtag group."

"You aren't one?" I asked. I'd assumed they were all a variety of psychotic.

"Oh no, darling, I am. Six here just happens to be one of the most emotionless of us all. A great actor if he was able to woo you before he abducted you." The cadence of his voice was almost lyrical. Smooth and transitioning, an almost feminine quality. Much different from Six's monotone, masculine one, and somewhat out of place for a killer.

Then again, I could be stereotyping again based on Hollywood. Though, most of the Killing Corps men I'd met fit that box.

"Let me guess…you've never been in love either," I said to Five as I sat down on the edge of the bed. Love seemed to be an off topic for them.

"I've loved many women in my time, and many men, but only in the physical sense. An emotional love has no place in a dealer of death."

Obviously love was not for undercover, cold-blooded, government funded killers.

Good to know.

Bad to learn when my feelings for Six were morphing and growing every day, against all rational thoughts.

It really was true—you can't change a man. Especially not the crazy variety.

Five crossed the room and sat on the edge of the bed next to me. The caress of his eyes could almost be felt, and the small smile on his face should have been reassuring, but instead held a bit of a frightening edge.

Six huffed and headed toward the bathroom, the door slamming behind him.

"He's going to kill you." The flippant way Five said the words caught me off guard.

"I know."

He gave a wistful sigh. "Kidnapped, held hostage, possibly forced into sex, and yet I get the impression you care for him."

I shook my head. "It doesn't matter."

He pursed his lips. "No, it doesn't, but it is interesting. Stockholm Syndrome, perhaps." He stared at me again, then took in a hard breath and looked away. "He had a job, and that job isn't finished until you stop breathing."

Tears stung my eyes, but I locked down my jaw and blinked them back. "You know, you don't have to remind me. I've lived with this knowledge and the psycho himself for quite some time."

He nodded. "True."

Six came back out of the bathroom, zipping his fly as he walked.

"You have quite the interesting pet," Five said as he stood. "She's feisty. Care to share?"

Share? My heart stopped for a beat, and I stared at Six. He wouldn't...would he?

"No."

"You won't even consider?"

"No."

The playfulness drifted from Five's face, hardening. His spine straightened, and he cracked his neck and shoulders. "Interesting."

My brow furrowed as I stared at him. The word was lower, deeper, like in those few seconds he'd transitioned between personalities.

"Are you done fucking with her now?" Six asked.

Five shrugged and smirked. "She's fun."

I rolled my eyes. "An act?"

He smirked at me and winked. "Baby, if he let me, I'd fucking spear you with my dick and pound you into the mattress all night long." My eyes popped open wide, which only made him grin and grab his crotch. "Gotta be flexible. You never know who you'll encounter or the orientation of the target. And it's been long enough that I'd fuck either or both of you."

"Where are you headed next?" Six cut in, changing the direction of the conversation.

"Hard to say," Five said with a shrug. "I had to grenade a wetwork team to get away from my last job. If Home really is getting rid of us, they better know we aren't going to go quietly."

"I think the best thing to do is get us all together."

"That's going to be a hard job with Home being on the silent side and Jason in hiding."

"Maybe. I saw Nine and One in Paris."

Five's eyebrows shot up. "And?"

Why did it seem out of all of them I'd met, Five was the only expressive one? He seemed the most normal, which left me wondering how he was there.

"Their plan was to head back and meet up when their job

was done."

Five groaned. "Why is getting information from you so difficult?" Six looked to me and Five followed. "Then why are we talking in front of her?"

"Oh, so me, the victim here, is to blame? Fuck you very much, assbutt."

Five's eyes went wide as they flipped from me to Six.

"Lacey."

I sighed and waved my hand in front of me. "Yeah, yeah, just keep on with your conversation. The only one I've got to talk to is the wall anyway, and I don't think this paper is going anywhere for a while."

I fell back onto the bed and stared up at the ceiling. My stomach muscles clenched when something hard hit and bounced onto the bed.

The TV remote.

I glanced up to two killers looking down at me. One gave me a smirk and looked like he wanted to eat me, while the other looked like he wanted to fuck the shit out of me.

Turning on the TV, I gave them the privacy to continue their hush-hush Cleaner talk. There were more channels than the shithole outside Atlanta, and I soon found myself lying on one of the two beds watching *Supernatural*.

I awoke with a start, my heart pounding in my chest.

Damn stupid falling dream.

The room was dark, and Six was wrapped around me as usual. The thought that he was there, protecting me, seemed to relax me, an irony which was not missed.

After I calmed, I pulled away and sat up. When I turned to look down at him, he was silent as he stared back in the dim glow of the room.

I stood and stumbled my way to the bathroom. That was when I noticed I was only in my shirt and panties. I didn't know when I fell asleep, but apparently he'd been able to get some of my clothes off without me noticing.

The best place to sleep really was in the company of killers.

Finishing up, I startled at the figure in the doorway. "Fuck, are you trying to scare me?"

Five smirked. "Just making sure you're all right and don't need a hand."

I rolled my eyes. "Are all of you perverts?" I reached down to grab my panties, pulling them up as I stood.

His tongue swiped across his lips. "No, but killing does give a jolt to the system. Gets the adrenaline and blood pumping." His hand moved down his bare chest to the hard-on that was trying desperately to get out of his boxers. "Gives you a high and a fierce need to fuck."

I stepped to the sink. "No." My hands began to shake as I rubbed them together under the water.

In the mirror I watched him shake his head. "I can be just as domineering as him." He reached out and caressed his finger down my arm. "But I make a better lover."

"Not looking for one."

Fuckity fuck.

Six was in the other room. He had to be awake. He was when I got up. Why was he letting Five do this? Had they silently agreed while I was passed out that he could use me?

He stepped behind me and whispered into my ear, "I'm not looking to go steady, darling. I just want to put my dick in your pussy until it squeezes the come from my balls. All I have to do is lean you over." He pressed against my back while I braced my arms against the counter. "Just stand there and let me get off."

Cha-click!

My eyes shot up to the mirror. Five wasn't concerned at all, but Six was all business.

"I don't share toys."

Five turned. "I was just having a little fun."

Six lowered his gun. "Fun. Right." His fist shot out, landing square into Five's stomach. Five's eyes popped open, and a small grunt came out as he bent over. "Don't touch." Six looked back up to me. "Get back in the bed."

I squeezed past Five in the doorway and walked around Six on my way back. They both followed, Five running his hand over the spot where Six's fist landed.

Six turned me so we were chest to chest on our sides, blocking me from Five's view. I quirked my brow but he didn't do or say anything, just wrapped his arms around me. Only I was nuzzling into his chest instead of a pillow.

Hot and cold, as usual.

Trapped in a room with one assassin for a few days was bad enough, but two of the horny bastards was torture. Especially after watching two hot bodies working out in front me.

Naked, sweaty, toned chests doing push-ups, sit-ups. One-handed push-up contests, then one-handed with one leg.

Athletic, strong, and lean, begging to have my tongue lick them.

They were turning me into a horny bitch, and I was fairly

certain Five was doing it simply to flirt, which only drove their competition.

It was a little weird sharing space with Five. I was used to running around the room anywhere from half-naked to full Monty with Six, but with Five I felt a bit on the shy side. After his prank—and I was pretty certain it was at least half for show and the other half seeing if I'd go along with it—he didn't exactly stop.

Then again, Six made it pretty clear.

"Are you serious right now?" I asked as my hand whipped out and slapped Five in the stomach.

Five laughed and shrugged, my hit having neither the strength nor force behind it like Six's. "Face it, bit bit, you got caught up in his mysterious aura, didn't you?"

I rolled my eyes. "There were a lot of things that night, including a lot of alcohol and a front zip dress on a body that hadn't been fucked in months."

"Trolloping whore, huh?"

My mouth popped open. "Ass."

"Did she meet the desperate-woman-seeking-dick look?"

Six nodded. "She had the added bonus of being the hottest woman there."

Hold the phone…

He paid me a compliment. Six, in all his fucked-up-ness, had just said one of the first nice things to me he'd said since he had a bead on me.

"Check and mate." Five clapped his hands together. "She's a tasty cookie, and I love her feistiness." His tongue wet his lips. "Are you sure I couldn't—"

"Don't make me shoot you, man."

"Guess I'll have to go pick up my own hostage." Five wagged his eyebrows.

I watched as Five stood and walked to the bathroom, then returned my focus down to the book I was reading. Three sentences was as far as I'd gotten when the end of the bed dipped. I glanced up and right into the dark eyes of my captor.

He grabbed on to my ankles and twisted me, pulling my body down the bed as he climbed between my legs. Heat flooded my cheeks as he slowly worked his hands up my stomach, wrapping his hands around my arms, moving them above my head.

Leaning down, he pressed his lips to mine. A sensuous kiss, one that made my thighs tighten around his hips, drawing him in closer. Slow, devouring strokes of his tongue. His hips flexed into me, pushing his cock against my clit.

We didn't get the all night fuck-fest he'd mentioned when we left to see Jason, and it seemed he wanted to make up for it right then.

"Five's here," I whispered. For days, he waited until Five left on some errand before getting his rocks off, but it seemed there was no more of that.

His mouth sucked warm trails down my neck while his hands pulled my shirt up and over my head. "And?" I bit my lip, then hissed as he took one of my nipples into his mouth, sucking on it, flicking it with his tongue. "It's not like I haven't fucked you in front of someone before."

My head tipped back onto the bed. He switched to the other nipple and I shuddered, arching into him as my breath sped up.

Within seconds, Six had me from slightly chilly to burning inferno.

The door to the bathroom opened, and his lips attacked mine. I ran my hands up and wrapped them around his shoulders, gripping on the hair at the base of his neck. Bare chest against bare chest as we kissed—nothing felt better.

For such a frightening man, his testosterone filled intensity still made for a panty-wetting attraction.

Sitting up, he grabbed on to my shorts and panties and pulled them down my legs.

There was excitement, a tingling that ignited my cells, knowing the fine male specimen in front of me was about to unleash a torrent of primal need. Skin to skin contact for base urges that I refused to deny.

I dove in head first, because going with the flow was easier than resistance. Pleasure better than pain.

I watched in a hypnotic trance as his fingers worked open his jeans, my hips rotating each second he upped the anticipation.

"Beg."

My eyes widened. "You want me to beg for it?"

The corner of his mouth moved up into a smirk. His arm stretched down, fingers pressing against my clit.

I reached out, my fingertips skimming across the bulge he was teasing me with. "You play dirty."

There was a groan somewhere in the room, but my attention was focused on the carnal demon in front of me.

"Get your fucking cock in my pussy and make me come."

There was a flash in his eyes before he reached out and wrapped his fingers around my throat.

"I make the rules," he snarled through clenched teeth.

His hold was loose, but a shiver ran through me at the monster about to shatter me. "I like to break the rules, remember?"

He let go, his hand trailing down, stopping to grope my breast before returning to the task of getting his dick out.

I smiled at him, then decided to give him what he wanted with only a little bit of sarcasm. "Please… I need your cock in me, stretching my pussy." A sweet sarcasm. "Make me scream out that it's yours and yours alone."

The last words were barely out when he leaned over and

slammed his dick into me. My eyes rolled back as a shuddering, muscle tensing moan ripped its way through me.

There was only a second before he drew his hips back and thrust them forward again. It was a hard, sensual rotation that hit in all the right places.

Low moans slipped from my lips as I drowned with each pounding stretch.

"Fuck."

I opened my eyes to find Five sitting on the edge of his bed. His hand fisted around his cock, moving in fast strokes.

No shame amongst killers.

I couldn't take my eyes off him, off the large cock in his hand. It was more erotic than I could have imagined—I was in a live porno. The girl getting fucked while he was the voyeur.

Six moved down so that our chests were mashed together. One arm slipping underneath my back, fingers lacing around the base of my skull. He kissed me again, drawing my attention back to him, back to his cock. Not that it ever left.

His teeth nipped at my neck, scraping their way up toward my jaw.

"For the rest of your life, you're mine."

What he said shouldn't have sent fire through me, because he would be the one to end me, but the possessive edge in his voice was unmistakable.

My thighs clamped down around his waist, keeping him closer, right on the spot that was scorching my mind blank. Muscles tightened, and I pulled him so tight against me in case I did melt, so I could fuse with him.

A tight whimpering shook me as my mouth opened in a scream as he forced an orgasm from me. No sound came out, but the moment after I broke, nothing could keep my pleasure filled wails down.

His thrusts sped up, his grip on my shoulder and hip tight as his muscles tensed. Sitting up, he gripped my hips in both of his hands, using the leverage to slam harder into me.

The groans next to me grew in volume, and I looked over in time to watch the angry red head of Five's dick let out thick droplets of pearly white all over his chest and legs.

The sight had my pussy clenching again, and Six moaned. He usually came inside me, so it surprised me when he pulled out. A few short pumps with his hand and come exploded out all over my abdomen and breasts.

Warm, heavy drops of his seed, painting my skin. Marking me.

His fist moved slowly up to the tip shaking, pushing out the last few drops.

"I totally get why you're ranked higher than me now," Five said, his arm thrown over his eyes as he lay on the bed.

I let out a small laugh and as I did, I heard a much deeper one. Opening my eyes, I looked at Six. He was smiling. It wasn't a huge grin, but both sides of his lips were drawn up.

I realized immediately that I was staring at the most genuine smile I'd ever seen from him. Not some act to pick a girl up, or to play for the normal world.

I was struck, once again, by how handsome he was.

Fucker.

WAITING TO HEAR FROM JASON WAS JUST AS BORING AS all the previous waits. The only difference being the hotel we found Five in had a much larger television channel selection. That, and Five was entertaining to be around.

The night before was a power play, but when Six pulled out and came all over me, I realized what was really going on—he marked his territory. Leaving no room for debate—I was his.

Possession was added to the growing list of things I was other than a person. Though something inside me liked the idea of being *his*.

With Six I was able to knock some things off my kink bucket list—it was hot seeing a guy stroke his cock while he watched me get fucked.

My bucket list was growing with new things and being checked off almost every day. I didn't even know I had a kink section of the list until Six.

"Are you ever going to tell me what all the numbers mean?" I asked Six from my usual position on the bed. It was a question I was tired of speculating in my own head, especially after what Five had said.

"They're our ranking system." The way he answered was

like I'd asked if he was hungry, his eyes never leaving the computer in front of him. "Our only form of identification."

Over the past week our dynamic had changed, though I had no doubt this was "if I tell you I have to kill you" information, but since he already had that all planned out, it was no biggie.

"Okay, so is bitchy blonde whore extraordinaire top dog or bottom feeder?"

He made a small little laugh-like sound, but I doubted he'd ever own up to it. "One is the lowest ranking of our elite agents."

"The Killing Corps."

He ignored my nickname. "Nine is highest."

That explained a lot. Nine had an arrogance that could be from knowing he was the deadliest.

My stomach rumbled, and I rolled around on the bed and let out a groan. "He's been gone so long."

Five was the official food runner. Six didn't trust him enough to leave me alone with him. I couldn't leave because we were in a more populated area where my face could be recognized, especially being in the same state as the motel where he killed two people.

The beep of the electronic key went off and I sat up, my stomach's call answered.

"They're coming," Five said as he stepped in, throwing a few bags onto the table.

"Are you sure?" Six asked as he shut the screen and put away the gun he'd been cleaning. In my opinion, he had an unhealthy relationship with his firearms.

Five tossed me a bottle of water, then handed me a bag. "No onion, right?" He winked at me.

I rolled my eyes. "It's not like I'm going to be kissing you.

Why are you denying me vital nutrients?" Inside the bag was a sandwich, along with two new books. I smiled up at him. "Thanks."

He grinned. "You looked bored."

"Back to the subject," Six called out, directing our attention back to him. "Nine and One are coming here?"

Five popped a fry into his mouth, chewing as he nodded. "They'll be here today. Jason talked to them after you got here and they headed out."

"Great."

Two killers turning their attention to me was never going to be a comfortable feeling, less so when Five's lip twitched.

He tossed another fry into his mouth and stepped back to the bed. "Which is it—you can't stand Nine or you want to scratch One's eyes out?"

"Why is it one or the other?" Did it make a difference?

"Just answer."

I let out a huff. "I want to scratch One's eyes out."

"Because he fucked her?" he asked.

I gave a reluctant nod as the unwanted jealousy flared inside me. "She rubs me wrong."

"We've all fucked her," Five said in that tone like it was no big deal.

I blinked at him. "W-What?"

"Sex is sex, Lacey. One's just as fucked up as we are."

My jaw dropped open. "Oh, God, she's probably some disease ridden skank. Ew!"

Five's head tilted back as he let out a loud laugh.

"There is nothing funny about that! You shitheads could have given something to me. That's gross."

Five wagged his eyebrows. "Condoms and constant testing, darling."

"Condoms? That's it?" I looked to Six, my jaw jutted forward. "Would you have still fucked me that night if I didn't have any?"

Five's eyes widened, and he turned to Six. "No you did not try to play that card."

"You," he pointed to Five, "shut up." His attention then turned to me. "And since I didn't have any on me, yes. I would have been taking more risk fucking you raw than you would have on me."

Risk?

Six didn't take risks. Not like that.

"Not prepared and you picked her up, huh?" One of Five's eyebrows twitched up as he looked at Six, whose gaze narrowed.

What Five said, or rather didn't say, had me reading between the lines. Their exchange implied things that indicated maybe that night didn't go down exactly how I believed.

A knock at the door a few hours later made me freeze and two hitmen grab their guns. It was a few ticks in before they relaxed. Whatever pattern sounded seemed to be a signal.

"Be normal," Six said, looking to me as he headed to the door.

"Oh, I'm super normal. If I had my phone, I'd hashtag the hell out of that shit."

"What does a hashtag have to do with anything?" Five asked, chuckling at me.

I shook my head. "All you killers need to pop into the real world once in a while."

With the door open and no words exchanged, a familiar blonde stepped in carrying a large case and a bag followed by Nine with a few more bags.

As soon as they were in, they dropped their gear and One turned to Six with a smile.

"I have a surprise for you," she said, setting the long case on the table.

Six's eyes widened, and he placed a reverent hand on the case. "Oh, baby, I've missed you."

My brow scrunched, watching as he flipped the latches and lifted the lid. Inside was a gun, one I recognized to be a rifle. It wasn't like most found at the local sporting goods store—it was military grade.

A sniper rifle.

"Told you I'd take care of her," One said.

All of their attention was on the weapon, staring intently as Six picked it up and shouldered it.

Nine shook his head. "I can't believe you still have that."

Six set it back in the case. "You're still mad I outshot you."

Nine quirked a brow. "Only by fifty meters."

Five let out a chuckle. "Yeah, he's still mad about it."

"You snipers and your rifles," One said with a shake of her head.

"Sniper? That's new." The moment the words were out of my mouth, One and Nine looked my way, while Six buttoned the case back up.

There wasn't surprise, so they knew I was there, just chose to ignore me. Based on the sour, utter look of disgust on One's face, she was not happy I made my presence known.

"I see you still have your toy," she said.

"Still shiny." I smiled real big while I flipped her off in my head. The urge to do it to her face was tempting, but she was one of the Killing Corps after all.

"Best pet I've ever seen," Five said, giving me a wink.

One pursed her lips and straightened her shoulders before strutting over to Five. She reached down and grabbed his junk, drawing his gaze to her.

"Let me know if you need to let off some steam."

Her seductive act had me vomiting in my mouth.

Granted, I got it—their work was a lonely business. I was certain there was some study that linked their personality types with high sex drives. I'd seen it firsthand with Six.

"Mmm, I think you could use some right now." Her fingers twisted around the hem of her boatneck tee as she pulled it up and over her head. Nothing but a lacy bra underneath.

"Oh, come the fuck on!" I threw my hands up in the air. "Are you so sluttastic you just wave that shit around for any dick to come knocking?"

Her lip curled up, and she turned my way. "Listen up, you little shitstain, I will fucking end you right here and now."

"Whoa." Five stepped between us. "Ladies, let's take it down a notch."

Six moved to stand next to me.

"I'm about to take *her* down a notch." She turned to Six. "Seriously, why do you still have this thing around?"

"She has information."

One's eyes widened. "You're keeping her around for that, or to keep your dick wet? Because last time I checked, you broke every bone in a guy's hand until he told you what you needed to know. If that didn't get it, you filleted their skin."

Ouch.

Nine stepped forward. "She's unnecessary baggage. Get the information and get rid of her."

"Wait. I don't think that's needed," Five said. "I don't think you're seeing the bigger picture. She's pure fucking camouflage gold."

I had no clue why, but I had Five batting for me, while Six became more and more tense beside me.

"Lacey's life isn't up for discussion. She's alive, for now, because she is of use." His eyes narrowed on One. "And not just to keep my dick wet. That's an added bonus."

Five licked his lips. "Are you sure I can't—"

"No." Six cut him off.

One pursed her lips, face red as she shot murderous daggers at me. She picked up her shirt and pulled it back on.

"Come on," Five said as he walked past her toward her bags. "We rented the adjoining room."

She didn't break her glare, and I didn't back down. Because I was insane, it seemed. Pissing off an assassin.

Maybe I needed some caffeine to get my head on straight before she took it off in a literal sense.

Moving back to my perch on the bed, I watched silently as they interacted. Nine and Five moved bags through the connecting door and into the other room while One directed, and Six cleared his rifle from the table.

They were oddly the same and different in the way they moved. Fluid, assured, and strong. Precision and accuracy. It was amazing how in tune Nine's aura was with Six's. They even had matching blank expressions.

I didn't know how old any of them were. Even the ME's report on Three only gave an age range, but I had a feeling they all fell into the same.

One, who was beautiful on the outside, showed fine lines around her eyes and her hands no longer held a youthful fullness. She was snotty, superior, and slutty. With what she did to Five, I could tell she was jealous of me. She'd probably used her pussy to gain favors with the men, to gain some control over them, but with another female around, she became furious that they weren't fawning all over her.

Five appeared a bit younger, but then again, that could have been his personality. Something told me he was the baby of the group, but even being the baby put him in his thirties.

Nine was all business—a lot like Six. But he held that air of authority, of cockiness. Being the highest ranked of elite killers could do that to an ego, I supposed. They all seemed to respect him.

Then there was Six. For weeks I'd studied him, tried to figure him out—my Mr. Mysterious. The best guess I had was that he was on the upper side of thirty-five.

All in all, I was rooming with a scary bunch of people, whose combined body count was probably in the hundreds. They were all cold and calculating, but there was something in Six, a detachment, that seemed to make him the bigger threat of them all. Then again, I knew him the best. I hadn't seen the rest in action.

And I thought being in a room with two of them was bad.

Four was bound to be an adventure.

For almost half an hour, they'd been spinning theories. It started after Five returned with dinner. Most of it I didn't understand, code words and super-secret spy things.

So, I sat there, listening, perking up at a name I recognized.

"What about Jason?" Five asked.

Three deadly heads stopped talking and turned to look at him.

"Jason?" One's eyes were wide. "Impossible."

"Why?" Five asked as he shoveled another fry into his mouth.

Nearly every meal since we met him involved fries. He was a fry-aholic. They were offset with vegetables and meat, but there was almost always fries.

"No." One shook her head. "He knows everything about us."

Six nodded. "Exactly. He'd be the last person we'd suspect."

"Or the first," Nine said. "It could be that Home is just using him as a mouthpiece. He could be sending us to our deaths and not even know it."

"Why now, though?"

Six shrugged. "Disbanding us could be costly."

"How so?" Nine asked.

Five threw his empty fry sack on the table. "Too much information."

"Meaning we could never retire? Go freelance?" One asked. "I don't want to be a henchman my whole life. If I wanted that, I would have gone to work for the mafia."

"I think we need to make a go at Langley," Five said.

"What good would that do?" Nine asked. "No one knows who we are. We have no identification."

Six leaned back and folded his arms. "Wolesley is still there."

Five shook his head. "That assnugget wouldn't know us from his own secretary." He let out a sigh. "Face it, we're exactly what they wanted. Invisible. There are probably three people besides Jason who know about us."

"We have no forms of identification. Not CIA or even our real names, if we can even remember them."

My brow scrunched. "Remember them?"

Four deadly sets of eyes turned to me, one set in particular spitting venom.

Nine took a sip of water and passed it to One. "It's been a long time since we've used our real names."

"But it's your *name*." The whole conversation seemed impossible. Even if the prior five or so years had been spent under a multitude of identities, how would it erase thirty some years of the name they were born with?

Five patted my head. "Doesn't matter, buttercup. Even that fades after a while."

I shook my head, unbelieving the possibility of what they were saying. "I can't even imagine that."

"Can't you?" Six quirked a brow at me. "When you talk to yourself, what name do you say in your head?"

"Paisley."

"Your name is Paisley?" One asked in a snarky tone before letting out a demented cackle.

Fuck, I hated the bitch.

Six ignored her. "I say Six. It's more my name now than any other. My only constant title."

I stared at him, stunned. "Are all of you like that?"

They all nodded.

Badass enough to have a code name, not able to live enough to remember their real names.

They returned back to the topic and I lay down, staring up at the celling, lulled to sleep by their conversation.

My eyes snapped open what felt like seconds later, but by the dark room, was probably actually hours later. Six climbed into bed, startling me awake. He let out a sigh as he settled in behind me, sliding his arm under me and pulling me close.

I turned and for reasons unknown, slipped my arm around him and nuzzled his chest.

Maybe it was just that some way, somehow, in the company of killers, he was my safety.

My captor. My killer. My security.

When did my executioner become my lifeline?

Life with One was not fun.

Less than forty-eight hours in and I wanted to smack her, but that would be unwise. Even the bottom of the Killing Corps scale probably had more killing capability than a hundred soldiers.

Maybe it was an exaggeration, maybe not.

"Are you really going to keep her around?" Nine asked Six as they sat at a table overlooking some paperwork.

My head popped up to look at them from where I sat at the edge of the bed, Five next to me. I was holding the barrel of his own rifle while he adjusted something.

The muscle in Six's jaw jumped. "I thought we talked about this."

Nine's brown eyes—his natural color—locked with Six's similar. They both had strong profiles, similar shaped noses, and strong jawlines.

Why were all of them ruggedly handsome? Should they have been a little more average?

Technically, they were. Their good looks were just on the upper side of normal.

"She stands out. What if that makes you more visible?" Nine's words and tone struck me. They weren't dismissal like in Paris. It sounded a bit like worry, but that seemed out of place for them.

Then again, they were two down, seven to go. Worry for their lives, and maybe even each other, was bound to leak out a little.

"She can't be that good of a lay," One said.

Two days was all I could take.

"What is your fucking problem, you twatapatomus?" I snapped.

One's eyes widened, and Five stopped what he was doing and scooted a little closer to me, his arm crawling across my back until his hand rested on my hip.

"Excuse me?"

"From the moment you laid eyes on me, your claws were out. Am I stepping on your turf? Is that it? The only woman in a man's land, and when the attention is on something new, you can't deal."

Fuck. Fuck. Fuck. Oh fuck.

Her lips twitched, jaw clenching and unclenching, brow furrowing before the hard gaze I was used to softened.

"I'm the only woman, you're right." She nodded, then swung he arm around, gesturing to the others. "For years, it's just been us. We pass each other every now and then, but in all the years I am the one constant woman in their lives. So, as much as I hate to admit it, I don't like that you've encroached. They're my boys, and I'm *very* protective of them."

My brow scrunched. "I'm just a toy he's going to discard." I made a gun shooting gesture with my hand to my head. "No threat here. When I'm gone, you'll still be here, right beside them."

"You can't fault us for having our hackles up around you," Nine said from across the room, his gaze rising to meet mine. "Outside of Jason, it's been years since someone besides our little group has known anything about us."

Five tickled my side, and I snapped back to him. "You may not be a psycho killer like us, but you still unnerve us."

I let out a little *ha* sound. It wasn't the first time I'd heard that. Six long ago said I unnerved him. Though I believed the reason differed from the one the Killing Corps presented.

Six had remained silent, not even moving when Five wrapped his arm around me. I stared at him, curious if he'd weigh in an opinion.

"You've been with him so long, I've been wondering if he's going to be able to go through with it," One said as she turned to Six, her eyebrow raised.

That got Six moving. He stood, grabbed his gun from the table, swung his arm up, aimed at my head, and fired. I heard the silenced *snap*, eyes wide, heart stopped, frozen and waiting for the pain, the feeling of blood.

But it didn't come.

"Does that answer your question?"

Shaking, I turned to look behind me. In the wall there was a small, round hole.

Fuck.

None of them questioned him, returning to their tasks. Five took his rifle from my shaking hands and put it away. He gave me an apologetic smile.

Why was he the most human of them?

Frightened, thinking he was going to off me right then. Left scared in a huddled mass of shock. I moved back on the bed until my back hit the headboard, and pulled my legs up.

There was no empathy in them. No sympathy. And even with Five being nice, he was still the same. Just as dangerous and deadly. If he hadn't taken a liking to me, I was certain I wouldn't have gotten that small bit.

A little while later, Nine and One left on a food run and Five jumped in the shower, giving me the opportunity to talk to Six alone.

"Did you have to shoot at my head to prove your point?" I asked from my tucked-up place on the bed.

His head rose, eyes locked with mine. "Yes."

"Why?"

He looked away, pausing, probably questioning if he should say anything. "They think having you is a weakness. I had to prove myself."

"By shooting at me?"

That damn blank expression of his stared back at me. "I didn't hit you."

"That's beside the point."

"I will be hitting you, though."

I froze, my voice lowering. "Yeah, I know, but don't be an ass trying to show off to your buddies."

He stood up and walked over to the bed. "Are you telling me what to do?"

"No, just saying if you want me to be cooperative, don't shoot at me."

He nodded the last few steps. Cupping my cheek, he ran his hand around to the back of my neck. What was a soft gesture became painful as his fingers fisted my hair and he tilted my head back.

I hissed, leaning toward his hand to relieve the pain.

"I'll do what I want. And you will cooperate, or you'll die sooner."

Through my watering eyes I could see something in his own—emotion. Not anger, but something I couldn't name, but was akin to pain. What type, I had no clue.

I reached up and cupped his face. His eyes widened just the slightest. Adjusting my position, I was able to get onto my knees, moving closer to him as I pulled him down.

When our lips met, the hand in my hair relaxed. Every kiss with him was full of energy, but instead of a lust-filled craze, we tasted. Teasing tongues as his hand moved to my waist and he pulled me closer.

As much as he was fronting, I could see that things weren't that simple on the inside.

The line between captor and captive were blurred.

THE NEXT DAY, WE SPLIT OFF FROM THE OTHERS AND headed out in search of the missing Killing Corps.

"Four of us hunting down three Cleaners and a handler hiding somewhere in the world. Easy." Five chuckled as we headed out of the hotel room.

"Just remember to check in," Nine said. "We'll set a meeting place and work our way there once we have everyone."

"And if something happens to one of us?" One asked.

"Try not to die," Six said, giving One a little smirk.

She rolled her eyes and gave him a hug before moving on to Five and Nine for hugs as well. It was kinda strange.

"You boys are my favorites, so stay alive, okay?"

She stopped in front of me. "Goodbye, Lacey." She held out her hand and after a beat, I took it. "I'm not sorry for who I am or what I've said to you, but I am sorry I was intimidated by you and thus treated you poorly. You were right—I won't see you again and they'll go back to being mine alone."

She turned and stepped away, leaving me to stare after her, too stunned and confused to say anything back.

Five stepped up beside me. "Wow, that was as close to an apology as I've ever heard her give."

I turned to him. "That was an apology?"

His lip quirked up. "It was a pleasure getting to know you, Lacey. I hope to see you again, but I don't know if that's in the cards for us."

He pulled me in for a hug and I wrapped my arms around him, smiling into his chest.

"Thanks for being awesome."

He pulled back, and I looked up. His eyes were intense, serious. "If only you could die happy, having known my dick inside you." He leaned down and pressed his lips to mine, catching me by surprise.

"That's it," Six said as he pulled Five off me.

My lips tingled, and I could feel my face heating up.

Five held out his hand to Six. "I hope to see you again. You're one of my favorites in our little ragtag group."

Six nodded. "Till next time."

We climbed into the car to drive back to Atlanta. We needed to stop at the studio apartment to drop off his guns before boarding a plane to Las Vegas.

Jason hadn't been heard from in days and they couldn't get ahold of him, so Five was headed out to find him. One was searching for Seven while Nine was going to look for Two.

Six and I were headed to Vegas in search of Four—the last place he'd been dispatched.

In the time I'd been with Six, I'd traveled more than in the entire decade prior. Las Vegas wasn't new to me, unlike some of the other areas we'd been to. I'd visited the adult playground two years prior when Digby and I had gone on a long weekend trip. We stayed at The Venetian and had a blast. It helped that Digby won almost a grand playing poker.

With Six beside me, I knew it was going to be a *vastly* different trip.

Pulling up to yet another seedy motel, way off the strip near the downtown area, I let out a groan.

"Are we staying at the cokehead special for a reason?" I asked as I looked through the window of the car that, like Miami, was mysteriously waiting for us in the long-term parking lot.

After it happening multiple times, I figured they must have had some sort of in with one of the rental companies to discreetly supply them with a vehicle. Or at least, that was my theory.

We made one stop for a weapons pickup before driving into the what was probably the worst part of town.

Six looked around, then back to me. "Stay."

I stared at him and rolled my eyes. "I doubt the druggies are going to be any help to me."

He didn't take his eyes off me as he walked into the lobby, if you could call it that. I stared at the neon sign as he passed by it and shook my head. In the window was a sign that read "Cash Only" and below that "We rent by the hour."

It was actually the first time since the motel outside Atlanta that he'd left me alone. Since it had been a while, his warning was almost amusing. At that point, I was in too deep to go back. Even if I did get home, the government or CIA would probably knock down my door soon after and drag me away.

The wait for his return was only a short minute or two, but when he came out he was angry.

"You didn't kill anyone, did you?" I asked as grumpy pants climbed in.

His gaze narrowed on me. "Almost."

My mouth popped open. "You showed restraint?"

"We're not staying here."

Someone woke up on the wrong side of the bed. Considering I was the one woken up by a cock sliding into me, I would think it would be me, but something had crawled up his ass from the time we got up. Agitation from leaving his brethren maybe.

All I knew is that I was getting grumpy as well. Hangry, topped with a three-hour time difference that made me sleepy.

"Why?"

"It's not clear."

I quirked a brow at him. "Not clear?"

He shook his head. "It's no good."

I sighed. "Fine by me."

We drove around for a few minutes before pulling into another motel that looked a bit better than the last, but still in a shitty area. Six went to rent a room while I stood outside, soaking in the warm sun.

It was finally April, so it was a nice, dry heat in the desert city, making the sun feel that much warmer.

I closed my eyes and relaxed a bit, or as much as I could. There'd been a constant fear laced adrenaline pumping through me in small doses since he took me. Almost two months of that, and it felt good to soak up some sun.

"Hey, sweet thing, how you doin' today?" a strange voice asked.

I opened my eyes to find a man in front of me licking his lips and acting all cool like he was the shit. Dressed in an oversized shirt and jeans down past his ass, he was the epitome of the stereotypical ghetto gangster, but he could've been a wannabe. I couldn't tell the difference with the area we were in.

"Good."

He stepped forward. "You lookin' for a party, baby?"

"No. Thanks."

Another step closer, he placed one hand on the car next to my shoulder and leaned in.

"You sure? I bet I can make this sweet body sing. A little love drug and my love club can make you feel real good, baby."

It was incredibly hard not to laugh at his cheesy lines. Being with Six had desensitized my danger warnings. Normally, I would have been uncomfortable in that type of situation, but the one I feared the most would kill the guy without even thinking. The wannabe in front of me didn't stand a chance.

Maybe cokeheads or hood rats went for the bullshit he was selling, but not me. Besides, some of the best sex I'd ever had was holding me hostage. Though I'd become more of a companion.

In the background noise there was the distinct *ca-click* of the slide being pulled and flying back in place. The guy recognized the sound as well and froze.

My gaze was still locked on his eyes that had widened significantly. "I think he has a problem with it. I'd run before he pulls the trigger. I don't want blood on my shirt."

He nodded and scurried away, tripping on the curb as he hauled ass.

I chuckled as I turned to Six, who was stowing his gun. There was no amusement. All serious and businesslike and maybe even a little pissed.

"Don't talk to anyone."

I rolled my eyes. "Oh, come on! You think I initiated contact?"

"You were flirting."

"No, I thought it was funny," I said with a shake of my head. "Maybe a bit flattering as well. You may be giving me the goods, but you're lacking in many other areas."

He slammed one hand onto the car, blocking my path, the

other hand grabbing on to my hair and yanking back.

"This isn't fun and games. I'm using you before I kill you." His teeth pressed against my neck, biting hard before pulling away and letting go of me.

"Such a charmer."

The side glare he gave me only made me want to bait him more, because the jealousy he'd begun to display was one of the last reactions I expected from him.

The trunk was filled with our two suitcases, his book bag holding the super-secret laptop, and the bag full of weapons.

"You really would love it if the world went into some nuclear war or something equally as population devastating so there wouldn't be as much cattle around, wouldn't you?" I asked as I took the book bag from him.

He stared into my eyes, unblinking. "Yes."

Nothing but truth behind his fake baby blues.

Speaking of, I couldn't wait to get the stupid contacts out of my eyes. They'd bothered me for the last twelve hours.

The room was on the second floor, which meant hauling all of the shit we'd acquired up.

"Why do you always stay in such shitholes?" I asked as we entered a '70s version of the previous shitholes, only with early '90s updates.

"Because a lot of the people here don't snitch on illegal activities."

I sat down on the edge of the bed. "It's not like you're buying drugs or are wanted."

"No, but right now, you're wanted and I don't want my face on cameras."

Point.

I steered my suitcase closer and turned the dials of the lock. When I set it up, I used the last four digits of my phone number.

A phone that was blown up almost two months prior.

Strange how it was always attached to my hand for games, music, Facebook, but I'd hardly missed it. There was no desire to check anything. Only the desire to live, and I was doing it the only way I could.

Thankfully, I had the foresight to put my toiletries bag in the front, but it was a tight squeeze getting it out. With it in hand, I walked to the counter that contained a sink and mirror just outside the rest of the bathroom.

I opened the case and reached into one eye, pinching the edges of the brown lens, letting hints of the bright blue hidden beneath peek through. First one, then the other before I deposited both into the case and closed it up. I blinked in rapid succession as I located the eye drops.

The cool drops burned before soothing my dry, tired eyes.

"That's better."

Six stepped up behind me, pushing and pinning me against the counter's edge. We locked eyes in the mirror—his fake blue with my real.

"I missed your eyes."

"You did?"

He nodded and leaned forward, running his lips along the length of my neck. "They're so beautiful."

I froze, gaze locked on him.

Beautiful?

I turned in his arms and looked up at him. "You know you don't have to throw fake compliments my way to get into my pants."

He shook his head, lips twitching up. "All too real." He leaned down, his lips millimeters from mine. "I do know beauty."

His lips pressed against mine and I kissed back, my hand running up his chest.

"Too bad even beautiful things eventually die."

Insert splash of cold reality.

I pursed my lips and glared at him. "Thanks for the re-minder." I slapped his chest. "You are such a shit sometimes."

He pulled back and smirked. "I'm hungry."

I let out a chuckle. "That doesn't surprise me."

The beginning talks of food were interrupted by a knock at the door, making both of us freeze. Six glanced at me, then picked up his gun from the table and stuffed it in his waistband as he moved quietly toward the door. He looked through the peephole and remained silent.

"Hey, puta, open up. We know you're there."

Six sighed, probably in annoyance, and tilted his head to the side, releasing a few loud cracks. With a flip of the deadbolt, he pulled the door open.

From my vantage point there were about five guys, all dressed like the idiot from earlier. They were all shorter than Six, but then again, he was just over six foot.

"You the pendejo that pointed a gun at my cousin?"

Six's fingers flexed, wrapping around the grip of his gun. "If he was the idiot trying to pick up my wife, then yes."

"Who the hell do you think you are?" the guy asked, his voice almost a yell.

The situation did not look good, and I had a feeling it would be wise to pack my bag up again. Luckily, I hadn't taken much out.

Six pulled the gun from his waistband and pointed it at the guy who was talking. "Look, I'm tired and really don't want to run out of here and find another motel. That is *the* single reason I haven't pulled the trigger. You and your homeboys need to go."

The leader stepped up, his jaw jutted forward, eyes in slits. "You think you can take me and my boys, cabrón? You're nothin' but a yuppy with a gun."

Oh, boy…

I stood up and walked to the doorway, my arms wrapping around his waist as I peered out.

"You're nothing but a poser. This guy here is the real deal. Leave on your own now, or leave in a body bag."

The confidence and the words were not normal for me in that type of situation. But I had confidence in Six. He wasn't going to put up with them.

"Shit, puta, shut your fucking mouth." He reached down and grabbed his crotch. "Or better yet, come over here and I'll keep it occupied."

Six groaned.

"I hate your shitty motels."

The words were barely out when every cell in my body jumped, my ears going deaf for a second before a loud ringing set in.

The leader fell back from the force of the bullet moving through his skull. His friends didn't even have time to get over their shock before four more shots deafened me, and all five of them were on the ground.

The correct response was to scream or hyperventilate or throw up. While I was suddenly on the nauseous side, Six killing them had me running for my suitcase instead of the hills. I prayed nobody else came out of their room in our escape, because they too would join the body count.

In trying to get them to go away, I riled them up instead. Everything was mushy and my ears were ringing as I stuffed my toiletries bag back in my suitcase.

"I hate this shit," he said as he picked up his weapons bag and grabbed on to his suitcase. He looked to me. "Hurry up."

I stared down at them, transfixed, watching as the blood

seeped out of their lifeless bodies.

It was the longest I'd gotten to look at Six's meticulous and deadly handiwork. It was the first time in weeks I was reminded how ruthless and savage he was.

"Come on."

My hands shook as I blindly reached for my purse, his book bag, and suitcase. The ground seemed uneven beneath my feet as I dragged the suitcase behind me. At the threshold I glanced down at the bodies surrounding the entrance.

"Don't step in the blood," he said with a calm coolness. It was the same tone one would use when talking about wet paint.

He turned back to grab my bag as I continued to stare down at his handiwork.

The death before me was a reality I hadn't seen from him in weeks. But their fate was the same as mine. I would soon be the one bleeding on the floor, eyes void of life.

My head was swimming, and everything seemed to pulse around me.

"Lacey!" Six's voice broke through.

I looked up at him in confusion. He shook his head, jaw clenching as he reached out for me. Holding on to his arms, he helped me step over the blood.

Once on my feet outside the massacre, he grabbed on to my jaw, forcing me to look at him.

"You need to focus on me."

I gave a shaky nod and blew out a breath. He let go and handed me the weapons bag as he took my suitcase. Steel steps clanked beneath our feet and in the distance, I heard sirens. Six didn't say anything, but he picked up the pace. He was at the trunk loading the bags in when I reached him. After tossing in the ones I was carrying, we climbed in. The engine roared to life and with a quick switch of gears, we were off.

I looked back at the hotel and the few windows with the curtains drawn watching us go, then close up.

"They were never leaving alive, were they?" I asked as we sped down the road, away from the sirens and flashing lights.

"No."

"Why?" I didn't understand why someone wouldn't walk away when threatened like that.

"Because they're cocky assholes who don't back down, even when their insides are screaming at them to."

"**O**H, COME ON! HOW MANY SHITHOLE MOTELS DOES this city have?" I asked after an hour of driving. We'd pulled into an almost identical architectural stain as the blood covered one we fled.

"A lot," Six said as he turned to me. "Vegas, baby."

I groaned and reached for the handle.

My hands shook as I exited. While the adrenaline had worn off, there was some residual aftereffects that prevailed. Weakness and fatigue being some of them. Luckily my ears had stopped ringing, but there was still a strange feeling in them.

Once again, the room was out of date and well worn. I collapsed onto the bed as soon as we entered.

The images of the dead gangsters were on my mind. I couldn't shut them off. I'd seen enough death to last a lifetime since Six.

Death chased him and the other Cleaners. And only I knew why Three was able to be taken out.

"You aren't as great as you think you are," I said, my face half mashed into the comforter. "The Cleaners aren't invincible."

He stopped unloading his computer and stared at me. "Are you actually going to tell me what you know?"

Was I? Thinking back on what my tired brain said, it was a sort of interlude. Did I want to tell him? But what did I really know?

Would telling him end me now?

"I know that you aren't impervious to death. I know you are susceptible to drugs."

Six stood and climbed onto the bed to lie next to me. "What drugs?"

"Three."

Six nodded. "That explains a lot."

"There was a cocktail of drugs in his system, including Ketamine." I thought the word would register, but by his blank expression, it appeared it didn't. "I don't know what your date rape drug knowledge is, but it's fast acting and can impair motor function and distort the senses."

"Ingested from a drink," he said, thinking to himself.

"You need me more than I need you," I said, knowing for the first time it was true. "There have been plenty of times I could've run away, gotten help, but I didn't."

He reached out and brushed a lock of hair behind my ear. "Because I'd kill you."

"At this point, I'm trying to live as long as I can. Therefore, I don't want to piss your psychotic ass off."

"You push my buttons constantly."

I let out a little laugh. "Yeah, but that's fun. You make it too easy."

"Why are you such a sarcastic pain in my ass?"

I shrugged. "Sarcasm is my defense mechanism, so…shut up."

One corner of his mouth twitched up. "I should punish you for that."

"Yeah, Mr. Killer, what are you going to do?"

"Hmm." He looked around the room as he tried to come up with something. "I could fuck you."

"Pfft, that's no punishment."

"No, but I just killed five guys and now I want to fuck your brains out."

My brow scrunched. "Is that a side effect?"

"I guess you could call it that."

"I thought you were hungry." We never did get to eat before those dickwads showed up.

"After." He smacked my ass, making me jump.

"Fine, but I'm just going to lie here because the day's shit wore me out."

"Undo your jeans."

I quirked a brow before reaching down and flicking the button and drawing the zipper down. His hands wrapped around the waistband, then yanked my jeans and panties over my hips and ass.

They weren't all the way off, just down enough to expose the necessary areas.

"You're determined," I said as he pulled my hips up and back, forcing me onto my knees.

He flexed his hips against my ass, letting me feel just how turned on he was. Hard cock straining against his jeans, ready to fill me in all the ways I loved.

"Mmm, fuck."

His hand smacked across my ass and made me jump again. A few seconds and the sound of a zipper later, there was another smack, but with his cock.

"Just wet enough," he said as he rubbed the tip along my slit.

Even with as many times as he'd fucked me, the feeling of his cock pressing in, spreading my pussy, filling me completely, made my eyes roll back and my mouth fall open.

"Fuck."

Leaning over, he pressed his chest to my back, a loud moan moving through him, vibrating against me. One hand slipped around my waist, running up between my breasts and resting around my neck. He straightened back up, pulling me with him.

"You're right," he whispered into my ear as he rocked his hips in small thrusts. "I do need you more than you need me."

A moan crawled out of me as his cock rubbed my walls, lighting up every nerve, sending a tingling shiver from my head all the way down my spine.

His breath was hot against my neck as he nipped and licked. Moans slipped from my lips with each increasingly strong drive of his cock. The pleasurable grip of his fingers tightened around my neck. What was a light, guiding hold became constrictive as his muscles tensed.

Trembling took hold as my body shook in clenching convulsions, my eyes unfocused and mouth open in a silent scream as I shattered in his arms. Pussy pulsing quakes of my orgasm sent him over the edge, his hips slamming against my ass as he bottomed out, groaning against my skin. I felt his powerful dick twitches as he emptied all the way inside me.

My head fell back against his shoulder, arms lax at my sides as he sat back on his haunches, our hard breaths in time as aftershocks pinged through me.

"Hungry now?" I asked between breaths.

"Famished."

My stomach rumbled. "I want tacos."

"Okay."

The next morning I woke and sat straight up in the bed. Sunlight filtered in through the sheer curtains, lighting up the entire room.

The bed was empty, as was the room. My mouth stretched open in a yawn as my arms did as well, my back arching with a groan.

Stupid bed.

It was as bad as every other hotel, minus the one in Paris.

The only sounds were of cars and people on the street below. The door to the bathroom was open, but it was silent inside.

I stood and walked in, confirming something I was finding hard to believe—I was alone. Turning, I surveyed the room. Everything was in order, all of our bags, including all of his weapons.

My sleep addled brain attempted to figure it all out as I sat on the toilet, then went about my morning rituals before jumping into the shower.

Was he testing me? Or was he trusting me?

I could easily grab a gun and shoot him the moment he walked through the door. I could be free of him.

But.

The flip side was a great unknown.

I let the warm water beat down on my back as I stared at the blonde tips of my hair resting on my breasts. Another bit of evidence of my unending change, but could it be reversed?

Sure, if he was dead I would be free, but then what? There were three other highly trained killers who knew of me, and had the ability to track me down. Six wasn't the only one I had to worry about. After seeing Jason, and hearing what he told Five, I was certain the rest of the Killing Corps knew about me.

That was if I could even do it, could kill him.

I stepped out of the shower and grabbed the towels hanging,

patting the water droplets before wrapping it around my body.

Could I do it? Kill Six?

I threw my hair up into another towel and stared at my reflection. Let the feelings take over. Noticed the vice around my chest at the thought of him being gone.

He was going to kill me and had no qualms about it. Even after almost two months, it would be nothing for him.

I was nothing but another body in his wake. The latest in a long trail of blood.

He was a good actor—something I had to remind myself of. The moments where he seemed real, somewhat sweet, were nothing more than a ruse.

He didn't care about me.

My face scrunched up and tears welled in my eyes.

"Get a grip, Paisley."

It wasn't logical, made no sense whatsoever, but the thought of being without him caused me pain and sadness.

I was a rational being. The emotions brewing within me were chaotic and stronger than comprehension for a man who had done terrible things and in the end, would snuff out my life.

Moving back into the room, I hauled my suitcase onto the bed and opened it up. With no idea what the day held, I threw on some panties and a tank top to wait for him to return.

I was running a brush through my wet hair when I heard the door click and turned in time to watch him glance first to the bed, then around the room.

"Hi," I said as I continued with my task.

He stepped in, a few bags in tow, and shut the door.

"You're here."

I quirked my brow, knowing what he meant, but still playing confused. "Where else would I be?"

The corner of his mouth twitched up, his head nodding. "I

wasn't exactly sure."

"But you thought I might test the boundaries?"

"Wouldn't that be the rational thing to do?"

"Perhaps."

"Are you no longer a rational being?" he asked as he handed me a paper bag and a bottle of water.

"Oh, I am." I sat down on the bed and took a sip from the bottle. "I'm rational enough to know that there are three other highly trained killers who would be after my ass, plus your threat of killing my ex-boyfriend. That results in a pretty easy answer that the devil beside me is my best bet."

He moved to the table and opened a second bag. "Okay, I'm glad we've come to an arrangement."

"So, what's on the agenda?" I reached in and pulled out a container with a fork and some napkins.

"Waiting to hear from a contact."

I pursed my lips, thinking about the boring afternoon ahead. "There's a lot of waiting in your line of work, isn't there?"

"The more information you have, the better prepared."

"Ah, the control aspect you're so fond of."

I opened the container and took in a whiff of the most wonderful smell, my mouth salivating. "Where did you get a tenderloin sandwich out here?" The thing was huge, taking up the entire container and then some.

"There was a place around the corner."

I picked up the bun to survey the giant breaded hunk of meat. It was two meals or more worth. Spots of red caught my eye and I stared down, trying to figure out what was on it.

"Ketchup?"

"Hm?"

The corners of my mouth turned down as I scraped the bun off on the container.

"What the hell? You don't put ketchup on a tenderloin!"

Ew, just ew.

"Why?"

"You just don't. I've never seen ketchup on a tenderloin, it's just not done."

"How are you an expert?"

"My grandparents lived in Indiana. The tenderloin is like the state sandwich, if there was such a thing."

He shook his head at me and took a bite.

I let out a moan at my own bite, memories of a different life flooding in.

It was a surreal moment. Sitting with the man who kidnapped me, almost as equals eating a sandwich that reminded me of my former life.

I was still there because I didn't leave.

I was still there because I couldn't.

In the early evening a few days later, Six's phone rang. More elusive words, and after only a minute or two, the call was done.

The instant the phone was down, he started stripping. "Your outfit from Paris." He pulled both of our suitcases up to the bed. "Put it on."

"Oh, we're going glam." I pulled out my makeup case and curling iron. "Same underneath?"

He stopped searching in his bag and looked up to me. He reached up, running his fingers across his lips as his gaze drifted down and back up.

"Just…get dressed," he said, turning back to his search.

I had to admit, making a strong, ruthless killer into a

man ruled by his dick was quite empowering, especially in my situation.

It took about an hour to get to the level of dolled up my outfit called for, but the groan of approval that left Six made it worth it.

The drive to our destination was longer than I expected, and suddenly brighter as we neared the strip. The sun had set, yet it was as bright as day on the streets. People flooded the side-walks, drinks in hand. The flashing of slot machines was visible through open doors, calling people in with their pretty-pretty lights and air conditioning.

Not that the air conditioning was needed right then, but in a few short months it would be a strong pull from the desert heat.

We ended at the far end near the airport, at Mandalay Bay, leaving the car with the valet and entering the gigantic establishment.

"Shit, this place is huge," I said in awe.

While the gaming floor was comparable to the Venetian's, the high ceilings and dark décor area was packed with people.

"Stay close," Six said as he slipped his hand in mine.

I stared down at our hands that were joined like any other couple. It wasn't like we hadn't held hands in public before, it was the way he did it was such ease. The way my chest warmed and my heart raced.

That feeling scared me more than he did.

We weren't really married. He wasn't my husband, but in some ways, he was.

The more people we waded through, the more he squeezed my hand. Cut off, people stopping in front of us to stare—I be-gan to wonder how close he was to pulling out his gun.

It wouldn't happen, but they were testing his patience.

We made it to the blackjack tables and took two of the open

seats. There were seven spots in all, and only two remaining open. There was another couple, probably in their forties, and an older gentleman in a suit with a glass of what I guessed to be whiskey.

The dealer was a short statured Asian man who was probably in his thirties.

Was he really our next contact?

Six pulled out four one-hundred-dollar bills and handed them to the dealer. He stared at them for a brief second, glanced at Six, then made the change call. He slid over a large pile of chips, and Six gave me half.

We played for a while. I lost about a hundred dollars, while Six was up about five hundred. The couple left, and we sat there with the older man. I didn't know how much longer we were going to be, but my stack was dwindling.

Counting cards was not my strong suit.

"Hot night tonight," the gentleman said, tipping his glass to us.

I stared down at the cards in front of me—a king and five—trying to decide to hit or not. Tapping the table, I cringed as the dealer turned over the next card, blowing out a sigh when a four appeared.

"It is," Six said.

I glanced over at him, surprised he responded. When I looked back down at my cards I hissed a "yes!" when the dealer busted at twenty-four and I finally won a hand.

"You've got an awful pretty kitty with you tonight," the man said.

That stopped me, and I understood. "Oh, come on!" I cried out, pissed that, once again, I was being referred to as an animal. Luckily my outburst happened when I hit and bust, making perfect sense.

"Cards aren't being too kind to you tonight, are they, kitty?"

I turned my head and glared at him.

"You've got a feisty one," he said with a smirk.

"You have no idea," Six said.

"Where you two from?"

"Virginia."

"And her?"

Six's lip twitched. "I took her from her boring life in Ohio."

I wanted to object, but he was right—my life was boring.

The man nodded. "My drink's gone dry. Think I'll head over to the sports bar for a refill and place a penny or two on some ponies."

"Good luck."

He nodded at us. "Night."

Six and I were left alone at the table, the dealer waiting on our new bets. Reluctantly, I pushed a ten out, while Six pushed an entire stack out—almost four hundred dollars.

That was a lot, and when the cards came out, my eyes grew wide. There was no way he would hit on twenty, which would be a nice payout.

I only had six, and hit three times before busting at twenty-two. When Six knocked on the table I turned to him in wide-eyed horror.

What was he doing? The odds of him getting a one were astronomical.

Three.

He tapped again and I was shocked when the dealer continued.

Eight.

Again.

The dealer ignored him and went on to his own hand.

"Dealer wins."

"Too bad," Six said as he stood.

Everything in me wanted to go off on him, but I couldn't cause a scene. Instead, I stared at him as I took his hand and waved goodbye to the dealer.

"What was that about?" I asked as we merged in to the flow of human traffic.

Holy shit, Six was right. A herd of cattle walking together.

He didn't respond but kept me close, even going so far as to wrap his arm around my shoulders. There was an opening in the crowd, and we rushed through. After weaving through a few slot banks, we ended up at the sports bar and went in.

There were a tiny handful of people, maybe four including the bartender, inside. One of them was the man who'd been sitting at the blackjack table with us.

"Nice night for a race," Six said as he sat, pulling me onto his lap.

"You're looking good." The man's eyes never left the screen.

Six ran his hand up and down my thigh. "Retirement has aged you."

"Nah, just age catching up to me. I'm trying to live the good life in my golden years."

Six chuckled. I hated to admit how the deep, resonating sound made me tingly. Flashes of alternative scenarios jumped around my brain of a regular life, of making him laugh.

Of being with him longer than my death sentence.

What the actual fuck?

"Your boy was down at the Golden Nugget, but that was nearly a week ago."

"Nothing since?"

The man shook his head.

"Did he finish his work here?"

The man nodded. "Two days ago. That was the last I could

find of him."

"Any idea on where the meeting was?"

"Say, do you two like tacos?" he asked. Segue much? "There is this fantastic taco truck that drives around. I sometimes see it just outside of town headin' to this industrial complex."

"We may have to go for a drive, then."

"Watch out, though, there are some rats that hang out in those things."

Six nodded and stood. "Good luck."

"You, too. Take care."

Six stood and wrapped his arm around my waist, guiding me back out to the madhouse of the casino floor. Diving between gaps of people, we wove through throngs of mindless walkers the entire way back out to the front to pick the car up from valet.

Standing and waiting for them to run and get it was strange. Surrounded by people, next to a sociopathic hitman, I realized I would rather be standing there with him then just about anywhere else.

When we were back in the car and headed back to the motel, I turned in my seat. "Okay, we're out of there. What's going on? Who was that guy?"

"He's an informant."

I gave a slow nod. "And what did we learn?"

"Three and Eight are dead and that's all that they know."

I threw my hands up. "We already knew about them. How did you get that anyway?"

"The dealer."

My eyes widened. "The *dealer* was an informant as well?" He looked like any other dealer in town. Guess informants were everywhere.

"Yes."

"All right," I said with a nod as I caught up. "What was all the cryptic talk in the sports bar?"

"Four was last seen in an industrial area about an hour outside of town."

Two down, possibly three.

Six didn't say anything more, instead lost in his thoughts. Probably calculating fifty different next moves and analyzing them.

But more than that, his brow was knitted together. For the first time, he was showing me the slightest hint that beneath his cool, calm exterior were rough seas.

FOR HOURS I WATCHED SIX METICULOUSLY CLEAN EACH piece of the arsenal he picked up. Boxes of bullets emptied, pushed one by one into a clip for backup.

He had a shoulder holster, and as soon as two guns were ready, he strapped them in, setting it aside. What looked like a smaller pistol was slipped into some other type of holster and set next to the other one. That left one more along with half a dozen full clips and at least two knives.

"Are you going into battle?" I asked, completely enthralled and totally terrified.

He stopped and glanced at me. "Preparing for as much as I can."

Preparing.

I continued to watch him and realized that it was for that rarity he talked about—a firefight. If there was, what would happen to me? Caught in the middle, nowhere to go and no way to defend myself?

"What about me?"

He quirked his brow. "What about you?"

"I'm just going to be left undefended?"

"Lacey, this is a precaution. This is being prepared for the what ifs I can't answer. The control I'm lacking going in there with little to no information other than this is where Four last was seen."

There was no John Doe in the area, no found bodies. No evidence Four was alive or dead.

I nodded, but I couldn't help but worry. I was on board for Six killing me, but the prospect that it could happen by someone else didn't sit well.

It all may have been a precaution, but as I watched him put a vest over his T-shirt, the panic began to grow.

"You're wearing a bulletproof vest?" I scrunched my brow at him while he pulled on the Velcro straps.

"We're going into the unknown. I don't like that. I'm a killer, not stupid."

Fair point.

"I hadn't seen you wear one, so I guess I assumed you were that badass."

"I am that badass. But I'm also a badass who has enough bullet wounds in his torso."

True. There were at least five.

He threw another shirt on top of the vest, then paired it with some cargo pants in which he stuffed the extra clips. Setting his foot on the chair, he attached the smaller gun with what appeared to be an ankle holster.

Shoulder holster on, knife strapped to his other ankle, and the last gun he had prepped stowed in his waistband. He threw on a jacket and stashed the second knife into one of the side pockets of his pants.

Seeing as he was getting ready to go, I got ready as well. However, my options were extremely limited.

A sundress.

And a jacket.

Flat strappy sandals.

Cherry lip balm and a bottle of water.

Oh, yeah, I was a force to be reckoned with.

I held my arms out and motioned between us. "There is a major imbalance going on here."

"Don't worry. I've got you covered."

It was odd, but his words did relax me. Because I'd seen his brutality first hand. The safest place for me was next to him.

After about fifteen minutes of driving, civilization fell completely away, replaced by the barren desert landscape. The flat of the bowl shape that the city sat in morphed into rocky hills and cliffs.

Asphalt gave way to bumpy dirt roads. What seemed like driving into nothingness opened up to a large metal structure. Concrete exhaust towers, flanked by steel and rock from the hillside. Large conveyor belts reached for the sky, moving from one tower to another.

Bright lights flooded the exterior, cutting through the dark. Its dayglow ways reminding me of the strip.

Two cars sat in what appeared to be a parking area, but based on the dirt, anywhere was a parking spot.

Six's fingers drummed on the wheel as he drove around at near idle speed. After a minute, he threw the car in park and turned to me.

"Stay behind me," he said in an almost whisper.

"That sounded almost chivalrous."

He turned to me with his usual blank face. "I just want to fuck you later, and I'm not into corpses."

I pursed my lips and nodded. "I guess I'm flattered that my pussy means that much to you."

"Don't be. It's a convenient hole."

What was I thinking earlier? Fucking bastard.

Smacking a psycho killer across the face hard was probably not advisable, no matter how much he deserved it. Seeing as I didn't want to be a rotting corpse in the desert, I swallowed the urge and got out of the car.

It was about fifty feet to the nearest door, and Six's cautious steps were somehow creepy and sexy at the same time. He put his head up to the door, and when he didn't hear anything, turned the handle and pulled it open.

It creaked, echoing off the metal walls and up the stairwell that we walked in to.

It was a little odd walking right into a staircase instead of a room like I expected, but it was probably just the door we chose.

Each step up the metal grate stairs was a soft clang, making more noise than I felt comfortable with.

Reaching the second story platform, Six reached for the handle, but it wouldn't turn. He didn't say anything, just continued up the next flight of stairs.

Same thing.

Looking up through the railings, there were at least three more possibilities before we had to retreat back down. Luckily, third was a charm, the handle clicking.

He pulled the door open a tiny bit and listened. When I assumed he heard nothing, he slowly opened the door and glanced out.

My senses were on full alert as we passed through the doorway into the hall. Listening, looking, feeling for anyone.

Six pulled one of his guns out and held it at his side as we moved through the hall, checking doors as we went. Finally, one opened up into a large room filled with conveyor belts and other large equipment.

Maneuvering through it all was tricky and hot. The temperature seemed to be rising as we moved around, making our way to the other side.

Six stopped a few feet from one of the doors, and I almost ran in to him.

"What?" I asked.

His head was tilted, a serious expression on his face as he listened to something I couldn't hear or decipher over the machines in the room.

"Fuck."

"Six?"

Before he could respond, one of the other doors opened and a team of men in what looked like S.W.A.T. gear came rushing in.

Shit!

"Run!" he yelled with a push on my back.

Gunfire, followed by the ping of bullets ricocheting around had my arms flying up around my head and my eyes fighting to close. One foot in front of the other, flight response adrenaline propelled me down the hall, blood thumping in my veins.

Fingers wrapped around my arm and yanked me, pulling me down another hall. We slipped between two large crates and through a door. There were empty desks and miscellaneous furniture stacked, filling the room.

I leaned against one to catch my breath, my heart hammering in my chest. All the fears I had made sense. There were half a dozen guys shooting at us, and the only protection I had was a thin layer of cotton.

"Shit," Six cursed.

"Who are they?" I asked, still listening at the door for any signs that they were headed our way.

He moved around the room, looking for something. Probably another way out, but being a storage room, I doubted he would find one. Though, there were some large panel glass windows which overlooked the outside.

"Not friendlies."

I rolled my eyes. "That's a duh. What gave it away?"

"Lacey." His voice held that edge of warning.

I canned my sarcasm. "What are we going to do?"

His jaw ticked, teeth grinding. There was a lack of control of the situation, but I was certain he could handle it.

"There's a fire escape." He didn't seem to be talking to me, but to himself.

"With a building this big, there better be."

His eyes narrowed on me. "Normally I don't have baggage to carry around."

"Cattle. Baggage. Yeah, I know, I'm a burden." One step forward, two steps back. "If you'd give me one of your guns, maybe I wouldn't be such a hindrance. I could help, you know."

"By shooting me?"

"Really?" I threw my hands up in the air. "We're being chased by half a dozen lunatics with Uzis. I don't stand a chance against them, and I highly doubt they'd help me out. Plus, I've somehow grown kinda fond of your psychotic ass. Especially when being shot at by other people."

He stared at me with that emotionless expression while he contemplated what I said. "It is a nice ass."

I rolled my eyes. "Gun for some head?"

"I'll get head from you anytime I want." Reaching behind him, he pulled out a gun and presented it to me, grip first. "There are seventeen rounds. Make them count by actually hitting something and not me."

There was a surprising heft about the metal in my hand. Probably about two pounds.

It was the first time I'd held one, and there was a wave of fear and excitement that moved through me. In my hand was a match for the gun he constantly pointed at me.

"Where's the safety?"

Six's brow scrunched up and he let out a chuckle. "There's no safety."

"What do you mean?"

"A lot of guns are made without external safeties these days."

"Oh." I took it in one hand and clasped my left hand over my right.

He stepped behind me and repositioned my left hand. "Move your thumb or you'll get slide bite and bleed all over the place." Uncrossing my thumbs, he moved my hand higher up the handle, making my left hand mirror my right. "Hold it like this. It will help offset the recoil. Use your thumbs as a guide for shooting."

"Why my thumbs?"

"We're not going to have time for you to get them in your sights. Your thumbs are closest to the barrel and pointing in the same direction. Not the best indicator, but a good guide for the right direction."

I nodded and shook a little bit. When I was a teen, I'd shot a rifle a few times, but I'd never held or shot a handgun. It sounded like a good idea, but my insides clenched. Releasing my left hand, I held it in front of me.

"One more thing."

"Yeah?"

He pulled his gun back out and held it sideways, his trigger finger was parallel to the barrel. "Get your finger off the trigger until you're ready to shoot. I don't need an accidental bullet in my ass."

I nodded and moved my finger up. Thumbs on top of each other. Point and shoot when ready.

He moved to the door, turning the handle and opening it just enough to hear and see any activity outside.

Adrenaline coursed through me, my insides shaking as fight or flight kicked in. I wanted to flight, to run my ass away from a scenario I never should have been in, but the only way to do that and live was to fight.

We had to fight our way out. Fight to live one more day before he put a bullet in me anyway.

I took a few hard, deep breaths, locked my jaw, and nodded to Six. He held his finger up to his lips and slowly opened the door, looking both ways before stepping out. Following right behind him, I let the door lightly close behind me.

In the distance, the sound of a walkie-talkie could be heard, the words gargled by the static and echo. The reverberation down the hall made it hard to determine which direction it was coming from.

Six grabbed my arm, pulling me behind him.

Ten steps and stopped.

Listened.

Continued.

When we reached a cross hall, he flattened his back against the wall, and I followed suit. I didn't hear anything, but Six didn't move, didn't even attempt to look down the hall.

He released my arm and held it out flat for me to stay, but never looked at me. All of his attention was focused as he took slow, silent steps.

Before I could blink, he grabbed on to something and pulled. A man came around the corner in time for Six's elbow to connect to the side of his face. His arm straightened and fired off two shots before aiming down to the man he'd hit for another.

The concussion wave of each shot slammed every cell in my body. My ears rang as the shots echoed around the halls.

I expected him to grab on to me again and pull, but instead he kneeled down. A few steps revealed two other bodies—all three shot in the head and dressed head to toe in black.

"Shit," Six hissed as he pulled on a thin cord that led to a box on one of the guy's waist.

I looked down the way we came and back to Six, watching as he put an ear bud up to his ear. Moving my hand in front of me, I gripped the gun with both hands, folding my left on top of my right as he showed me.

Each second we stayed there, the faster the thumping in my chest and the itch to run grew. But Six knew what he was doing, and I had to follow his lead.

The faint clopping of shoes in the distance turned my head back to the way we came. My attention focused on the sound, trying to decipher if it was coming toward us.

I glanced back down to Six who was still crouched down. He was frozen, his head angled toward the same sound.

My fingers tightened around the grip of the gun, each second seeming to pass like minutes.

"Six?" I asked in a whisper as the footsteps grew louder.

"Come on."

He reached for me and we started toward the direction the men we encountered had been heading.

I took one last glance down the hall, and my eyes grew wide as a figure stepped into view.

I'd never fired a handgun. Never even held one before. Somehow, instinct took over and I pulled my hands back together around the gun and lifted it up, my finger moving to the trigger.

The force of the shot rang through my hands as the gun kicked back. I jumped in surprise, the bullet clipping a wall.

The figure dropped and raised his own gun.

I continued to fire off a few more shots as Six pulled me. Before we were out of sight I watched the guy grab on to his arm, dropping his gun on the ground.

Elation filled me. One down, one who was hurt and might not continue to pursue us.

Time lost all meaning as we ran down the hall. Sound wasn't right, and I felt almost high.

There was no telling how many more there were. It seemed with each turn, each hall and doorway, the sounds of more were heard.

Six fired off three more shots, taking out two more men in black as we rounded a corner.

They didn't stand a chance.

I kept as close to Six as I could. When shots fired off somewhere I cringed, waiting for pain. Six turned, his arm held out, sweeping me behind him as I snapped off five shots in the direction the sound came from.

He tensed at one point, but swung us back around.

Not ten steps later I cried out as pain zipped up my leg, causing me to trip, but I managed to recover. Running became stunted, and I felt warmth slide down my thigh with each shaky step.

He stopped a few feet in front of me, ushering me through a large steel door, another few shots ringing in my ears.

Three more figures appeared at the end of the hall and my steps faltered, almost sending me to the ground. My heart stopped for a brief second before I raised the gun and pulled the trigger.

And pulled.

And pulled.

And pulled.

Two of them fell to the ground, one of them taking a bullet

to the skull. The third one bore down on us, gun raised.

I stumbled back, firing off randomly when Six moved in front of me. Two bangs and the third guy was on the ground.

There was no time to think, to process what I'd just done. The need to get away, to live, was all that mattered.

The fear and adrenaline made for a strong cocktail.

We pressed on, searching for a way out, an opening. Through one door, down another hall until we found ourselves in a large room with another group closing in on us.

"Fuck." Six raced around the room, pushing things out of his way.

The room was at the end of the hall, and it seemed it was a one-way-in, one-way-out design.

He ejected the clip from his gun and fished another from his pocket. After pushing it in, he slapped the butt of the gun and pulled the slide.

The stomping of boots grew closer and Six grabbed my arm, pulling me toward the only other way out. On the other side of a large window was a platform.

He opened the window and jumped out onto the dizzying metal grate catwalk. Sticking his head back through he reached for me, helping me out. It seemed stable enough, but my hands still shook, legs failing to cooperate, making my steps on a no-rail, probably-not-meant-for-people platform even more labored.

Six still had his arm around me when a shot rang out from within the room. He pulled me close, turning as he fired back. The groans indicated he'd struck them, but the rip in his jacket and the blood dripping down his arm told me he wasn't the only one whose bullet made contact.

There was no pause, our feet clanking against the metal below us. I tried not to look down, but with no railing, I was forced to or risked falling off the edge. Unfortunately, that also meant my eyes focused on the ground some four stories below.

My head spun and I clutched onto Six's jacket, helping to guide me.

Before we could reach the other side, a figure stepped out from around a large piece of equipment the platform was attached to. He raised his gun, but Six reached out, hitting his arm as he fired, sending bullets ricocheting around and Six's gun to fall from his grip.

With his left hand, Six jabbed at the guy's throat, making his eyes go wide as Six grasped at his neck. Pulling out one of his knives, Six thrust it into his stomach and angled it up.

A gurgling sound came out of his open mouth. Six pulled the knife out, and when the man fell to his knees, Six kicked him in the chest, sending him down to the grate.

I stared at the man and for the first time, had no care about who he was. It was him or me. The gruesome way in which Six killed him didn't even startle me. I felt a sick sort of satisfaction in knowing he could never even attempt to hurt me again. I had never seen anyone killed with such brutality, and it scared me, but excited me. Six didn't do it just to save himself. He saved me as well.

Blood covered his hand, and there was a spray of red across his clothes. He wiped the knife off on his pants before stowing it away. As he leaned down for his fallen gun, there was the sound of multiple people clamoring about the platform.

We froze, listening for the direction of the sound. It came from the window we crawled out of, so we started in the other direction.

About twenty feet from the other side, the men appeared and I raised my arm, firing off a shot at the same time Six did. One fell, but the much larger one only dropped his gun.

The clanking of footsteps behind us drew Six to turn

around, blocking me from them as he fired. The concussion of each shot jolted my whole body, almost as if I was being pushed in the back.

The hulk of a guy who was gunless scowled at me and stomped forward. I pulled the trigger, but missed. My hands shook the closer he got, and I missed again.

One of his huge, meaty fists swung out, connecting with my cheek. The force twisted my body as the momentum of my shifted weight threw me off the edge of the steel catwalk.

Time seemed to slow down, even though only a second passed as I realized there was nothing but air below my feet, that I was falling. It was still enough time for fear to grip me, for me to realize that the fifty-foot drop was probably going to be the end of me.

I couldn't even process the vision of Six jumping toward me at the same time he aimed at the asshole who hit me. It wasn't until I jerked to a halt, body swinging in the air, that I noticed the fingers wrapped around my wrist.

Six was laid out on the catwalk, arm over the edge. The bracelet on my wrist was the only thing keeping me from slipping through his grasp.

He caught me.

Six *saved* me.

His jaw was clenched tight, eyes fluttering closed.

Pain. He was in pain.

Everything flooded back to me: sound, time, gravity which was causing strain on my arm, and most of all, pulsating, adrenaline laced fear that I hadn't experienced since he burst into the lab and took me.

"Grab on," he yelled.

I glanced down, which was a bad idea, then back up. My vision spun, my heart hammering so hard, breath so ragged it felt like I was going to pass out. His grip released the tiniest bit, but the drop on my end felt like feet. It was enough of a jolt to clear my head, and I reached up to grab his hand.

It didn't work, the dropping of my arm shaking us. Pain radiated through my stretched muscles.

"Lacey, grab my fucking hand," he said through gritted teeth.

I blew out a breath and twisted up as I swung my arm.

Contact.

Calm began to settle in from my triumph as I held on to him with both hands, securing our grip.

"I can't pull you up like this."

I blinked up at him, panic settling back. "What?"

"My shoulder is dislocated. Keep a firm grip. I'm going to turn and get you high enough so you can grab on to the ledge. Then I'll be able to stand and pull you up with my other arm." He began without confirmation of my understanding, grunting as he rolled onto his side. "Grab the ledge."

A deep breath and I let one of my hands go, reaching for the curled metal edge. Once I had a secure grip, I quickly let go and connected my other hand.

Left hanging as he stood, my grip was the only thing between me and a drop of doom. I wasn't strong enough to lift myself, not hanging like that.

He stood, his left arm hugging his side. I stared up at him as he walked to the ledge and looked down at me. If he hadn't just hurt himself trying to save me, I would worry he was about to stomp on my fingers and send me falling.

But he did save me.

He kneeled down and held out his hand, and I latched on without pause. With a slow, strong pull he stood, dragging me back onto the catwalk. The second I could, I hitched one leg up, then the other.

Once standing, I threw my arms around him. He couldn't hug me back, but his good hand did wrap around my waist.

The moment I pulled back, my jaw was in his grip, moving my face as he surveyed the damage.

His gaze met mine, and I was almost dumbstruck by the intensity. "Are you okay?"

I nodded. "It hurts. My leg was shot and my arm is sore, but I think I'm fine."

He nodded. "We need to get going."

"What about your arm?" I asked, noticing the way the left shoulder of his jacket didn't look right, his arm hugged tight against his torso.

"It'll have to wait," he said, looking down and then up to the window.

"Don't you need it?"

He shrugged with his right shoulder. "Maybe."

"I lost your gun," I said as we headed toward the far window, realizing my hand was empty.

He bent over and picked up one of the men in black's and handed it to me. It was larger, heavier, but I felt better with it in my hand than without.

Maybe that was how Six felt all the times he had to be without his when we traveled.

The halls were quiet, but we continued with our cautious steps, avoiding bodies as we went. At every corner we waited for the sound of more footsteps.

The stairwell was empty, as far as we could tell, and we descended each floor as quietly as we were able. It was difficult, the searing pain in my leg flaring with each step.

When we made it to the bottom, he opened the door an inch. Confident that it was safe, we crept out.

There wasn't the sound of another soul in the building.

Did we kill them all?

The thought had my stomach twisting. The words *we* and *kill* together.

I killed.

Without hesitation.

Truly doing anything to survive.

Even taking another life.

We made it out to the parking lot without incident, which only seemed to confirm that everyone inside was dead. There were two large black SUVs parked behind us. Vehicles that obviously weren't there when we arrived.

Where were the owners of the two other vehicles? The ones that were there when we arrived and still remained in their spots.

Questions for later as we rushed across the dirt.

Silence as we got into the car and peeled out.

THE ADRENALINE WAS WEARING OFF, THE PREVIOUS HOUR playing on loop. My ears hurt from all the shooting, and I probably had a little bit of hearing damage.

"Was that a wetwork team?" I asked, remembering the term he and Jason used.

He nodded. "They knew we were coming."

"Late?"

"Four was here days ago. If he was killed there, there would be no reason to show up."

I stared at him. The gravity of what that meant was heavy. "So, there's a leak in the system."

He nodded again. "That many men? They wanted to make sure I didn't leave."

"Why?"

His grip on the wheel tightened. "That's the million dollar question. Two of us, maybe three, are dead. Hunted down and killed."

"You're contemplating something," I said as I studied his expression.

The muscle in his jaw jumped. "You said Three probably drank the drugs."

"Yeah."

Six shook his head. "I just don't see that happening."

"Why?"

"We're all very careful, paranoid, about where our drinks come from."

"You drank from the bar." He'd ordered for the both of us.

"But I kept careful watch over where he was pulling it from."

Well, shit. "What do we do now?"

"First thing is get patched up. You're going to have to go into a drugstore and get us some supplies."

I hadn't been anywhere on my own in two months that wasn't a hotel room. "Me?"

"You're less bloody."

I looked at him, then down at myself. People would be wondering where the body was, while I just looked injured.

A half hour later, we pulled into a drugstore and I climbed out of the car. Six handed me a few twenties and listed off some necessary items.

There was no covering up the wound on my leg or the trail of blood, and as I walked in, I tried to think up a plausible scenario.

Dog scratch? No, too big.

Rope burn? Too bloody.

Cooking accident? Yeah, right.

Blowtorch experiment gone wrong? Not in my outfit.

A few heads turned my way as I hobbled to the first aid section. With the adrenaline gone, the pain had settled in.

The odd bit of relief I had from the small amount of freedom was strange. Six wasn't there breathing down my neck, making sure I didn't step out of line.

Six said he had some supplies back at the hotel, but gauze and a larger bottle of hydrogen peroxide was needed. He also needed a sling for his arm, and we both needed some Biofreeze for muscle pain. Some aspirin, a few cold bottles of water, and I hobbled my way to the checkout, picking up a bag of M&M's as I greeted the checkout clerk.

"Oh, honey, what happened to you?" she asked in a sweet southern accent.

"Contact burn." The words popped out and were quite perfect. It was possible I leaned against something super hot, burning off the top layers of skin.

Then again, I hadn't actually taken a good look at it.

She looked down at my basket of goodies and nodded. "This should help. Maybe throw in some tequila shots to take the edge off."

I smiled at her. "That's a great idea. Thanks."

Change in hand, I headed toward the door just as a cop walked in.

The expression about blood running cold was very applicable.

He smiled at me, and my lips twitched to match. I watched his eyes widen.

"Are you okay, Miss?"

I held up my bags and smiled. "Yup. Teach me not to pay attention when my boyfriend tells me something's hot."

He let out a little chuckle, but the humor didn't spread to his eyes.

"You should let a doctor take a look at that."

I nodded. "First thing in the morning. Have a nice night!"

I was out the door before he could respond and searching for the car. Six had moved around the corner of the building, and I quickly climbed in.

"Go. I don't think he bought it."

There was no pause, no questions. He understood. He

made sure not to cross in front of the storefront in our getaway.

"Think it might be time for a new car," I said once we were a few miles away.

Six let out a surprising laugh and shook his head.

"What?"

"You're officially my companion."

I blinked at him, my brow scrunching. I couldn't decide if that was a good thing, or a bad thing.

Over the course of the evening, I had done many things that were not Paisley like. The dynamic in our strained relationship had changed.

It had been changing for weeks, but it was the first time I'd really noticed how much.

And how much I was losing myself.

But that was part of the bargain, I supposed.

Anything to survive.

The moment we were back in the motel room, I set the bags down and grabbed some towels from the bathroom. Six was trying to work his jacket off, but it wasn't cooperating. I grabbed both sides of the collar and flipped it over his shoulders, allowing him to let it slide off his arms and down to the ground.

His right arm was painted in rust-colored trails while the left shoulder was dropped and hanging at an awkward angle.

"How do we fix this?" I asked, motioning to his arm.

"It's easy," he said as he lay down on the floor. He moved his arm out. "Grab hold around my wrist and put your foot under my arm."

I sat down and removed my sandals, my own rust-colored leg stretching out so I could tuck my foot just under his armpit. I took hold of his arm and waited.

"Don't yank, just pull slowly. Roll it. Arching up, like in a swoosh." He demonstrated the motion with his good arm, and I nodded in understanding.

I began to pull, moving just as he instructed. He made no sound, his breath even. I stared at his shoulder as I continued to steadily rotate. When the skin bulged and his shoulder moved back into place, he made a small grunting noise as he blew out a breath.

He sat up and turned to me. "Thanks."

"Has that happened before?"

He rotated the arm around, testing out the motion. "A few times."

"What happens when you're alone?"

"I can do it on my own, it's just easier with another person."

He stood and grabbed hold of the hem of his shirt, pulling it away from his chest.

My eyes widened as I noticed multiple tears in the fabric. I grabbed hold of the fabric and stretched it out, looking at five holes.

He pulled it off and underneath, imbedded in the bullet-proof vest, were five mashed pieces of metal in the same spots as the holes.

My mouth dropped open as I stared at the remnants of five bullets that would have killed him had he not been wearing the vest. In the back of my mind I remembered a few times where he seemed to step back due to what seemed like a strong force.

They were all times he had been shielding me from them.

Yanking on the Velcro straps, he got the vest off and threw it onto the table. On his skin were five impact points surrounded by pink areas that were turning purple.

"You took those bullets for me," I said as I stared at the blossoming bruises. He didn't respond, turning his attention to the bags. "Why? And why didn't you just let me fall? Either of those, and I would've died and you wouldn't have to bother doing it later."

His forehead crinkled a bit, and his lip twitched. "I'm not ready to let you go."

In a move that surprised us both, I threw my arms around his neck and pressed my lips to his. It took a moment, but his hands moved to my waist.

The second our mouths parted, tongues touching, something ignited in both of us. The force of his kiss arched my back as his hands moved up to my ribs, fingers spread, flexing as he lifted me from the floor. I drew my legs up, wrapping them around his waist as my back hit the wall.

He pinned me there with his body. Low groans rumbled in his chest as he tried to suck the life out of me through my mouth.

We parted for breath, eyes locking for the briefest of moments. His were heavy and dark, filled with lust. His mouth latched on my neck in hot, wet, teeth scraping nips as he worked his way back up to suck on my bottom lip.

My pussy ached for him to fill me. Heat flooded every part of me, my blood burning for him. Need wasn't a strong enough word for my body's cry for his skin on mine.

Frantic hands reached between us, but all I could concentrate on was his mouth. A nudge between my thighs, then a thrust, and everything was fuzzy. Thoughts stopped.

"Fuuuck," I groaned, my eyes fluttering.

The first push always got me.

There was no pause, his hips rocking back and forth, pushing and pulling him in and out. His hands dug into my ass, holding me to him as he leaned in and rammed his cock into me, knocking me into the wall like he was trying to fuck me through to the other side.

My fingers curled up, nails digging into his skin.

Hard. Rough. Primal.

Base instinct fucking, and I'd never felt anything so good.

Every cell tingled, my body moving on its own and submitted to the onslaught of his cock trying to destroy me. All I knew was one word—

"More."

More pleasure, more need, more of his cock. Faster, harder, until I couldn't stand.

His entire body was tense from the beginning, and strained even tighter with every passing second.

A shuddering whimper tore from me, every muscle clamping down. Mind wiping pleasure as my head fell back and a scream tore through me.

Hot breath fanned across my neck in waves as convulsions shook me along with his quickening thrust. The groans moving through him made me moan in response.

Fucking sexy.

A few more hard pushes and he slammed into me so hard, I heard the drywall make a crunch.

Teeth bared, muscles locked down, he let out a loud, stuttered groan. Each pulse of his cock pushed him as deep as he could possibly go.

His body shook as he came down, relaxing and falling against me. I couldn't keep my legs up and he couldn't hold them or me any longer, so we slid down to kneeling on the floor.

As I came down, catching my breath, the pain of my injuries started to flare.

"I should give you a gun more often," Six said against my neck.

I let out a small chuckle, my body nothing but jelly.

Yes, he should. Especially if it led to more of that.

The next day my hands hurt. An ache in the muscles needed to fire a gun. Muscles I didn't normally use to such an extent. My thumb muscles were the worst. They didn't want to move much, and I understood the struggle of all creatures without opposable thumbs.

The shooting did the majority of the damage, but I was certain holding my body suspended on the edge of a metal catwalk fifty feet above the ground didn't help.

My leg was sufficiently cleaned and wrapped, Biofreeze and aspirin working on my shoulder muscles and the lump on my cheekbone, along with the cramps from my period that started in the night.

Six's chest was painful to look at, the bruises fully in black and blue hues. He said he felt fine, the vest did its job. His arm was also wrapped in gauze, the other in a sling.

And after a lot of work and pain, all of the blood was gone from our skin.

"Fuck, this is hard," I cursed as I pressed the bullet down with my useless thumb. "How many clips do you have?"

His brow scrunched as he leaned against the headboard loading another. "Clips? There are no clips here."

I held it up and waved it in front of him. "Then what am I loading?"

"A magazine."

I quirked my brow and wrinkled my nose. "That sounds weird. And if they're magazines, why do they always call them clips in movies?"

"Because that's Hollywood. I'm sure some high-up long ago

decided clips sounded better and the average Joe wouldn't know the difference."

Sounded logical.

"What's a clip, then?"

He held up the *magazine* he was loading. "This feeds the gun bullets. A clip feeds magazines, which…"

"Feeds the gun bullets." I rolled my eyes and shook my head.

He smiled and nodded. "Good girl."

"Do I get a cookie?"

"No, but if you keep playing that way, you'll get a cock."

"Well, you know how much I like that." I pressed down the next bullet, only the fifth one, but I couldn't get it down before the two rounded sides slipped off each other. I tossed the bullet down onto the bed and put my poor thumb in my mouth. "Thith thucks."

He chuckled and raised his brow as he held up the magazine in his left hand and a bullet in his right. "The trick is to press down on the back of the last bullet, then press down the tip with the new bullet and slide it back with your thumb."

He demonstrated the action a few times, and I glared at him when each bullet seamlessly slid in.

Taking my thumb out of my mouth, I picked the bullet up from the bed and tried to recreate his actions. With the strength in my hands gone it was difficult, but pushing on the back of the bullet did help.

It took some time and a lot of whining, but I finally filled the magazine with as many bullets as would fit.

In the duffle bag of doom, he had a least a dozen empty magazines along with a couple boxes of ammo. The empty magazines from the other night were just left there, thrown away, which was probably why he had so many.

I spun one of the bullets in my fingers. On the flat end there was some writing which seemed to indicate the caliber and man-ufacturer, as the name matched the box I pulled it from.

The tip had a divot in it. "Why does it have a hole in the top?"

"It's called a hollow point. When the tip hits water the bullet flattens out, slowing it down and stopping it from passing through the body."

My jaw dropped as I stared at him. "What's a full metal jacket then?"

"The tip comes to a point and isn't hollow. Without that tip to slow it down, it can rip right through a body."

My eyes popped open. "Oh my God!"

"Sometimes it's better than having the bullet lodged in your body. Trust me."

"You took those hits like they were nothing."

His head tilted to the side, and I watched the muscles in his jaw jumping. "I've probably been shot over fifty times."

"What?"

"With the vest on I'm not as worried about being shot, which gives me an advantage."

"So…you willingly take them? Take the risk?"

"Whatever to get the job done. After the first time, you know what to expect. You lose some of the trepidation."

"That leads to cockiness."

He shook his head. "No. Confidence. By wearing a vest, I've greatly reduced my target zones. Accuracy decreases with less area. I'm more confident in my survival chances. Cockiness gives the wearer the belief that they are invincible, and stupid mistakes are made."

It made sense. Six didn't do reckless.

Even in a situation out of his beloved control, he wasn't flustered. Cool and calm, and with deadly force. He knew everything that was going on. Knew where his targets were. Knew when to reload.

"Why does the slide stay back when there are no more bullets?" I asked, remembering the night before when he switched magazines.

He picked up one of the guns and slipped in one of the empty magazines, then slapped the bottom. He then pulled on the slide until it stayed back. "See that tab there." He pointed to a small piece of metal sticking up in the slide. "When there are no more bullets to load in that pops up, holding the slide back."

He ejected the magazine and released the slide before replacing it with a loaded one. "Now the gun is loaded but not chambered."

"Meaning?"

"Meaning there's no bullet ready to go." He pulled on the slide and that familiar sound filled my ears. "That's cocking the gun. The hammer is now in position to fire."

"Huh. Do you walk around with it not ready to go?"

He shook his head. "That's a bullet in my ass waiting to happen."

My lip twitched before a full, loud laugh sprang from my chest as the image popped in my head.

Gripping the magazine, I tried to slip it in the slot, only to have to turn it around because it was backwards. I pulled on the slide—no easy task—and released.

But it didn't go back all the way. My lips pulled to the side as I inspected it, trying to figure out what was wrong when Six reached out and took the gun from me.

"Out of battery."

"Battery? There are no batteries."

A loud laugh sprang from him, one I'd never heard before. "No batteries." He pulled the magazine out and pulled the slide back, a bullet popping free. "The slide stays back because the gun is recoil driven. If there is a bullet that isn't properly seated, the slide doesn't fully return, and can't be fired… Well, most of the time."

"And the rest of the time?"

"Basically the gun having a mini-explosion in your hand."

"Ouch." I stared at the smile on his face. It was natural and easy and new. "You like talking about guns, don't you?"

He nodded. "How can you tell?"

"Because you're all casual with me, not lifting up a bullet and telling me that it was mine and how you were going to put it in my skull. That, and I've never seen you smile like this."

The smile dropped, the fun fading. He was not amused.

"Right on all counts. I love talking about guns," he picked up one of the bullets and, just as I described, held it out, "and this *is* still coming for you."

"Why?"

"Because until then the job isn't done."

"Can't you just say you killed me?"

He shook his head. "It doesn't work that way."

My gaze moved from him down to the bed, watching as he gathered up all the full magazines and guns, placing them back in the bag.

"I already let your boy toy live, which goes against the job."

Boy toy? "Digby?"

He nodded. "You two were pretty cozy. He obviously means a lot to you." He scooted down the bed, settling in for a nap.

"He did. I just… I wasn't as in love with him as I thought." A nap sounded like a good idea, so I fell next to him onto my back and let out a heavy breath. My whole body was exhausted. "But I didn't want him to die because he happened to run into me."

His gaze turned my way, brown eyes studying me. "Such a

strange, selfless creature."

"No, I'm pretty selfish, actually."

Turning onto my side, I ran straight into his arm. My bottom lip jutted out, and I lifted up his arm and snuggled into his side, resting my head on his chest.

He didn't say anything, but his fingers did brush my hair back.

I PULLED BACK THE DRESSING ON MY LEG AND CRINGED. IT wasn't pretty. It was healing, but I kind of expected it to look better after a week.

We stayed in the motel room the entire time, with only one trip out to a grocery and to switch out cars. Laying low in an entirely different fashion than before.

And by switch out, I meant steal. It wasn't one of the set-up, ready and waiting ones.

During that time, he tried to get more information about Four while I learned the mechanics of guns, from safety to disassembling and cleaning. Not to mention the cabin fever that was beginning to consume me.

"Does this look okay?" I held my leg out, and he stood up and walked over to examine it.

His hand ran up the inside of my thigh as he took hold of my leg and turned it in the light. "It's healing nicely. How does it feel?"

"The pain is pretty much gone, just depends on how I move the skin."

He nodded. "Sounds about right. You should keep that off, let it get some air."

I moved to resting on my knees, then placed my hands on

his waist, working my fingers under until they met skin. Slowly, I moved my hand up his abs, etching into memory the warm, hard flesh beneath.

"Then you should too."

He smirked at me and cupped his hand around my neck, thumb under my chin, angling my head back. Twisting my head, I placed an open mouthed kiss on the pad of his thumb, flicking it with my tongue.

There were so many tells to his arousal—parted lips, labored breath, clouding dark eyes, and the primal edge to his touch. Then again, he could go from zero to sixty in a few seconds.

"My bruises don't need to be aired out."

I swirled my tongue around his thumb. "No, but your wound is under your sleeve. It's best if we just take this off." I pushed again on his shirt.

"Are you bored? Want me to shove my cock in you for a while?"

"If you're feeling up to it."

"I'm always *up* for it."

I pulled on my bottom lip with my teeth as I smiled up at him. "Then why are you resisting?"

Normally he would have his hands and mouth all over me by then, body covering mine, hips rocking against me.

"Because it's going to have to wait."

"What's up?"

"Lead. We need to check it out," he said. I sighed and pulled away, but Six jerked me to him, lips inches apart. "But when we return, we're picking back up."

I smiled up at him. "I like that idea."

Back to the strip we went, this time parking the car in a back parking garage and walking in versus valet. We also weren't dressed to the nines, just some everyday wear. Something to hide our wounds.

The Luxor had a huge open area with rooms lining the edge of the pyramid. My eyes ate everything up, the slot machines calling my attention.

If only it was a normal situation and I could spend a few hours trying my hand at the various games. Them's the breaks when you're tied to a CIA hitman.

We loaded into an elevator with half a dozen tourists, bound for the fourteenth floor. Six was all business and quiet as we made our way to room 14207. I still had no idea what we were doing there or who was inside.

He knocked on the door, and we waited. A few people passed by and I looked over the balcony onto the huge area, taking in the stand that sold the yard of margarita.

Oh, what I wouldn't have done for a strawberry one.

He knocked again, and once again there was no answer.

We were in Vegas, after all. Did he expect them to stay in there waiting?

His jaw locked, the muscle bulging, accentuating his sharp jawline. Such a public place with so many cameras, and then to be stood up? Not a happy killer.

To avoid being noticed, we left, heading back through the throngs of drunk vacationers to the parking garage.

"What do we do now?" I asked as I tossed my hair up into a ponytail. It was hot out that day, even in the black of night.

Six frowned at me. "We need to touch up your hair."

It had been two months since he bleached my strawberry-blonde-turned-brunette hair to platinum blonde. With my hair back, my roots showed that much more.

"That's the next step?"

"No, but pulling your hair back, I see how much it's grown out," he said as he reached behind him.

"You probably don't have to deal with that much, being a guy and all."

Six's arm snapped up, gun ready to put a bullet in someone, and I jumped. I didn't hear or see anything, but apparently his super-duper self did.

He stepped in front of me as a man came around the corner, also holding a gun out.

"It's been a while," the man said.

I peeked around Six's waist to find a man who looked to be in his early forties. He had the lines of age and graying temples of his brown hair. Overall, add in the suit, and he looked very distinguished.

"It has," Six said in response.

"Why are you here?"

"I'm looking for Four. You?"

The man lowered the gun, and Six followed suit.

"I'm here on a job."

"Four?"

He shrugged. "There was no name, only a place."

"A morgue?" I asked from behind Six, curious if my guess was right.

The man craned his neck to see me. "Stray?"

I rolled my eyes. Seriously? Were all of them assholes?

"She's pretty tame now."

"She's right."

I stepped out from behind him and resumed walking toward the car.

"Lacey." It wasn't a question, just a name. Almost like Six was saying stop. Hell, it wasn't even a warning.

I turned back to them. "My pussy is only one reason I'm still alive, remember?"

Six started walking, and the killer guy followed suit. It was almost midnight, which if it were run like my lab, would be a minimal crew. Then again, it was Las Vegas, a place where the strip was open just about twenty-four-seven.

All I knew was that if there was another Cleaner, then everyone in that building was dead. Going late at night was the only way I was going to save the most people. There was no stopping them from killing the staff, so my objective was for them to kill as few as possible.

Wetwork teams were different from innocent bystanders.

Which led to the fucked-up state of my mind that I was actually helping them kill.

But that wasn't right either.

There. Was. No. Stopping. Them.

That was what I knew as truth. There was no way for me to change their minds or divert them. All it would do was get me my bullet that much faster.

Deals with devils.

The whole situation I was in was fucked up from day one, and now I was bartering lives.

"Who is he?" I asked once we were in the car.

"Seven."

One. Three. Five. Six. Seven. Nine.

The Sesame Street Count would not be happy with my counting skills. Only single digits had been mentioned and though I hadn't seen him, I did know Eight was killed in Indianapolis and we were searching for Four.

"So Seven is better than you," I said, remembering our conversation in Tennessee. His lips formed a thin line. "Is that wounded pride I see?"

"Seven is marginally better than me. Like I said, with a group like ours, there is very little that separates the top from the bottom."

"If you're so close, how did they rank you? Is it possible to climb ranks? Like, can you become Nine? Or can Nine fall?"

The sure sign of his annoyance showed—the dreaded jaw clenching—and he took a turn a bit on the fast side. Just to jostle me, I was sure.

"Why the sudden curiosity?"

"Well, according to all your buddies, I am a cat."

Nothing. Seemed he would still only answer some questions.

He sighed and glanced at the rearview mirror. "When we get in there, stay behind me."

I glanced back as well. "You don't trust him?"

"I don't trust anyone."

Walked right into that response.

"Changing the subject won't stop my questions, you know."

He glanced at me. "Yes, you've been annoying me with them for two months. I've already told you too much."

"Who am I going to tell?"

With another right, we pulled into a parking lot, the sign lit up in the headlights—Clark County Nevada Coroner's Office.

There were only a handful of cars in the parking lot and only a few more than that of illuminated windows in the building. Six pulled a silencer out of the glovebox and screwed it on the end of his gun.

I pulled the door handle, popping the door open, but Six grabbed on to my arm. The look in his eyes when I met them was the same deadly cool and calm from when he burst into my lab.

"Don't try anything. Don't say anything. You are here for one reason and one reason only. Anything out of line, and you'll be just another body in the wreckage."

I nodded as a shiver ran through me. The relaxed atmosphere evaporated. Business. And I was a loose end.

After nine weeks, there was no way anyone would believe my story. In fact, it was getting harder and harder to see that even if I got away from Six, I'd ever be able to return to my old life.

Bottom line—I'd never be normal again, let alone see my family and friends.

Yes, I'd come to accept my situation. In fact, I'd almost turned into someone else. Paisley Warren seemed like a distant memory, while Lacey Collins was globe trotting with a hardcore bad boy sex god.

Sex god? Really, Paisley?

Asshole did have me there. I placed all the blame on having fucked one of his alter egos when we met. It totally messed me up.

Seven got out of his car, his eyes flashing to me before he stepped up next to Six.

"I was able to hack into their system earlier today."

"No cameras, then?"

Seven nodded. "I was going to wait until the morning, but due to the location…" he looked around to the built-up area "…this works better."

In the back of the building was an employee entrance that required a card to enter. Just as I was about to scold myself for not thinking of it, Seven pulled a blank card out of a backpack and swiped it. The lights on the keypad changed to green and the lock clicked open.

Good thing killers came prepared, because I really didn't want to come back when there were more people.

It hit me then, really hard.

Everyone in the building was going to die. They weren't going to let anyone out alive, all to cover up the death of one of their Killing Corps buddies.

My hands shook as we walked down the hall. When we reached the lobby, I closed my eyes and took a deep breath. There was the familiar suppressed bang of a silenced gun and the sound of a body falling to the ground.

I opened my eyes and glanced over, instantly wishing I hadn't. Slumped against a filing cabinet was a man, probably in his thirties, with dark skin and a small hole in the center of his forehead. There was a splatter of red on the wall behind him and some bits that I recognized as brain matter.

My stomach turned.

I wasn't made for unfeeling killing. Gruesome I could handle, but being there, standing next to the person who did it, knowing I would be sleeping in the same bed as him, his arms around me…

But it wasn't the first time. That wasn't the first person he'd killed in front of me and fucked me soon after.

Even with as lax as things had become, almost normal routines, I was still a captive even with my new companion status. The threat of death is what kept me beside him as much as I kept myself.

I tried to push the image out of my mind as we made our way through the building.

Tried not to think of my family and friends.

"The morgue is this way," Seven said, directing us to the large metal doors at the end of the hall.

There was another swipe pad by the door, but his magical electronic skeleton key didn't work.

"Looks like we need help," Six said.

They changed direction, heading to the other end of the

long corridor to one of the few lights on. The first room was empty, or at least seemed that way, as were the next two. Finally, at the far end, there was not one, but three people.

Two snaps as Seven and Six walked in, followed by a shrill scream.

"Get her card," Six said, his tone leaving no confusion on who he was talking to or room for debate.

I stepped between them, trying not to look at either of their fresh kills or into the eyes of their next victim.

But then I did look and there was a gasp along with my name, my real name, slipping from her lips. "Paisley?"

Fuck.

No.

I looked into soft, familiar olive green eyes. Her brown hair was up in the most perfect mussy bun like she always wore it.

Marissa Wade.

"Rissa?"

Complete and total shock rolled through me. I blinked at her as I covered my mouth. Tears started to fill my eyes.

No. Oh, no. Why? Why is she here?

They were going to kill her.

We went to college together, had the same major. We were always partnered up because our last names were next to each other. Over those years she became one of my best friends.

"What are you doing here?" I asked, my voice shaking. We hadn't talked in a long time, years really, but her Facebook status said she was still in Phoenix, and mentioned nothing about moving.

She looked between Six and Seven, and their guns out, then back to me.

"I transferred last month. What...what's going on?"

"You're going to let us in to the morgue," Seven said as he

pushed past me and grabbed her arm.

That moment, watching him drag her down the hall, was like seeing what happened to me from the outside.

"No!" I reached out for her, but I didn't make it two steps before Six's hand wrapped around my neck and he slammed me against the wall. Pain radiated down my bones when my head hit the cinder blocks behind me. The barrel of his gun pressed against my temple as I watched Seven drag her away.

"What did I say?" Six asked with a snarl.

I looked back at him. "Please, no. Not her. Please, don't kill her."

"Do you want to die with her?"

The blood in my veins froze. It was our first week all over again. Any progress I thought might have happened, especially after he saved my life, was nonexistent.

In front of me was the hardened killer. The assassin.

My eyes squeezed tight when I heard more of the distinctive snaps.

Six's fingers tightened around my throat more, causing me to gasp for air.

How could I be so stupid? Everyone Six killed had friends and family who loved them. Sure, the body count at night was lower, thus less of an overall tragedy, but I was still aiding them in taking lives.

"She's my friend," I managed to choke out.

There was no softening in his eyes, just the hard gaze of a killer.

He pushed the tip of the gun harder into my head. "Now or later?"

I swallowed hard and closed my eyes before whispering, "Later."

He released me, and my body sagged as I drew in a deep

breath. That was all I was allowed before he grabbed hold of my arm the same way Seven had Marissa and pulled me down to the morgue.

Once we got there, it was like reliving my abduction all over again.

Marissa cowered against the wall, sobbing as she stared at the fresh body and the deep red blood that seeped all over the concrete floor.

Seven opened each cooler door, pulling corpses out. The ratcheting of the drawers, the jarring slam when they reached the end.

I stood in the middle of the room a few feet from Six.

"Fuck," Seven whispered as he stared down at one of the bodies. He turned the head and looked behind the ear, the same as Six had done. "It's Four."

Six turned to Marissa. "Bring up his file," he said as he raised his gun and pointed it at her.

My chest clenched watching her shake, her steps unsteady as she moved to the computer. The shaking was so bad, she messed up the password three times before getting it right.

Seven pulled her back as Six pushed me forward. I gave Marissa an apologetic look before taking over.

My eyes perused the files. Their John Doe had almost identical attributes to ours.

"The trajectory of the bullet is execution style, just like Three," I said as I read through the examiner's notes and drawings.

Distinctive markings listed the shadow of what the examiner believed to be a removed tattoo on the right side shoulder blade, and four small black dots in the same place Dr. Mitchell found three on our John Doe.

Four markings for Four and three for Three.

Did Six have six?

"Lacey." Six's voice held an edge of urgency.

"Give me a minute." There was as little information about the victim as was in ours, with the exception of the numerous detailed prior injuries both had sustained. "It's not here."

"What do you mean?" Six asked.

I turned back to them. "The toxicology report is missing."

Six and Seven were both bearing down on Marissa. One of them was frightening enough, but combined they were literally the worst nightmare I could imagine.

"Where's the toxicology report on John Doe?" Six asked Marissa.

She could only squeak, terrified out of her mind. I pushed my way between them and stepped up to her.

"Has it been run?"

My heart broke to look at her. Tears flowed down her face from her glassy green eyes, her muscles tensed so hard her shoulders were almost in line with her ears. She was able to nod.

I stepped forward and took her hands in mine, a tear slipping down my face. "I'm so sorry," I whispered.

"Lacey." Six stepped forward and grabbed my arm again, spinning me around.

"It'll be back in the lab," I said.

He looked up to Marissa. "Show us."

Her eyes widened as Seven stepped forward and did the same he'd done earlier, and dragged her back down the hall.

I moved to follow, but Six held me tight.

"Is there going to be a problem?" he asked. I couldn't look at him, couldn't speak. Inside my torso was a tornado, twisting and tumbling my organs around. He made a growling sound. "Don't make me shoot you tonight."

I looked into his eyes. He meant it. He didn't want to kill me right then. It was still going to happen, down the line, but what he said to me when he saved me still applied—he wasn't ready to let me go. Whether that was due to feelings for me, or need for cover, I wasn't sure.

My chest clenched, for unknown-to-my-rational-brain reasons. Did I really think what he said and how he said it and what it meant was sweet? In what world? In the fucked-up one I was residing in?

The longer I stayed with Six, the more deranged I became.

We made our way down the hall where Marissa was frantically searching through a stack of files.

It was a hard thing to do on a regular day, but under a literal gun, the pressure was worse.

"Come the fuck on," Seven said with a sigh.

About two-thirds down, she was triumphant and handed the file to me.

There were so many questions in her eyes, so much confusion, but no fear of me. I wish I could tell her why I was there, but she was smart. Maybe she'd already figured it out.

I flipped open the file and scanned over the readings. Over and over I read the results, unbelieving the striking similarity.

"They're the same," I said. My memory was a little sketchy after so long away from the file, but they were close enough to where there was no denying it—whoever killed Three also killed Four.

"Shit."

I turned to look at him, to say more, when Seven raised his gun at Marissa.

"No!" The file fell from my hands.

Six stormed forward and grabbed on to my neck again, then forced me backward, slamming me onto the floor. A shot rang out, reverberating through my ear, setting off a loud ringing.

My vision blurred for a moment and everything lost focus. Six's hand was tight around my neck and I looked to my left to find a gun in his hand.

He shot. Not me, but a warning. Possibly the last one I would get. There was a turbulence and anger swirling in his eyes.

I craned my neck to the right…

Everything stopped.

Time. Breath. Heartbeat. Blood.

Empty green eyes stared at the wall, a bead of blood trickled down her forehead while a puddle formed beneath her.

"No! Marissa!"

Six squeezed hard, blocking me from screaming again.

I tried to calm down, but the tears wouldn't stop.

She was my friend.

Seven aimed his gun at me, and I froze. Six snapped up to standing and pointed his gun straight at Seven.

"You need to let the stray go," Seven said, eyes locking on Six's.

"Not yet," Six growled out.

Seven's brow scrunched. "Don't you see how it's interfering and holding you back? It's a helpless thing that's only good to fuck. Pets are frowned upon."

"I still need her. You're going to need to get some cover as well."

Seven cocked his head. "Why?"

"If it's like Cincinnati, we're going to have a firefight getting out of here."

"Cleaned?" Seven asked, his eyes growing wide.

Six gave a nod. "That's my thought."

Seven lowered his gun. "Fuck that. Nobody is getting rid of me yet."

I glanced over to where Marissa had been standing, to

where she was lying.

Dead.

All the late nights at the library, being lab partners, and going to parties together flashed through my mind. Her smile, her laugh. The day she came over after she found her boyfriend cheating on her. Graduation day when we sat next to each other, got our diplomas seconds from each other.

Never again.

Just like my memories, she was in the past. Only retrievable in my mind.

Another piece of Paisley's life that was unattainable.

Pain spiked in my head as Six yanked on my hair. "Are you here?"

I nodded, shaking another tear loose.

It wasn't over yet. We still had to make it out.

"Shit!" Seven cursed.

Six followed his gaze. There wasn't a second's pause before he snagged my hand and pulled.

We ran out and down the hall, bodies flashing by along with a blinking.

We ran, I realized, because something was wrong.

Adrenaline kicked into high gear, pulsing through me as the danger warning erupted into panic mode in my mind. Six pulled on my hand as we made it to the door, shoving me through in front of him.

We didn't stop, didn't slow down until we made it to the car. Key in the ignition, Six kicked it into drive as he slammed his foot on the gas. The car had barely lurched from the spot when I saw the fireball explode from the windows. The boom was a fraction of a second later.

The blast concussion shook the car and shattered the back window. I threw my arm up to block the flying glass as my body jolted, everything inside me giving a jump as we sped away.

I looked back and watched the spinning flames completely engulf the building.

It was then that a numbness spread through me.

Over the last two months, I'd changed and somehow forgotten how I got to where I was. How I was still alive and why.

How I was still breathing when so many weren't.

Because I'd embraced my situation, the situation forced on me. Knowing I only had a short time left, I took it as an opportunity to check things off a someday list that suddenly became a bucket list.

I was living, probably in the truest sense. More than I ever had before, because every moment counted. And because of that, I'd already done things not to be proud of and seen horrors I never wanted to.

With my fingers, I brushed out the bits of glass from my ponytail as we raced down the streets, Seven right in front of us.

We only drove for about ten minutes before pulling into a used car lot.

Getting out, Six and Seven headed right for each other as I lagged behind, shaking more bits of glass from my hair.

"How did someone know we were there?" Six asked. It was an actual question and not an accusation like I thought it would be.

Seven shook his head. "I did recon, and everything seemed legit."

"You used your computer?"

"Of course," Seven said with an edge of annoyance in his voice.

"How was Jason when you talked to him?"

"Normal."

"He didn't seem scared or on the run?"

Seven shook his head. "Same shit, different day. We joked about the casinos and how I might have trouble finding my target with all the drunks on the streets."

That didn't sound like the Jason we'd met with a few weeks ago. Given that Six and the others also had trouble getting ahold of him was solidifying their terrible theory.

Maybe Jason wasn't on their side.

Six ran his fingers through his hair. I tilted my head as I stared at him. That was his sign of worry and agitation. There was a lack of control in a situation that should have been well controlled. Not that he wasn't able to adapt and change, but that was when his idiosyncrasies showed up.

"I met with Five, One, and Nine a week ago. I know One was looking for you. We're trying to get everyone together."

"For what?" Seven asked.

"A go at Langley," Six said. I watched Seven's eyes widen a small bit. "Stay close and I'll find you when we're ready."

"Do you think we've been hacked?" Seven asked, finally seeming truly concerned about what was going on.

"I don't know, but I'd watch your back." Six held out his hand.

Seven took it and gave it a firm shake. "You, too. And get rid of that cat sooner rather than later."

My eye twitched at being called a cat again. I flipped Seven off as he moved back to his car, right as Six turned around.

He stepped up to me, his face as stoic as ever, and reached up, plucking a piece of glass from my hair.

"Let's go."

I heaved a sigh, then climbed back into the car.

It was silent the entire way back to the motel. Silent as we walked up the stairs.

Silent as we entered. Silent as I stripped off my clothes and threw on a T-shirt before climbing onto the bed.

Silent as my mind was numb.

"She would've died even if you weren't there," Six said as I stared at the wall.

No. Shut up.

"She might not have. If he'd gone in the morning like he was thinking," I said, my voice low and notably lifeless.

I suddenly found the combination checkered and floral pattern of the wallpaper very interesting.

"Then many others would have died."

Why was he still talking?

"What the fuck do you care? We're all just cattle to you. Stupid animals that roam the earth." A tear slipped from my eye, landing on my wrist.

"I know life is important to you."

I turned to look at him, my brow furrowed. "Why are you talking to me? You never do it willfully. I'm always poking and prodding, so why now?"

He stood next to the bed, arms at his side, looking almost confused. "Because you're upset."

"And? With all the times that you've hurt me, how is this one different?"

His jaw ticked, and he looked away.

"That's what I thought." I turned back to my wall.

He stood there for another minute, then moved to the bathroom.

The anger at him letting Seven kill her tore at me. I knew he couldn't stop it, and there was relief that it wasn't him who killed her, but deep inside, I wished he'd let her go.

But he didn't. He couldn't.

I knew it wasn't a possibility. They were *absolute*.

Except me.

Six had kept me alive for over two months.

The sound of the toilet flushing filled the room as he stepped out of the bathroom. There was a rustling of clothes and then a dip in the bed, the awful springs bouncing.

I wanted to tell him to sleep on the couch, but he wasn't my boyfriend.

He was my captor.

Six was an unfeeling machine of death, not a lover.

All the times we had sex held no emotional ties. They were fucking and nothing more. Just as he said—the purpose was pleasure.

Like a stupid, crazy ass girl, I began to think maybe it meant more.

When his arm wrapped around my waist, I jumped. But just as with every night, I melted into his bare chest. Molded my body to his.

Yes, he made it obvious in more than one way that night that he didn't want to kill me yet, but that didn't equate to emotional ties. I was alive because I was of use. Nothing more.

"Just because I'm a sociopath doesn't mean I don't know what love is," he whispered.

I froze as I tried to decipher his words. "Can you love?"

There was a pause, then close to my ear a very distinct. "Yes."

The breath left me as tears filled my eyes again. A heat spread through me.

What was wrong with me?

The love of a sociopath, a killing machine—was that really what I wanted?

As a tear slipped down my cheek, I knew the answer. An answer that not only scared me but made me question myself.

Yes.

SAT IN A DAZE THE NEXT MORNING.

No snarky remarks. Not even many words.

There was blackness and a fracture and a huge ass identity crisis happening within me.

The death Six and the Killing Corps dealt was real. It was rivers of blood and piles of bodies.

And I was a part of it.

I'd added a drop to the bucket that overflowed with red.

Lacey was a different person from Paisley, and the lines between them were no longer blurred by obscurity. It was hard and absolute, and cracked, because I cracked. Because I saw for the first time what I had become. The difference between Lacey and Paisley.

Lacey was a role I played, not the real me, but somehow I'd forgotten. Nothing of the last two months had been my life. The way I looked, the clothes I wore, the way I traveled, or the company I kept.

I, Paisley, had killed people.

They were people who were trying to kill me, so it was self-defense, but I couldn't forget the high and the way I fucked Six after.

"We've been here too long," Six said as he began packing up his bag.

I shook my head.

He stopped and stared at me. "You have to let it go."

"How?"

"Turn it off."

I clenched my jaw, trying to keep the tears away. "And what? Start thinking of people as nothing but cattle? I'm not fucked up like you!"

"Are you done?" It wasn't a question of if I was done ranting. He was asking if I was ready for my bullet.

I shook my head, and my face scrunched up as the tears fell.

"Then get your ass up and start packing. We need to get moving."

Anger, sadness, confusion—I was a mess of emotions. I couldn't seem to get myself together. The chaos made me want to lash out.

"Why do you care so much more about your life and the lives of the Killing Corps than people? Do you have family?"

"I have a mother and a brother."

The shock that he gave me something so personal wasn't enough to stop me.

"And would you shoot them, kill them?" I asked.

"Yes," he said with that blank face and even tone of his.

I stared at him. *Really?*

"So, you don't love anyone enough to die for them?"

"No."

And there it was. Even if he did love me in some way, it would never be enough to give his life for mine.

"Why do you assume that just because I have family that I love them?"

I balked at him. "You don't?"

"By your reaction, I should."

"Then getting back to a long ago question—have you ever been in love?" I asked, needing to know the answer. "Or even to last night. If you can love, is there anyone you love?"

He didn't flinch, didn't break, his expression as blank as before. "I've loved and I've lost, but it doesn't change who I am."

He *could* love. He *had* loved. But at the end of the day, he was still a sociopath.

"You don't miss that love?" I asked. I knew I did. "Don't you ever crave affection? Have that skin crawling need to snuggle into the arms of someone you love?"

He stopped zipping up his suitcase, pausing as he stared down at it. "I'm an unfeeling killing machine, remember? I do the job, and the job is death. Love has no place in my life or in me." His gaze moved up to me, his brow knitted as he lightly shook his head. "I do very bad things, Lacey. I'm not blind to that."

Tears filled my eyes, lips pursed as I fought the scrunching up of my face.

Broken. Bruised and my heart bleeding.

I admitted to myself I wanted his love, but at what cost to myself?

"Where are we going now?" I asked after we were loaded up in the car.

"We're staying here, just moving to the other side of town."

I turned in my seat. "People tried to kill us here, more than once, and you want to stay?"

He looked out the windows, waiting for the opportunity to

turn. "The response to the situation would be to run, to move on. That's what they'll be expecting."

I didn't like moving. I didn't like Six much right then. I especially didn't like Seven.

I didn't like anything at that moment. Everything was wrong with me and my surroundings.

The drive was silent as I stared out at passing buildings and people. The sun beating down on the desert city, baking everything in a dry heat. Strangers moved all around us who had no clue that people like the Cleaners existed.

I envied them and their ignorance.

To go back to February and take a different path. To pretend it was all a nightmare.

Six left me to my thoughts. Not that he was one for talking anyway.

Across town, in yet another piece of crap motel, we dropped our bags and moved to the table to eat some food we'd gotten on the way.

The room had more of a '70s vibe. Old wood paneled walls were dark, matching my mood. Maybe the cave was what I needed.

We sat down and ate in silence.

The night before played on a loop, from every time Six stopped himself from killing me all the way to Marissa's empty eyes.

I wiped a tear away and tried not to think about her family. Darren, her brother, was once a crush of mine, and when we were in school, they were very close, even living states away.

The devastation of not only her family, but the families of all the other people who perished. Which reminded me of Indianapolis and Cincinnati.

All the lives lost to cover up the death of three men.

Three men with a distinct marking.

"Do you have them?" I asked as I toyed with a fry.

"Have what?" he asked in return as I failed to say what I was thinking.

"The dots behind the ear? Three had them, then Four. Do you have Six?"

He stared at me for a long moment. I wasn't sure if it was awe or if he was contemplating my mental health, but it began to be a few beats too many.

Stepping forward he kneeled down, left ear toward me, and folded his lobe over.

Sure enough, in a straight line were six small dots.

"What are they for?" I asked. A curious tattoo, but it held some meaning.

He moved back to his seat and his sandwich. "Identification."

My brow scrunched as I looked at him. "But I thought you said you had none."

"Not in the conventional sense." He took another bite of his sandwich. "It's mainly for our own safety from each other."

"How so?"

"For instance, do I look like the same man you met in that bar?"

I blinked at him. No. No, he didn't. It was a cosmetic difference, but enough to change him.

"We change looks so much and don't run into each other all that often."

"Why didn't they just put a barcode on you?" It wasn't really a question, and I rolled my eyes as I said it.

"They thought about it," he said, even more deadpan than normal.

I quirked my brow and took a sip of water. "But?"

"But that would be too much of an identifying marker."

Shifting positions, I pulled one leg under the other. "So, back to a question from a while ago… can you change ranking?"

He shook his head. "No."

One word answer, which was at least an answer. With a sigh, I returned to nibbling on my sandwich. I didn't have much of an appetite, but I also hadn't eaten since lunch the day before.

"We were ranked out of fifty candidates. The top nine made the cut."

I stared at him in shock.

Twice that day he'd shared personal information. Maybe it was his way of letting me in. Could it be that he did care about me?

"Did you know what you were a candidate for?"

He shook his head. "An elite task force."

"Do you wish you'd have known?"

"The reason didn't matter. My country wanted my skills."

My country. The words didn't sound right. His country was my country, and knowing they had people like him was unsettling. That they tasked a crew of killers that seemed above all laws.

The next morning we stopped off at a pharmacy, shopping for some supplies and bleach for my roots. With each aisle we traversed, I picked up something new. Half the time he didn't say anything, the other half he simply quirked a brow at me. It was a silent question, but he didn't voice any corresponding thoughts.

The dye was the main event of our trip, a necessity to get rid of the budding strawberry blonde of my hair that had become much more noticeable. So much so, he had me wearing a ball cap.

Cherry Carmex to battle the arid weather, a few toiletries I was almost out of, a package of Dove dark chocolate, playing cards, a new book, restocking of wound care, a box of Fruit Loops, a couple bottles of green tea, and a case of water.

All logical and nothing out of the ordinary.

Then I topped it off with a stuffed animal.

Still, he did nothing.

The soft, fluffy bunny was a leftover from Easter, and my new best friend. I hugged him in my arms all the way up to the cashier. The woman on the other side of the counter didn't even look at me strange. Then again, most of what I'd purchased looked like period necessities—especially the chocolate and pre-emptive package of tampons.

That was a better explanation to a general population than depression after watching one of my closest friends murdered before my eyes.

The bunny never left my arms as we returned to the motel. It stayed even as Six sat me in a chair and worked on my hair.

I did have to let him go when I jumped in the shower to wash out the bleach, but the moment I was mostly dry, he was back in my arms.

"Lacey?" Six finally spoke after a morning of nothing.

I lifted my gaze to him. His brow was scrunched, and he stared at me in almost confusion. I supposed my sudden obsession with a stuffed animal was strange to him. He didn't seem to have a wide emotional range.

Or maybe he did, but not an understanding.

"Comfort," I said as I buried my face in the top of the rabbit's head.

I couldn't take comfort in Six, and there was nobody else.

Me, my bunny, my heartbreak, and my tears.

Crying not because of my situation, but for the loss of the person I was, all the lives in my wake, and the death of a good friend. The remaining amount of my time before I was another casualty was approaching, and I mourned myself.

Everything was changing.

Six's hips slammed against mine, causing me to arch under him and a moan to rip its way out of me.

Mouths devouring, taking, enticing with lips and tongues. Frantic, soul-eating kisses as each thrust wiped my mind, emptying out all thought.

For two days he let me mope, caught up in his own head as he talked to Five and tried to locate Jason.

Six was a man of few words, but his body spoke volumes. His hands were rough, his touch strong and hard, and he used them to turn me into a shuddering mess, begging for him.

He pulled my legs up, resting them on his arms while his hands pinned me down. Forcing me to take every slam of his cock pounding my pussy. Making me feel so much my skin tingled, muscles protested, and I forgot everything and everyone but him.

Six.

Six.

Six

My Six.

I tensed, frozen before breaking, convulsing beneath and around him. Eyes locked, there was nothing but lust and desire as I came.

He sped up, making me thrash in his arms. It was too much, too intense. I hadn't come down at all, and he was driving me insane.

His sweat covered forehead fell to my neck as his muscles strained, teeth digging into my skin, holding in a scream as hips flexed forward, bottoming his cock out. I could feel each twitch inside as his come filled me. A few shudders and his grip relaxed, his arms slipping from under my legs, and landing beside me as the weight of his chest pressed against mine. My legs had no strength and relaxed down to the bed, my arms still in the position he had them pinned.

We were both breathing heavily, both coming down from a euphoric high, our bodies limp.

I didn't know if he knew what he was doing, if he understood, but I felt awake and out of the fog that held me for days.

Fucking magical dick.

"You the man," I said in my mushy, congealed blob state. There would be no moving for a while.

He didn't say anything and no sound came out, but his chest did give a slight shake and I felt his lip twitch against my neck.

The lovely post-coital bliss was interrupted by his cell phone going off. With as much weight as he had resting on me, I was shocked at how fast he pulled off and out of me. Then again, we were sweat slicked up, and all he had to do was give a little push and the puddles could propel him across the room.

"Yes," he said into the receiver. There was a moment's pause as the person on the other end spoke. His face showed no emotion. Was it Jason? "Yes…Fine." He hung up the phone and I stared at him, waiting. "We need to shower and get dressed."

"I can't move."

He said nothing, just walked over and grabbed onto my ankle, pulling my legs off before bending over and tossing me over his shoulder.

"Shit!" I let out a little laugh that turned into a moan as I stared down at his firm ass. I wanted to smack it or pinch it, but before I could he set me down in the tub and turned on the shower.

A scream rocketed out of me as the cold water sprayed down on me and I tried to jump out, but he held out his arms and blocked me. Even in my freaking out state, I heard the little chuckle he made.

"You think this is funny?" I asked, my arms folding over my chest as I shook in the starting-to-warm water.

He didn't say anything, just nodded as he climbed in. It was tight in the small space, but we managed.

"Did you have to make such a mess?" I asked as I cleaned between my legs.

"Yes."

I rolled my eyes and shook my head. Of course he would answer with that.

It took a little longer to wash off sharing the shower, but a few minutes later we were getting dressed and heading out the door.

"Where are we going?" I asked as we pulled away.

Due to his antics, I'd forgotten to ask who was on the phone.

"We're going to meet Nine."

"Nine? He's here?"

Six nodded.

"How? Why?"

"He knew I was coming here and by the news, thought I might still be in the area."

Instead of another outlying shit-tel, I was surprised when the strip view became larger and larger until we were pulling into the parking garage of the Venetian.

"Boy, he stays in nice hotels," I said as I climbed out of the car.

"He's always been a bit flamboyant."

Hand in hand we weaved through the casino floor. His steps were confident like he knew exactly where he was going, which was good, because the place was a maze and I swore at one point we'd gone in a circle.

Sitting in a central bar was a man who hadn't changed a bit in the weeks since I'd last seen him. In fact, he looked the same as when I first met him almost two months ago. Unlike Six, the only difference I saw in Nine was the green eyes I'd seen in Paris versus the brown of Tennessee.

"There you are!" Nine gave a broad smile and held out his hand. "So good to see you again."

Six smiled back and took his hand. "How are you doing?"

The change in demeanor surprised me. Friendly was not a word I associated with Nine, but then again, Six was very friendly when I met him. The Cleaners were all great actors.

"Let's go sit over there," Nine said as he picked up his drink and started walking.

We followed, the two of them sitting in the corner a low wall created while I had my back to the casino.

"What happened here?" Nine asked, his voice changing to the hardened killer voice I knew so well.

In vague terms, Six gave him a brief overview of the wet-work team we encountered, and what happened with Seven.

"Wait… Neither of you set it up?" Nine's eyes grew almost imperceptibly wider at the knowledge that someone else set the coroner's office to explode. "And Jason sent Seven?"

Six nodded. "Gave him the access key, too."

Nine shook his head. "No." He sat back and crossed his arms in front of him. "I can't believe he would betray us."

"I can't either, but we can't ignore the signs."

Nodding in agreement, Nine downed the rest of his glass and slammed it down on the table.

"I'm going to help One search for Two since Four and Seven are now accounted for."

Six gave a nod. "I'll find Five and help him locate Jason. See if we can get some answers."

Nine glanced to me. "Why do you keep her around?" Nine's voice no longer resembled a hardened Killing Corp member, but more like a friend.

Granted, I was certain they all knew each other and some of them probably for a long time and were once friends before they were nothing but government killing machines.

"I have my reasons."

"Do you care about her?"

My heart stopped, and I waited. If he did, would he admit it to Nine? Or would that be seen as a weakness?

"Lacey isn't a topic of discussion."

Shot down.

I might never know the answer. Things weren't the same as when he took me months prior. He was still Six, still a killer, but on more than one occasion, he showed me the man beneath. The one who could care for me. The one who maybe could love me.

They stood, and I realized that was the abrupt end.

"Have you ever thought about just walking away?" Nine asked.

Six's eyes widened. "What are you talking about?"

I stared at Nine as he studied Six's face like he was searching for something. He glanced down to Six's left hand, then to mine and the rings that were for show but were never taken off.

"Nothing. Forget it." He held out his hand and shook Six's.

"Hopefully I'll see you soon."

We split off, heading in opposite directions. I couldn't help but glance back at Nine.

For the first time since I met him, he seemed almost like an actual feeling human being. Then again, facing death could do that to even the most hardened sociopath.

STATS:

- 17 – number of times I'd been called some form of cattle or sheep or a cat
- 8256 – times I tried to convince myself I was not developing feelings for my executioner
- 8254 – times I succeeded in convincing myself I was not developing feelings for my executioner
- 2 – times I failed at convincing myself I was not developing feelings for my executioner

Fuck me

Things were beyond complicated. I was a rational human being, so logic dictated that you *do not* fall in love with a man who constantly reminded you he was going to kill you.

The problem was, his dick was so good at helping me forget logic. He made me *feel* for him.

The saying is you can't help who you fall in love with, but really? Did it have to happen with a psychopathic killer?

Though I didn't think it was quite love, but…

I'd never felt as alive as I did with him.

Although I never thought I would develop any feelings

other than loathing toward my captor, somewhere along the line, I had.

Maybe I was looking too deep into what he said after he saved my life, or the fact that he *saved my life*.

The man was charming and sexy, mysterious and alluring, on top of being dangerous. All things that attracted me in the worst ways.

Heart stopping danger, swoon worthy man, and a deadly mystery.

Maybe it was Stockholm Syndrome. Maybe I was a masochist. Then again, maybe I finally found a man worth fighting for. Who knew?

Whatever it was, I was his…for however much longer I lived.

"Are you ever going to stop hugging that thing?" he asked as I sat in bed, the bunny in my lap, playing a mindless game of solitaire.

"Want me to hug you instead?"

He glared at me, and I smirked in return.

Sir Flopsalot, as I was affectionately calling my stuffed bunny, was so soft and cuddly, how could I not hug him all the time?

The fact that Six seemed a bit jealous of the fluff stuffed fabric amused me, and made me snuggle it more.

It was early in the morning, and Six had been up since before the sun trying to get in contact with Five. Simply by his agitated behavior, the talk with Nine the day before had riled up his suspicions of Jason.

One third of their ranks were gone, which would amp anyone up, but it was something Nine said that lit Six.

I let out a sigh and rolled over to reach the remote on the nightstand. He gave me a glare, but I ignored him as the TV came to life.

I didn't even get a chance to change the channel or process what show it was when I recognized a photo of the Las Vegas Coroner's Office plastered on the screen.

A few seconds later, pictures of multiple ME and coroner's offices popped up, and I unmuted the volume.

"Around the country there have been a slew of explosions to local morgues. Police are still on the lookout for Paisley Warren, a lab assistant wanted for questioning from the devastation in Cincinnati." The photo from my ID popped up, and the image I hadn't seen in months almost scared me. "There is nothing to place Warren at the site in Indianapolis or the explosion in Las Vegas, but police have confirmed that similar explosives were used at all three facilities."

My mouth dropped open, and my eyes widened.

Shit. Motherfucker. KicktheshitoutofthesefuckingKillingCorpsAss holes.

Officially wanted across the country.

I slammed my head into Sir Flopsalot and whimpered.

"It could be worse."

I turned and glared at him. "How?"

"There's been no trace of you. The police aren't even sure you're alive."

"Jason's helped with that, hasn't he?" I asked. Six nodded. "This is a disaster."

"You're overreacting."

"Really? I thought I was supposed to be your cover. How does my face being blasted all over the place not qualify as a bad thing? Dyeing my hair and sticking contacts in my eyes doesn't hide my features."

I hopped off the bed and began pacing, biting on my thumbnail.

"People aren't that observant. They see the colors first."

"Maybe, but don't even get me started on the fact that the person supposedly helping to hide me is also someone you suspect of trying to off you."

That was the moment I realized there was not one, but two guns trained on me—Six and whoever was taking out the Cleaners.

Late in the evening or early morning hours, Six's phone rang, scaring the shit out of me as it felt like I'd just drifted to sleep.

"Jason?" he said into the receiver.

I couldn't hear the words, but I could tell they were rushed, worried.

"Where are you?" He dug a piece of paper out of his bag and started scribbling on it. "Yes... Fine... I'll see you soon." After hanging up, he turned to me. "Time to get packed again."

I crawled to the edge of the bed and swung my legs over. Glancing over to the clock, I groaned at the 4 a.m. reading. "Where are we going now?"

"California."

I sighed as I sat down next to my suitcase and started loading it back up. "At least we can drive there."

He didn't respond, instead rushed around, throwing things into bags.

Ten minutes later the room was empty of every item that we brought in. Our bags were in the car, while the trash we'd collected was deposited in a dumpster a few miles away.

"Do you ever check out of motels?" I asked as we merged onto the interstate.

In the rearview mirror, the sky was lighter and I dug into my purse to pull out my sunglasses in preparation for the coming sunrise.

"No."

"No?"

"Less of a trail."

I thought about it and nodded in agreement. If someone came looking, they would only have a paid through date but nothing on when he actually left.

Our drive out of Las Vegas was beautiful, watching the landscape change from desert to almost tropical as the sun rose over the horizon.

Close to the border, we stopped for gas, and I took the opportunity to use the restroom and get some coffee. Caffeine had been a luxury over the past months, and I smiled as I held the cup up to my nose and breathed in a substance that was once my lifeblood.

Walking back out to the car, Six was staring down at his phone, his jaw clamped down tight.

"What's wrong?" I asked, pulling some flyaways behind my ear.

His jaw twitched. "Jason isn't responding."

"Do you know where he was headed?"

He shook his head and stuffed the phone away. "Come on."

Back on the highway again, I convinced him to roll down the windows, letting the warm breeze in. Sure, my hair flew everywhere, even pulled back, but I loved the calm that took over, reminding me of carefree times long ago.

"Ooh, that looks like a shit-tel," I said as we drove into Los Angeles. "Oh, there's another one." Six glared at me. "I'm just saying. Every hotel you've chosen but Paris has been the same. I assumed L.A. would be the same pattern."

"Shit-tel?"

"Yeah. Short for shithole motel. Shit-tel."

Half an hour later we pulled into another very '60s looking motel, but it looked in better shape than the past drug dealer specials.

"Better?"

I pursed my lips and looked around, pausing before nodding. "Yeah, not as afraid of stabbing myself with a stray leftover needle here."

The places in Vegas were all ripe with hard drugs, prostitutes, and gangs. Besides the guys Six killed the first day we arrived, they'd all left us alone. Then again, Six did have an aura that screamed "Don't come near me or I will fuck you up," which all but the idiots seemed to respect.

The interior of the room was an improvement. Instead of out-of-date prints or paneled walls, everything was plain. Very little color deviation, all neutral, and even the mass produced artwork on the wall was pretty bland.

Once again, it was sit and wait. We'd made it to California, but without a meeting point, we were dead in the water, which didn't sit well with Six. With nothing else to do, I pulled Sir Flopsalot out along with my book and used him as a pillow while I dug back into my story.

"You know, a watched pot never boils," I said after he'd stared at the phone for an hour, willing it to ring with some word from Jason.

He refused to look at me, but I could tell he registered what I said when his gaze flickered between the phone and the window.

With a sigh, I put my book down, marking the page with a leftover receipt. The tension coming off him was infecting the whole room and making it hard to enjoy my reading.

As I walked over to him, he glanced to me but always back

down to his phone.

"Enough," I said as I kneeled in front of him between his legs. I reached out and pulled at his belt, working it loose.

"What are you doing?"

I didn't answer until I popped the button and had the zipper down. Once his cock was out and in my hand, I looked up at him.

"You need to relax." I ran my fingers up and down his hardening length, watching his reaction.

The crazed energy that seemed to be crackling in him simmered down, his gaze no longer on his phone but intently on my actions.

"I know you don't like things to be out of your control, and what's happening is hard for you to compute." I ran my tongue up the length of his shaft. He was only half steam, but growing harder with each second. "You're a warrior fighting an invisible enemy. You always know your target." I took the head of his cock into my mouth and sucked, earning a groan and causing his body to sag a bit. "You don't cope well with blindness."

"How do you know?"

I removed my mouth and fisted my fingers around him, sliding up and down. "Because I've watched you for months. I know your personality more than you think I do."

I wet my lips with my tongue before diving back down. One hand working the base while I swirled my tongue around much of the soft, hard flesh. Sucking, licking, bobbing up and down.

It didn't take long before his hands tangled in my hair. His hips joined in, thrusting up, trying to get more of his dick inside my hot mouth.

I let go of him and let him take control. Fucking my mouth, pushing past my gag reflex, groaning when my throat tried to eject him.

My jaw started to get tired, but I didn't do anything, just let him continue to face fuck me as I tried to suck the life out of him.

"Fuck!" His hips bucked up as he pushed my head down, forcing him deeper into my throat as he released stream after stream of come down my throat.

I choked, gagging around him, but he held me there until he dropped back down to the chair, his muscles finally shedding the tension that had taken over.

Swallowing around him, I pulled back, sucking until he popped from my lips.

His eyes were closed, chest heaving when I pushed on his thighs and stood. I smiled down at him, taking in his jelly-like posture.

It was empowering to see him like that, knowing I'd brought down an elite killer with the power of my mouth. There was a smile on my face in the mirror when I walked into the bathroom and wet a washcloth to clean my face.

"Lacey?"

I turned back to him, still in the position I left him, as I wiped all the saliva and escaped drops of come from around my mouth. "Hmm?"

"Thank you."

I froze and stared at him as I lowered the towel and blindly sat it by the sink.

Two small words that in my old life I was used to using and hearing multiple times a day. But hearing him say them, to me, after all the time we'd been together, made my chest clench.

There was no thought, just my body taking me back to him. Leaning over, I stroked his face with my fingers before pressing my lips to his.

When I pulled back, his eyes opened. I thought there might

be some emotion there, but if there was, he'd buried it.

Nothing but empty brown eyes that gave nothing away.

Another four hours later, after grabbing some lunch and Six's tension growing again, I couldn't take it anymore and jumped in the shower.

It was the only thing that got me out of the same space as him and helped me to relax some.

Six wasn't the only one nervous. Meeting with Jason, the one who may have been responsible for all of our near death experiences, had my stomach in knots.

I put on a strong face, because I knew how I ended my time on earth. However, with everything that was going on, I wasn't certain anymore that Six would be the one to do me in.

Three Cleaners down made all the rest of them nervous.

And nervous killers weren't a good thing.

Stepping out, I patted down and began to wrap a towel around me and walked out. I was expecting him to still be sitting, leg bouncing, waiting for the phone to ring. Instead, he stood in the middle of the room. Dark eyes stared at me as I looked down.

I'd been so distracted by him standing that I didn't even notice his lack of clothes or the hard dick pointed right at me.

"Holy shit," I whispered, heat flooding me and my pussy clenching.

I hadn't even gotten my towel all the way on when he grabbed me around the waist and hoisted me up. A scream ripped from me, but before it went for more than a beat, I was thrown down onto the bed.

My eyes were wide, staring at my attacker and nearly fucking coming from the absolutely powerful, dominant energy radiating off Six.

I watched in rapt fascination as he crawled onto the bed and tore my thighs apart. Not that I gave any resistance.

He dove down, settling between my legs. His tongue swiped up my slit making me jump when the tip flicked my clit.

"Shit!"

Spreading my lips, he shoved his mouth against my pussy, trying to fucking devour me.

Fuck.

Sex was usually a wham-bam thank you ma'am kind of event with him. Rough, passionate, and base instinct.

Eating me out had only happened once or twice since the first night when I cried out Simon.

My nails scratched his scalp, fingers tangling in his hair as I held him close, riding my pussy across his face.

"Fuck, fuck, fuck," I chanted as my thighs shook.

The suction on my clit had me screaming and thrusting my hips in the air. A shuddered cry left me and I bit onto my hand to stifle my moans.

"Stay," he said as his arms wrapped around my legs, holding me to his face.

My eyes rolled back, mouth open. Too much, it was too much.

I fell apart screaming, but he didn't stop. He continued on, easing me down as I relaxed back to the bed.

Wet trails of his saliva and my come were left on my skin as he nipped and kissed his way up my abdomen. When he reached my lips, there was no pause, no fumbling, just hot, hard cock pressing into me.

My sensitive pussy clamped down, a mewl leaving me.

"Fuck, that's good," he said against my mouth.

Nothing but the sound of skin slamming against skin echoed off the walls. My mind blank with nothing but pleasure firing off, holding any thoughts hostage. His assault on me wouldn't stop or even slow down, driving me to another orgasm at lightning speed.

I gripped the bed sheets, twisting my hands in them. Unable to take everything he was giving.

Fast, hard, frantic thrusts made the bed squeak and had my back arching as I came again. There was no reprieve as I thrashed beneath him.

Drops of sweat fell down on me, his eyes barely open, almost unseeing as he pumped into me.

"Fuck," he hissed as his hips slammed against mine, cock jerking inside me.

We were both breathing hard as he fell on top of me.

Fast and hard and done. Even sociopaths got stress and anxiety that could be cured by a good fucking.

Left in nothing but a mess of limbs. A mash of two bodies locked together.

For the second time in days, the phone rang with his cock still stuffed inside me. Still coming down, he sprang off me, come spilling out onto the bed as he ran to pick up the call.

I stayed where I was, watching his hot naked ass and his still hard cock bounce around.

"Yes." His jaw clenched, and he nodded. "Right, I'll meet you there." He hung up and tossed the phone on the table. "Tonight."

Climbing back on the bed, he fell down next to me, one arm flopping over my waist before pulling me closer. The tension was gone and finally hearing from Jason wiped him out. In what seemed like seconds, his slow, steady breath blew across my skin.

Assassin's sex drives were insane.

26

WHEN THE SUN BEGAN TO SET, WE GOT READY. SIX double checked the two guns he was going to take and grabbed two full magazines while I armed my jeans with my lip balm.

"Where are we meeting him?" I asked as I slipped on my flats.

He held the door open as I walked through. The car was parked right in front of the room.

Once out of the parking lot and on the road, he finally answered me. "Up the coastal highway, past Santa Barbara. There's an abandoned restaurant."

"Why was it abandoned?" I wasn't really expecting a response, just curious.

In true Six fashion, he ignored me. Instead, he kept his eyes glued to the dark pavement.

Once out of L.A. and past the Santa Barbara area, the traffic decreased and it became pitch black. The exception was the moon shining onto the great expanse of the ocean to our left, leaving a streak of light on the water.

It was an amazing view, the beam extending for miles. There were a few lights from boats, but otherwise it was empty.

After about an hour, he turned off the headlights. It freaked me out as we were still going over fifty on a windy, cliffy road.

"We're here," he said, his foot releasing the gas.

My eyes slowly adjusted to the black and stared out at the structure blocking the shine of the moon.

When we were stopped, I opened the door and stared out at the eerie building.

It was a large restaurant sitting on the edge of a cliff over-looking the Pacific Ocean. Six pulled out a flashlight from the car, and we made our way toward the door. As we went, I was able to see the fragile edge it precariously sat on. The cliff side was rocky, and probably a thirty-foot drop below to the water.

Six led the way in, and as we passed the front door I noticed the shadow of a sign that read *Rusty's,* but that was all I could make out.

The building was abandoned and probably hadn't been in operation in a few years, judging from the height of the weeds and grass invading the parking lot.

The wooden steps were misshapen and some dipped, threatening to break.

As we entered, the moonlight shone through holes in the ceiling and broken windows. There were a few chairs and tables, some lying on their sides, others covered in a thick layer of dust. Add in the faded artwork and cobwebs, and I half expected a ghost to appear. Talk about creep-tacular.

The moonlight helped with the lack of light, since Six was holding the flashlight as we moved through the dining area. It was two stories, the upper veranda overlooking the main area with a huge wall of windows. Beyond was a very large wooden deck overlooking the ocean.

Six was silent as we moved, listening for anyone or any-thing that wasn't us. I didn't hear anything but our steps, some creaking, and the crashing of the waves against the cliff below.

He started up the steps, and I followed behind. Up one, then flailing as I caught my toe on the second, nearly falling down.

"Shit!" I grabbed on to the handrail as I lurched forward.

Six turned, shining the light on me. He didn't say anything, and I didn't offer anything, just righted myself and continued on.

When we reached the top, he moved left while I went right. It was brighter, large skylights letting the moonlight in. Dilapidated booths and more leftover tables, complete with napkin holders and condiments, lined the wall and balcony rail.

Six moved behind me, his flashlight bouncing around, creating shadows. There was one in the dust of a table that caught my eye, but when the light moved, it remained. It was as if something had brushed against it, wiping it off, exposing the dark top beneath the layer of dust.

As I moved closer, I jumped as a foot came into view. Six stopped, his flashlight pointed at me as I took small steps forward. Legs, then a torso, dark skinned hands, and a familiar face.

"Oh my God." The words rushed from me as I stared down at the body on the floor.

It was Jason.

"What?" Six asked as he rounded the corner. He stopped just behind me and cursed under his breath.

I kneeled down next to him to examine him closer. With the back of my hand, I reached out and touched his.

The skin wasn't warm to the touch. "He's been here a while."

"How long is a while?"

I shook my head. "I'm no ME. A few hours maybe."

"It's the same as the others, isn't it?"

Was it? Walking around the body, I made sure not to touch or disturb anything.

There wasn't an exit hole in his skull. There was a crater. "Hard to tell."

I moved back around to the front and looked closely at the entry wound. Around the entrance was a ring of abrasion and another of soot. The soot was closer to the hole from the bullet at the top than the bottom.

"Close range and at an angle. The top of the barrel was closer to his skin than the bottom."

I glanced around the room and took in his position. One of his legs was bent, that foot tucked under the other leg that was straight. Once again, I stood and walked to his feet. Raising my arm, I held it at the approximate angle his killer would have if he was on his knees. Sure enough, the splatter from the back lined up.

"Same."

"You're getting good."

My brow scrunched as I looked at him. "What does that mean?"

"I figured that out five minutes ago."

"How?" He was a dealer of death, not an crime scene investigator.

"Years of practice."

"Practi… Oh." I stopped myself, understanding.

Something nagged at me as I held my arm out. Jason was about six foot.

I grabbed on to Six's arm. "Down on your knees."

"What?"

"I want to check something."

Reluctantly, he did as I asked and I held my arm out with my finger gun. "Bang!" I pushed against his forehead and after earning a glare, he caught on and fell back.

I compared the two and they were the same but one

thing—Jason's right leg was sticking out straight while Six's remained bent.

I held out my hand, and he grabbed hold as I pulled him back up. "Bring your right knee up, like you're tying your shoe."

He glanced over to Jason's body and understood where I was going. Replicating the position, I stuck my finger gun on his forehead again and pulled the imaginary trigger. Six did his fake deadfall and landed in almost the same position.

My brow furrowed, and I shook my head.

"What's going on in that brain of yours?"

I stared down at Jason. "I don't think he was expecting it. And it wasn't someone taller like you, it was someone shorter, like me."

The nine-inch difference between us meant the one who shot Jason was closer to my five-four than his six-one.

"Otherwise the bullet would be more at the top of his skull."

"He bent over, probably to tie his shoe or pick something up and when he lifted his head…*bang!*"

Six immediately pulled out his gun before reaching down and pulling the smaller weapon from around his ankle and handing it to me.

I took hold of it, pulling on the slide before wrapping my other hand around it. "Do you think they're still here?"

"Yes."

I stayed behind him as we moved through the building. Silence prevailed as we moved back down the stairs.

In the main dining area, there was a wall of sliding glass doors, and one was open that wasn't before.

We stepped out onto the deck, the floorboards creaking beneath our feet. I walked over to the banister and looked down. I could hear the waves crashing against the cliff, but they were difficult to see in the dark.

"Oh, good, Six, you're here," a female voice said from above us.

We both looked up twenty feet to a rooftop deck and the familiar blonde.

Six knitted his brows. "One?"

"Still have your little toy I see." One held her nose up in the air as she looked at me.

Superiority complex much? Yeah, she could probably kill me just as easily as Six, but her attitude made me want to slap the smug smile from her RBF.

She walked around to a set of stairs that led to a second story balcony to the right of us. It was much smaller than the deck we were on, only able to hold a few tables and was probably the smoking area at one time.

"Jason is dead," Six said, his gaze never leaving her.

One stopped in her tracks and glanced over to Six. "You found him?"

"He was killed the same way as Three, Four, and Eight."

She continued, stopping on the middle balcony and staring down at us. "The killer must be close. Do you think it was a team?"

Six stared and shook his head. "Tell me it wasn't you."

My eyes shot open, and my gaze snapped to her.

"What?" One gave an incredulous laugh. "You can't be serious."

Six's jaw ticked. "It was a .45 caliber."

"And?"

"I find it a little odd that here you are, a few hundred feet from our handler's cooling body and you also use a .45."

"Many people use that caliber." Her objection and defense was weak, even to me.

"Then tell me what you're doing here and how you got all

the way up there without me seeing or hearing you."

She paused, her lip curling up into a sneer. "He was going to tattle, and I don't like tattlers."

I stared in utter disbelief. The woman who was so pissed at me, who was jealous of me taking her attention away, who said she was so protective of *her boys,* was in on it all.

"Why?" Six asked, his voice going up in pitch and strength. There was an edge of anger and devastation.

The door leading from the second story opened, and out stepped Nine. He said nothing as he stepped to stand next to One, then stared down at us, his expression blank, emotionless. "Times change, Six. I'm tired of killing at their whim for little pay."

My mouth dropped open as I looked up at them, at the ones responsible for everything. The ones who betrayed their brethren in death. The time we spent with them, the conversations, all an act to throw off suspicion. They tried to put the blame on Jason, even while they were adamant it couldn't be him.

"There are other ways of leaving," Six said.

"Are there?" Nine quirked his brow. "The only sure way is if I clean us all. That's the only way to disappear and not be hunted down."

Six let out a harsh laugh. "So to avoid the possibility of one of us coming after you, the best decision you could come up with was to kill us all?"

A maniacal giggle escaped One. "We're the most ruthless and highly trained. You said it yourself—a Cleaner sent to clean another Cleaner."

"Haven't you put it together yet?" Nine asked, shaking his head. "Since we killed Three, Home has sent countless crews after all of us and none have been successful. Once one of us was dead, they started the chain reaction of trying to get rid of all of us. But, the only way to accomplish that is from our own rankings."

Six shook his head, lowering it as he closed his eyes, his body shuddering as he tried to hold his anger in. When his head rose again, there was an emotion I couldn't name etched into his features. "Eli…"

"No, Six. They took our names away, gave us new ones." Nine locked eyes with Six. "Join us, little brother."

Little brother?

Six glanced back to me, then to Nine. His arm snapped up, and he aimed toward them. "No. Your name is Eli, my blood, my brother, and despite that, I won't let you do this."

"When did *you* become so noble?" Nine snarled. "Fine. If you won't join me, you will die like the rest."

"I'm not noble," Six yelled, his voice rising. "You've given me a choice of joining you or joining them. I won't die by you, and I won't be ordered around like her." Six motioned toward One.

"Fuck you! You don't know shit." One raised her arm, lining her gun up to me. "Join, or I'm going to blow your fucking toy's brains out."

Nine pushed on One's arm, making her lower her aim. "I hate that it had to come to this. You're my brother, and I wanted you by my side. Family should mean something."

"If it meant something, you wouldn't be making me choose. But we both know it doesn't mean shit. This is just another fucking way for you to try and prove to yourself that you're better than me."

"I *am* better than you! I'm Nine. The best."

Six shook his head. "You're a cocky asshole sociopath that was always jealous of me."

The corners of Nine's lips curled down. "Fucking die." He

held up something in his hand, thumb pressed down, then tossed it toward us as they turned and walked away.

I recognized it, and what it was registered just as I heard the loud *boom*. I felt the wave that moved through the floorboards as the other side of the building blew out in a rain of glass, shrapnel, and fire.

The explosion rocked the deck, splintering the posts holding it up. My arms flew up, trying to keep my balance as the surface beneath my feet surged and buckled. The floor shifted, dropping down and back, holding on only by the supports to the building.

I stumbled, tripping over my feet until my hips hit the railing. It stung as I stared down at the thirty-foot drop to the ocean. The wood groaned, nails creaked, and my heart stopped. My gaze flashed to Six. He'd been about ten feet away, but now he was ten feet to the side and six feet above.

His eyes were wide, filled with what looked like fear, but Six feared nothing.

Another creak, and the banister broke away.

"Lacey!"

A scream exploded from me as my stomach flipped from the weightlessness, then came to a sudden stop a second later when I hit the hard surface of the salt water. It took me a moment before panic set in and I opened my eyes. I kicked my feet and moved my arms, but the blurry surface began fading away, becoming darker.

It wasn't working. My clothes were heavy, dragging me down. I pushed harder, kicking as I fought to surface. The pressure in my ears felt like my head was going to explode. Fire burned in my chest, my lungs begging for a breath as my mind fought for consciousness.

After everything I'd been through, death by drowning was

nowhere in the spectrum of ways for me to shed my mortal coil.

No matter how hard I swam, I couldn't do it. When I was almost ready to give in, something grabbed my wrist and pulled. It moved up my arm until my hand rested on a shoulder as I was chest to chest with him.

We broke the surface and my mouth opened wide, taking in a hard breath. There was no strength left in me, all of it concentrating on circulating the next gulp of air.

There was a stretch of beach near the cliff we'd fallen from, and Six's strong arms and the current pushed us toward it as fire continued to rain from the sky.

When we reached the shallows, Six threw my arm over his shoulder, carrying me onto the beach. The sand was soft and squishy beneath my bare feet, my shoes lost to the water. He dropped me down on my back where I continued my struggle to get oxygen back in my body. He fell onto his knees, looming over me, panting as well.

I could barely see his eyes in the darkness as he cupped my face, staring at me, his forehead dropping to mine. "Don't ever fucking do that again."

I blinked up at him. "W-What?"

"I say when, where, and how you die. Not you or anyone else, so stop trying to kill yourself."

My lips twitched into a smile before I reached out and grabbed his face, smashing my lips to his. They were salty, but I didn't care, because for the first time I realized he did.

Six did care about me.

"You like me."

His brow furrowed, and he grabbed my arm as he stood. "Come on."

I was about to protest that I needed another minute when he reached down and scooped me up in his arms.

"Are they still around?" I asked, my head leaning against his shoulder.

Another explosion rocked the cliff side, the dilapidated restaurant exploding in a fireball reaching high into the sky.

"Shit!" My eyes were wide as I stared up, the blast wave slamming into us, blowing my hair back.

The second explosion was much stronger than the first, much like the one from the coroner's office—meant to cover up all evidence.

Up in the black we heard an engine roar down the coastal highway.

Six continued walking toward a wooden staircase in the cliff's edge that led from the restaurant to the beach.

"Do you think they think we're dead?" I asked.

"I don't know."

He started up the stairs, carrying me the whole way, refusing to let me down.

When we reached the top, flames licked high in the sky, engulfing everything. Luckily, the car was, for the most part, okay. There were a few busted windows and a piece or two of shrapnel imbedded into the side. I had no idea how we would get back as we were in the middle of nowhere.

Soaked, sandy, and salty, Six set me down next to the car and we climbed in.

My teeth chattered, arms wrapped around my waist. Six reached over and turned the heat up to high. It was a nice gesture, but with half the windows destroyed, there wasn't much that was going to take the chill off.

BY THE TIME WE GOT BACK TO THE MOTEL I WAS CHILLED to the bone. My teeth wouldn't stop chattering, and I was dying to get out of my clothes.

"I'm going to take a shower," I said, my voice a bit raw, body sore and sluggish.

He didn't respond, but there was no need. Six wasn't one for unnecessary conversation, and I knew there was a lot going on in his head.

I stripped off my still damp clothes that were covered in salt and sand, and let them fall to the floor as I turned on the water. My skin felt ice cold to the touch.

As I stepped in, the warm water felt like it was burning my cool skin. I let the warmth fall over me, roll across my skin, and tried to forget.

To forget that Six was betrayed by two of his own, one being his own brother. To forget that we were probably still being hunted, and with a greater ferocity than before.

The sound of the shower curtain rings sliding across the rod made me open my eyes. Six stared at me, completely naked, as he climbed in with me. His eyes were off, his expression confused.

For the first time in months he looked at me like any other man looking at a woman, instead of a captor at his captive.

He was looking at me as more of an equal.

No words as he stepped forward. One hand moved to my waist while the other cupped and caressed my cheek. I leaned into his touch, a different kind of need than I was used to seeping through.

It was difficult for him, the struggle evident in his eyes for such an affectionate touch, but I could tell it was also something he needed. He wasn't completely unfazed by the events of the evening. Still the same, not changed, but there were definite emotions there. What they were, I wasn't quite sure.

He leaned down, lips pressing against mine, mouths opening and tongues touching in light strokes. His fingers made trails down my body, wrapping around me and pulling me closer.

I did the same, caressing my way up his arms and chest, slipping my hands up his neck and into his hair, pulling. A moan vibrated through him into me.

We were both panting when he pulled back, our bodies mashed together under the spray of the showerhead. In a quick movement, he bent down and grabbed one of my legs around the knee and pulled it up to his hip.

The heat of his hard cock slipped across my slit, twitching as he groaned. He grabbed my other leg and lifted me up, pressing me against the wall. The tile was cold against my warmed skin, making me hiss.

No time was wasted adjusting us so that his dick pushed right into my pussy, stretching me, filling me. His eyes never left me as mine fluttered from the intense pleasure, or when he began moving his hips in long, slow undulating thrusts.

No frenzied, frantic movements. It wasn't the need to

come that drove him, it was the need for comfort.

Skin moved against skin in a sensual dance. Each deep push forced out a moan from me and into his mouth, sliding across our tongues.

Steady strokes, hips coming together. In and out in waves of pure, pain fueled need. Pleasure for a reset of mind-wiping release.

Our eyes were locked and while soft, they were devoid of emotion. Not fear, sadness, pain or love. Nothing.

I really was in love with a sociopath.

He let out a loud groan, his cock bottoming out as his thrusts sped up in hard slaps. The muscles beneath my hands tightened. Hot breath against my skin as he buried his face in my neck, arms tight around me. He held us there, under the warm water as his cock jerked inside me.

Even after the last pulse, he stayed.

There was no rush to move, no need. Holding each other tight, trying to forget, for just a moment, that everything had changed.

War had come, and only the last Cleaners standing decided the new world order.

The motel room was a mess of sandy, wet clothes and salt en-crusted weapons. Six's lips formed a thin line as he looked down at his favorite gun.

"Will it be okay?" I asked as I toweled my hair off.

He nodded. "It'll take a while, and I need to get all the salt off it."

Instead of beginning to work on it like he normally would,

he crawled onto the bed and stared up at the ceiling. Throwing the towel over the shower rod, I joined him, lying on my side and staring at his lifeless expression.

The man beside me wasn't broken, but inside he was beaten up.

"He was really your brother? Like, you grew up with him, have the same parents?"

Six nodded. "His name is Eli. We're just over a year apart."

"So when I asked if you had family, he was the brother you were talking about?"

"Yes."

"And even then, you said you would kill him."

He was silent and I thought it was like normal, ignoring that I said anything.

"When I was twelve, he shot me."

I let out a gasp, my mind reeling as his fingers traced around to a wound in his lower abdomen.

"Then he killed our father." He paused, letting me process the very personal information. His eyes searched mine as if he was deciding to continue or not. "Our mother told the police our father shot me, and Eli shot him in defense, to stop him from killing our mother. After that, Eli got whatever he wanted because she was afraid of him. "

"Were you afraid of him?"

He shook his head. "He used fear to intimidate, but I've never been afraid of him because I'm just as fucked-up as he is. We're both psychopaths created from come poured from the dick of another psycho into the unsuspecting womb of an otherwise normal woman."

"You believe it's your nature?"

"It is. It was also my nurture, if you're going to try that argument."

Somehow, he knew where I was going. "You never retaliated against him? Against Nine?"

He shook his head. "No, but that was the first time I realized he was jealous. In many things, even at that young age, I was better than him."

"But when you were ranked…"

"I did what I do. There was nothing that drove me other than completing the tasks. I didn't and still don't care about the ranking. It was arbitrary."

"So, he put in more effort?" I asked, trying to get it all straight. "Are you better than him?"

"I don't know."

"But you're good at what you do?"

"Very."

All the information swirled around my mind, trying to figure the two of them out. "But his psychosis and need to be better than you and others drove him to push himself to the limits in order to be ranked the highest. To be ranked higher than you. Proof to him that he was better than you."

Again, he nodded. "Yes."

"You are one badass, frightening motherfucker."

He quirked his brow at me. "You're just now figuring that out?"

"Oh, no. I've known for months."

"But?" he asked, prompting me for more.

"But I also know you're more than just a killer," I said, knowing that I meant it.

He furrowed his brow. "What else am I?"

"A man." I slipped my fingers in between his. He'd shown me many times that night he was more than just the unfeeling killing machine that I'd labeled him as. "One that I, for some fucked-up reason, care a lot about."

"You shouldn't. Even as a man, I'm still going to kill you."

I pursed my lips, then rolled them into a thin line. "Yeah, I know."

"That doesn't scare you away from caring for me?"

I shook my head. "It's not news. I've known it from day two."

He gave a nod, his jaw ticking as he let out a sigh and returned to staring at the ceiling.

"What do we do now?" I asked. It was the first time we'd been in a true limbo. The situation was way beyond out of control.

He shook his head as he stared back up at the ceiling. "I don't know."

"You talked about a go at Langley… Should you warn them of what's going on?" I asked, trying to pull him out of his funk. Trying to get him to think about anything other than his brother's betrayal.

"Without Jason, there's nobody we can contact."

"You mean there's no backup? That's stupid. There should always be a failsafe."

He turned and looked at me. "There's that logical mind of yours." He reached out and stroked my face. "You are the strangest hostage ever."

"You risked your life for me twice now. There's no more getting around that you like me."

He made a *hmm* sound and went silent.

There was no protest when I lifted his arm up or when I snuggled into his side, my head resting on his chest. In fact, his fingers played with my hair and he tangled my hand that was resting on his chest with his own.

Even with the sun starting to create slivers of light from the gap in the curtains, we were both asleep in minutes.

Four days we stayed locked up. Four days he spent doing nothing but fixing his gun and lying in bed with me.

That, and taking apart his super-secret laptop to find a GPS transmitter inside and changing all access, including disabling a back-door entrance. It all sounded like gibberish to me, but I at least understood that much.

The phone never rang. He didn't call anyone. It was complete blackout. We had no idea if anyone else was alive or dead.

The world was just the two of us.

"Shit," Six cursed. It was the first time in hours either of us said anything. He had his laptop up and had been digging around for information.

"What?" I asked, setting my book down and sitting up.

He shook his head, jaw clenching and unclenching, his leg bouncing. "An informant just sent out an all call on a Cleaner."

"Which one?"

"It doesn't say, but being just one, it could be Two, Five, or Seven."

Nine and One were doubtful to leave each other.

"Close by?"

He nodded. "A few hours. Down near Sacramento."

Scooting to the edge of the bed, I put my feet on the ground, ready to move. "What are we waiting for?"

It only took a few minutes to pull on some clothes and load up on firearms before we were headed out the door.

"Here," Six said, handing me one of his 9mm Glocks.

I glanced from him to it, then back to him. "Really?"

He nodded. "If we run into them, you'll need it."

The gesture left me shell shocked as I reached out and took the pistol from him. It was for more than my help or to protect myself. It was trust.

Six trusted me—the woman he was going to kill—with his life.

The restaurant on a cliff was spooky, but the old, falling down warehouse was a whole other kind of creep-tacular. Both looked right out of a survival horror video game, and the mess of bodies dressed in black we waded through was a perfect match.

A wetwork team had come, and a cleaner or two emerged victorious from the rubble.

"Fuck." The carnage was unreal, blood everywhere, the floor a sticky mat of dark red. "This is about the same age as your email."

"It was probably set up by the wetwork team to draw one or more of us out."

"Looks like it worked," I said as we waded through to the other side.

There had to be another side.

He stopped and held out his hand. I froze, eyes wide, ears listening intently, but there was nothing. Moving again, he headed toward a staircase that was also covered in blood, a body lying limp on the landing.

On the second story there was a wide open space with one light that held power. Lit up was a lump that looked like a possible body.

We inched closer, Six keeping all his senses on high alert. Wide open spaces probably made him nervous. No cover in case someone was waiting.

Within twenty feet, it was obvious it was a body. Within ten, it was obviously not one from the wetwork team.

Shit.

The body was beaten to hell with multiple knife wounds and topped off with a couple of bullets. The face was mashed in. So much so, it was hard to tell who it was.

Many of the visible features resembled Five.

My chest clenched. Of all the Cleaners besides Six, Five was the only one I liked. He didn't try to kill me and stood up for me. He saw the value in me the others couldn't.

"I don't think they're trying to be sneaky anymore," Six said as he crouched down to try and identify the man.

Six's arm snapped up and he fired, hitting the floor, scaring the shit out of me.

"Whoa!" Five yelled as he jumped back. "I just got here."

My eyes widened and I ran forward, flinging my arms around his neck. "Five!"

"Hey there, baby," Five wrapped his arms around me, making sure to give my ass a squeeze. "Ooh, Six, I think your woman is starting to see and appreciate what fine attributes I have."

Your woman.

It was a title that I really liked. To be his. Our relationship was so different from the last time we'd seen Five, but still, maybe he saw something in Six I couldn't.

"Let her go," Six said. He still had his gun out and pointed at Five.

Five released me and I stepped back, glancing between the two.

"What are you doing here?" Six's finger was on the trigger.

My eyes widened as I looked between them. Six was serious. He was going to kill Five if he didn't give the right answer.

Five held his arms out. "Whoa, chill, man. It's been radio silent, so I continued on with the mission."

"What have you been doing?"

"I haven't found Jason, but I located Seven and he told me

what happened in Vegas." Five gave me a sad smile. "Sorry about you friend, darling."

I swallowed hard and nodded. "Thanks."

"Jason's dead."

Five's expression dropped. "Fuck."

"It was Nine and One."

"What?" Five asked in disbelief. He shook his head. "No. There's no way."

"They tried to blow us up."

Five continued to shake his head. "He's your brother. I mean, I know you two aren't close, but still… Guess there really is no honor among killers."

Six didn't say anything, just kneeled back down and held out his hand toward me. "Give me your napkin."

My brow scrunched as I looked at him. Napkin? He reached out and dug into my jacket pocket, pulling a folded-up napkin I'd stuck in there days before.

Whoops. I was shocked he even remembered it was there.

Turning Mr. Dead's head, Six used the napkin to wipe away as much blood as he could from behind the guy's ear. It took a few passes to get the sticky, dried red to leave the skin, exposing two small dots.

"Damn, it is Two."

Five sighed. "Down four now."

Six stood. "And we're about to be down six."

Five nodded. "Let's take them out." He was getting pumped up at the idea of going after Nine and One.

Six shook his head and started walking back toward the staircase. "No. He's my blood. I have to do it."

"Why?" Five asked, saddling up next to him. "He's a target just like any other."

We descended the stairs and walked in an opposite direction

of the sea of bodies to find another way out.

"But he's not. He made it personal. If anyone ends Nine, it's going to be me."

A busted garage door provided the perfect exit. Six held out his hand, helping me climb over the fallen panels.

"What about One?" Five asked as we made our way across the broken asphalt back to the car.

"She'll be with him," Six said.

It made sense. I had a feeling they never really separated when we left Tennessee.

"Can you take them both?"

"We can."

Five looked between us and my brow scrunched up, then he nodded. "Okay. I'll find Seven, and we'll start to get things prepped for a go on Langley."

"It's going to be a fight to talk to Wolesley."

Five's lips spread into a grin. "Not fun any other way."

As Five stepped away, the thought itching in the back of my mind clicked. "We? As in, you and me?" I asked, turning to look at Six.

Over the last almost three months and he always said *I*, never we.

"Do you think you can do it? Kill?"

Could I? I'd done it before when my life was on the line, but could I hunt them down with him?

The answer was an easier conclusion than I was expecting.

Yes.

It was their actions, their first betrayal, the death of Three, that put Six in my life. If they hadn't, we never would have met in that bar and my life would still be going, boring and all.

That meant, for months, they'd tried to kill me.

They played us in Tennessee because Nine wanted Six on

their side. That was probably the only reason they didn't kill us then. Two Cleaners could have easily been taken out, but they chose to wait.

"I already said I would do anything to survive." I placed my hands on his chest, moving them slowly up and linking them around the back of his neck. "And the only one I want to kill me is you." I pulled him down as I stood on the tip of my toes, reaching up to press my lips to his.

He pulled me closer, deepening the kiss.

What I said was true. If I was going to be killed, I wanted it to be him.

STARED INTO THE MIRROR ABOVE THE DRESSER, AT MY LESS-than-like-me new haircut, to go with my so-not-me dye job. If my eyes weren't their normal bright blue, I would seriously question the reflection as being me.

But it was me, or rather Lacey.

So much had gone on the last few months that my entire twenty-eight years leading up to now seemed like an entire life-time ago.

Paisley Anne Warren lived a lifetime ago.

I couldn't tear my eyes away from the mirror, from the changes I'd endured that morphed me into Lacey Collins. But I could hear the life going on in the motel room. The TV spouting some news about something terrible, as they always seemed to do. There was the buzzing of the phone against the wood table-top—an oddity since Jason's death. The spray of the shower, and then the squeak of the knob as it turned off.

Steam billowed out a minute later as the door opened, but Six didn't come out. Instead, the next sound that filtered through my ears was another buzzing. My gaze flickered to the door, then back to my shortened locks.

How long had it been since I'd had a bob? Such a small

change, but needed. We'd both been stagnant in our looks for months.

I reached up, my fingers skimming across the newly snipped edge. A surreal feeling came over me, a tingling sensation.

"Lacey?"

His voice echoed around my head.

"Lacey?"

I turned to look at him and gasped, my eyes going wide.

Like mine, his hair was gone. Only, all of his was gone. Nothing left but a fuzzy buzz of light brown.

"Are you okay?"

"Your hair…" I trailed off.

One brow twitched as he stepped closer. There was nothing but a towel wrapped around his waist, his skin glistening.

I moved from sitting cross-legged to my knees as I reached out. The soft fuzz beneath my fingers tickled as I glided them around his head.

He let out a small moan—the kind that made my clit dance. His hands gripped onto me as he stepped forward, pulling me closer.

"Damn, you look sexy," I said, my mouth only a few short inches from his.

"Sexy?"

I nodded, pulling his lips down to mine. "Fuckable."

I yanked him down onto the bed and stood before him straddling his hips. Watching his eyes darken as his hands moved up my waist only made me hotter for him. I let out a small moan at the feeling of his cock growing hard between us.

One last ride.

Just in case.

If I was going to die that night, I needed his cock in me one more time.

Lifting my hips, I guided him to my opening and lowered down. He groaned, leaning back to watch as inch by inch disappeared between my pussy lips.

I rotated my hips as I used my thigh muscles to push off and gravity to pull me back down. My eyes drifted closed, concentrating on the pleasure, of the feel of him stretching me, hitting all the places that made my mind go blank.

Primal need drove my body. The search for pleasure, release. The need to be one with him for just a little longer.

My lover.

My killer.

"Fuck," he hissed. His hips flexed up, making me shudder as he got even deeper.

My muscles began to tense, making it harder for me to move. He didn't miss a beat. His hands gripped my waist, lifting me up and down as he pumped into me. I let out a shuddering moan, my nails digging into his skin, and let go.

Uncontrollable tremors shook me. I was so far gone, too blissed out, that I almost missed him grunting as his cock jerked, spilling all his come inside me.

My arms went lax as I slumped against his chest. All energy gone, he fall back, taking me with him.

Calm spread through me for only a few minutes before the fear flooded back in.

Even an orgasm wasn't enough to forget that it might be my last day alive.

A tear slipped from my eye, landing on his skin.

I didn't want to die.

Getting ready was surreal. I'd never prepared for a fight, let alone a battle. Which was exactly what we were doing.

One last hurrah, one last time facing those that tried to kill us. Facing Six's own brother.

Brother versus brother, and by the end of the night, only one would walk away.

It would be Six.

It *had* to be Six.

If it wasn't, we were both dead and they won. They'd find Five and Seven and hunt them down next.

However it went, that night was the end of the Cleaners.

Quite possibly my last night on earth. I'd been living on borrowed time, anyway, and was actually, strangely, thankful for it. The things I'd experienced left scars and nightmares, but others were magical.

Warped and tangled, I wasn't the same person. I'd come to terms with my new identity and the loss of the old me.

I would kill, more blood to stain my hands, but in the end I hoped to still be standing beside the man I foolishly loved.

Sick and twisted. Broken and wrong. I wasn't a *good* person anymore.

I'd lived in the psychology of evil, had it rub off on me. Surrounded by monsters, I'd become one. Not like them, but a demented version of myself.

Killing was still difficult, but reservations of killing for self-preservation were gone.

I'd said it before—I'd do anything to survive. And I would do what was necessary to ensure that at the end of the night, we were the ones still standing.

I went over the bag and the contents. There were five pistols with eleven fully loaded magazines. All were Glocks, ensuring they all matched up. Three knives, multiple holsters, along with a few unusual weapons, like the icepick, rounded out the assortment.

One duffel that sat on the bed contained the explosives Six had rigged up. I didn't know what all was in the concoction, but I did know there would be no evidence left when it went off.

"What are you doing?" I asked as he pulled his bulletproof vest over my head.

"Just in case."

"No! This is for you," I said as I yanked at it, trying to pull it off.

He grabbed my hands, and I stared into his eyes in confusion.

"You need this more than me."

"Why?"

"Because this is the only way I'm going to be able to protect you in there."

Tears welled in my eyes.

Protect me? They were foreign words, and even more foreign coming from him.

I ripped it off and shoved it back at him, tears stinging my eyes. "I'm collateral damage. What does it matter if I get killed?"

His jaw ticked and he threw the vest back over my head. Fingers wrapped around my chin, lifting my gaze to his. It was electric, furious and pained.

"Nobody is going to kill you but me."

"Why?" I asked, my voice breaking.

His lips ghosted across mine. "Because you're mine. Remember, I say when and where. Only me."

A shuddering breath left him as he pulled back, his jaw ticking as he stepped back to the bed.

Mine.

Mine.

His…

I was *his* and nobody else's.

After months of being with him, I'd fallen in love with him. Maybe, just maybe, he'd fallen in love with me too.

After all, he did say he could love and had loved.

Was it too much to hope for that Six loving me would save me? Or had my badgering questions already answered that with a resounding no?

When it came to the job, the Cleaners were absolute. I was an anomaly. A wild card that would be eradicated when I was no longer of use.

He said that was how it had to be, but was it too much to wish for to have a few more years trapped at his side?

I tossed on a T-shirt over the vest to conceal it and added my jacket on top. Between the two, the vest was barely noticeable.

"Here," Six said, catching my attention as he grabbed hold of the vest and twirled me around.

There was a strange sensation as he stuffed something in my waistband. Before I could reach back, he began filling my pockets as well.

"What's all this?" I asked when I finally got to reach around.

Cool metal grazed my fingers as I traced the item. Barrel, grip, and trigger—one of his Glocks.

"You're giving me a gun?" I asked. He'd never given me one until the fight was on.

"Yes."

First the vest, then a gun and pockets loaded with magazines? He was suiting me up, preparing me to defend my life.

A life he was going to take.

It had taken days to figure out where they were hiding, but in the end, it wasn't that hard. One and Nine weren't so much as hiding as they were chilling. They believed they were four Cleaners down with only two to go, celebrating their power.

Cocky.

Conceited.

My hands shook, and I drew in a deep breath to try and get them to stop. Nervous didn't cover how I felt walking into the lion's den. I was an average woman. I wasn't a Cleaner, but side by side I stood next to one as some strange form of equal. Not behind him, shielded by him—next to him. In the front.

There were two men standing outside the building, which seemed odd for Cleaners to have a need for guards. Then again, maybe they weren't guards, but fodder. A human alarm system made of bloodied, dead bodies.

Two shots from Six's silenced barrel and they slumped to the ground.

There were no cameras that we could see, and as we approached, Six stopped in his tracks.

"Shit."

"What?" I asked, freezing on the spot.

"They're agents."

"What does that mean?"

"It means either they've corrupted others, or someone at the top is pulling the strings."

Neither of those sounded good. If they'd turned others, how many were there? Would there ever be a safe place?

The building appeared to be an old factory. On the first floor, though, there was only a few doors. The second and third floors held huge glass windows with many broken panes.

"How many do you think there are?" I asked.

He shook his head. "Let's find out."

The metal door was heavy, the screeching of the old, rust covered hinges echoed off the walls. If it wasn't a call to anyone who was inside, I didn't know what was. Hopefully, they just thought it was the guys outside coming back in.

"Jesus, Pete," a voice called out. Footsteps shuffled across the floor and Six lifted his gun. "Would you stop com—"

Bullet to the eye.

He made a gurgling sound, blood streaming from his empty socket before making a thump as he crumbled onto the ground.

Bile churned in my stomach, the gruesome sight almost too much, even after everything I'd seen.

We moved through in stealth mode—no talking, quiet footsteps, and cautious moves. Three more agents were downed before we found the stairs and made our way up.

Large wood plank floors and metal I-beams that stretched two stories high filled our view. Evidence of large equipment could still be seen in ghost image outlines on the floors. Pages of newspaper floated around, piled up in corners and layered in pieces on the wood.

Such an open space, lit by huge lights that buzzed. Not all of them worked, leaving shaded spaces. In the middle was a large table and some chairs, even a couch. Computers lined the table, and sitting in front of them was Nine and One.

"You found us," Nine's voiced boomed out. He didn't even look our way.

There must have been cameras outside.

Six pointed his gun straight at One, but before he could fire, there was someone beside us, his sights on me.

"You didn't think we wouldn't be prepared, did you?" One asked, her lips twitched up into her bitch smirk.

Six's jaw clenched. There was only one of the stray we didn't find, or so it seemed.

"You can go," Nine said to the man beside me, sending his goon away.

"Can't watch your own back?" Six asked. "Or have you gotten that lazy?"

"You're alive," Nine said, his expression blank. "I wasn't expecting that after your ocean dive to save your pet."

"You of all people should know I don't die that easily."

Nine's gaze hardened. "No, you always have had a way of avoiding death. It's almost as if you're a cat." Nine's arm rose, his gun aimed at Six. "Let's see if you've reached your ninth life."

"After everything, you want to end it that way?"

Nine's lip twitched. "What do you have in mind?"

"You and me. Let's finish the fight we started decades ago." Six held out his gun and let it drop to the floor.

Nine followed, setting his own gun on the ground. "Fine by me. You need a reminder who's better before I kill you."

Six dug his feet in and ran full speed, knocking his shoulder into Nine's stomach, forcing him back. Nine beat on Six's back, trying to get him to let go. When he did, a dance of fighting artistry began. Blocked punches, avoided kicks, all making a fairly even match.

Nine struck the first blow, whipping Six's head around.

My chest clenched watching the two of them brawl. A fight to the death where the winner would determine my own fate.

Six promised me a bullet to the head, but I had a feeling Nine and One might make me suffer.

When I looked back to One, she wasn't watching them. She was smiling at me, and in her hand was the weapon that killed all four Cleaners and Jason.

A .45 caliber gun.

One held it high, her aim on my head. "Time to finally end you, little toy."

I didn't flinch. It wasn't the first barrel I'd stared down, and it wasn't going to be the last.

But still, she had the drop on me. I'd been preoccupied watching them fight, not paying attention to the twatwaffle bitchapotomous.

Life wasn't supposed to end this way, and it wasn't going to. Not by her hand.

Six was too far away, his fight with Nine still going strong with no clear sign of a winner. Perhaps my naiveté was in believing he could come out of anything and would always be there to save me until the day he ended me himself.

Anticipating her firing, I dove toward the ground, pulling out the gun Six had slipped into the back of my jeans. Both of our shots rang out at the same time.

The bullet grazed my arm and exploding pain fried my brain, but my gaze stayed focused across the room on One. I landed hard, but forced myself to get right back up. I pushed up from the floor and walked over to her, gun still in hand.

Her face screwed up in disbelief, one hand on her stomach, the other lifting the gun at me again. I stopped breathing.

She fired straight at my chest and the force nearly knocked me off my feet. The pain was intense, excruciating, but I was alive. The bullet didn't pierce my skin.

Her eyes widened as she stared at the hole with no blood coming through, at the realization I was wearing a vest.

Another *Click!*

Nothing.

Her lip curled up in anger, finger hitting the trigger over and over. Strength left her with the blood flowing down her body and she fell to the floor, landing hard on her knees. When I was within a few feet she tried again, oblivious that the slide was back.

"You know the definition of insanity, right?" I lifted my hand, gun level with her head.

She looked over to the fight. "Nine!"

I followed her gaze and tried not to gasp. Six was on the ground, struggling to get up, with Nine standing over him. My chest clenched while my stomach turned.

I knew the order. Nine was the best.

But Six, my Six, was better. He had to be.

He had to win.

Nine's bloodied and bruised head snapped over, anger and contempt flashing across his face. "Really?" He tsk'ed. "You've gone downhill, One, to be beaten by an ant. I'll squash her as soon as I'm done with my brother, but you'll probably be dead by then." There was no emotion in his tone, none of the affection I'd seen in the past or indication that she would be missed. More annoyance that the pawn in his game had been defeated.

Behind him, Six rose to his feet, blood dripping down his face from multiple cuts. He ran forward, gripping Nine's neck with one hand while his other arm swung out, fist colliding with Nine's ribs with a dull thud.

I turned back to One. Her hand was outstretched, reaching for another gun, but it was too far.

"Looks like he doesn't care about you after all." I smirked down at her.

Her lip curled up as she sneered at me. "You can't pull the trigger."

"No?" I asked as I moved my finger down.

"You're not a killer. You can't finish the job from your shot of self-defense and preservation."

I gave a small shrug. "Maybe, or maybe Six has rubbed off on me."

She scoffed. "You're nothing more than a little toy. A pussy to play with, to fuck, before he kills you."

"Think what you want. It won't stop him from killing Nine, from me killing you, and the two of us leaving together. After what Nine said it's obvious who the toy is, and it isn't me."

I took sick pleasure in the sadness that filled her expression when she realized I was right, then I pulled the trigger.

The shot rang out just after the bullet pierced her skull and exploded out the back. Her face relaxed, her eyes dimming as she slumped over onto the ground.

Ringing filled my ears, cancelling out everything else but the reality before me.

I killed her.

I killed One.

Bile rose up my throat and my hand shook, radiating up my arm and throughout my body.

Inside I screamed at myself that it was okay, because she'd been trying to kill me for months, but it didn't change the fact that what I'd done was still so wrong to me on many levels. I'd spent my working life around death, but dealing it myself, especially in such a cold-blooded manner, was different. It didn't feel good, but there was also no stopping the sheer relief that flooded me.

A cackle exploded from my mouth, my muscles released the tension I was holding as the stinging pain in my arm from my wound made itself known.

One was dead, and Six would finish Nine.

We'd finally be free from all the running.

Six.

I had to force myself to stop staring at her body to find him.

Shots filled the silence, and fear rocked my body. My eyes were frantic as they searched for the last man standing, praying it was Six.

I let out a hard breath at the sight of Six standing in the middle of the room, Nine on the floor a few feet in front of him. He let the empty gun drop, clanking as it hit the floor, and turned toward me.

He was beaten, badly, and barely standing, but from the evidence on Nine, minus the bullet holes, it was an even match.

I ran forward, wrapping my arms around his waist. "Six!"

He stumbled a bit, his breath coming out hard.

"Are you okay?" I reached up and visually took stock of his injuries.

He shook his head. "But I will be. We need to destroy this place and get out of here, now."

"Is the bag in a good place?" I asked, glancing at it across the room.

He nodded and reached into his pocket, pulling out the small detonator. "There's enough explosives to level this building and leave it a blazing mess for days."

All evidence long gone.

"Can you walk?"

"Not my first show." He took a few unsteady steps before resting one arm on my shoulders. "Maybe I need a little help. Worst show ever."

"Good ending, though."

He quirked his brow at me. "How so?

"You won."

"Was there ever any doubt?" he asked, brow scrunched up.

"Doubt?" I shook my head. "No. Fear? Yes."

He grabbed my chin and tilted it up, his lips pressing to mine. The rusty tang from the blood on him couldn't stop the fluttering of my heart.

"Come on." He pulled me to the door, bending down to pick up one of the stray guns on the floor as we walked.

I took one last glance back to the bodies of One and Nine. I half expected them to get up, but it wasn't going to happen.

Six killed his brother in order to save not only himself, but me and the other Cleaners.

I expected a firefight trying to get out of there, but it didn't happen. Nine and One had minimal security personnel, and Six took care of most of them on our way in. Still, it was eerie, especially since we knew one of them was still alive and seemed to have disappeared or was hiding.

We got in the car like nothing happened. That we hadn't just killed two of the government's best killers.

My stomach was in knots, waiting for someone to come chasing after us like they had for months.

Six started the car and hit the gas. A few blocks later he pulled out the detonator and pressed the button.

The explosion was ear splitting a half-mile away. In the mirror chunks of debris fell back to earth and flames licked high into the sky.

The ringing in my ears stopped, and the only sound was the revving of the engine along with the traffic on the interstate as we entered.

"One was the definition of cocky," he said a few miles later.

I blinked and turned to look at him. "Huh?"

"Tying back to our conversation that first day."

My eyes widened. "Wow, that was literally another life."

"She was the lowest ranked," he continued on, ignoring me.

"Of elite trained killers." I pointed out.

"And she was beaten by you because she believed you so inferior and that you would never in any life be able to touch her."

"And you won because of all your self-confidence?" I asked.

"No, I won because I'm a highly trained killer and I got to a gun first."

I grimaced. "Good thing, too."

"Why?"

I slipped my fingers in his blood covered ones. "You don't remember? You're the only one I want to kill me."

He glanced to me, his fingers flexing around mine.

There was no letting go.

He only held on tighter.

AFTER OVER THREE HOURS OF DRIVING, A PHARMACY STOP an hour in, and a vehicle change, we checked into some obscure motel in the middle of nowhere. It was a welcomed sight. We were both tired, hungry, and injured.

The moment we were in the door and Six latched it, I was dragging him into the bathroom, pharmacy bag in tow.

I sat him down on the toilet and looked him over. His left eye was swollen shut and he was so covered in blood I couldn't tell where it was coming from or if it was even his.

"We need to get this off," I said as I pulled at his shirt.

He blew out a breath and took hold of the hem, his movements stiff. I pulled from the back, working his head through the hole and sliding the rest down his arms.

With his shirt gone, I looked over his chest. There was some swelling and some bruises starting to blossom, indicating there might be some broken ribs. By the way Nine was hitting and kicking him, I wouldn't doubt it. There were no pulled punches.

I tried to turn off my emotions to get the job done. Six needed to be cleaned and patched up.

Though I did let the relief in, even if it didn't seem real to me on some levels. Nine and One were dead. I saw the bodies, created one of them. Even with those facts, I couldn't shake the knots in my stomach.

Six's head bobbed, his eyes drooped, and his body began to slump.

"Whoa, none of that." I gave his face a slight slap, the sting making his eyes jump open.

He let out a hiss and glared up at me, but I ignored it.

Wetting a towel and running his hands under the faucet in the sink, I was able to clean off a lot of the blood to get a better look at his hands. They were also swollen, and there were multiple lacerations.

I continued up his arms and his face until as much blood as I could get was gone. His face had a few cuts, but none of them needed anything more than a butterfly stitch. A little antibiotic ointment and some bandages did the trick on the rest.

His hands required a few more of the butterfly stitches, along with some ice to help with the swelling.

"We need to do you," he said, grabbing my wrist and pulling me to sit on his lap.

I'd been so concerned with him that I hadn't even registered the pain in my arm or the ache in my chest. Copying my motions, he wet a towel and cleaned up my arm.

The bullet had only grazed me, but it was enough to make a mess.

I let out a whimper, trying not to cry as he cleaned the wound. Each pass stung like a motherfucker. Like sandpaper digging into my skin as it lit it on fire. In a motion I wasn't expecting, he pressed his lips to my shoulder and when he pulled back, I saw for the first time an emotion I equated to love.

Reaching up, I lightly cupped his face and leaned down, pressing my lips to his.

No more signs of affection as he bandaged me up. One

small glimpse was all I got, but it was enough.

Once done, we headed back into the room and as he stripped, I saw the beginnings of black and blue marks on his back. It had been a knock-down drag-out fight to the death and his battle scars, while painful, were proof of him being alive.

He turned to me, ripping the Velcro off and pulling the vest over my head. Once the bottom shirt was off, we both looked down at the red splotch on my breast, just above my heart.

He said nothing, but leaned down and kissed it as well, before guiding us to the bed.

"How are you feeling?" I asked as we climbed on.

He collapsed down on his back and turned to me. "I'll be fine." He held out his hand, beckoning me forward.

"You may have a concussion."

He didn't say anything, just grabbed my arm and pulled me down to him.

Slipping into the crook of his neck, I settled into my safe spot. With a sigh, I relaxed into him, my head on his chest, his arm wrapped around my shoulder.

The safest place I could ever be, wrapped in the arms of my killer.

Three days of healing had passed. Three days of nothing but the two of us.

When I awoke, the bed was cold beside me. Panic surged through me, and I sat straight up. My eyes swirled in confusion until I found Six's brown eyes studying me.

He was dressed, fresh bandages on his wounds and a packed bag at his side.

"What's going on?"

He slapped his hand down on another bag sitting on a table next to him. "This bag contains cash, a gun and ammo, keys to a Ford Taurus parked outside, and all the paperwork you'll need to continue to live as Lacey Collins."

"Six?" None of what he said made sense to my sleep addled brain.

"I have to go."

I blinked at him. "Why?"

"Because it doesn't end with Nine and One. They started a war between us and Home. I need to find Five and Seven and we need to end this, or we'll be running forever."

He stood and walked to the edge of the bed as I crawled over to it. I swung my arms around his shoulders pulling him tight, mashing our bodies as close together as I could. He indulged my need for affection, but his own need for it seeped out.

Six had become my world—what was I going to do? Where was I going to go?

He stepped back and picked up his bag, slinging it over his shoulder. "Lay low somewhere and don't try to contact anyone you knew, no matter what."

I reached out, my fingers fisted into his shirt as I held in the begging wail that wanted to slip out. "But you haven't killed me yet."

He stared at me for a moment. "I'm not ready to let you go."

"What does that mean?"

He gripped the back of my neck and pulled me forward with a harsh tug. "It means I finally figured out when I'm going to kill you."

I froze. His tone was lighter, but the words were what they'd been all along. "When's that?"

"I'm going to consume you. Slowly. Over years and years, just as you've consumed me." His lips crashed against mine, tongue forcing its way in. Passion and need, taking just as he always did.

Then he was gone, the door slamming behind him, leaving me bewildered. I guessed that was as close to "I love you" as he could give me. Maybe one day I'd hear it, though.

One day.

I stared at the door, a sense of loneliness and confusion coming over me.

What now?

Never in my mind was there a life after Six plan. His departure was abrupt and left me reeling. My chest was suddenly filled with anxiety.

An hour later, I loaded my suitcase and the bag into the car and drove off. It was going to be a long drive, but as I packed up, there was only one place I could think of to go. A place where childhood memories could keep me company.

It was a start. My death had been postponed, and I had the chance at a new beginning.

A new *life.*

I wasn't dying anymore.

It was time to live.

4 months later…

"WOW, LACEY, HUNGRY?" SUE SNICKERED ABOVE the small half wall that separated our cubes.

I looked up but continued to chomp away on my pretzels, giving a small shrug to my coworker. "Seems to be an hourly thing lately."

She chuckled. "I remember those days."

It was true. In the last few weeks my hunger had kicked in to overdrive. I'd gained five pounds in the last two weeks alone. The second trimester seemed to be making up for the lack of food I was able to consume during the first. If it didn't slow down, I was going to end up a whale by the time the baby arrived.

The thought stopped me, the pretzels suddenly very unappealing. I tossed the bag onto my desk in disgust and frustration.

Six didn't know.

I had no way to contact him and hadn't seen or heard from him since he left.

So, there I was, all alone in Florida. Pregnant. Scared out of my damn mind.

My family thought I was dead, and it was better that way. Paisley Warren died the moment Six barged into her lab and pointed a gun in her face. The whirlwind months that followed was the birth of Lacey Collins.

Six left me with a hundred thousand dollars and all the papers for my new identity—more than enough to start over with. It wasn't hard to decide where to go. I'd spent many family vacations in Florida's Ft. Meyers and Sanibel Island area.

Once there, I found a duplex a block away from the beach for rent from a sweet older lady and found a part-time office job.

My phone's calendar went off, reminding me of my mission for the day.

I had a phone call to make.

It wasn't a conversation I was looking forward to, but it needed to happen.

"All right, Sue, I'm out," I said as I shut down my computer and loaded up my bag.

"See you tomorrow, Lacey. Have a good night."

I smiled at her and waved.

It was just under a mile to my work, and I preferred to walk versus drive. What was I going to do with my time anyway? Besides, the exercise helped keep my anxiety down.

That was just it—I was biding my time.

There was no rush like in my old life. I felt stagnant. The money Six left me wasn't going to last forever, especially when the baby came. Then what?

I had no friends, no family, nobody I trusted. What the hell was I going to do?

Too many in his organization knew about me. Another reason I could never go back to being Paisley. The inquisitions alone if I did show up would be too much. The FBI or CIA would probably whisk me away.

Paisley was still a person of interest in the destruction of the Hamilton County Medical Examiner's office along with the deaths of all her coworkers. Not to mention my connection with Six, a secret government cleanup op.

"Hi, Esther," I said as I approached the porch of my duplex.

"Good afternoon." Her lips pulled up into a sweet smile that had her blue eyes shining. "How are you feeling today, honey?"

I smiled at her. "I'm doing good this week."

Esther spent most of her time on the front porch playing solitaire or listening to the waves down the street. She was seventy-eight, and only once had I seen any family come by in the time I'd lived above her.

"That baby not givin' you any more fits?"

I shook my head as I reached into my tote bag and pulled out a brown paper bag. "She's being nice to Mommy lately." I held the bag out. "Here, I brought you something."

"What's this?" she asked as she unraveled the top, her hands shaking—a lasting side effect from a past stroke. Her face lit up even more, and her hand rested against her chest. "Oh, Lacey, thank you. I love strawberries. There's so many... enough to make a pie."

"Ah-ha! You discovered my ulterior motive." Esther made fantastic strawberry pie. She'd spoiled me my first week. "The farmer's market was going on this morning, so I picked up a few things."

She let out a laugh and shook her head. "Better get going then so we can have it for dessert," she said as she stood.

"I've got to run an errand and I won't be back until late."

"Fine, fine." She waved me off. "I'll hold it hostage. You come over for lunch tomorrow."

Her use of the term hostage had my heart hammering against my ribs, pulse racing, but I forced a happy face and smile.

"It's a date."

As she entered, I hopped up the exterior steps that led to my portion of the house. One deadbolt and a lock later, I let the door swing inward, checking the flour I laid out on the floor for footprints before stepping in.

Since Six, I'd become a bit paranoid, even more so when I found out I was pregnant.

I would say she was a parting gift from him, but when I finally broke down and went to a doctor, conception had actually happened almost a month before he left.

After putting my farmer's market finds away, I headed back out the door, sifting some more flour. It may not have been the best way to check for intruders, but I thought it was pretty clever.

A tightness grew around my chest as I pulled out of the driveway, still in the Ford Taurus Six left. There had been one thing weighing on me besides my impending baby. So heavily, I drove for four hours and picked up a prepaid phone with cash for a single phone call before I planned on tossing it.

Deep breaths as I punched in the numbers, trying not to hyperventilate as tourists passed by in droves.

"Digby Torheim."

I froze, unsure what to say. Six told me not to contact anyone, but I didn't want to risk not keeping my promise to Digby for fear he'd alert some authority that could get me killed. Or worse, him.

"Hello?"

"H-Hi."

"...."

"I can only talk for a minute."

"Paisley? Is that you?" There was surprise in his voice, and I could just imagine him scooting to the edge of his chair like he used to do when something interested him.

I nodded, which was stupid, because he couldn't see. "Yes."

"Are you all right?"

I rested my hand on my stomach. "Very much all right."

"Where are you?"

"I can't say."

"Please. I've been so worried about you."

"I'm fine, don't worry."

"… What do you mean you're fine?"

I swallowed. He was not going to make it easy. "I'm…on my own."

"Let me come get you." There was frantic movement, a few things crashing, and what sounded like keys tingling.

"No, Digby."

"Why?"

"Because it's never going to be safe. Nobody can know I'm alive. If even one person knows, you risk my life." I swallowed hard and told the biggest lie I could tell him, but there was no other way to get through to him. "I… Digby, I'm in the witness protection program."

"What?"

I swallowed hard. It was the best way, but it didn't make it any easier. "I'm breaking so many rules contacting you. I really wish I could tell you more, but all I can tell you is that I'm alive and I'm okay."

"Why?" he asked, his frustration evident in his voice.

My chest clenched at his tone. It was gut-wrenching.

"Because I made a promise to you. So here it is. I'm calling you. I'm alive, but you still can't do anything other than forget about me."

"Forget about you? Paisley, I can't forget about you. That's the whole problem."

My hand twisted in the fabric of my dress. "You need to. I

can never go back to my old life. I've seen and done too much."

"Done?"

"I'm far from the woman you knew. I've changed in more ways than you could imagine."

"Jesus, Pais."

"I want you to be happy," I said as a tear slid down my cheek. "Fall in love, get married, have kids, and be happy. You know, that whole American Dream your parents came over here for."

"What did he do to you? What did that asshole do to you?"

I wanted to call him out on the asshole comment, but it was true. Being in love with the guy didn't get rid of that.

"I did what I had to do in order to survive. I'm on my own now and…I'm in love."

"With who?" By the tone in his voice, I had a feeling he'd guessed the answer. *"Don't tell me him."*

"I can't say."

"I need to know."

"Look, I know you want more answers, but this is all I can give you. I loved you, Digby, and part of me will always love you, but in order for me to live, everyone has to believe I'm dead. I can never be with you again."

It felt like his proposal all over again, emotionally draining with me having to break his heart.

"I wish things were different, but I promise I will do what I can to keep you safe."

"Thank you, Digby," I said, trying to choke back my tears. "Goodbye."

I didn't wait for a reply before hitting the button to disconnect the call.

Tears streamed down my face as I walked into the mall, through the herd of people coming and going. Some were waiting for reservations, others for the nightly celebrations to begin.

They didn't know me or my pain. What I'd seen and done. They didn't care that I willed my tears to stop so they wouldn't look at me. So that I could blend in.

Just another cow, making her way through a weathered path.

I located the restrooms and sent the burner phone on its way to fritzville, giving it a goldfish farewell.

A final goodbye to Paisley Warren.

Esther's pie was fantastic, per usual. After our lunch, she sent slices home with me in little plastic containers. Mostly old butter packaging.

It worked and gave me easy to carry containers for work to make my coworkers jealous.

I let out a moan as I took a bite at my desk, earning a glare from Sue. "Next time, buy her two bundles and bring a pie here."

I chuckled and nodded. "Okay."

"Hey, Lacey."

I spun in my chair, fork in mouth, to face the receptionist. "Hi, Amanda. What's up?"

She fidgeted with the cord that led to her headset, a blush spreading on her cheeks. "Well, there's someone here to see you."

"Me?" I asked, my brow scrunching as I looked at her. Everyone I knew in my new life was sitting somewhere in this office. Minus Esther.

"He's really good looking, and…he says he's your husband."

I rolled my eyes as I let out a little laugh. "My hus—" I couldn't even finish the word when it dawned, my eyes widening.

I jumped out of my seat, tossing the pie down as I pushed past her to run down the hall.

Six.

It had to be.

I skidded to a halt just inside the lobby, nearly crashing into the doorway. "Six!"

His back was to me and when he turned, my breath caught in my throat. Dirty blond hair, familiar brown eyes, and the body I knew so well.

Tears sprung in my eyes as I ran to him and jumped up, throwing my arms around him. "Six."

He stumbled back a bit, but his arms wrapped around my waist and after a minute, he buried his head in my neck. "Lacey."

"I wasn't sure I'd ever see you again," I whispered into his ear.

"I made you a promise, didn't I?"

I nodded and pulled back a little. "Yes."

He rested his forehead against mine and stared into my eyes. "And now I have all the time in the world to consume you, little by little." His gaze flickered down. "But there seems to be more of you."

I stepped back and bit my lip as I smoothed my hands over my dress, revealing my little baby bump. "I didn't have a way to contact you."

He stared down in what I could only tell to be horror, before locking eyes with me. "A baby?"

I nodded. "Without my birth control and you coming in me all the time, it was bound to happen. I just didn't think I'd be alive."

In a tentative move, he reached out, his fingers flexing as he neared, and placed his hand against my abdomen. Just then she kicked, bumping the spot where his hand was. His eyes widened and he swallowed hard.

"I…I…"

"Let me go grab my bag and we'll go…home. We can talk about it there."

He nodded, expression blank.

Telling an assassin he was going to be a father was easier than I thought, but I worried about his reaction. Would it change his mind? Would he leave me again?

My heart hammered in my chest, and I hoped in the few minutes I was gone that he wouldn't leave.

"Who is it?" Sue asked when I returned to my desk.

Pulling open my drawers, I grabbed my tote and purse, and threw my water bottle inside. "My husband."

"Your husband?"

I nodded. "I'll see you tomorrow."

"Wait! Lacey!"

I jogged back down, eyes wide, praying he was still there and sighing in relief when he was right where I'd left him.

I held out my hand. "Come on."

His brow furrowed and he slowly reached out, slipping his hand in mine.

The walk was silent and not leisurely. He kept looking at me, glancing down at my stomach. I couldn't get us back fast enough.

Thankfully, Esther wasn't out when we arrived. Up the stairs and unlocking the door, I stepped in, but he remained outside. His gaze was on the floor, to my flour.

All I could think was if that was the moment he left, unable to come in. Unable to deal with the life he created. The devastation it would cause me. Months of wondering if he was okay, if he was coming back. He stood in my door, so close, and I waited for his decision.

One step in, then another, before he slammed the door behind him. I started to smile, but the look in his eye as he charged toward me made my eyes pop open.

Large hands grabbed on to my waist and lifted me up onto the counter as his lips attacked mine. Frenzied, needy, all-consuming want took over. I was so lost in the sudden confusion, I didn't even notice what was going on until his cock pushed its way inside me.

The sudden and unexpected filling of my pussy had me gasping for air as my fingers fisted his shirt.

"My child." His thrust rocked me on the edge of the counter, and I could do nothing but hold on. "My wife."

His words sent shivers down my spine. *His*. I was forever his.

As warped as it was, it made me happy.

He wrapped his arms around me, pulling me as close as possible. The pounding of his hips increased, the pleasure rippling through me. Fast and hard until he let out a roar.

He held me in a crushing grip as his cock twitched, filling me with his come.

A moan rippled through him, vibrating against my chest as I ran my fingers through his hair, holding him to me.

My death was beginning again, and for the first time, that made me happy.

"So, are you going to tell me what happened?" I asked a few hours later as we lay in bed, completely spent after another round. My skin prickled in soothing tingles as his fingers caressed my shoulder and arm.

"I found Five and Seven. You should've seen the look on people's faces when we walked into Langley."

I gasped. "They knew who you were?"

He smirked. "No, but their sophisticated security didn't like the hardware we brought with us."

"Did you shoot your way in?"

"Only a little."

I sat up and stared down at him, resting my hand on his chest. "Seriously?"

He tucked an arm behind his head. "It's hard to get into a place you work for when only a few people know you do and you have no identification to confirm it. They tried to detain us."

"But you wouldn't let that happen."

"No fucking way after everything. An hour into a Mexican standoff later and someone finally came. He tried to get us to drop our guns, so I shot him in the leg."

"What?"

He shrugged. "Five semi automatics aimed at me, I get antsy. I told him not until we saw Wolesley, and even then he couldn't have my gun."

"Why didn't they shoot you?"

"Oh, they tried."

"What happened?" I asked, completely enthralled with his story.

"Five and Seven were there with more weapons, including some nasty ones. They weren't going to risk lives over it." His lip twitched as he thought back.

"Wow."

"The Cleaners are done," he said, his lips pursed in a thin line. "Basically, we retired. We came to a consulting agent status and training position settlement versus in the field."

"Does that mean we're moving?"

He ran his fingers over my bump and let out a sigh. "I'm not sure anymore. This changes things."

"Would they know who I am? Who I was?"

He nodded. "I took care of it. The destruction of the ME's office was deemed a gas line explosion. Paisley Warren was inside."

"But the news…"

He shook his head. "Your involvement with me, all that happened with Nine and One, your knowledge of the Cleaners. It was decided you know too much to go back."

"So, you have an identity again?" I asked. He nodded. "Am I ever going to know your real name?"

He smirked and reached over the edge of the bed, down to the floor. "Now that I'm official." He held out a badge—Isaac Collins.

"Isaac…" I trailed off. "You used your real last name?"

He nodded. "Sometimes the best camouflage is hiding in plain sight."

My brow scrunched up. "What do I call you? Six or Isaac?"

"Say my real name again."

"Isaac."

He made a humming sound. "That one."

"Me too." Leaning down, I pressed my lips to his, savoring what was the first of many kisses in our new life.

For the first time since he pointed his gun at me, I felt like I had a future. Funny how things changed. Sometimes, when I closed my eyes, I could still see the barrel of his gun. It was a sight I'd never forget.

I'd never forget any of it, but I did forgive him. Because loving him was so much better than hating him.

My devil.

My captor.

My husband.

My Six.

The End

AFTER ALL THE WORDS AND STUFFS

Sooo…. This might be cheating as *Six* was written in 2016 and doing this is new to me, but here goes.

If you're reading this you've finished my sociopath. You made it to the end alive!! If you love him, that's okay, it's not a bad thing. Many others love him as well. You're in good company.

When I set out to write *Six* it was to push myself. I wanted dark and gritty and an anti-hero who didn't soften. Well, Paisley didn't exactly go along with that whole dark hostage vibe, now did she? Honestly, she had me cracking up. Her snark and sarcasm in the literal face of death had me in tears sometimes.

I have to admit, no offense to my other titles ("I love you all!" she says, knowing they're not real, but she's getting dirty looks from the characters in her mind) but this was my favorite book to write. Make no mistake, it was hard. It had rough patches, but Lacey and Six were a challenge and so different and interesting. I didn't hold back. I let it take every direction Six demanded.

Once upon a time I had a dream. One that was so vivid and clear that in the morning I wrote it down. I was running around with an undercover agent that went by the last name Isaac. I remembered his brown eyes, and the fine lines around them so vividly I drew them that morning. Now, Six is nowhere near the type of agent dream guy was, but I decided to take a few of those elements and make them part of him. In a way, I made my dream come true.

Thank you for taking this crazy ride with me. Thank you for taking a chance and letting me take you hostage for a few hours.

ACKNOWLEDGEMENTS

First and foremost… Thank you to everyone for taking a chance on this book and me. Without you, I wouldn't be able to do what I love.

Next up on the thank you train is to my poor, neglected husband. I have left him alone many a night, shut in my office when he got home, so I could work. He'll never read this, but I love him.

My assistant Kaylee who tirelessly worked on graphics and marketing. Stayed up late to talk things out and bounce ideas off each other. Who didn't get too mad when I constantly teased her.

To Dani for supporting Six and for her wicked dream. It made for a badass addition.

Carol for allowing me to tease her for weeks on end and giving me great feedback.

T for her excellent catches and thought inducing insight. Also, for helping me to make this piece of unbelievable fiction more believable.

Vanessa, for understanding that I will never understand some things. And her cohort Manda, for helping me fix things I didn't know were wrong.

ABOUT THE AUTHOR

K.I. Lynn is the *USA Today* Bestselling Author from The Bend Anthology and the Amazon Bestsellers, *Breach* and *Becoming Mrs Lockwood*. She spent her life in the arts, everything from music to painting and ceramics, then to writing. Characters have always run around in her head, acting out their stories, but it wasn't until later in life she would put them to pen. It would turn out to be the one thing she was really passionate about.

Since she began posting stories online, she's garnered acclaim for her diverse stories and hard hitting writing style. Two stories and characters are never the same, her brain moving through different ideas faster than she can write them down as it also plots its quest for world domination…or cheese. Whichever is easier to obtain… Usually it's cheese.

Website—www.kilynnauthor.com
Facebook—www.facebook.com/kilynn.breach
Twitter—twitter.com/KI_Lynn_
Instagram—www.instagram.com/k.i.lynn
Get my Newsletter—http://bit.ly/1U9NSoC

MORE BOOKS FROM
K.I. LYNN

Welcome to the Cameo Hotel

I get what I want.

When I walked through the door of the Cameo Hotel I didn't expect such a beauty to be working the front desk.

The effect she has on me is intense, and I make her life a living hell because of it.

I love her spirit, her internal defiance when completing the most inane task I assign her. My two week stay has turned into unending, just to be near her.

She's under my every command if she wants to keep me happy.

There's one last thing I want.

Her.

Find out more here
books2read.com/WelcomeToTheCameoHotel

Cocksure

A life altering lie, ten years, and one wild night later, the game has changed.

Niko

My life is great. I love my job, have awesome friends, and a great family.

Women love me, even if they know it's just for a night.

I always thought love at first sight was bullshit. Then she came storming into my life. She tore through my every rule, rocked my world, and knocked me on my ass.

There's only one problem…she lied.+

Turns out my best friend's little sister isn't so little anymore.

Everly

I stole a night with my fantasy. Lied to him.

After ten years of not seeing each other, Niko doesn't even recognize me.

So I take what I want from him, what I need from him. Without worry. Without consequence.

What I didn't count on was the lingering need for him.

Once the truth is out, the game changes. There are consequences.

I should have known nothing in my life is ever simple.

My brother is going to kill his best friend and I have nine months to figure out what I want.

Find out more here: books2read.com/Cocksure-Lynn-Kelley

Becoming Mrs. Lockwood

Every girl has dreams of meeting Prince Charming, or at least I
know I did.

A fairy tale-like meeting of love at first site.
Real life and fairy tales are very different.

I'm just a small town Indiana girl that had a chance encounter
with one of Hollywood's golden boys. You may think you know
where this story goes—not even close.

Life is different. Marriage is hard. It's even worse when you're
strangers.

Find out more here: books2read.com/BecomingMrsLockwood

Breach, Book 1

Existence is more than just a word, it's a state of being. More importantly, it's my state of being. Day by day I go through the motions of living—eat, breathe, work, sleep.

That is until I finally get some help at work in the form of Nathan Thorne. He's sexy, cocky, arrogant, an asshole, and total bullshit.

I see through the façade to the turbulent man beneath, but I'm not the only one who can see through masks.

One late night the tension between us explodes, starting a lust filled craving for each other. All it takes is that night and his dirty talking mouth, and I'm his.

Now sex is in the mix. Violent and dirty and passionate and everything I need to fill the void inside me but one thing is missing—he can never love me.

It's not enough for me to leave, even though I know I should.

More than my heart is on the line, and I don't know if I'll survive our breach.

Find out more here: books2read.com/Breach

Need, Book 1

I was Kira's from the first moment I saw her. Maybe it was love at first sight, but I was only ten.

She became my best friend.

My crush.

The girl I can't live without.

But I have to.

She was almost mine, but my father took away my chance.

Now she lives across the hall from me. Instead of the title of girlfriend, she's now my stepsister.

But that doesn't stop how I feel, how I want her. Thankfully, I'm off to college two hundred miles away, but even that doesn't help.

She's under my skin, all around me, and I watch her morph from a sexy teenager to an irresistible woman.

I can't take it anymore, I need her.

Is it possible to ever be happy without the one person you *need*?

"I'm Brayden, baby. The man you've been dreaming about your whole life. And I'm about to fucking show you why."

Part 1 of a 3 part series.

Find out more here: books2read.com/NeedSeries